HOLLIS'S HOBBY

A Killing Quill Book

Courtnee Turner Hoyle

Pale Woods

Hollis's Hobby

A Killing Quills Book

Cover design: Taylor Dawn, Sweet 15 Designs, LLC

Author Photo Credit: Tosha Cannon

To Legacee and my mama
I'm glad you're aware of the monsters so you can keep them away.

To Tosha, Journee, Jubilee, Avalee, Ellawyn, and Kinidy
Walk tall, carry pepper spray, and wear whatever makes you happy

Pale Woods Mystery Series

My Brother's Keeper
Pinky Swear
Rose Colored Glasses (January 2023)

It's About Time Series
Finding Emma
Finding David (Coming Soon!)

Pale Woods Suspense
Solomon's Tears

Under Archard's Spell Series
Cascade
Under Archard's Spell (2023)

Rasputin's Dynasty Series
Rasputin's Scorn

Hollis' Hobby Playlist

1. "Tiptoe Thru the Tulips with Me" Tiny Tim

2. "Angry Johnny" Poe

3. "Stricken" Disturbed

4. "Down Boys" Warrant

5. "Shots" Imagine Dragons

6. "Possession" Sarah Mclaughlin

7. "Open Your Heart" Madonna

8. "Unskinny Bop" Poison

9. "She's a Beauty" The Tubes

10. "Midnight Blue" Lou Gramm

11. "Snuff" Slipknot

12. "I Stay Away" Alice in Chains

13. "Your Love" Outfield

14. "Vermillion Pt. 2" Slipknot

15. "Coma White" Marilyn Manson

16. "Monsters" All Time Low (featuring Demi Lavato and Black-
bear)

Content Warning

Sometimes, serial killers are made from difficult situations. Readers should be advised that this novel contains sensitive subjects. Some of the material details murder, abuse, and even though it is not discussed in detail, teenage rape is mentioned.

Prologue

She stared at the electric saw, willing it to disappear. She had reached a clear mental focus, making it possible for change, but there was too much blood on her hands.

She had taken a break that had turned into change for the better. She had created a new life without missions or killing. *Shouldn't that count for something?*

But that wasn't entirely true, was it? She had gone through all the motions, and now, another man was dead, or dying a prolonged tortuous death, because of her.

Strangely, she didn't regret it. She would do it repeatedly to save people from their forced burdens.

There was no saving grace for the man she had killed. She had debated it for months and waited until the time was right, watching him and hoping for a small kindness in him, a fondness for animals or concealed giving, but he had been hopeless. He had been a scar on the landscape of a caring community that had welcomed and embraced her.

So she had killed him, committing a murder that she had, in so many words, promised never to do again. *Was her soul too dark for redemption? After so many murders, would this be the one from which she'd never come back?*

Chapter One

Robbie

The sun retreated into the mountains, leaving only traces of the light she had enjoyed. It was easier for her when the sun's rays caressed her, warming her flesh with its comforting solar touch. She filled her day with bright activities, like gardening, hiking, and identifying plants when she was out for a run. When the sun went down, though, it drew a curtain on the radiance of the day and brought shadows. They crept into her mind and pushed out her positive thoughts.

She looked at her watch.

He had told her he'd be there by eight o'clock, but the superintendent of roads, John, had left him early in the afternoon to oversee their paving job, claiming he had a dentist appointment. Robbie, her boyfriend, had dutifully finished the work, stripping the road down to the rock on the length of Harris Hollow Road. The road was deep in the outer reaches of the county, and he had been out of service for most of the day, but he had called her when he went with one of the tandem drivers to pick up a load of dirt.

Just as she was about to throw their dinners into the trash, she heard the familiar rumblings of his pickup truck. It idled for a moment, as if the truck hesitated to stay, before Robbie switched off the ignition.

She pretended she wasn't watching him, as if all her nerves weren't tingling with anticipation for his arrival. She washed a solitary dish and put it in the drainer while he clomped across the stone steps to her back door.

Robbie didn't knock, but the door stuck, causing him to push his one hundred seventy pounds against it. The old wood expanded in the early July sun, popping loudly in the mornings and afternoons as it warmed and cooled.

He sighed heavily, but the moment he saw her, a smile inched across his full lips. "Good golly, Miss Holli."

She ran into his arms, encouraged by his usual greeting, but he put his hands up. "I'm filthy. I sent most of the boys home an hour ago, but I stayed to lay some of the dirt."

She was familiar with the terminology. Robbie had taken her to several of the county road crew's paving sites over the past few months. A quick learner, Holli had soaked

in all the information as they stared at the stars from the cab of a backhoe or excavator. After spending Robbie's free time with him, she was so familiar with the process of paving a road that she could almost oversee a project herself.

He walked over to the fireplace and faced the kitchen. "Where's your car?"

"It's in the shop," she told him. "It started clicking when I started it, and—"

"It sounds like the alternator," he said, interrupting her.

"You're probably right," she replied. "They'll call me when it's ready."

He shook his head at her. "I would have fixed it for you this weekend. I could have gotten to it on Friday after my chiropractic appointment, and you wouldn't have had to pay the steep prices they charge at the shop." He looked thoughtful. "Did you take it to Mason in town?"

She wrung her hands when she answered him. She knew he wouldn't be happy with her answer. "I took it to Hot Shots in Bristol."

His eyes widened, and he ran a hand through his closely cropped brown hair. "They're gonna rip you off. If it had been Mason's shop, I could have called him and tried to get you a better deal."

He sat down on the cold hearth, and she knelt in front of him, folding her legs beneath her. She carefully removed his boots, untying his thin boot laces and slipping them off his feet. They smelled of old sweat and tar, with black marks clawing the sides. She sat them on her shoe mat at the door and washed her hands.

Holli stole glances at her boyfriend as she dried her hands with the hand towel he had bought her. It was part of a kitchen set he had given her one night after he picked up a meal from a restaurant that also functioned as a country store.

Robbie brushed the debris from the soles of his work boots off his socks. Most women would be bothered by his habit, but Holli was happy he felt comfortable enough
to be himself.

She tilted her head to the side and took in his golden tones, the result of working all summer outdoors. His Roman nose fit beautifully between his hazel eyes.

Robbie stood and stretched. Working for the county had kept him trim, even though most of the men she knew who were in their forties boasted larger bellies. He wasn't
taller than her five feet, eight inches, but he maintained good

posture, keeping his back straight when he moved into a chair at the kitchen table.

"Dinner smells nice," he commented.

"It's only soup beans and sweet cornbread muffins."

"You're speakin' to my country boy heart." He laughed, and the rough sound stirred a smile out of her.

"I guess I know what you like," she said, sashaying to the table and settling into his lap. Her kiss silenced his objections to the state of his cleanliness, and he wrapped her in his arms.

"I really need to take a shower," he laughed.

She pulled her cherry lips into a pout. "But dinner's already gettin' cold."

"Can't you put it back into the pot while I rinse off?"

Her pout deepened, and he ruffled her hair. She despised the gesture but made her face impassive.

"Okay, sweetheart. I'll eat before I shower."

She brought their plates to the table and put Robbie's favorite bottled beer in his hand. He took it from her gratefully. "After a fourteen-hour day, I could suck the bottom outta this." He took a long drink.

Holli watched on with satisfaction, motioning for him to begin eating while she poured a glass of water for herself. He hummed as he ate, enjoying each bite. "I can't believe you put applesauce in the cornbread mix, just like my mama." He dipped his spoon into his mouth, popped it out, and pointed it at her. "You should let me take you to meet her this Sunday." His words came out around a mouthful of beans.

Suddenly cold, she stuck a hand on her hip. "You haven't told her about me, have you?"

The spoon clanked against his bowl when he dropped it. "No, I haven't told my mother about the woman who has made me happier than anyone else."

She grew still but forced her voice to remain calm. "We talked about this, Robbie."

"Yeah, months ago."

Her eyebrows shot up. "But you agreed."

He turned his honey-colored eyes to her, the lines around his mouth longer on his fallen expression. "Haven't we been together long enough yet? Don't you know by now that I won't break your heart?"

She took a deep breath and tears pricked her eyes. "I can't believe you're mad at me. This was supposed to be a nice evening."

Seeing she was distressed, Robbie crossed the kitchen and took her in his arms. She breathed in the almost mechanical scent of oil and metal that reminded her of
him.

"You're right," he said. "I made a promise and I aim to keep it." He gestured to the table, where his beans and cornbread were mostly uneaten. "It's a small price
to pay when you treat me like a king."

Holli's doubts about the evening were further assuaged when she joined him at the table. She took small bites as she listened to him talk about the fight he broke up between two coworkers.

"Andy shouldn't have run over his lunch box, but Sam should have kept it in the truck." He showed her the bruise on his arm. "I can report Sam for tryin' to hit me, but it's not worth it. John would look over it, and it'd seem like I couldn't handle myself on a job site."

She nodded her head, covering her mouth with her hand, and chewing quickly. After she swallowed, she said, "You've told me

about Sam's temper before. This isn't
the first time he's lashed out at you."

He sat back in his seat, unbuttoning the top button on his pants. "Yeah. We fought a couple of weeks ago in the parking lot at work. It was over something stupid. I
don't even remember—"

"It was over his girlfriend," she reminded him. "You had asked her what she was doing in the county's parking lot, and she told you she was waiting on him."

He let out a dry laugh. "Sam thought I was hittin' on that stringy haired thing when the most beautiful woman in the world shares her bed with me."

Holli blinked at him with lidded eyes. "I have a surprise for you."

"Well, I'm gonna have to take a shower before we get tangled up." He opened his mouth into a wide yawn. "And then I'll need to turn in."

"Not that kind of surprise." She flicked her napkin at him and laughed at his eagerness.

"What is it, sweetheart?"

She pulled two amusement park tickets out of her apron and pushed them across the table. He held them up and cocked an eyebrow. "They're for tomorrow and Thursday." He put them down. "I have to work, honey."

She averted her eyes, grabbing the tickets and stuffing them back into her pocket. "I just thought it'd be a nice escape with all the drama at work, and you'd already taken off Friday for your chiropractic appointment."

He reached across the table to pat her hand. "It would be nice, but we have to finish pavin' the road, and John's really countin' on me."

She starred at the black and white tiles on her kitchen floor. "I thought it would be kind of special, since we haven't been out of this house together."

He thought about what she said, taking a long pull from his beer. He sat down his bottle and looked at Holli, who had lifted her eyes with his movements.

"You know what? Let's do it."

She glanced up at him hopefully.

"You're right. It's about time I stepped out into the world with you by my side."

"Really?" she asked.

"Yeah," he returned. "And the park's close enough that we can come back here each day, unless you want me to rent us one of those motel rooms with spinning beds." He
waggled his eyebrows.

She laughed. "No. We can come back here."

His jaw stretched into another yawn. "I'm gonna have to get in the shower before I camp out on your kitchen floor." He patted his belly. "A hard day's work and fillin' up on good cookin' is puttin' me right to sleep."

She winked at him. "Save a little energy for me."

"I'll splash some cold water on my face," he told her. "I don't want to miss it when you take off that dress." He nodded to the simple black sundress she had on under
her apron.

He got up and placed a kiss on her lips. She tasted the beans and smelled the beer on his breath.

"I'm gonna take a shower," he announced. "You can join me if you want."

"Shouldn't you call John to let him know you won't be in?"

"I can call him in the mornin'."

"But I thought we could sleep a couple extra hours. If you wake up at dawn to call him, I won't be able to go back to sleep."

Robbie looked like he could almost go to sleep while he was standing in the kitchen. "Yeah, that's not such a bad idea. Hand me my phone."

Robbie plopped back into the chair and put his head in his hands. Holli flipped the phone up and scrolled through the numbers until she located John's number. She

almost stopped at a number labeled Misty, but she pressed John's number and handed the phone to Robbie.

Robbie swirled the last of his beer in the bottle and turned it up before he responded to his boss's voice.

Holli listened while Robbie told John he was coming down with something, and he'd see him on Monday. The older man asked Robbie for a report on the road they were

working on.

"There's a couple of loads of dirt ready," he told him. "Bob left the backhoe, so Sam can start pushing it in the mornin'. I put a little dirt down, but he'll have to finish the job."

Robbie slurred his words, and his boss remarked that he sounded sick.

"I think I've been goin' at it too hard," Robbie replied. "It'll be good to have a break."

Holli sat down and stared at Robbie as he finished his conversation. From her place at the table, she could hear every word of their exchange.

"I'm gonna have to stay home tomorrow, too," John told him. "It feels like that dentist ripped out every tooth in my head and filled the holes with cement."

"I hope the crew will be okay without us," Robbie returned.

"Most of 'em don't know their butts from a hole in the ground, but they'll be okay," John joked. "It's just pavin'." Hearing no response from Robbie, he hopped to another subject. "I hope you feel better by Sunday, so you can see your mama and bring us some of those chocolate chip muffins she makes."

Robbie tried to smile and rubbed his thumb and forefinger over his eyelids. "I'll tell Mama to wrap some…"

The phone slipped from his hand and Holli caught it. She listened as John called to Robbie. He gave up, commenting to someone that Robbie had fallen asleep before he hung up.

Holli stared at Robbie from across the table. It was time for her work to begin.

The belladonna had done its job, lulling an already exhausted man into a deep sleep. Holli laid him on her floor, careful not to hit his head on the tile. She watched his breaths, steady and even.

Without wasting another minute, she stood behind him and grabbed under his arms. She bumped his head on her porch steps, but she smoothly slid him across the grass.

Holli was in excellent shape, running frequently and working out five days a week in her home gym, but dragging her boyfriend from the house to his truck had winded her. She took a minute to prepare the truck bed as her heartbeat regulated.

She unrolled a black garbage bag over the bed of his truck. She dragged Robbie to his truck and placed him on a black garbage bag, crinkling a couple of soda cans as she pushed his head against the back of the cab.

Robbie's phone was still on the kitchen table and his boots were by the door. She wiped his phone with bleach and erased her contact information. She didn't bother to

erase her number from the list of recent calls. It was a burner phone, and she'd dispose of it soon. She left the screen with Misty's number at the center before she shut it off.

She couldn't wear a hairnet, but her thick, blonde hair was pulled into a tight bun. She scolded herself for forgetting to use her lint roller in case one of her hairs had fallen on Robbie. Deciding it wasn't too late to be careful, she took it outside and rubbed the sticky sheets over his body, pulling any rogue hairs that may have fallen.

She put her lint roller in the outside trash can and put on a pair of latex gloves, stretching them over her fingers until they fit. Holli would wipe down the house she had rented by the month with bleach, and since she had given her landlord advanced notice of her move, the house would only be empty for a week before the keys arrived in her landlord's mailbox.

She grabbed Robbie's boots and trudged back up to his truck. She put them on him carefully, tying them in a double-knot as she'd seen him do when preparing for

work in the mornings.

She hurried inside for a couple pairs of gloves. She shut the door and pulled on the knob before she locked the deadbolt. You never knew what kind of crazy people were out there.

• • • ● ● • ● ● • • •

Holli pulled off the road and marveled at the drop down the embankment. No wonder the road had to be replaced; erosion had been quick.

They were alone. She hadn't passed anyone on her way there and the windows had been dark in the few houses alongside the road. She guessed the closest house to them was half a mile away.

She stayed on the paved area, careful not to step in the dirt or grass. A footprint could give her away, especially a size eight in a place where a bunch of men had been working.

Holli pulled the body off the truck bed, and Robbie's head smacked the pavement. The plastic bag had come with him, so she used it to slide him to the spot on the road where the dirt ended. It wasn't a significant drop, only several feet, so she doubted he woke from his herb-induced slumber, if he was still alive. She wadded up the plastic bag and put it in the grass by the truck.

The backhoe was parked just off the road, the red and white county symbol emblazoned the side. Holli climbed the step and lifted herself into the cab. Once inside, she used the key to start it, thankful that the company who made the equipment designed their keys to start any of their backhoes. She turned on the light.

Holli used the front bucket to collect dirt and rolled the machine over to the edge of the road. Robbie had placed some dirt there, so she dumped the dirt over his body, covering most of it with one scoop. She repeated the process until the area where Robbie lay was completely covered. She rolled over the collection of dirt, making it look as level as the dirt Robbie had placed on the site before he left.

The result was seamless. No one would know Robbie hadn't added ten more feet of dirt to the project. And no one would guess Robbie was buried under the road.

She jogged down the street, her dress bouncing around her legs. Her feet hardly touched the pavement, but every footfall sounded louder than the hooting owls and buzzing insects in the trees.

She had left Robbie's truck at the site locked up with his phone and keys inside. Tomorrow morning, his coworkers would arrive and fill in the last eighth of a mile with dirt, and by the end of the day, the road would be paved.

John was the only one who knew about Robbie calling in, and he would be at home in pain after his root canal. It may seem odd that Robbie's truck was parked at the

site, but with it locked up, it would only seem like he had left it there so he could work at another part of the county. The workers might talk about the missing man when they all gathered back at the shop, but no one would suspect he was missing until the road had been paved.

And so what if they dug up the road and found him?

Holli had left his cell phone and keys stuffed in the side of his truck seat. When the authorities looked through his phone, Misty's number would be discovered, and Sam would be their primary suspect.

Although, if they didn't find Robbie's body, and she guessed they wouldn't, then Sam would be free to live his life in peace. Well, after he dumped his cheating girlfriend.

Holli had been out for a run on a trail that looped beside the county's highway department, when she saw Misty drop off Sam, kissing him tenderly and handing him a lunchbox. Minutes later, as Holli jogged past a fast-food restaurant, she was surprised when Misty's car pulled into the lot.

The dark-haired woman scanned the parking lot with wide eyes, and Holli recognized the look. She didn't want to be caught at whatever she was about to do.

Holli settled onto a bench and watched the car. When the county vehicle pulled up next to it, she watched as Robbie got into the car with her. People zipped through the drive-thru at a comfortable distance while they hurried through their pleasures. Hollis only had to wait fifteen minutes before Robbie was in the county truck again, ready to go back to work. Misty was smiling when she left, her stringy hair more bedraggled.

Holli marked Robbie that day. She despised cheaters, and if left to their own devices, she knew exactly what they were capable of.

In the days that followed, Holli amassed a wealth of knowledge on Robbie from his social media accounts. Nothing was private, so she saw almost every milestone in his life from the past ten years.

After she had the necessary information about him, she faked car trouble by his workplace. She knew he was the first person to leave after work, so she faked car trouble and positioned her car and her body in view just after his work shift ended.

As expected, he pulled over to help her, eyeing her spandex running shorts and tank top. When he touched her elbow as he made

his way under the hood, she knew
he was hers.

It was easy to get him to follow her home, under the guise of making her feel safe, and her demure look overpowered any of his reservations about her. He asked her
to go out on a date, but she told him a story about a boyfriend who had paraded her around and broken her heart.

Robbie believed her fabrication about her preference to staying home, and he indulged her with food while they watched a mixture of documentaries and meat roasting competitions to pass the time.

When she finally let him into her bed, he was gentle, but every time after was a little more forceful, his true personality winning out against the face he tried to
show her. Afterwards, he was kind to her, as if an animal didn't lurk beneath his pretty country words.

Holli was used to that, though. The type of men she chose had a violent nature, whether they wanted to admit it or not. They thought she was a meek little mouse, eager
to please them, when, in reality, she was a tiger stalking her prey until it flashed its jugular.

Holli spotted her car. She had left it in a lot where hikers parked before climbing to the falls. It was a mile and a half on the other side of the mountain from the job site, so she felt confident no one had seen her car.

When she had left her car, she had feigned car trouble, and a young man from Bristol had given her a ride back. He had been kind, talking about his wife and newborn baby. He hardly glanced at Holli's breasts and legs in her short dress and spaghetti straps, so she had him drop her off two blocks from her house.

She unlocked her car and drove back without spotting another car. She walked into the house with only the running refrigerator and air conditioner to greet her.

Anticipating her activities, she had slept earlier that day, so she was full of energy for the task ahead. She put two boxes of personal items in her trunk and folded up

her exercise equipment. It slid easily into her back seat.

The police had no reason to suspect her when Robbie was reported missing, but she chose to cover any possible traces of herself from the house in which she'd lived for the past six months.

She bleached everything, from the tile in the kitchen to the surfaces in the bedroom and everything in between. She rented the house furnished with utilities, so her name wasn't associated with anything tied to the residence. Even the pictures of Irish landscapes that adorned the walls belonged to an elderly lady who allowed her to pay rent in cash without a lease.

After dying her hair and treating herself to a hot shower, Holli cleaned the bathroom. She shoved the door closed against the stubborn wood frame and hopped into

her car. Robbie was gone. He wasn't the first to fall victim to Hollis's hobby, and he wouldn't be the last.

Chapter Two

Hollis removed her ID to show the store clerk, careful to pull out an auburn-haired Hollis Bradshaw instead of the license with a blonde Holli Holiday smiling up at her. He hardly looked at it, other than to type the mandatory digits of her birthday into his register.

She took the tall, brown paper bag with the wine, twisting the bag around the neck to afford her a better grip on it. She hopped back into her car, easing onto the interstate, and taking the next exit.

She drove under the amusement park's awning and eased into the fifth spot from the entrance. Her hair flipped in the wind while she locked the car and it beat against her eyes as she rushed to the ticket booth.

A familiar figure stood at the ticket window, and she stopped her before she purchased admittance. "I have the tickets already." Hollis showed her friend the two pieces of paper she had printed yesterday after she'd invited her out for the day.

Josie tumbled out of line, catching herself, her hand over her chest. "You startled me!"

Hollis threw her arms around Josie, taking in soft jasmine perfume and honey hair products. Her friend's alpine blue eyes widened when she noticed Hollis's appearance. "Your hair!" She stepped back to fully appraise Hollis in her olive-green tee shirt and light blue jean shorts. "I'm so glad you changed your hair back."

Hollis didn't comment on her altered appearance. It had been ill timing when her friend had run into her during one of her runs. She'd had to fake a migraine to get away from Josie.

They rode a couple of the roller coasters but nothing that spun them upside down or through water. They got stuck on a ride for almost a half hour, and the tops of Hollis's thighs colored to a shade of pink darker than the rest of her skin. Josie simply seemed overheated until her skin evened out into an almond tone.

They stopped at a small sandwich kiosk and ordered lunch. Josie ordered a Philly cheesesteak and Hollis asked for a vegetarian delight.

Josie rolled her eyes. "You're not saving any more animals by starving yourself."

"I'm not starving myself," Hollis insisted. "I just don't want to think about how many animals were murdered to make my sandwich."

"You're one to talk."

She gave her friend a sideways glance and tried to keep her heartbeat steady. "What do you mean?"

Josie raised one threaded eyebrow. "I've seen the fur coat in your closet."

Hollis let out a louder laugh than she'd intended. "It's a faux fur coat."

Her friend smiled and threw a piece of her steak at Hollis. It hit her leg and stuck. Josie chuckled and wiped it away with her napkin. "I'm sorry. I grew up on the farm, and we loved our animals, but we also had to eat them."

Hollis put her arm over her friend's shoulders. "I'll tell you what. I'll stick to my fruits and veggies, and you can eat all your animal friends. I guess Mage should watch out!"

Her face dropped. "Now don't talk about my little baby!"

"Little? Mage is one of the biggest German Shepards I've ever seen!"

She put her nose in the air, "He's my sweet baby, and I won't hear anything against him."

"Okay, okay," Hollis conceded.

She looked at her phone. "Speaking of Mage, I need to start back soon. It's almost a two-hour drive."

Hollis sighed and nodded, wrapping up the last of her sandwich and throwing it away. When she turned back around Josie was studying her.

"What's wrong?"

Hollis and Josie were sitting in the shade of a tree, but Hollis could feel her face grow hot. She didn't want to explain to her friend that she had a sense of hopelessness between the men she assigned to herself, but Josie was waiting on an answer. "I don't feel like I have a purpose." Josie shook her head, ready to argue, but Hollis continued. "I'm in my late twenties, and I don't have a child in my care or a mate. I don't even have a dog to look after." Tears well in her eyes, but she blinked them away.

Josie smiled, waiting a couple of beats before she consoled her. "Oh, honey, is that what this is about?"

She scooted close to Hollis and put an arm around her shoulders. Hollis could smell the beef from the sandwich her friend had eaten, but she didn't mind.

"I only have Mage," Josie commented. "He's all I have since Cotton—"

"I'm so sorry." Hollis buried her face in her hands. "I wasn't thinking."

Josie waved her hand dismissively. "Don't give it another thought."

The friends were silent while the screams of unexpected drops sounded from the nearby roller coaster. The wind picked up and a heavy cloud covered the sun.

"It'll be two years this week." Josie turned the gold band on her left hand absentmindedly.

"You still haven't heard anything?"

"No," Josie confirmed. "They had an anonymous call from someone who said he was in Nashville, but it doesn't make any sense. He doesn't even like country music."

Tears were rolling down her friend's face faster than she could wipe them. Hollis jumped up and grabbed napkins from the dispenser on a nearby table, and by the time she returned, Josie had gotten control of her emotions.

"I ruined your special day."

"No," Hollis told her. "No one ruined our time together. We're just doing what friends do. Sharing our feelings."

"I just wish we could do it more often." She waded up the napkin in her hand. "Are you going to sign up for another four years?"

Hollis looked away. "I love serving my country. I'm considering it." It was one of her biggest lies, and unfortunately, one she had to maintain in order to explain her long absences to her friends and family.

Josie looked up hopefully. "There's a job opening up at the school."

Hollis wrinkled her nose. "You think I could teach a bunch of teenagers?"

Josie laughed. "I do it, and it's not that hard."

"Yeah, but you have patience."

"So do you," she argued, and waggled her eyebrows. "You have me for a friend, so—"

Hollis held up her hand. "Point taken."

"Hey!" Josie slapped her thigh playfully.

Hollis recovered quickly from her mirth. "Seriously, though, could you see me teaching a group of kids?"

Josie angled her head. "Actually, yes. You may need to work a little on a certification, but you have almost everything they want in a P.E. teacher." She took Hollis's hand. "It doesn't take a rocket scientist to figure out that you're not happy. Maybe it's time for a change."

Hollis saw Josie's determination and decided on the best response. "I'll think about it."

Josie took a deep breath, and her lips formed a thin line. "Okay, Hollis. But maybe you could consider the other end, too. You've never really opened up to me about it, but I know you had a troubled time in your teens." She shrugged her shoulders. "You could use your experience helping one of them."

Several days later, Hollis continued to scout for her next mission. She had gone north of her last residence. She always went in a circle around her hometown, even if it was into the next city.

She had zeroed in on three potential candidates, but they had all been cleared. She quickly checked their social media accounts, if they were careless enough to flash a bank card in her direction, or she'd just watched them, looking for the tell-tale signs of infidelity or heckling.

She unscrewed the cap off her water and took a long drink. She had been sitting in her car outside the gas station for two hours, so it was almost time to move along before she was noticed.

Gas stations were the easiest ways to find them. Sometimes, there were obvious red flags, like the type of beer they drank or the way they walked, stalking across the parking lot with their eyes straight ahead like a predator. Other times, their hints were more subtle, leading her on a social media chase to figure out their personalities more plainly.

Her mind kept going back to her conversation with Josie. After lunch, they'd left the amusement park, but Josie had revisited the topic of switching jobs when Hollis walked her to her car, highlighting more reasons why Hollis would be a good educator and how easy it would be for her to join the faculty. She told Hollis that she could stay at her house, mostly empty since Cotton had left.

Hollis thought there was more to her friend's invitation. *Did Josie need her? Was the mention about the job opening a ploy to get Hollis to move in with her so she wouldn't be lonely?*

Hollis shook away the thought, but it wouldn't leave her mind. *Could she teach at a school?*

A certificate for the physical education program wouldn't be hard to obtain. She had served four years in the navy, so she had discipline and a firm resolve, and kids caused less trouble when they were active, right?

She couldn't believe she was actually considering the idea. She turned her attention back to the people moving in and out of the gas station. Five more minutes and she would move on.

She enjoyed her self-assigned missions, and she didn't want to stop. There were a lot of men out there who needed her brand of justice, and she couldn't stop now. She'd made a vow that she'd rid the world of as many of them as possible. But maybe she could take a little break.

She had been moving across sixteen counties in three states since she was honorably discharged from the military, and she was starting to feel a pull to settle down. *What if she took a year to explore other possibilities?* She could do some research while she lived a simple life, so it wouldn't be a complete waste of time, and she might help Josie, too.

A pain threatened to push the bones of her head together. Whether it was real or imagined, Hollis felt it acutely. *No. She needed to find another one.*

Just then a man in a loose black tee shirt and red and white basketball shorts sauntered out of the gas station's automatic double doors. He clutched a twelve-pack of Moon Walker beer and a green and white pack of cigarettes. She watched his eyes, shifting over the cars at the pumps. *He could be the one.*

He stopped at a late-model Honda and lit his cigarette. A young boy jumped out and hugged his waist. The man held up his cigarette, cautioning the boy against burns. A blonde woman with a straight nose and too much lipstick climbed out of the car and joined them. After she got the boy in the car, she kissed the man and he hugged her to him, still holding his cigarette at arm's length.

Hollis bit her lip. He definitely wasn't the one.

She glanced at the clock, realizing her five minutes were up. She left, intending on going to a gas station in the next town, but she found herself turning onto the interstate. For the first time in years, Hollis was going back home.

Chapter Three

Quillen

Quillen pulled up to a long line of cars. Glancing over, he noticed Rose's smile as she swiped across her phone's screen.

"It's a private school in a small town. You'd think there would be a shorter drop off line." He chuckled, but Rose didn't notice. She was busy with whatever app was popular.

He tried again. "School doesn't even start for twenty-five minutes." He waited for her response.

She finally noticed his stare. She flicked a button on the side of her phone, darkening the screen, but she didn't put down the device. "What do you want me to say, Dad?" She gestured to the cars. "I have to go to school in a new place for" —she rolled her eyes up, pretending to count— "the *fifth* time in two years, and you're upset because the drop-off line's a little long?" She huffed. "I'll make it easy for you." She grabbed her bag and the door popped open before he could voice his apology.

It seemed like he was apologizing a lot. He was sorry they had to move, he was sorry she couldn't stay with her friends, he was sorry she couldn't play sports. The list went on and on.

He moved out of the line, holding up his hand to a pretty set of teachers who seemed to be overseeing the drop off. They waved back. The blond returned the gesture cheerily, but the auburn-haired woman stared at him with skepticism. He supposed he had gotten out of line while students were moving around, but he'd thought it was the more courteous move since his daughter had already stormed into the school.

He drove to work and stopped at the water fountain on his way to his post.

"No coffee?" Dan asked him.

"I've never been much of a coffee drinker," he told him, lifting his plastic cup up in a mock toast.

Dan waved some files in the direction of his office as an excuse to cut their exchange short. "Paperwork." His shoulders peaked. "You know how it is."

Quillen understood Dan's point well. Mortgage rates were the lowest he had ever seen them, so mountains of people had tried to buy homes or refinance existing loans. It was hard to dash the dreams of so many people at once. They'd show up with bright eyes, telling him about lowered interest rates, as if he didn't know, and then he'd have to deliver the sad news two days after they told him their plans to remodel a room or buy a starter home, usually after viewing a low score on a credit report.

He'd always had to dash people's dreams, but it was more common in the past month. The area was expanding, so opportunities to buy newly constructed homes were popping up all over the county and surrounding areas. Fortunately, he was in a position to see some of the best deals when they surfaced, and he had recently purchased a house based on the increasing realty opportunities and prime mortgage rates.

He and Rose had recently moved to town, following a promotion in his company, and they were living out of a hotel. Rose enjoyed the pool and free Wi-Fi, but he had been constantly searching for something more permanent. They had moved several times over the past couple of years, and rental homes were nice, but they didn't provide the sense of home Rose needed. On some level, he supposed he needed something more solid too, but he wasn't sure if he'd be able to stay in the small town, even though the surrounding mountains reminded him of his childhood home.

A client had approached him a week ago, ready to sign a loan for a single-level ranch-styled house. It had been updated with digital ports and all new appliances, so it was move-in ready. Quillen had stared at the specs on the house and gapped at the description. It was on a two-acre lot within walking distance of the town, and it included a cellar and a two-car carport. It would have been the perfect place for Rose and him. *How could he have missed it?*

He begrudgingly filled out the paperwork, but his spirits were lifted when the credit report came back. The client's credit score had dropped in the past month, due to several high-dollar purchases. He wouldn't be able to approve the loan!

Quillen called the realtor and arranged a viewing. She told him the house had just been placed on the market, but someone had already made an offer on it. Quillen was certain that offer was going to fall through, so he asked to view the property anyway.

He and Rose toured the house that afternoon, and she seemed happy, pointing to her chosen room and the bathroom she had marked as only hers. Quillen had made an offer before they left, and he denied the client's loan the next morning. He placed the obligatory call, ready for his guilt to be fully realized.

"That's not possible!" the client barked at him.

"I assure you, Mr. Stevens, I have your credit report right here, and it falls well below the number required to obtain a loan on the home."

Mr. Stevens cursed, but it wasn't at Quillen. "I'll straighten it out and be back by the end of the week."

Quillen acknowledged him but closed his file. Usually, credit disputes took thirty to ninety days, so Mr. Stevens would likely have his eye on a new property by the time he came back into the bank.

Quillen's offer was accepted, and he and Rose prepared to move in the following month. They celebrated by eating pizza, Rose's favorite food, even though she hadn't eaten it a lot over the past two years.

Mr. Stevens came in at the end of the week. "Check my credit now," he said.

Quillen had objected, but he relented after Mr. Stevens told him that his son had applied for student loans and a motorcycle. "He has the same name," he explained. "The credit agent had to switch it on our reports because he signed as a junior. It was their fault."

When Quillen ran the credit again, it came back well above the score needed to secure the loan on the house. The client asked for his pre-approval letter and left, presumably to track down the realtor to solidify his offer.

Monday morning, Quillen was called into the branch manager's office. Mrs. Hender cut her eyes at him, fixing her pink plastic frames over her severe nose. Quillen thought she was marginally attractive, with her azure eyes and lithe movements, but her thin lips pressed into a line, and it put him in mind of an old school marm, diminishing her looks.

Mr. Stevens sat in the chair opposite of her, but he looked like he was ready to bounce out of it at any moment. His arms rattled over the arm rests and his feet jumped in small movements, as if a bolt of electricity was coursing through his body.

At the sight of Quillen, Mr. Stevens jumped up, pointing his bony finger at him. "He's the one!" he shouted. "He bought my house right out from under me!"

Mrs. Hender put out her hands, palm up. "Now gentlemen," she admonished, even though Quillen had merely walked through the door of her office. "I'm sure there's a reasonable explanation." She glared at Quillen like she was pressing him to come up with something to diffuse the situation.

Quillen stuck to the truth. "Mr. Stevens entered my office last week and filed for a loan."

Mr. Stevens crossed his arms and tapped his foot. He eyed Mrs. Hender and licked his dry lips like every word Quillen spoke only proved his accusations.

Quillen resisted the urge to roll his eyes. "He was denied based on his credit score."

"Which wasn't true!" Mr. Stevens almost shot out of his chair again, but Mrs. Hender gave him a withering look.

"Is that true, Mr. Stevens?" she asked him. "Were you denied based on your credit score?"

Color crept up from his shirt collar. "Yeah, but—"

Mrs. Hender interrupted him by holding up her hand. She addressed Quillen. "Did you look at the house before or after you denied the loan?"

Quillen knew it was in his best interest to lie. "I inquired about it after Mr. Stevens's loan had been denied."

"Awfully convenient." Mr. Stevens huffed.

"How so?" Mrs. Hender asked. "As far as I can tell my employee has done nothing wrong. You were denied the loan, so he viewed the property and put in an offer."

To an outside observer, it would look like Mrs. Hender was defending him, but Quillen knew when she called him her "employee" instead of by his name that there would be some sort of repercussions for his actions. Right now, though, she was doing damage control.

"But my credit was fine!" Mr. Stevens insisted. He pointed a finger so close to Quillen's face that he could have bitten it off, and he thought about doing it.

"You've told me that your son's purchases were reflected on your report, but did you share your suspicions with my employee when he called you about your application?"

Mr. Stevens raised his chin. "I didn't know I had to."

Mrs. Hender took off her glasses and bowed her head, rubbing the bridge of her nose. "That's true. You don't have to discuss personal matters with bank employees." She put on her glasses and turned to Quillen. "Did you think Mr. Stevens would be able to secure the loan on the house?"

"No," Quillen answered her honestly.

"Then I don't see the issue here."

Mr. Stevens catapulted out of his chair. "The problem is that piece of—"

Mrs. Hender cut him off. "Watch your language, sir."

Mr. Stevens wasn't finished. "He stole my grandparents homestead out from under me. " He was shaking, almost vibrating with his finger pointing at Quillen.

Quillen hadn't known that the property had belonged to Mr. Stevens's family. He looked away, shame threatening to overtake him.

"What do you want me to do?" Mrs. Hender asked. "My employee was well within his rights to—"

"I want you to fire him!" Mr. Stevens shouted. Quillen was glad they were in a back room. He doubted it was soundproof, but no one could see a customer berating him.

"I think it's time for you to go." Mrs. Hender picked up the phone on her desk and pressed a button. "Please tell Martin we may need him to escort a customer out of the building."

Mr. Stevens blanched, but he quickly regained his fervor. "You can call off your dog. I'll leave." He bent at the waist, leaning onto Mrs. Hender's desk to meet her eyes. "But you can bet I'll never do business here again."

"We'll be sorry to see you go," Mrs. Hender replied without inflection.

He put his finger back in Quillen's face. "You better watch your back, boy."

He stalked out of the room. Martin glanced at Mrs. Hender for direction when he'd almost passed him, but she shook her head. There was no reason to escort him out.

Now that Mr. Stevens was gone, Mrs. Hender turned her slow-boiling wrath on Quillen. "Mr. Stevens has over one hundred thousand dollars in CD's at this location. What were you thinking?"

Quillen crossed his legs and leaned back in his chair. "I really didn't think he could get approved for the property."

Her eyes darted left and right, as if she were trying to read him. She took in a long breath and let it out.

He tried another tactic. "You know I've been trying to find a house for Rose and me. This house is two blocks down from where you live. I'd thought we'd be close enough for Rose to reach out to you if she needed to. You know, if she needed a woman's perspective."

The flattery worked on Mrs. Hender. Her hands fluttered from her face to her paperwork. "You know I'm always available if she needs to talk."

"I appreciate that so much." He dipped his head. "After what's happened in our family, I—"

Mrs. Hender raised her hand, trying to manage a blush that had flushed two roses of color on her cheeks. "Say no more," she said. "Just try not to buy any more houses out from under our patrons."

He smiled to himself, realizing he had won her favor. He still had it.

If it were possible, Rose slammed the door harder when she got into the car than when she'd exited it.

Quillen winced. "Easy." The white SUV was leased, but he didn't want to pay extra at the end of the term for preventable dings.

Rose pretended not to hear him, pulling out her phone and clicking her fingernails across the screen. He imagined she was typing a message to one of her friends from a previous high school about her first day, so he tried to wait until she was finished before he spoke again. They were almost to the hotel before he interrupted.

"How was school today?"

She paused, but her fingers never left her phone. "Fine."

"Could you elaborate?"

She sighed, not even turning in his direction. "No."

He willed himself to stay calm. It was always like this when they moved. Every new experience reminded Rose of the friend's she'd lost, so she punished him for it.

Quillen supposed most of it was his fault, but he wouldn't take responsibility for the reason for their first move. No one could have stayed in that house after what had happened.

Rose trudged into the hotel room behind him. The room had been cleaned by hands more skilled than his own, and a scent of lemon cleanser and Rose's perfume lingered. He put two large files on the table and fell into the chair. The room had two beds, a television, and a small table with two chairs. A mini fridge made it possible to keep a couple of canned drinks and a half gallon of milk cold, but without a way to store food or cook it, all their meals had to be ordered out.

Rose kicked her shoes onto the rug between their beds, her eyes still glued to her phone. Quillen wondered if taking it away might bring her closer to him, but he dismissed the idea quickly. He didn't want to isolate her any more after he had moved them again. If the truth were told, he agreed with Rose, and almost condoned her emotional hostility. It was time for him to find a more permanent place for them, and he was glad he had secured a home, even if he had made an enemy in the process.

He was thankful for his schedule at the bank, and he was glad he had smoothed things over with Mrs. Hender, since she controlled his hours. For the past two years, the bank had offered him flexible hours. As long as he processed all his loan requests, he could have office hours while Rose was at school and finish any application requests on his own time. It allowed him the opportunity to pick his daughter up and drop her off at school. Once she made friends, it afforded him the ability to watch them from a distance without Rose's knowledge.

His daughter was very dear to him. She was all he had left, and he was determined to keep her safe.

He didn't feel like going out again to grab anything else for them to eat, and the food delivery services hadn't reached the small town yet, so he ordered a pizza for dinner.

Rose sat in her chair, scrolling down the screen. He hated to shut off the light he saw in her features, but he couldn't allow her to start using her phone at the table. He had to set boundaries on devices.

When he told her to put her phone away, she tossed it onto the bed. It had a protective case and insurance, but Quillen wished his daughter treated her belongings more delicately. She threw her phone and laptop around, and her clothes were stuffed in drawers. It was like nothing was truly precious to her.

Quillen's side of the room was neat. He could easily find and gather his items within ten minutes and move to another location. Rose kept her side in a disarray. Her clothes were littered on the floor, and she never bothered to make her bed, claiming the sheets were changed daily by the cleaning staff.

Quillen was embarrassed by his daughter's lack of respect, but instead of talking to her about it, he picked up her clothes and made her bed. She had been through enough.

She glanced up at him, the starbursts in her cerulean eyes more visible under the low-hanging light. Combined with her straw-colored hair, her eyes stood out starkly from her coffee-colored skin and full, dark eyelashes. She was taller than most of her classmates, her resulting height causing boys to think she was older than her fifteen years. Quillen had chased off some of her admirers, but Rose usually pushed their attentions away, choosing instead to focus on her studies and the friends she had picked up in the towns where they had briefly lived.

Quillen had already asked her about school, so he refined his question. "What are your classes?"

Rose finished chewing before she answered. "I have biology and English before lunch, and law and P.E. after."

"Only four classes?"

She shrugged. "After Christmas break, I'll have four new classes. Well, I'll have three new classes. English will be the same."

"That's interesting," he mused, wiping sauce off his chin. "You'll still have seven classes every year, but they're finished sooner."

Rose surprised him by continuing the conversation. She usually bored easily, rolling her eyes at his attempts to communicate with her. "Yeah. The classes are longer, though. I'm worried Geometry will take forever next semester."

He took another bite and nodded along. He didn't want her to lose interest in their conversation, but he had little to contribute. He enjoyed math, and geometry had been one of his favorite subjects.

"Do you have a favorite subject?"

Rose tossed her head back and forth a little. "Law is cool, and P.E. is okay." She paused. "The P.E. coach asked me if I wanted to play basketball."

He stopped chewing, and then forced himself back into the mechanics of moving his jaw up and down until his tongue could comfortably slide the bite down his throat. "What did you tell him?"

"Her," Rose corrected. "I said I'd have to ask you."

He rubbed the napkin over his mouth and leaned back in his seat. "And you know my answer."

Rose's pained expression broke his heart. "It's been two years," she cried.

It never ceased to amaze him how fast his daughter's mood could change. She could transform from joyful to a soppy mess in under twenty seconds. If it weren't for the melodrama, teenagers would make great thespians.

"There's still a threat."

She rolled her eyes. "Do you really believe that, Dad? Do you really think we've been followed when—"

"That's enough!" He spoke more harshly than he'd intended.

She recoiled, pushing her chair back. With no bedroom to flee into, Rose bolted to the bathroom. She turned on the fan, but he could hear her sobs. He tried twice to apologize, receiving no response.

Finally, she left the bathroom and crawled into her bed. Her back was to him, but he found comfort in her presence. *Was he wrong for holding on so tightly to her?*

As Quillen shut off the light by his bed, he decided to look into the school's basketball team. He drifted easily into sleep, but dreams of masked men stalking the last member of his family plagued him until morning.

Chapter Four

Her first day had been one of the worst days in her adult life! She'd murdered people for less than the infractions the school allowed to pass.

She entered Pale Woods Academy at seven o'clock. She had never liked early morning activities, preferring to stay up late, but the State of Tennessee insisted that children should begin learning just before eight o'clock in the morning. That put her waking up at five o'clock, so she could have a proper workout before she showered and stuffed something in her mouth as she ran out the door.

The building was breezy when she walked down the hallway. Part of it was in the two-story brick's construction, and the open doors at the front and back of the building. She flew into her office, a small compartment just before the gymnasium, and typed her passcode into the computer. A flurry of messages appeared on her screen, part of the school's intranet. She ignored the welcome messages from other educators and their invitations, and she clocked into the record keeper. Her time was recorded, and she was satisfied that she was five minutes early.

Hollis put her hands on her hips and surveyed the room. She had bleached the floor and walls, but the smell of sweat was soaked into the concrete walls. She was provided with a desk and a filing cabinet, so she had decorated them both with three pictures, but the only one visitors could see was the picture of Josie and her on the filing cabinet. The other two faced toward her.

Her office was mostly open. Two walls were made of glass, and she could see into the gymnasium and the hallway leading into it. It helped her keep an eye on her surroundings, but it also let others look in on her. She constantly reminded herself that she was always watched while she was there.

She hurried to the front of the building where the older students were dropped off. She stood just outside the door, welcoming sullen teenagers who were just as excited to be there as she was to receive them. She was a skilled actress, though, and she mirrored Josie's enthusiasm as each child climbed the steps to the school.

Josie held a container of coffee in one hand and waved with the other. "This isn't so bad," she told Hollis. "It gives parents the chance to see you."

Hollis resisted the urge to roll her eyes.

"Hey, Mrs. Gouge." A lanky-haired boy with braces and glasses waited for Josie's response.

"Good morning, Gregory," Josie chirped.

He stood on the steps, looking from her to Hollis. Josie took the initiative to introduce them.

"This is Mrs. Bradshaw. "She'll be your new physical education coach."

"I don't have physical education," he told them. "I'm in the band."

A dark-haired boy, twice the size of Gregory, bumped into him on his way into the building. The action was slight, and Gregory ignored it, but Hollis sensed his hostility. She said nothing, knowing that it would be harder on Gregory if she did, but she mentally marked the boy who had bumped into him.

Gregory exchanged pleasantries with the two women, and Hollis learned that he aspired to work for NASA. He showed them pictures of his experience at space camp before he scurried inside.

"When you take the time to speak to them in the morning, you get to know some of the kids really well," Josie said, sipping her coffee.

"Hello, Laura," she spoke to a girl ascending the steps. She looked up and smiled at them quickly. She wore a pink dress that brushed her knees and had her dishwater blonde hair pulled into a low ponytail. Light makeup brushed her features. Soft pink eyeshadow and tan lip gloss enhanced her round eyes and plump lips.

"Hey," Laura said back. Her greeting was forced, but her smile seemed genuine. She gave Hollis a look she couldn't quite dissect before she disappeared into the school.

Josie strategically pointed to an SUV in the drop off line by raising her mug in the vehicle's direction and then taking a sip. "That's a sad story."

The kids usually waited until they were at the mouth of the school before they jumped out of the vehicles, but as Hollis turned her attention to the SUV, a girl practically jumped out of the passenger side door and raced to the double doors.

Hollis didn't have time to ask about the situation before the girl was running up the steps.

"Good morning, Rose," Josie said.

Her blue eyes darted up. "How do you know my name?"

Josie laughed. "I gave you and your father a tour of the school on the day you were admitted."

The girl seemed puzzled but nodded. "Good morning," she returned before going inside.

"She has no idea who I am," Josie commented. "But it may have to do with the number of schools she's attended in the last two years.

The SUV had been nudging its bumper into the other lane, and it had finally pulled into it. As it passed, Hollis noted a man driving. She could tell he was tall, even though he was sitting in the vehicle, as his head was within an inch of touching the ceiling of the cab. His hair was pulled into a bun at the back of his head, and he wore a suit, but she couldn't tell much more through the darkened windows. He threw up a hand as he passed.

Josie waved and Hollis did the same, but she couldn't bring herself to match her friend's open smile. The man was in the wrong lane in a student drop off. *Did he think he was more important than the working parents in front of him or the teenagers running around his vehicle?*

"Quillen Banes," Josie sighed. She noticed Hollis staring at her in surprise and let out a chuckle. "Hey, I might be married, but I'm not dead."

"I couldn't see him well through the tinted glass. Is he attractive?"

"Positively dreamy," her friend replied with a giggle. "Dark hair, crystal-blue eyes, toned."

Hollis was certain her friend would be swooning if she weren't in the company of adolescents. She had a far away look in her eye as she recalled her last meeting with Rose's father.

"Mrs. Bailey grabbed me in the hall last week and asked me to give a tour of the school to a new girl and her father." She waved her hand. "She had an appointment or something, so she had to leave."

"I saw Rose first, and she is breath-taking, but then her father stepped out of the office." She fanned herself, and a blush rushed across her cheeks. "He has that clean-cut, but wild, look that I love."

She took a minute to compose herself as they welcomed a rush of students. They were arriving faster now, as the bell was about to ring.

"Anyway," Josie continued. "I don't know what rooms we went into and what I said about them. He kept joking with me, and his daughter was sweet. It was easy to feel comfortable around them."

"You said they had a sad story," Hollis remembered.

Josie nodded and took a sip of her coffee. The bell rang, ending their conversation.

"Duty calls," Josie said. Hollis couldn't help but feel like one of the students as her friend gave her an encouraging pat on the shoulder. "You're going to have the best day ever!"

Her first class gathered in the usual fashion. She spaced them across the polished gymnasium floor and asked them to sit with their legs crossed.

"Criss-cross applesauce," one of the boys mocked.

Hollis turned around and examined the group. The academy was filled with students who had above-average intellect, but they were still teenagers with a range of emotions and a flood of hormones.

"Okay, let's jog around the perimeter."

"Perimeter?" a girl echoed.

"Yeah," she said to them. "I was going to read some rules, and tell you what you'd learn this semester, but I think I'd rather start getting you in shape right away."

The students looked at each other. Mumbles of "Is she serious?" and "She can't do that!" carried across the room. It wasn't until Hollis blew her whistle that they begrudgingly hopped to their feet.

"I was in the military," she informed them. "The perimeter is the outer area of this floor." She motioned to the royal blue lines that marked the edges of the basketball court. "Jog on those lines."

They groaned, throwing their heads back and stomping to the line. Some of the taller boys took off from the center of the court, obviously no stranger to the activity. *They're probably athletes*, she thought.

Several of the girls held back, walking and chatting while their classmates went around them. Hollis walked beside them, picking up swatches of their conversation about the tallest boy in the group.

"Aaron is so hot!" the first girl said. "I don't know what he sees in Laura."

"He probably thinks she's pretty," Hollis commented.

One girl grabbed her chest above her heart, and the other one startled. They gaped at her with wide eyes.

Hollis addressed them firmly. "I said to jog."

They took off without a word.

After two laps, three of the kids sat down on the bleachers. She recognized one of them was Laura. Another boy joined them, lying down with his arm over his eyes.

"What's going on here?" Hollis asked.

Only one of them looked at her. He said, "We're tired."

"After two laps?" She raised her eyebrow. "You can walk if you can't jog, but you have to keep moving."

The kid laughed and turned back to his friends. One of them moved their arms to mock her attempt to keep them active during class.

She hadn't been a teacher for long, but she knew she had to assert her position, or the kids would run all over her. She thought about the range of disciplinary actions discussed when the principal spoke to her about classroom conduct. She pulled out the first one she remembered.

"You can run, or you can be suspended."

The kid with his arm over his eyes spoke up. "You can't do that. You have to give him a detention first."

Hollis was momentarily caught off guard. *Could she follow through with the punishment?* She decided to stick with it and hope they didn't call her bluff.

"I may be new here, but you'll do what I say. Now, get up and run around those lines, and if I see one toe out of—"

"I thought you said for us to jog," Laura said.

The boy shielding his eyes— she remembered his name was Zach— spoke again. "It's easy for her to say. She doesn't have to do it."

"Zach."

She only had to speak his name to get their attention. Once their eyes were on her, she ran in place, waiting for the leading boy, Aaron, to run past her. As soon as he was level with her, she matched his pace and jogged a little ahead of him. After she rounded the corner, she saw Zach, Laura, and the other boy and girl joining the ranks.

After fifteen minutes, kids started to walk. Even Aaron alternated walking a lap and jogging another. Hollis maintained her speed until the bell rang. Zach had jogged since he'd rejoined the group. He didn't quit until she officially dismissed them.

For some reason, she felt like she should extend a kindness to him. "Good work today, son," she said, falling back into the language she'd heard from her sergeants.

He turned a little, barely glancing at her with one eye. "I'm not your son."

• • • ● ● • ● ● • • •

Her second class was more compliant. She didn't know if it was because they were happy lunch was soon or if they'd been cautioned about her by the kids from the first period. She ran around the gym with that class, too.

She was famished by lunch, and even though Josie wanted her to join her in the teacher's lounge, Hollis decided to eat her lunch in her office. She feasted on an oversized salad she had prepared in a container. Luckily, she had a small refrigerator in her office, something left by the last coach, and she'd planned to eat the salad for two days. She ate the last bite in the plastic container as the bell rang for third period.

She didn't have a class during that time, as she was supposed to make detailed lesson plans for each day during that period. She set to work on the next week's lesson plan, as she had already complet-ed the current week's plans and turned them in to the principal.

The fourth bell rang, and students steadily streamed into the gym. Rose was among them. Some of the local girls seemed to have adopted her into their group, and they sat on the floor and chatted with her. Knowing that there was something sad in her history, Hollis didn't separate Rose from her new friends, opting against alphabetical order.

It was odd that she was drawn to the girl when she had only spoken to her when she called role. Some people might think it was the mention Josie had made of her that morning, but Hollis knew it was something deeper. She had seen it in her eyes when she'd looked up from the steps that morning. Hollis recognized the anger that burned behind her soft features, and she understood something about the teenager without the need for confirmation: Rose was like Hollis. They had both known pain and they were still running to get away from it.

Chapter Five

"Did you have a good day?" Josie asked casually just before she took a bite of her baked tilapia.

Out of all the meats, fish offended her the least. It didn't put off the rancid odor, like pork and beef, that reminded her of a dead body.

"Yes." She responded simply. She cooled her alfredo, blowing gently over a forkful.

Josie raised a skeptical brow. "Honestly, Hollis. How long have we known each other? Eight years? A decade?" She motioned to Hollis's hand with her empty fork. "Do you think I don't recognize when you're lying?"

Hollis looked down at her fingers. She'd pushed back the cuticle of her thumb with the nail of her ring finger.

"It's a tell-tell sign," she added nonchalantly.

Hollis laid her hand flat on the oak table. She and Josie preferred to share their meals in the kitchen, as the dining room seemed too formal, and the wooden kitchen table was more than roomy enough for all their food.

Josie was still eyeing her. "Spill it."

Hollis looked up from her food. "It wasn't great," she conceded.

"Can I help?" Josie asked.

Her friend was a fixer. She listened to every word Hollis uttered, but her goal was always to help Hollis remedy whatever problem she was experiencing. It wasn't a terrible attribute to have in a friend, but sometimes Hollis just needed to vent. Not every problem needed solving.

"Not unless you can go back and teach years of manners to the kids in my classes."

Josie laughed, a little piece of fish landing on her hand. "Then I'd have to do that with all my classes, too."

Hollis thought for a moment. "There is this boy, Zach. At first, I thought he was a troublemaker, but when I showed him I was willing to do whatever I asked the class to do, he joined in."

Josie had been nodding along. "Zach's really a sweetie. He comes from a bad background, but he's smart. He has a way to break the cycle, but most of the teachers don't really give him a chance."

Hollis could think of several toxic cycles. "What's his cycle?"

Josie spoke around her last bite of tilapia. "Violence. His father beats him."

"Why doesn't his mother leave?" Hollis asked, her temper flaring.

Josie looked up, startled by Hollis's tone. "She died."

Hollis regulated her breathing and relaxed until she could almost feel the anger slipping off her face. "Did his father kill her?"

"I'm not sure," Josie admitted. "The news said it was asphyxiation, but Zach said his father drowned his mother in her own vomit."

It was becoming harder for Hollis to keep her cool, but she maintained what she hoped was a conversational tone. "And no one believed him?"

Josie got up and carried her plate to the sink. "I don't think anyone really cared. She was a drug addict, and the pieces seemed to add up to the police."

Hollis bet that Zach cared. She was willing to guess that he cared very much.

Before her thoughts continued to spiral, she picked up on her friend's body language. Josie had finished her meal, but she was looking at the cabinets.

"I bought some wafers. Do you want to eat some with me?"

Josie touched her flat stomach. "No. I need to keep my figure."

It had been years, but Cotton's words still echoed through the house. Josie still had her husband's pictures on the walls and her heart in her hands, even though he had taken off after their last fight.

Hollis wanted to tell Josie that she was beautiful, and she would be even more lovely with full cheeks, but she decided against it. They'd had the discussion many times, and Josie was still living by the rules set in place by a man who never deserved her.

Josie had prepared their meals, so Hollis washed the dishes, glad to be of some service to a friend who would never ask for her help. Josie wondered out of the room as Hollis ran the dishwater.

Josie was already grading her students' work when Hollis walked into the spacious living room. An eighty-five-inch television hung on the far wall, but Josie's back was turned to it as she scanned the answers her students had provided.

Hollis flopped onto an oversized beige recliner, identical to the one next to it. They hardly matched the sea foam walls, but Josie hadn't had the heart to part with the furniture her husband had chosen when he'd moved into her family's farmhouse.

Hollis had sprayed the chair with fabric cleaner half a dozen times, but the stale smell of cigarettes clung to it. She had tried to sit on the couch, but it was stiff and uncomfortable. She also hoped her presence in it would keep her friend from looking over at the empty chair like her husband was going to materialize in it.

Mage's toenails clicked across the hardwood. He stared at Josie before he laid his head in her lap. She rubbed his ears absent-mindedly.

Mage was the only thing Hollis was grateful Cotton had left behind. Mage had always preferred Josie to the man who considered himself the dog's master, and they had a much more loving bond than Mage and Cotton would have ever had. He slept at the end of Josie's bed and guarded the house. The nearest neighbor was a little under a mile away, so it gave Hollis some peace of mind to know that Mage was standing sentinel over her friend.

Josie swiveled in the chair at her desk and Mage sat, waiting for her to speak. "It's so much easier to grade papers on the computer."

"I can't believe you already have papers to grade," Hollis replied. "You should have given them a break on the first day."

Josie laughed dryly. "Like you did when you made your students run for half an hour?"

Hollis had been relaxing in the chair with her feet propped up, but she looked over the back of the chair and smiled. "They jogged. Most of them couldn't sprint to the end of the gym and back without doubling over."

Josie shook her head. "It's not nice to judge." She glanced back at her computer. "Besides, this wasn't really an assignment. It was more of an assessment."

Hollis raised her eyebrows.

"Well, today you assessed that the students in your class were out of shape— "

Hollis held up a finger. "Most of them *are* out of shape."

Josie rolled her eyes. "Anyway, I need to assess how much my students know about the material I plan to teach them."

"How much do they need to know?"

Josie swiveled back around and clicked on an icon. A list of fifty names popped up on the screen before a summary followed.

"It looks like I'll have to sharpen their fluency and rhetoric skills this semester and reassess in December."

Hollis stretched until her feet moved past the leg rest. "Sounds like fun."

"Do you want to watch a movie?" Josie asked without looking away from the screen.

Her friend wasn't committed to her request, so Hollis told her she was going to bed early. Josie remained downstairs, alone with her thoughts.

Hollis had been skeptical about returning to Josie's family home. She'd lived there when no one knew she had been honorably discharged from the military, and she hoped things would be different.

Thankfully, people who said friends shouldn't live together were wrong about Hollis and Josie. The extra time together had made them closer. So when Hollis showed up on a July afternoon with her shoulder bag over her arm and a gas station slushie in her hand, Josie was thrilled. Both women looked forward to long talks into the night, shared meals and responsibilities, and living with someone familiar. Most of all, despite Mage and Hollis's victims, neither woman would feel alone for the first time in years.

The next day, Hollis applied for a position at the academy. She called in a favor, and a teaching certificate was waiting in her email inbox the following morning. If it were verified, the provided number would substantiate her ability to teach physical education to minors.

With her military background and the forged certificate, Hollis was almost guaranteed the position. The first day of classes was quickly approaching, so she didn't have to wait long for the call. The principal of Pale Woods Academy, Mrs. Bailey, welcomed her to the staff and told her about what to expect in the coming weeks.

Josie claimed Hollis was going to get the job from the moment she applied, but she seemed relieved when Mrs. Bailey confirmed it. She suggested a huge celebration. The women reminisced and played gin rummy well into the wee hours of the morning. Gin wasn't only in their cards, and Hollis and Josie slept most of the next day. Hollis didn't get hangovers, so she was the first to rise, fixing her friend toast which Josie promptly threw up.

After drinking water and getting another good night's sleep, Josie was ready to show Hollis the campus. Pale Woods Academy was positioned on a mountain next to a river the Native American Cherokee had named Nolichucky, or river of death. The outside of the building was constructed from the rock from the river and boasted plenty of room for the five hundred, or fewer, students who roamed its halls.

Hollis was amazed by the school, but she was glad to ride back to her new home with Josie. The farmhouse was only fifteen minutes away, so the ride to and from school was quick.

The animals greeted them as they wound up the dusty drive. Sheep and pigs vied to be the loudest, and Mage ran freely with the horses and checked on the cows.

The hundred-year-old farmhouse showed most of its age. Josie had used some of her parent's insurance money for updates, like cream-colored siding and new kitchen appliances, but the home creaked in the night, and the only air conditioning came from two window units, one in the living room and the other in Josie's room.

She had offered for Hollis to sleep in her room during the dog days of summer, but Hollis had declined.

Heat rises, and by the time Hollis lay down each night, her room was sweltering. Between the heat and the constant popping and cracking in the house, it took a lot for Hollis to fall asleep. Her chosen lifestyle had made her a light sleeper, so she woke up frequently to the pops in the floorboards and the creaks in the doors that shouldn't be moving while all the life in the house was tucked in bed.

She enjoyed the nights when she and Josie drank a glass of wine and talked before bed, but she quickly noticed the nights when her friend was more contemplative. She called those nights "Cotton Nights," and left her alone to think about her husband.

It was one of those nights. Hollis had tried to learn Josie's triggers to see if she could keep her friend's depression from looming over her, but she hadn't been able to assess a clear pattern. Josie should have been excited about a new school year and tired from the excitement, but she had plenty of energy left to brood over her absent husband. *Josie had received a letter from Cotton in June, but her friend shouldn't still be worried about that,* should she?

Once in her room, Hollis checked her laptop for news. A light breeze flicked the sheer curtains and circulated through the sparsely decorated room. Josie had told Hollis that she could make the room her own, but Hollis hadn't touched the faded pink walls and the worn flowered rugs. She simply placed her suitcases of clothes next to the cherry wood dresser and wardrobe and put a clean pair of gray linen sheets on the bed.

Her laptop blinked to life, and Hollis was thankful for the WIFI connection Josie had asked the electric company to install the previous year. She had never looked for reports of her killings, but since she was staying very close to the same town as her last victim, she decided she needed to know if his remains had been discovered. So far, there had only been a brief write up about a missing person's report filed for a county road worker.

Hollis leaned back and congratulated herself on another successful mission. *How many disgusting men had she sent to their dooms?*

She resisted the urge to check the reports of her other victims. Some of them had been found, but others were in places no one would ever look.

Chapter Six

Marshal

"You're covered in filth!" he said.

She'd gotten back early from her run, but he'd met her at the door. His meeting had been canceled, and she'd been caught.

He held open the door, but he stood in the doorway, repulsed. "You can't possibly expect to come in here with dirt all over you."

She spoke before she thought it through. "How else am I supposed to get clean, Marshal?"

He raised his eyebrows so high she though they might touch his hairline. "Go use the hose, and I'll meet you at the back door."

She gritted her teeth and walked to the side of the house with the frosty grass crunching beneath her sneakers. She took off her running shoes and beat the caked mud out of the recesses. Next, she turned on the hose and washed the dirt off her hands and legs. She braced herself for the frigid feel of it running over her face and arms, but she was too angry to feel the full effect of the water in her heated state, at first. A late November chill had settled over Arkansas, and the air sent shivers across her exposed skin after she'd washed most of her body off.

She climbed the steps on her toes, trying not to touch the cool concrete with her heels and arches. Marshal stood on the deck, two bags and a towel in his hands. He indicated that she should put her shoes in one of the bags and gave the other bag to her.

"Put your clothes in there," he demanded. Holli took the bags and tried to go around him. He held up his hand, careful not to touch her. "You can disrobe here."

Holli looked at the homes around her. Each one was worth at least half a million dollars and had any number of housewives and small children inside, possibly staring out at them as they ate oatmeal or made coffee.

"You can't be serious? There's no way I'm going to take my clothes off out here."

He put a hand on his hip, the gold band on his left ring finger catching the sunlight. "You will if you want to gain access to the house."

Holli knew he was unmovable. After six months, she was aware that he wouldn't let her go inside if he saw a speck of dirt on her.

"Fine." She undressed quickly, throwing her leggings, shirt, and windbreaker into the bag.

"And the rest?" he said, shaking the bag with a small smile tugging the corners of his mouth. She hated his bemused tone.

There was no sense trying to argue. She thrust her bra and panties into the bag and stomped into the house.

Marshal picked up the stick he used to open the outside trash receptacle and tossed the bags inside. He pulled out a container of hand sanitizer and poured it over his hands.

"What are you doing?" Holli shouted from the doorway. "Just put them in the washer!"

"And wash them in the same machine as the other clothes?" he admonished.

A breeze brushed her naked body, and Holli started to shake. Before Marshal could delight in her regrettable state, she ran up the stairs to the shower and jumped inside. She had locked the door, but Marshal used the master key he carried in his pocket to barge into the room midway through her shower. He pulled out a gallon-sized container of bleach from under the sink and put it on the counter.

"Wash the shower after you finish, and take another shower when it's clean," he commanded. "You know where to find me when you're done."

Holli took her time in the shower, using the soap physicians usually gave to patients before surgery. She scrubbed the tile and fixtures, and showered again, repeating the process of her first shower. By the time she was finished, her scalp and skin burned, and her hands had pruned.

As promised, he was waiting for her. He rested against steel gray linen sheets with a condescending look on his face. His tanned skin had no creases, even though he was in his mid-forties, and his dark eyes danced over her naked flesh.

"I thought we could take advantage of your cleanliness," he said, inviting her to slip into the bed beside him.

She lay rigidly on the pillow as he prepared himself. "Turn your head to the closet," he told her.

She faced the closed doors as he mounted her, careful not to breathe on him. She'd made the mistake of blowing against his neck once, a move that had won her past favor in the bedroom, but he had jumped out of the bed and ran to the bathroom. After his shower, he had finished while he held her jaw in the opposite direction.

He wore two condoms, even though she told him about the disadvantages, and he didn't kiss her. He simply entered her and took over her body until he was finished. Holli laid on the pillow, feeling his thrusts, and hating the heavy breaths that covered her shoulder.

He didn't look at her, so he was spared the venom in her eyes. He was too busy meeting his own needs to care about her, so after the first couple of experiences, she let him direct her. At least he didn't put a layer of cling wrap between them anymore. After he realized she didn't sweat during sex, because she was only allowed to lay beneath him, he took away the unnecessary protective layer.

The signal for his release sounded in her ear and his body went rigid. When he relaxed, he rolled away, darting to his personal bathroom.

Holli stripped the bed, made it with sheets that were the same color and texture, and took a shower. When she reappeared, she was dressed in a navy blue evening dress. Her blonde hair was pulled into a tight bun and light makeup enhanced her features.

She glanced at the contents of the refrigerator. "Would you like fresca?" she called to him.

He shuffled into the room. "There's no need to yell."

"I'm sorry," she replied, and in a softer tone repeated her question.

"That will be fine." He rubbed his thumb and forefinger over his clean-shaven face. "Will you fix me a drink?"

"Would you like a beer?" she asked hopefully.

He scrunched his nose. "Not today. I usually drink them in the summer."

Holli's hopes fell. She couldn't imagine waiting another seven months to carry out her plan.

Holli spent Thanksgiving alone as Marshal visited his family in Chicago. She wasn't supposed to mention them, and she never did, but she knew about his sweet thirty-something wife and two blonde daughters. They were on the lock screen of his phone, the image flashing their picture-perfect smiles every time Marshal received a notification.

He rejoined her after the holiday weekend, ready to spend five days bouncing between meetings, showers, and her bed. He was in a foul mood when he returned, and she was privy to his insults.

"Why haven't you washed the dishes?" he asked her, pointing to the solitary cup by the sink.

"There was only water in it," she defended.

As fast as she had spoken, he crossed the room with the cup in his hand. He held it so close she could see the reflection of her eye in the glass.

"Does it look clean to you?" he shouted. A blood vessel had popped in his eye and the red, vein-like tendrils stretched to his iris.

"No," she responded quickly.

He lifted the cup, and she prepared to hear it shatter on the floor, but it connected with her jaw. When she turned away from the assault, he brought the glass down on her back and shoulders. At some point, the top of the glass broke, and she saw splatters of her own blood splatter against the stark white walls.

He stopped as suddenly as he had started. "Clean this up," he commanded and walked numbly up the stairs. She heard the water in his bathroom run through the pipes.

She assessed her injuries, careful not to move too quickly. Her jaw was swollen, but it was nothing compared to the cuts and bruises on her back. She rose gingerly and hobbled into the kitchen. She returned with a broom, dustpan, and bleach. She had the mess scrubbed away in less than twenty minutes.

The song of the water through the pipes indicated Marshal was still in the shower. She went to the garage and collected the white paint. Marshal kept several cans of it in case the walls were marked, and she'd had to use it many times.

The wall was still too wet to paint, so Holli stepped into the shower. The hot water stung her abrasions, but she cleaned herself thoroughly. She dressed her wounds, counting twelve long cuts and four large bruises on her back.

He was standing at the door when she opened it. She readied herself for his apology.

"You will need to paint the wall and take another shower," he said to her. His tone was cold, completely unfeeling. "You will join me in my bed afterward."

Holli opened her mouth to speak, but he cut her off. "Do you know how lucky you are? Someone like you could never hope to live in a place so nice."

She could see his anger rising. His fists were clenched in front of him.

"Thank you," she spoke meekly. "Is there anything else I can do for you?"

He huffed. "There's very little you're good for," he barked at her. "Paint the wall."

She watched him cross the room, wondering how she was going to survive the coming months. He paused at the door and fingered the ridges along the frame.

"And you can bring me a beer."

Holli painted the wall, but it wasn't until the next day, after it had dried.

She bleached the house, grateful that Marshal had gallons lining the shelves in the garage. No one would have questioned the number of bottles of bleach in the trash, but she put them in bags in her car, just to be safe.

After consciousness left Marshal's body for the last time, Holli wrapped him in plastic wrap, something else he bought in bulk. Anger from her recent beating made it easy to lift his body and carry it to the garage. Once there, he joined the empty bottles of bleach in her truck.

After running through her usual checklist in the house, and eliminating the traces of her presence, she drove to the woods where she had her morning runs. No one was parked in the spaces beside the trail, and the fading light made it unlikely that she'd bump into anyone.

She used her compass to locate the place she'd visited numerous times over the past several months. On the mornings when Marshal had been at the office, Holli would run for a mile, and then she'd dig with the tile shovel, shovel, and buckets she left inside a dead tree log. The hole was eight feet deep, and she'd had to use a rope and buckets to lower herself into it and bring the dirt back up with her. The deeper it got, the slower the process had been for her.

She'd had to walk to the hole with Marshal's body over her shoulders. If she met someone, there would be no denying her purpose off the trail, so she brought along a hunting knife. She hoped she wouldn't have to kill an unsuspecting hiker.

It was fully dark by the time she made it to the hole. The tree with branches that reminded her of a crouching cat marked the area. She had covered her hole with long tree branches and the dry leaves that still clung to them rustled like nails scratching across a floor as she pulled them away.

She wasted no time tossing Marshal's body into what she hoped was his final resting place. He landed at an odd angel, but she felt no desire to point his face to the sky. She pulled out the regular shovel and lifted it, flipping it around once.

It was well into the night and close to morning by the time the hole was halfway full. Holli had rested several times between piling dirt over Marshal's body and she may have fallen asleep once. Her warm clothes kept her body insulated against the cold but quickly caused her to sweat as she worked.

She jogged to her car and opened the trunk. She slung the crossbow and a quiver of bolts over her shoulders and crept back into the woods. It was too early for the morning hikers she usually met on her runs, but deer took advantage of this time to come out and eat.

Holli tried to find a deer close to the hole, but the deer must have smelled her there. She waited one click away, perfectly still against a red maple tree.

Half an hour passed, and Holli began to worry about the time. It was cold, but dedicated exercisers would populate the trails soon. Most of the paths were away from her location, but what if someone ventured beyond the well-worn paths designed for them?

A deer peaked out from behind some low-lying brush. The doe hadn't smelled her, and Holli guessed it was about twenty feet away. She had prepared her bow and lifted it carefully.

Holli didn't casually extinguish a life. After she reached adulthood, a killing was weighed against all the benefits of allowing the life to continue and the murder was methodically planned out. She hadn't killed an animal in a long time, and Holli took in the doe's wide black eyes and sleek movements against the light from a sun that had barely touched the horizon. Everything about the animal whispered nature's beauty.

She released the bolt and it hit its mark. The deer fell immediately, suffering very little.

Holli crouched down. The animal's eyes were open, and one leg twitched as if the doe were still trying to run away.

It took almost every ounce of her energy to pull the deer from the area where she had shot it to the hole. She could only remember a couple of times when she had been more exhausted.

After she removed her quarrel, Holli pushed the doe into the hole, and the deer folded. She felt sorry for the animal. It had been too beautiful to share a grave with a man like Marshal, but Holli had decided on the plan months ago, and she wasn't going to change it. If the authorities somehow found Marshal's unmarked grave, they would be dissuaded by the deer, and she doubted they would dig beneath it, assuming that a careless hunter had buried the animal during the off season.

She'd drunk a bottle of water she'd found in her car, but she wished she'd brought another one with her. Her throat ached for refreshment and her body burned and stunk with sweat. She was certain she was bleeding outside the bandages on her back, but she couldn't change them.

She listened to the rustle of the wind through the trees. The crisp wind felt so heavenly as it caressed her face that she didn't even feel herself slip into sleep.

• • • ● ● • ● ● • •

She awoke with a start. The sun was shining high through the trees, indicating it was well past morning. Holli wasn't as tired, either from the rest or the jolt of adrenaline she had upon waking, but soreness had set into her muscles. Her arms ached and the tops of her thighs were on fire from shoveling dirt and dragging a deer for over half a mile.

Holli walked around the hole, disparaging about the amount of work she still had to do. She started as soon as she stretched out her muscles, eager to complete her mission.

At first, she threw shovelfuls of dirt evenly into the hole, but after a while she began to question her process and started pushing dirt into the hole with the shovel. The result was uneven, so she was forced to resume shoveling the dirt.

Her breaks were more frequent, and when she wasn't in pain from the toll each shovelful of dirt put on her arms and back. She was convinced she heard someone approaching. At one point, she heard a branch break. She threw down the shovel and ran to the source of the sound. Whatever had been there was either an animal or a human who was too fast for her tired legs.

She leveled out the dirt as the sun completed its skyward rotation, and she dusted the area with tree limbs and leaves. She took her crossbow, quiver of bolts, buckets, rope, and shovels with her as she left the area for the last time. Thankfully, no one saw her on the trail to her car with her arms full of questionable objects.

Goodbye, Marshal.

Chapter Seven

"Spit it out!" Hollis demanded, pointing to the large trash can at the other end of the basketball court.

Zach stared at her without an expression.

"March, mister!" The way she addressed him earned her several snickers from the other students.

Hollis thought she had earned Zach's cooperation on the first day of class when he almost matched her stride for stride around the basketball court, but the weeks that followed had proven her wrong. Due to a mix up in scheduling, Zach had been moved from her first class to the last class of the day. By that time, he seemed to be finished with abiding by school rules and decorum.

He tried to switch places with the girls in the class, making the other students laugh when he responded to roll call in a feminine voice. Randomly, he'd break from whatever skill they were learning to bound up and down the bleachers. At first Hollis tried to ignore his behavior, but it became more of a distraction every time.

Hollis crossed her arms and glared at the offending teenager. "Spit your gum in the trash can or I will write out a detention form."

"Ooo," the boys in the class responded. A look from Hollis shushed them.

Hollis was prepared to stare down Zach all day, but she broke eye contact to march to her office. She took out a stack of pink sheets and wrote Zach's name and his offense on one of them. On the day Mrs. Bailey had handed them to her, Hollis had doubted she'd use them, but here she was, proving herself wrong.

She strutted out onto the court and handed Zach the paper. She shone with victory.

Zach didn't take the detention. He simply let the paper flop over in Hollis's hand.

"Hannah," Hollis said, without taking her eyes off Zach. "Go get Principal Bailey."

There was a slight shift in Zach's expression. Hollis had called his bluff, but he wasn't willing to back down.

They stood staring at each other for most of the class, Hollis with the paper in her outstretched hand, Zach with his arms crossed, and the rest of the class conversing from their positions on the court. Finally, Hannah reappeared with Principal Bailey right behind her.

"What are you doing, Zach?" Principal Bailey asked.

Hollis was moved to speak and defend her position, but she remained quiet. Zach's defiance was clear, and it helped her case more to stay silent.

"Zachery." She narrowed her eyes at him, but he wouldn't look at her. "It appears that Coach Bradshaw has given you a detention. I don't have to tell you that this is your third detention, so you will serve an in-school suspension."

Hollis blanched. She hadn't known her punishment would cause Zach so much trouble. She had only been trying to follow school protocols.

"Would you like me to make it a true suspension?" Principal Bailey asked him.

Zach blinked fully, as if he had been startled awake. He looked from Hollis to Principal Bailey, jerking the pink slip from Hollis's hand.

"Good," Principal Bailey said. "I don't expect to have any more trouble from you today." She turned on her heel and called over her shoulder, "Report to Mr. Baker's room tomorrow to serve your suspension."

Zach walked over to the bleachers and stayed there the rest of the class. Hollis let him go. Part of her felt badly about causing him trouble over a stick of chewing gum, and the other part just didn't want to deal with him.

At some point, he must have fallen asleep, because he didn't move when the bell rang. Rose gently shook his arm, and he bounced off the bleacher, yelling something at her. She stomped off as he apologized to her.

In the moment of confusion, Hollis saw something she hadn't noticed. All the kids in Hollis's class were required to dress in a white or gold shirt and black sweatpants. The colors represented the school, and the clothes provided more freedom for movement. When Zach had jumped off the bleacher, his black sweatpants were pulled up on one leg, revealing the skin and curly cues of black hair. Dotted along his ivory skin were old and new burn marks and bruises, easily seen under the unforgiving gymnasium lights.

An emotion welled up in Hollis that she hadn't felt in a long time. She understood that kids sometimes hurt themselves in an attempt to get attention, but that didn't seem to fit Zach's character.

Someone else had put those marks on Zach, and Hollis knew who it was.

Hollis had already collected the eggs that morning, but the sun had hardly risen, so some of the chickens had laid their eggs after she and Josie had left for school. Josie brought them to her in a collection crate, and Hollis stacked them on the truck bed.

"Why do you have so many chickens?" she asked her friend.

Josie pointed to the crate. "Because I can't eat all the eggs fast enough." She arched an eyebrow. "But they haven't laid nearly as many eggs since you've been here."

The women shared a laugh as they completed their chores. Owning a farm was hard work, but Josie maintained her schedule, and the animals seemed to love her.

Josie's father had been a tobacco farmer, but lawsuits and hard times had forced him to stop growing it. The family lived on their livestock until he secured a contract with a produce company. He grew fields of corn and beans until he passed away.

Upon her parents' death, Josie was too young to continue the contract, so she and her aunt fulfilled that year's obligation to the company and were glad to leave the fields bare afterward. Josie had tried to grow some of her own food, but she lacked her father's green thumb, so she tended to the animals. Some of them had been cared for by her parents, so she never entertained the idea of selling them or the property.

Josie brushed the horses and fed them, while Hollis slopped the pigs. It was her favorite part of the farm chores.

Wilber and Bacon rose and carried themselves to the fence. At nearly seven hundred pounds each, the boars could devour a mound of food a day. One of the workers in the cafeteria gave Josie the leftover food, even though she could lose her job for doing so. She argued that the food would be thrown out anyway, so Josie and her pigs should find some use for it.

The white Yorkshires nosed the air, and Hollis filled their trough. She petted them and scratched behind their ears. They snorted and nudged each other out of the way as they ate leftover corn, potatoes, and chicken nuggets.

The pigs were Hollis's favorite animals on the farm, even though Bacon had tried to bite her once. Josie was always nervous about cleaning their pens, but Hollis took over the responsibility gladly.

"Are you ready?" Josie called.

Hollis jogged to the truck, pushing the crate of eggs and her muddy work boots further onto the bed. She shut the tailgate, and the Farm Use Only tag stared back at her in white block letters. The limited use of the truck kept Josie from paying wheel taxes every year, but she had to keep it on her property.

Hollis hopped into the passenger seat, and Josie rode them past fields with haystacks as tall as Hollis. She was struck by an idea.

"You should sell the haystacks."

Josie glanced at her thoughtfully but shook her head. "I usually just donate them to the schools. The kids take pictures with them during their fall festivals."

Josie settled the truck behind the house, and they ran inside. After washing up to their elbows, the girls thought about dinner.

"We could order a pizza," Josie suggested.

"But then the smell of the meat from your half would be all over mine."

Josie rolled her eyes. "Okay, vegetarian princess. I won't have them put any meat on my half."

"Really?" Hollis asked. She couldn't hide her surprise.

Josie stared at her for a moment, and Hollis had the feeling her friend was trying to read her. "You've not had a lot of experience with nice people, have you?"

Hollis didn't mean to hang her head, but she found herself looking at the floor when she responded. "No."

Josie crossed the distance between them and hugged her. "You know you don't have to live that way ever again," she told her. "You can stay here with me, and you won't have to walk on a tight rope for anyone."

Hollis was reminded of her friend's past. "You, too."

Josie broke their contact and fumbled for a subject that would shift Hollis's focus. "Let's order that vegetarian pizza."

Chapter Eight

She eyed him from her place at the bar. He had a full head of black hair, and an angry scar traced his cheek from his eye to his ear. Above the scar, his eye was blind, a milky sheen over its gray iris. He drank Moon Walker beer from the tap, and his glass had a full head of foam at the top. The foam brushed his mustache every time he gulped it down, but he wiped it away with the back of his hand. He was middle-aged, with a medium build, but no other muscles than the ones on his arms had been developed. He deserved the low-lidded gazes of the woman gathered around the pool table. He could have his pick of any of the four of them, and he'd probably bedded them all at one point or another.

She watched his movements, from the nervous twitch in his good eye to the way he leaned into the pool table. She knew his kind.

She was almost ready to make her move when someone sat down beside her. He put his hand on her arm.

A predator didn't startle easily, so she turned her head slowly. A gorgeous man with startling blue eyes and coal-black hair had taken the seat next to her. His height was clear in the way he leaned over in his seat to speak to her. She guessed he was a little over six feet tall.

"Can I bother you a moment?"

Hollis raised an eyebrow and brought her glass to her lips. He misinterpreted her actions and asked the bartender to bring her another cocktail.

"It's a virgin," she reminded the bartender.

His eyes widened in surprise. "You're not drinking alcohol?"

"Not tonight," she replied.

As if remembering his manners, he held out his hand. "I'm Quillen Banes. I think my daughter, Rose, is in your class."

Hollis nodded, not taking his proffered hand. "She is. She seems to be a nice girl."

"Anyway, I saw you sitting here by yourself, and I thought you—"

"— might like for someone to hit on me?" she finished.

He blushed, and the bartender picked that moment to slide her daiquiri to her. He slipped a bill to the girl and waved away his change. Hollis was pleased when she calculated the tip he had allowed for the bartender.

"I'm sorry," she said. "I had a hard day, and I wasn't expecting anyone to join me."

"You mean it's not easy to hang out with a bunch of teenagers all day?" he chuckled. "I never would've guessed." He downed his drink, and based on the color and smell, Hollis guessed it was bourbon.

"I'm Hollis," she told him, twirling her thin red straw through her drink and not offering her last name. She didn't want a man who made her breath catch to call her by her last name.

"It's nice to officially meet you, Hollis," he said, handing his empty glass to the bartender. A hint of sage floated to her as his cologne drifted past.

"Is there anything to do around here?" He motioned around the walls with muted light and the town's bar flies. "I mean, besides frequent this wonderful establishment, of course." He winked at the bartender to soften the blow, but she barely offered a smile in return.

Hollis took a sip of her daquiri, and it turned into a long drink. "I wouldn't know. I'm new here, too."

Quillen seemed confused. "Oh, so you just started at the school?"

Hollis nodded once. "Josie —I mean Mrs. Gouge— told me there was a job opening at the academy."

"I think she's Rosie's English teacher," he mused.

"She is if Rose is studying Julius Caesar, because Josie has lived and breathed that play for the past week."

He smiled at her warmly, and she was mesmerized by his eyes. Thankful she hadn't consumed alcohol, she finished her drink and told him she needed to go home.

"Can I walk you to your car?" Quillen asked.

The bartender threw her a glance, but Hollis held up her hand. "It's okay, Missy. His kid is in one of my classes."

Even sober, Hollis had a little trouble negotiating the gravel parking lot in high heels. Quillen held out his arm, and she used it for support. Normally, she would have turned down the gesture, but he seemed kind, and she didn't want to fall in front of him.

She pressed the fob, and her doors unlocked. "This is me," she declared.

"I had a Jetta in college," he commented, surveying her car. "Mine was diesel, though."

"Well, I'm going home to get some sleep. It was nice— " She turned to quickly, and her foot turned in her shoe. He caught her around the waist and held her to him.

"— to meet you," he finished.

Hollis was so close that his warm breath sent shivers across her bare neck. If he noticed, he was too chivalrous to say anything, and steadied her in front of her car door.

After her failed attempt at a casual goodbye, she couldn't look at him. "Have a good night."

"Maybe we could have dinner one night," he offered.

She closed her eyes. She had almost made a clean getaway. *How was she going to tell this beautiful man that she wasn't going to date him?* Then it hit her.

"I'm Rose's teacher," she reminded him. "It wouldn't be appropriate."

He rested his hand on her car. "I'm sorry, Hollis. I just thought it'd be nice to get to know someone here, and when you told me you were new to town, too, I felt like you might enjoy the company."

She sighed inwardly. *It was a break, right?* She could be like any normal person, and normal people accepted friendly dinner offers from handsome men with eyes the color of island sea water.

She gave him her number, but she didn't give him the chance to offer his. She jumped into her car and was surprised when she saw him watching her leave. She threw up an uncertain hand when she passed him, and he returned her gesture.

Hollis was trying to be an average person, and if ordinary people had crushes, then she had the biggest one of all.

Chapter Nine

Asher, Part 1

Hollis fell into his arms, laughing until she was almost hoarse. "Stop it. I'm going to pee!" She tried to wriggle away, but Asher held her. His fingers stopped poking along her ribs, but his hands lifted her up to meet his eyes.

"I have never loved anyone more than you," he declared.

Hollis rolled her eyes. "What about Martina?"

"Martina who?"

She batted him with a pillow. She was used to his playfulness.

His chocolate eyes regarded her seriously. "Hollis, you know you're my whole world."

She rolled onto him and straddled him, letting her auburn hair fall around his face. "How can you love me after everything I told you?"

He caressed her face and let his fingers linger at her chin. "I'm not going to judge you for anything you told me." He took one of her hands and held it to his heart. "I'm safe." He knocked her hand against his chest to emphasize his point. "And you're safe with me."

She believed him. From the moment they'd met, Asher had been everything to her. He seemed to hold her on a pedestal, cherishing her fine points and dismissing her flaws. Any faults she had were forgotten when he held her and whispered her name.

She had been too scared to start a relationship with Asher right away, but he had been patient. He'd told her that he would wait on her, and she had dragged out the first part of their relationship for months, hardly allowing him to hold her hand. Part of her wanted to jump into his arms, but another part of her knew that he would run away when he saw the real her, so she strung him along without a hope for a real future. Finally, after too much liquor on a rainy night, she had told him her secret. All of it.

At first, he had simply looked at her as if he were expecting there was more to the story. Then he scrubbed his hands over his clean-shaven face. He realized he needed to say something, and he looked almost mortified at the prospect of speaking. He stared with wide eyes at a spot on the rug, one that she had scrubbed, but she couldn't get it clean, so she had decided to let it stay in her apartment, like another picture on the wall or a tiny trinket from her past. She kept her eyes on the spot, too, as if doing so would somehow connect them.

Please don't leave me, she begged in her mind. *Treat me however you want—I want to be punished for it— but don't leave me.*

She didn't want to admit to her attachment, but Asher had won a place in her life, and if he passed her test, then it was proof that they were meant to be together. She didn't speak until his mouth moved, and when it did, she was convinced she hadn't heard him correctly.

"You did what you had to do."

It was all he said, but his expression softened, and he pulled Hollis into an embrace. He held her to him, and she cried. Maybe her tears were over the terrible things she had done, but her mood was lighter. The guilt had been diminished by Asher's love and acceptance, so the worry about her past lifted like the fog off the mountains on a sunny day.

That night, she'd let Asher all the way into her heart and into her bed. She had declared herself a secondary virgin, never having a choice about her first sexual experiences. Asher was gentle with her, and it was everything her first time should have been like. Afterward, he held her in his arms and promised forever.

They were inseparable, going to parties together and lining up their classes at the same time. When she thought back to that night, she realized that her tears had nothing to do with her past. The distrust she had for men was still there, bubbling under her surface interactions, but she believed there were good men in the world. All of them didn't want to hurt her.

Her sobs had long subsided. They had been part of the effect of letting go and revealing her secret. She cried because she felt absolved, and she could finally move forward with a man who was her future.

Chapter Ten

"You're going on a date with my teacher," Rose said to him.

Quillen eyed himself in the mirror, checking for a stray hair or a rogue blemish. "I'm taking a beautiful woman, Hollis, out for a date."

Rose was adamant and threw both hands into the air. "But she's my teacher!".

"He turned to her, realizing the true reason for her distress. Taking her in his arms, he explained, "It doesn't mean I've forgotten our family."

Always pushing boundaries, Rose asked, "What does it mean?" Her words were slightly muffled against his chest.

"It means that I met a woman, had an interesting talk, and now I want to continue that conversation at a nice restaurant."

"Because you want to get her into bed."

He moved her out at arm's length. "Rosie!" He prepared to scold her, but she was so dejected that he couldn't bear to be cross with her. He let her lean against the door frame while he thought of the best way to address her.

"It's been two years," he started. "I think it's time I date again."

Rose crossed her arms.

"Just because I go out on a date, doesn't mean that anything more will come of it."

He was struck by a sudden thought. *Had Beth had time to talk to Rose about the birds and the bees?* It seemed like a conversation they would've had by the time Rose was almost fourteen, but he couldn't be sure. He asked Rose, and earned a look of such repulsion, that he moved on without mentioning any more about her knowledge of the intimacies between adults.

"So, what do you want from Coach Bradshaw?"

He sighed. "I only want to get to know her a little better." He was tired of explaining his intentions to his teenage daughter, so he treaded out into rougher waters. "Sometimes, men like to go out with women to see them smile." He squirted some high dollar cologne on a patch of skin just below his collar bone. "They want to look into their eyes, and—"

"Eww! Enough!" Rose exclaimed, covering her ears with her hands as if to block out her father's words.

Quillen's smile stretched across his face, but he was the only one who saw it. He kissed the top of Rose's head. "I'll be back around midnight."

Hollis lamented her punctuality. She should have done what Josie said, and entered the restaurant a few minutes late, but her military training, or her anxiousness, had won over, and now she sat in the restaurant at the exact time Quillen had specified, waiting on him.

Every time the door opened, sucking air into the foyer like a gasp, she looked up, ready to see him. Quillen messaged her five minutes after the agreed-upon time, telling her he was five minutes away. She appreciated the text, but she would've been more inclined to forgive his tardiness if he had phoned or messaged her five minutes *before* she was supposed to meet him. She didn't reply to his message and spent the next five minutes thinking of a way to gracefully get out of the date before he arrived.

Quillen breezed into the building, and her heart stopped. He looked handsome in his dark gray suit and stark white shirt, and a few heads turned when they caught a glimpse of his blue eyes and raven black hair. As soon as he saw her, he seemed to glide over to her with such confident moves that she found it hard to hold his gaze.

"I'm sorry," he told her. "I mismanaged my time, and I deeply regret it. Can you forgive me?"

Hollis had expected a number of excuses that placed the blame on everything from wrecks and traffic lights to the weather. She was startled by the way he accepted the blame for his actions and offered a sincere apology to her for it.

She found herself saying, "It's okay," and meaning it.

The host seated them in a more intimate section of the restaurant, surrounded by other tables with singular couples talking in low voices. Some of them were holding hands as they spoke, but others were as unfamiliar with each other as Hollis and Quillen, pausing their strained conversations for delicate bites.

The host had led them past bright booths with families sharing their days and their plates, but the section in which she and Quillen were deposited was hushed and encouraged a quieter exchange. Soft classical music played in the background, and Hollis imagined it was a skilled pianist's interpretation of Chopin's Waltz in D-flat Major.

Accepting the wine list, Quillen hardly opened it before he asked for a bottle of Zinfandel. He didn't consult her about the wine, possibly relying on his own expertise and the type of food offered, but she was glad when he didn't order her food. The waitress committed their requests to memory and disappeared after she complimented their choices. Hollis wondered if her hasty exit had more to do with efficiency or because she wanted to enter their meals before she forgot them.

Hollis and Quillen prattled through the usual pleasantries. She was feeling better about taking him up on his dinner offer until he asked, "Where were you born?"

It was a seemingly innocuous question, but it distressed Hollis. *Should she answer him honestly or give him the answer Holli gave to anyone who asked?* His glass was midway to his lips, but her changed expression had alarmed him.

"Did I say something wrong?"

She hugged her arms around her body without thinking and released herself into a more relaxed posture. She took a breath to consider her response.

"No, Quillen. You said nothing wrong." She took a sip of her wine. "I think I'm just out of practice with the whole dating thing."

His smile lit up his eyes. "You couldn't be any more out of practice than me. Rosie didn't know what to think when I told her I was going out."

She chuckled and then arched her eyebrow. "Is this your first date since..." She trailed off, not knowing the best way to complete her sentence.

He picked up on her awkwardness, but he fingered the stem of his wine glass before speaking. "It's the first time I've been out since my wife and I were together."

Hollis felt terribly when she noted the tear that slipped from his eye. Before she knew it, she picked up her chair and placed it beside him. She took Quillen's hand in her own, and he glanced up at her gratefully before shifting his attention back to the wine glass. He drained it in one long drink, the liquid traveling soundlessly down his throat.

"I'm sorry," she told him. She wanted to hug him, but she feared he would think she was too forward. "What can I do?"

He wiped away the track the tear had made down his cheek. "There's nothing you can do. There's nothing anyone can do now."

Josie had told Hollis some of Quillen's sad story while she was preparing for their date. She hadn't prepared to talk about it before they received their entrées, though.

Quillen took a deep breath and shook his head. "I'm okay," he promised. She loved his smile but worried that it wasn't as sincere as his usual one.

She moved back to her original spot at the table. Hoping to steer the conversation to a more agreeable topic, she asked, "Are you close to your family?"

He shook his head. "Rosie and I are it," he said. "My parents died when I was a teenager, and Beth's mom and dad don't keep in touch after"—he paused—"Well, you can imagine how strange our relationship would be after everything that happened."

Hollis nodded.

"Did Mrs. Gouge tell you?"

"Josie tells me everything," Hollis confirmed. "But I had no idea until I told her I was going out with you." She didn't want Quillen to think her friend gossiped.

His eyebrows shot up. "Why would you? We were lucky enough to keep it out of the news because of that big fire in the mid-west."

He allowed the waitress to refill his wine glass when she delivered their food. Hollis hadn't noticed when they ordered, but she quickly realized her companion's meal was meatless.

"Are you a vegetarian?" she blurted out. She was used to receiving comments about her lifestyle, and she regretted her outburst.

He took a piece of bread from the basket, breaking it, but not adding butter to it. "I'm actually vegan," he told her. "I chose this restaurant because their bread and pasta dishes are made without animal products."

"I'm vegetarian, so I can appreciate that," she returned.

He considered her. "You never made a jump into veganism?"

Hollis wondered if he was judging her until his face opened up into a wide smile. He took a bite of his roll and motioned to the butter.

"The butter is made with real cream, so I forgo it, but I can enjoy all this" —he motioned to his plate of pesto in olive oil—"and no one is any wiser about my proclivities."

"I never thought about checking a restaurant out before I went there," Hollis mused. "I just picked something without meat from their menu."

Quillen pointed at her. "You should take control of your life. Don't just go along with the crowd."

Hollis almost choked on her wine. Once she regained her composure, she said, "I doubt anyone would accuse me of that."

Hollis declined Quillen's offer when he asked her about dessert, and at Hollis's insistence, they each paid their portion of the bill when the check arrived. Quillen left a considerable tip for the waitress, telling Hollis not to contribute to it since she had paid for half of the wine he had selected.

Quillen held open the door and they stepped out into the chilly evening air. "It's a good night for hayrides," he commented.

Hollis glanced down at his moderately expensive suit and backed up. "I wouldn't have guessed you for a hayride type of person."

He stood up to his full height. "Why, you're lookin' at the winner of the Pike County Hay Heftin' Contest," he said with an accentuated southern drawl.

"You're from Kentucky," she asked. She hadn't heard a distinct accent before his admission, but she knew dialect could be erased over time. She had done it.

"That was years ago," he said, returning to his usual voice. "It was beautiful there, and the people were kind, but I moved out west when I was seventeen, with a head full of dreams, and" —he looked at her with a mischievous grin. "Well, you get the idea."

Hollis giggled, surprising herself. She liked Quillen's easy manner and openness. She felt perfectly at ease with him.

At her car, he spun her around. He looked at her for permission, and she nodded, almost imperceptibly.

He didn't close his eyes, but the feelings that swirled around her mouth and her body caused Hollis to lower her lids. She opened them once and noticed that he was watching her. She broke their contact easily but firmly.

He ran a hand through his hair, and it fell perfectly back into place. "Was that weird?" he asked.

Hollis had catered to a wide range of fetishes. It had thrown her off, but it was nothing from which she couldn't easily recover.

"Not at all," she told him. "I'm just not used to it."

His mouth raised on one side. "I'm a visual person. I like to see the effect I have on the women I kiss."

Hollis smirked. "So I'm not the only one after all."

It was dark, but she thought she noticed a blush creep up from his neck. It gave him a healthy glow.

He cupped her face and she looked into his eyes. He kissed her lips but didn't part them, and they stared at each other.

Hollis thought it would be uncomfortable, but it made her feel more connected to him. He released her and drew a finger down her jawline.

"No, Hollis. You're the only one."

Chapter Eleven

"How was it?" Josie asked.

Hollis stared at her friend and dropped her keys into the dish by the door. "It was a date. A simple date that you forced me to go on."

Josie didn't deny that she had applied firm pressure to get Hollis to meet Quillen for dinner. "But he was sweet, wasn't he?" she said. "I can tell he's sweet."

Josie had the ability to read people when it came to anyone beyond her romantic reach. She had failed to choose men who would be kind to her, but she had successfully set up several teachers at Pale Woods Academy who were happily married to the partners Josie had suggested.

"He was late, and he didn't text me until five minutes after he was supposed to be there," she told Josie. She watched her face fall, worried that she had urged Hollis into a terrible evening.

After Hollis was satisfied with the effect her words had on her friend, she sighed. "But then he gave me a real apology, not the kind full of blame, and it turned out to be nice."

Josie recovered quickly. "I knew it! I knew he was a good guy!" She spun around in the foyer.

Hollis smiled at her friend's reaction. She was happy Josie was excited about her night, but she wanted her to have similar experiences. Josie was waiting for a man who would never come back, and she needed to be living her life.

Josie grabbed a container of chocolate ice cream, two spoons, and met Hollis in the living room. Hollis kicked off her low heels, happy to be out of the pretty, restrictive shoes. She dug into the chocolate ice cream and noticed that Josie had gotten the kind with bits of cookie dough. She closed her eyes and savored the feel of the silky ribbons of chocolate as they slid across her tongue.

Josie lifted the leg rest on her chair and curled her legs into the seat. She turned her body to face Hollis and looked at her eagerly. "Okay, spill it."

Hollis told Josie about the food, the wine, Quillen's near break down, and her feelings about it. Josie took bites off her spoon, never breaking eye contact.

"Do you think he still misses his wife?" she asked.

Hollis twirled her spoon around the partially melted ice cream. "Yeah. But that's not a bad thing, right?" She looked up into her friend's sympathetic face. "If you take Rose's age into account, they were together for almost two decades."

Josie abandoned her temporarily happy mood. "I shouldn't have let you go on a date with him. It was selfish of me."

"What do you mean?" Hollis asked, but she understood. Josie wasn't going to reach for her own happiness, so she hoped to grab some residual dopamine from Hollis after her date.

Josie put her spoon in the container. "I've been really lonely lately. It's been years since Cotton left me, and I'm starting to wonder if he'll ever come back."

Hollis waited for her friend to cry, but Josie held her emotions in check. She pulled at the fabric on an old blanket she'd thrown over her legs.

"I thought the two of you would make a nice couple, but I didn't know him that well," she admitted. "I should have talked to him a little more before I pushed you on him."

Hollis held her finger up. "Hey. I'm not your responsibility." Hurt flashed over Josie's face, but Hollis continued. "You may have gently pushed me in Quillen's direction, but I'm the one who decided to go." She took her friend's hand. "This is *my* break, remember? After this school year, I may stay here, or I may go back into the military, but those are my decisions, and as much as I value your opinion, I don't want you to feel responsible for my mistakes."

Hollis had no intention of going back into the military, but it was a necessary lie to keep Josie away from the truth. If her friend knew the demons she had to fight every day, she would run screaming in the other direction.

Josie squeezed her hand. "You're right. But please don't let me influence you. Be sure Quillen is over his wife before you see him again."

"It'll be hard for me to stay away after our goodnight kiss."

Hollis had been waiting for the perfect time to release that bit of information, and she was glad to see Josie's features transform. Smiling wide enough to bring light back into her eyes, Josie picked her spoon back up and stabbed the coldest part of the treat. Hollis told her about every moment, sparing no details.

"That sounds so much like my first kiss with Cotton," she reflected. "You may be heading for a relationship with Quillen yet."

Hollis didn't comment on Josie's memory of her husband. She tried not to encourage her friend's misremembered contentment with a man who was way less than her ideal match.

"I bet he's good in the sack," Josie said, jarring Hollis from her thoughts.

Ice cream flew out of Hollis's mouth and nose. After her coughing fit subsided, and she'd wiped brown droplets off the arm of the chair, she asked her friend, "How would you know? If I remember correctly, your sexual experience amounts to exactly one partner."

She colored. "I just know these things," she replied with her nose slightly elevated.

Hollis and Josie talked about where Quillen might take her for a second date, and when he might call her again. By the time they'd exhausted every part of her experience, both women were ready for bed. Hollis watched Josie ascended the steps dreamily and smiled. She was glad that she'd brought some joy to her friend's life.

Hollis took their spoons to the sink and washed them after throwing away the empty container of ice cream. She climbed the steps, eager to slip out of her evening dress and thankful she hadn't gotten ice cream on it.

At the top of the stairs, next to Josie's room, hung the last picture Josie and Cotton had taken together. They had hosted a fall festival for the academy and had set up haystacks and pumpkins at the entrance to their farm. His white hair whipped in the wind, and her eyes were fixed on him, admiring a man who didn't deserve her.

Cotton was the worst thing that ever happened to Josie, but she held onto him with unfailing devotion. Hollis wished she could have kept them from meeting, but instead, she'd have to try to find a way to help her friend get over him.

Chapter Twelve

Cotton, Part One

Hollis stared up at her temporary home. The two-story farmhouse, with its tall windows, wrap-around porch, and wide-open spaces was the ideal spot for a little down time.

Josie had invited her to stay with her for a while, and Hollis had immediately agreed. The police were searching for her last victim, and a neighbor had provided them with a decent composite sketch of her. She didn't want to be interviewed as a person of interest, so she'd jumped at the chance to hide out until the situation cooled down.

She climbed the steps tentatively, and she heard people yelling. She recognized her friend's voice, tired and meekly protesting to the shouts of her enraged husband.

"You'll march right down there and apologize to her!" he yelled.

Hollis wanted to retreat to her car and stop listening to their marital disagreement, but she couldn't pull herself away. Couples had disagreements, but there was something in his tone that made her instantly protective of her friend.

"But I saw you with her," Josie protested. Her voice was small and pleading. "I'd never mistake your hair—"

"But you did!" he argued. "I was at the bowling alley, like I told you, and you saw Phyllis with another man."

Her friend's voice hardly carried to Hollis's ears. "I didn't even know her name was Phyllis."

Hollis imagined the silence that followed was due to his shock at her statement, but when he spoke again, Josie's husband was calm and condescending.

"Look, you're upset because you thought you saw me with another woman." He let out a forced chuckle. "I get it. You women can be possessive when it comes to your man. But there are plenty of blond men out there." He said something Hollis couldn't make out, so she took another step.

A loud creak announced her presence, and the conversation halted. She froze, unsure what to do, but their footsteps jolted her into action.

The light oak door swung open, and Josie ran out to greet her. The three adults were unwilling to discuss the exchange Hollis might have heard, so no one mentioned it as she was ushered into the house and shown each room.

After she had seen the three upstairs bedrooms, and toured the kitchen, dining room, and living room downstairs, Hollis was offered a glass of sweet tea. She declined, asking instead for water, and Josie hurried to the kitchen to get it for her.

In the melee, she had been introduced to Fred "Cotton" Jones, and her opinion was even less of him than it was after she'd heard the argument he'd had with Josie. She had shaken the hand he offered, but she had hardly looked at him when they were introduced. She didn't want to encourage the behavior she'd heard. As expected, his pride had been wounded, and he'd stayed in the living room.

They sat silently, Cotton staring at her, and Hollis pretending she was overly interested in a picture of Josie with her parents. After a few seconds, though, Hollis wondered why she was avoiding his gaze, and she met his cold, dark eyes. In that moment, an understanding passed between them. Hollis knew what kind of person he was, and he hated her for it.

Chapter Thirteen

The note was on her desk, written in big block letters.

STAY AWAY FROM HIM

She knew exactly what it meant, but she didn't know who had written it. She ran down the hall and asked everyone she met if they had seen anyone go into her office or in the direction of the gymnasium. No one could remember seeing anyone go in that direction, but the only people in the building were busy staff members, and they had other things on their minds. Too late, she realized that she should have been asking them if they had seen anyone who wasn't a teacher.

Throughout the day, she stretched her mind in different directions until she talked herself out of anything truly nefarious. Her leading theory was that Rose had planted the note because she was afraid Hollis was attempting to replace her mother, and by the time Rose shuffled in to the last class of the day, Hollis had convinced herself the girl had planted the note.

She didn't want to personally confront her, so she took the note and passed it under the eyes of every student in her class. She watched each of their expressions, but she paid careful attention to Rose.

Rose looked at the words with the same amount of interest as her peers. She seemed to be nothing more than generally curious.

"Who's husband were you with?" joked Darrin.

"Are you a homewrecker, Coach B?" Aiden's grin stretched across his face until he met her eyes. He quickly stuffed his hands in the pockets of his sweatpants and looked at the floor.

"I found this paper in my office this morning," Hollis said. "Someone laid it on my desk and ran off like a coward."

She remembered the meetings she'd attended that discussed the proper way to speak to students and it hadn't included insulting them. She changed directions.

"Does anyone know who would write a note like this or recognize this handwriting?"

Rose lifted her head. At first, Hollis thought she had caught her culprit, but then Rose's eyebrows drew together, as if she were bothered by something more.

That look was all it took to convince Hollis that Rose hadn't written the note, but she had a good idea who had done it.

Chapter Fourteen

Vinent

"You spoil me," Holli said in a heated whisper.

He held it in front of her, and she pushed her hair up. His breath tickled her neck as he secured the clasp. He knew what he was doing to her, and he laughed good-naturedly as gooseflesh raced across her arms.

The necklace was beautiful. A full karat diamond in a teardrop shape fell against her chest. She felt the weight of it, simultaneously comforting and incriminating.

He trailed kisses down her neck until he reached her shoulder. His tongue swirled around her clavicle, and she breathed him in. His rich cologne and minty shampoo gave off clean scents that attracted her, but the beer on his breath and the sweat on his skin created a darker layer of his essence. He pulled her to him, his eyes never leaving her as he lay her head gently on a pillow. She was drawn to him until he was satisfied.

Afterward, he played with the necklace as he held her. "Did you enjoy tonight, darling?"

"Yes," she cooed back. Then, knowing what he wanted to hear, she asked, "You don't have to go, do you?"

He lifted up on his elbow. The moonlight cast shadows across his high cheekbones, and his dark eyes were pools of ink in the absence of sunlight. She almost wondered if she had met a creature darker than herself.

His tender touch was out of place with her thoughts, and she looked at the wall just behind him, so she could concentrate on his words.

"I can wait to leave until tomorrow night, but I have to go."

She put her hand on his chest and he brought it to his lips, settling back onto the pillow. She lay against his chest, counting his heartbeats and wondering if they matched her own.

"I love you, Vincent."

Instead of returning the sentiment, he sang to her. His voice was deliberate and sweet, each line a tribute to her.

When he was finished, she asked, "Is the song about me?"

He hugged her arms to her body briefly, before whispering, "It is for you, mi amore. Soon, our love won't be locked away in a secret song."

Holli sat up, hating the hope that filled her. "You're leaving her for me?" She didn't dare say her name. His wife was a presence who hung between them, disturbing their calm or adding more fervor to their appetite for each other.

He nodded. "It is time."

Holli drew circles on his chest and kissed his shoulder. "But what about the children?"

"They are older now, so they will come here for visits." His fingers ran down the length of her jaw. "And we could have more."

Holli bristled at the mention of having children with him. Suddenly, fear gripped her, and she wanted to run.

He kissed her passionately, but she moved away.

"What's wrong, my darling?"

Holli excused herself to go to the bathroom. Once there, she opened the medicine cabinet. It took forever to crush all the sleeping pills into a fine powder, but she emptied the result into her hand. In the kitchen, she mixed the pills into his favorite beer, grabbing herself a glass of wine.

She entered the bedroom balancing the bottle and glass.

"That's how I always want you to serve me," he said, eyeing her naked curves.

"Always," she returned.

"Why are we drinking?" He placed the beer on the table. "I thought we were ready to sleep."

She needed him to drink all of it. A couple of sips would only make him go to sleep, and that wasn't her aim. She tried to be clever, and her mind landed on something believable, but she was loathe to tell the lie. It went against every fiber of her being.

"I wanted to play a game with you," she told him. His silence urged her to continue. "I've wanted to try this for a long time, but I've never felt comfortable enough with anyone to do it."

He moved up a little on his pillow. "Tell me your fantasy, and I will make it come true."

She sat on the bed and took a sip of her wine before she placed it on the bedside table. She leaned into him and whispered, fluttering her fingers down his chest as she spoke.

He didn't respond immediately after she finished, and she thought he was going to try to talk her out of it. Then he said, "With the beer bottle?"

She nodded and hoped he could see her in the absence of light. She didn't think she could say anything more to entice him, especially since it was one of the last things she'd ever want to do.

He stared off, seemingly at war with his feelings. She thought he was going to turn her down, suggesting some other socially acceptable fantasy.

"I want to do it." His voice was cold, almost distant, as if she had awoken a part of him that he kept buried in a far-off place. He jumped off the bed and grabbed the beer.

"What are you doing?" she asked almost too loudly. A hint of panic laced her question.

"I'm pouring it out," he said incredulously. "We can't do what you suggested with a full bottle."

"Vincent," she said, trying to return to her flirty voice. "Drinking the beer is part of my fantasy." She waited a moment and added, "I know you can understand the need to play out the scene in my mind."

He may have nodded, but she couldn't tell. Her eyes hadn't fully adjusted to the darkness, and she hoped he wouldn't see particles of the sleeping pills bouncing off the bottle. He sat down on the bed and gulped it down like a frat boy at a party. He pushed her onto the bed, without much interest at first, but once she cried out in mock surprise, he rushed at her, grabbing her hips so hard she had bruises from his fingers for a week. She dragged out the foreplay, thrashing around in the bed as if she were scared, but keeping her body close enough for him to hold. He started losing momentum after fifteen minutes and questioned why she kept dodging his more heated advances. Through slurred words, he turned her over and begged to fulfill her request.

Finally, she had no other option. Perhaps his years on the road had built up his tolerance to drugs, and the sleeping pills would merely knock him out. She steeled herself for him to carry out her spurious request just as his face dropped onto her back. He lay there as she counted out almost a full minute before bouncing back up. He tried again, but she dropped her body onto the bed and sighed deeply.

"That was fantastic!" She grabbed him and pulled him to her.

He tried to lift up, but he couldn't support his weight. "But I didn't do it."

She sat up, feigning surprise. "Yes, you did. And it was the best experience of my life."

She thought she saw his mouth lift up in the corners before his face fell. "I'll do anything to please you."

Holli ran her nails down his cheek, but there was no reaction. "I know."

She waited for him to stop breathing, but his breaths continued to puff. At one point, a belch escaped, and she smelled Moon Walker beer.

She wasn't disappointed that the pills had failed to kill him, but she was ready for it to be over. She pressed the edge of the pillow to his nose and mouth. There was little resistance, as his mind had shut down due to the effects of the drugs, and soon his chest stopped moving. She waited, ticking off the time in her head. After ten minutes, she rose and dressed.

First, she took the designer shoes, dresses, and jewelry in the spacious walk-in closet and stuffed them into bags. She organized his suits in the open spaces, carefully making it seem as though he was the only one who occupied the apartment.

Luckily, she hadn't waited long to complete her mission. A doorman noticed her coming in and out with Vincent twice, but due to his fame, they usually left through the back entrance. Vincent had asked her to wear a wig that resembled the hairstyle of his producer in case the paparazzi found them entering or exiting the building, so she doubted the doorman would remember her well enough to provide a description.

Vincent had leased the apartment when he had taken her as his mistress. The cathedral ceilings, ornate portraits, and crisp, designer furniture had been mostly depressing to her. She had chosen to stay in the bedroom, so she had less to wipe down than if she had truly relaxed within the confines of the apartment.

As fast as she worked, she was still thorough, so it took the rest of the night to clean. She left him sprawled on his stomach, but she moved the fabric away from his mouth. She put her toiletries in a bag with the clothes. She sorted through the trash, taking condoms and wrappers, but leaving the bottles of beer he drank before the last one she gave him. She put that one in the bag with the condoms.

"Goodbye, Vincent," she told the body.

She left the apartment with the bags of clothes, shoes, and jewelry, the bag of trash with the beer bottle, and the clothes she wore. The extra key Vincent had given her to the apartment was tucked into a drawer where he had put circulars and odds and ends.

An hour later, daylight was blinding her as she drove into a city only slightly larger than the one in which she'd just resided. Her first stop was a store that claimed donated items were given to women who had suffered from domestic abuse. She dropped off the bags of jewelry, clothes, and shoes. The lady behind the counter couldn't disguise her surprise as she skimmed through the designer pieces. "Ma'am, I don't know how to write you a receipt for this."

"No receipt," she told her. "I'm getting out of a bad relationship, and I don't want to keep anything he bought me."

The lady's expression reshuffled, and her mouth formed a thin line. "I can understand that." She glanced at the items she'd unpacked. "There will be a lot of grateful women who can profit from your donation. Showing up for interviews in these nice clothes may get them a better paying job."

Holli smiled and waved. Back in the car, she pulled at her wig. The dark hair framed her face, and the bangs covered the small scar on her forehead. Soon, she'd be able to take out the contacts that colored her eyes a muddy brown.

The post office was seven blocks away, and she hurried inside, grabbing a small shipping box. She waited in line for twenty-five minutes before a dark-haired man with olive skin and bright, green eyes waited on her. During her wait, she had unclasped the necklace, cleaned it with bleach wipes, and put it in the box. One lady wrinkled her nose from the smell, but Holli glared at her, daring her to meet her eyes. She didn't close it until she had been told the shipping cost.

"That's a real beauty," he commented. "Do you want to put insurance on it?"

Holli paid to insure its arrival. She couldn't write a note, but, hopefully, Vincent's wife would think he had mailed it to her.

Holli left the post office and pulled into the gas station adjacent to it. She stuffed the bag of trash from the apartment into a trash can as she pumped gas. She parked the car and watched the trash can and the people who moved in and out of the store.

Holli bid her time until the sun was low in the sky before one of the workers emptied the trash cans, carrying them to the dumpster. She waited several more hours, using an app to match faces with social media accounts, before she spotted her next target.

A black SUV with a green stripe squealed out of the parking lot, and Holli pulled out behind it.

Chapter Fifteen

Quillen didn't call Hollis for almost a week.

She tried to steer her mind off it by keeping herself busy. She wrote detailed lesson plans, went on long runs, and cleaned everything in sight, but she couldn't keep from checking her phone for a message or missed call at least every thirty minutes.

Her mood soured from her presumed rebuff, and it spilled over into other parts of Hollis's life. She was a little less patient with the students in her classes, handing out more detentions for misbehavior that she usually let slide, and shutting herself in her room instead of spending her evenings in the living room or kitchen with Josie.

After three days of Hollis's remoteness, Josie knocked on the door to her room and let herself inside. She offered Hollis a semi-warm cup of chamomile tea and sat on the bed facing her.

"Spill it," Josie said, nodding to Hollis's cup, "and I don't mean the tea."

Hollis had been in the middle of grading a quiz she had given the students about the circulatory system. They all had perfect scores, except Zach, who didn't try to answer them correctly. He breezed through the test on his tablet, and when Hollis's laptop had notified her that he was the first one finished, she had felt her spirits rise. But when she glanced over his work, she saw that he had chosen the letter "d" for all the questions. She had kept him after class and spoken to him as he eyed the exit and bounced in place like he was ready to make a dash out the door. When she had asked him why he had picked "d" for every question he had told her, "Because that's the grade I need to pass your bogus class."

Josie listened to Hollis talk about Zach. "He had a rough day today," she told Hollis. "They sent him to the office for throwing his tray in the cafeteria."

Hollis's eyes widened. "Did he hit anyone?"

Josie smirked. "No, but he probably should have. Pumpkin Thomas was calling him names."

Hollis was of the opinion that a child with the name "Pumpkin" should refrain from calling other students names. He was over six feet tall, and had a defensive lineman's build, so he could settle the difference with anyone who didn't like his brand of teasing.

"Does he have another in-school suspension?"

Josie confirmed it. "And I think Mrs. Bailey is at her wits end. She's going to have to expel him if he doesn't calm down for a while."

"She can't do that," Hollis blurted out. She regretted saying what she was thinking, not because Josie was untrustworthy, but because it felt like she was betraying Zach.

Josie was sipping her tea and lowered her cup quickly. "Don't worry. She'd only expel him for a week."

Hollis stared at the red and white swirling pattern on her bedspread. She muttered something Josie couldn't hear. When Josie asked her to repeat herself, she said, "He has bruises."

It surprised Hollis when Josie responded. "I know."

Hollis's eyes flipped up. "You *know*? Why haven't you done any-thing?"

Josie lowered her eyes. Hollis could sense her shame, and when she spoke, her frustration was clear. "There's not a lot we can do"—she shook her head— "as educators, I mean."

Hollis had been present for the meetings that discussed the pros and cons of an educator becoming involved in a student's homelife, and abuse had been discussed. She pressed Josie to express her feelings about the cases she'd seen at the school.

Josie bit the inside of her cheek before she answered. "It's never good to see a child suffering. Luckily, we don't see a lot of cases of abuse."

Hollis wondered how many children were in distress at home, but they were able to mask their concerns around their teachers and friends at school. Hollis knew there were more ways to abuse someone than physically, and she felt a draw to the children who suffered in silence. Maybe that was the reason she paid special attention to Zach, even though his attitude begged her to back off.

"We've talked about a hard subject, but Zach's abuse has been going on for years." Josie searched for Hollis's eyes until Hollis lifted her head. "Something has been bothering you for the past week, though. What's going on?"

Hollis gave up trying to hide her hurt from her friend. "He hasn't called me."

"Quillen?"

"Yeah," Hollis said. "Maybe I read too much into our kiss, or—"

"Don't do that," Josie interjected. "You've not done anything wrong or misinterpreted signals." She grabbed Hollis's hand and held it. "Quillen suffered a tragedy that eliminated half his family. He may have decided he's not ready to date. But whatever the reason, it has nothing to do with you."

Hollis squeezed her friend's hand and then let it go. "It's hard not to take it personally."

"Sure," Josie agreed.

Hollis closed her laptop and put it beside her. "I just wish I knew if he was going to call, or if I've been ghosted."

Josie seemed thoughtful. "I may have a way to find out," she said, hiding her smile with her cup as she took a drink.

Chapter Sixteen

Rose didn't wait for him to shut the door before she told him about the note in Hollis's office. "It's started again."

The wave of terror that crashed over him almost drowned him. He couldn't make out the words Rose was saying, and he could hardly breathe. Something in his demeanor or pallor clued Rose into his state, and she led him over to the sofa.

Time passed before he spoke, but when he did, his voice was calm and resolute. "I have a couple of things to tie up, but I can have us out of here by next week."

Rose's expression changed from sympathetic to furious. "I am not moving again!"

Quillen reached out to her, but she jumped up, moved away, and faced him. She was fiercely determined.

"We can't stick around and wait for something to happen," Quillen reasoned. "You know I have to do this."

Rose put her hand on her hip. "Fine. You do it then. Run away like you always do,"

"That's not fair, Rosie."

"Really," she shot back. "Let me tell you a little something about what's not fair." She threw her hand up, her voice rising with it. "Not fair is when I have to struggle to keep up in my classes because you insist on putting me in the best schools, but each one has a different curriculum. Not fair is when I have to say goodbye to the friends who have just gotten used to me so I can do it all over again at another school. And not fair is when your dad wants to run away from his problems because of one little note." She pointed at him. "You're my parent, aren't you able to protect me without tucking your tail between your legs?"

His defenses went up. "Of course I can protect you; I've been doing it for two years!"

"We're still getting notes," she pointed out.

"*We* didn't get a note," he reminded her. "A woman I went out with got a note."

Rose was quiet. She didn't want to concede the point, but she couldn't think of anything else to say.

Quillen got up and took her in his arms. "Look, I don't want to fight with you. Let's talk about it over dinner." He held her at arm's length. "Pizza and breadsticks?" He twisted her from side to side, swaying with her like they were dancing.

Finally, Rose rolled her eyes and smiled. "Okay. But make it pizza and cheese sticks."

Quillen didn't expect Hollis to walk into the bank on Friday afternoon. Her bright auburn hair was the first thing he saw before he embarrassed himself by standing up.

Rose was doing her homework in the chair opposite to him. When she saw her father get up and look at the woman in the lobby, she raised an eyebrow. "Why don't you go talk to her?"

Quillen had thought about Hollis all week, but he hadn't called or messaged her. By now, he was sure that Hollis was mad at him, and he didn't have an excuse prepared. Truthfully, he despised when people lied or tried to place blame on others for their mistakes, so he usually handed them a valid reason for his fault and hoped for the best. He was surprised by how many people preferred the lies and excuses of others to his honesty.

He owed Hollis an apology, and he hoped he wouldn't choke on it.

"I'll be back in a minute," Quillen told his daughter.

"Whatever," Rose sang out, clearly amused by the situation.

Hollis was almost to the counter when he approached her. "Hello, beautiful lady. May I help you?"

He was certain that she'd known who was speaking to her before she turned around, but she made a show of dropping her smile when she met his eyes. He'd have a lot of work to do if he wanted to salvage their budding connection.

"I'm sorry," he began. "I should have called you like I said I would." He ran a hand through his hair, looking around at his coworkers. Most of them were staring at him, but they weren't close enough to hear their conversation.

Hollis stood with her arms crossed loosely over her body, her less than designer bag hanging off her hand. She gave him a dismissive smile and alternated between looking at him politely and glancing at the line in front of her.

"It's okay. I was so busy this week that I didn't even notice."

It was clear from her too-wide smile and lack of eye contact that she had given his inactions some thought. She knew he worked there, but he had never seen her in the building, so he assumed she'd really entered the bank to see him instead of whatever errand she seemed to be fulfilling.

Hollis was next in line, but she seemed more nervous than relieved that she was the upcoming one in the queue. He wondered if she'd expected him to ask her to his office before a teller waited on her.

"May I help you?" asked one of the tellers.

Hollis stared at the girl, reluctantly approaching the counter. Quillen stayed in place, far away enough to give her privacy, but close enough to watch her body language.

Surprisingly, Hollis gave the teller a member identification card, and the teller handed her cash. After she completed her transaction, Hollis waited for Quillen to come to her. She stood off from the line, taking a considerable amount of time putting money into the brown bag she carried. It was clear that Quillen could address her, but she wasn't going to walk back to where he stood.

Quillen's pride got the best of him, and he turned around on his heel. Rose was staring at him from the window in his office, her mouth in a drooping frown. She waved her hand at him in a shooing gesture and Quillen raised his eyebrows.

"Go," she mouthed.

He rolled his eyes with great exaggeration, but when he turned around, he was the perfect picture of gentlemanly composure. He stood next to Hollis until she pretended to finish rummaging in the purse.

"I am truly sorry," he began again. "Rosie and I had some unexpected information that we"—he shook his head— "that I couldn't process right away. I should have called you."

Hollis looked up, finally meeting his eyes for more than a few seconds. "I'm sorry you were upset this week."

"It's my own fault," he admitted. "Problems won't get solved until you quit running from them."

Quillen thought he saw Hollis's hands tighten around the straps of the bag. "That's true," she agreed.

He asked her to have dinner with him and he was glad when she accepted. They made plans quickly and he almost skipped back to his office.

"So?" Rose asked when he strutted into the room.

He laughed at her. "Normally, I wouldn't discuss my dating life with you, but since you helped orchestrate it, I'll tell you that she's coming to dinner at the house."

"But I'll be at Katey's tonight!"

Quillen winked at her as he sat down. "I know."

Chapter Seventeen

Josie admired Hollis's casual selection. "I like your blouse. The olive-green color makes your hair and skin stand out and the V-line will give him easy access—"

"Whoa!" Hollis said, turning away from the full-length mirror. "No one said anything about making it easier for him."

"But it's the third date," Josie said, pouting her lip and falling dramatically on Hollis's bed. "One of us needs to see some action." She flipped over, grabbing one of Hollis's pillows and resting her chin on it. "It's been years for both of us."

Hollis looked back in the mirror to avoid her friend's gaze. Her eyeliner was detailed, but she pretended to wipe away a smudge.

Josie smacked the pillow. "What!" She stared hard at Hollis in the mirror until an involuntary smile lifted the corners of her mouth.

Josie pointed at her. "Ha!" She seemed triumphant in finding out a little more about Hollis's sex life. "What have you done? Spill it!"

Hollis sighed playfully. They both knew she wouldn't be leaving until she told her friend everything about her last experience.

"I was on a mission, so I can't tell you all of it," she said.

Josie nodded. "I don't want to know the military stuff, just tell me about the man."

A stab of guilt went through Hollis's stomach. She wished she could share everything with her friend, but she doubted Josie's open-mindedness would extend to her murderous lifestyle.

"He was a little older than me," Hollis started.

"Ooo! Was he an officer?"

Hollis shook her head. "He worked with machines and other equipment, and he taught me how to operate some of it."

"Did you have sex on the equipment?"

Hollis blushed at her friend's forward question. She was an adult, and she should be used to that type of question, but she was inexperienced when it came to intimacy. Josie was her best friend, though, and she needed to hear saucy details, so Hollis obliged. After she told Josie about her familiarity with the man and the machines he worked, Josie's eyes were wide.

"Was it really hard to, you know, get around the gear shift and steering wheel?"

"There are ways to get around them," Hollis answered with a smile. "You just have to be creative."

"I wonder if I'd even remember how!" Josie cried. "It's been so long!"

She buried her head in the pillow, but she lifted it quickly and kicked her legs on the mattress. Hollis laughed at her friend's mock tantrum.

"No one would blame you if you started dating again," she mentioned.

Her friend's face clouded over, and she sat up. All traces of good humor were gone.

"I'm a married woman," she reminded Hollis curtly. "I can't get involved with anyone else." She stared at a spot on the floor. "And I don't want to."

"How many years has it been?" Hollis asked, sitting on the bed and grabbing Josie's hand. "When will you be able to move on?"

Josie's body shook from the tears Hollis hadn't known she was crying. She regretted her question, but she couldn't take it back.

"He was my first love," she sobbed. After she caught her breath, she added, "Robbie was my first real boyfriend, but Cotton took me away from that monster."

Hollis had an opinion of both men, and it wasn't favorable. Josie didn't need to hear that she had a horrible taste in men, though. She was a fixer, and she always tried to correct the behavior of the men to which she attached herself. And they hated her for it. Her helpful suggestions earned her more battle scars than Hollis ever saw in her time in the Navy.

"I'm sorry," she said to Josie. She pulled her friend to her and stroked her hair, tugging the curls straight at the end.

Josie let her play with her hair for a few minutes before she spoke again. "First loves are hard to get over."

Tears threatened to spill from Hollis's eyes, but she blinked them away rapidly. It had been over a decade, and she still hadn't gotten over her first love.

Chapter Eighteen

Asher, Part Two

Hollis covered the chili, thankful for the cooking pot her mother had given her for her birthday. It had been a beautiful celebration, and her mother was recovering so well that Hollis thought she might be ready to start looking for another job soon.

She could hear Asher in the shower singing in a deep baritone. She thought about joining him but decided to make a pan of cornbread first.

Over the past year, they had settled into a comfortable existence. They lived in Asher's cabin and provided for themselves from the land around it. In the spring, they had planted a garden, and she had helped tend to and harvest it. He had taught her how to hunt, and their matching crossbows sat in the corner next to the door.

They had been out all morning looking for roaming deer. A startling snow had settled over the region, and the day had warmed up just enough for some animals to look for food. However, the night brought back the cold, and the freezing temperatures quickly froze the melting snow into icicles.

During their hunt, Hollis had been the one to spot the buck. He was beautiful, standing sentinel on the crest of an embankment. He seemed to be watching over a couple of does who were rooting bare patches of ground.

Asher had encouraged her to shot him, but Hollis had resisted. There was something so evil about taking the life of something so majestic, and it almost physically pained her to consider it.

Asher had told her he understood her reservations, but he said, "The meat from the buck could feed us for a couple of weeks. We're not killing it for the sake of killing it."

His argument made sense to her, and the way he said it, linked them to the act. She felt less alone, and more like a team.

Hollis lined up the shot and released it. Her quarrel hit the mark, and the buck ran a couple of steps before he fell.

Asher grabbed her hand and ran over to the place he'd fallen. The wide-eyed does had darted at the sound of the bolt whispering through the air, so no other animal or being was with them as the light faded from the buck's eyes.

Asher picked up the buck's head, surveying it. "He's only got eight points, but given his spread, I think you landed a good one."

Hollis's heart jumped into her chest. "Was he too young?"

Asher shook his head. "This guy probably had eight points when he was around two years old but with his spread"—he moved the antlers from side to side— "he was probably four years old."

"Shouldn't he have had more points?" she asked, trying the jargon she'd heard Asher use.

He looked thoughtfully at the buck and shook his head. "Not necessarily. Sometimes it's just not in their genetics to have more than a certain number of points."

He noticed her moist eyes and put the deer down so he could hug her. "Don't worry. Most of the bucks around here live about four or five years, so you didn't take anything from him."

Hollis disagreed. Every moment roaming the earth as a free creature was a gift and she'd robbed the buck of countless days in the mountain sun.

• • • ● ● • ● ● • • ·

Hollis had already learned about dressing a deer from watching Asher after one of his kills. He guided her through the nauseating process, insisting that she should do it since she had loosed the bolt. Hollis realized the necessity of the process, but it didn't make it less gruesome. It wasn't the first time Hollis had wished they could have focused more on a larger garden and less on hunting.

Hollis was thankful for everything Asher had taught her. He had shown her how to spot certain herbs and had watched as she discovered her own patch of ginseng. Hunting was one of her least favorite activities, even though Asher believed that they needed to do it for their continued survival. They had canned vegetables from the garden, but Asher insisted that meat would fill them up over the course of the winter.

Shouldering the spoils, the two headed back to the cabin. Mid-way there, Hollis spotted darkness on a nearby range.

"It's going to storm," she said.

Asher squinted into the distance. "Maybe. We better hurry back."

When they reached the porch, Asher stopped, digging deep into the front pocket of his thick coveralls. He smiled when he pulled out his phone, but when he noticed Hollis studying his reaction, his look was more uncertain.

"It was a picture of my niece," he said quickly, and slid his phone back into his coveralls.

It was odd for Asher not to share a picture his sister sent. They both loved seeing his niece's accomplishments and the occasional funny videos, even if the cell phone tower was only reliable on sunny days.

The sun had touched the western mountains, and the dark clouds in the south seemed closer. Asher watched them, inching over the blue, pinks, and oranges in the sky and devouring them as it edged closer to their safe haven.

Warm air met Hollis when Asher opened the door to the cabin. It had a lock and a dead bolt, but they left it unlocked. The security measures had only been installed to keep out animals.

Amazingly, they weren't so far away from civilization that they had to live without certain creature comforts. Asher was against buying a television for the cabin, but they had electricity, so they could enjoy hot water, overhead lights, and cooking on an electric range. Most times, Hollis liked to curl up with a book under an electric blanket until Asher was ready for bed.

Asher was a quiet and docile man. His body was well-developed from busting wood for fires and farming, but his hands were gentle when he touched her. His voice seldom raised, and even when they argued, Hollis knew she could end it with a kiss.

She loved her life in the mountains and the man who shared it with her. She couldn't imagine it any other way.

Asher sang another bar, and she grinned. She decided to pull the cornbread out of the oven and join him in the shower.

He had laid his phone on the table, and it lit up. Hollis wondered why he had silenced it. Curiosity won over and she tiptoed through the kitchen. Laughing at herself for being quiet, she shook her head and picked up the phone.

She expected to find a text from Asher's sister, possibly another picture or a reply to something he may have sent her in response to her last message. What she saw caused her blood to run cold and changed her view of the man she had once thought was perfect.

Chapter Nineteen

She pulled up to the ranch-styled home at seven o'clock. She was very aware of her punctuality and proud of herself for it.

Quillen answered the door, and before she could appreciate the care he had taken in his appearance, he held a finger to his lips. "Rosie's in bed."

"I thought you said she was going to a friend's house," Hollis said, skeptical about their date.

"She has a migraine, so she's gone to bed early."

Hollis was no stranger to migraines. They were much worse before she met Asher and for a time in her early twenties, but she hardly had them anymore.

"She'll be on the other end of the house from us," he told her. "I set up a table in my bedroom."

Hollis had been taking off her jacket, but she stopped. She was unsure about having a date in a man's bedroom while his daughter was home.

Quillen held up his hands, one of them still holding a serving spoon. "It's just a room," he defended. "I don't want you to think I have the wrong Idea." He thought about what he'd said. "I mean, it's okay if you like the idea of being with me in the bedroom, but I don't want you to think you have to—"

Hollis lifted on her toes and interrupted his rambling with a kiss. It was a short press of her lips against his, but the effect lingered on her mouth like the taste of a good wine.

A wide grin stretched across his features as Hollis did her best to hold his eyes without blushing. There was something in his stare that almost hypnotized her.

"So does that mean you want to skip dinner and just—"

Hollis smacked him playfully on the arm. "Your daughter is in the house!" She shushed him when he laughed.

"I guess that means I need to get back to the steaks," he said, motioning for her to come along.

"I thought vegans didn't eat meat," she commented as she wandered down the hall behind him.

"We don't." He pointed to the cast iron frying pan on the stove. "I thought I'd finally met a woman who could enjoy my cabbage steaks." He stopped and looked out the back window. The bitter wind sent a low scream through the eaves of the house. "I would have grilled them, but it's too cold outside."

Hollis glanced around the kitchen. It wasn't cleverly decorated, but it was functional. Quillen had every modern convenience, from an air fryer to a talking refrigerator. Except for the smaller appliances, everything was stainless steel, and it was polished until every surface blinked the light back at her. The floors were beige tile and the countertops appeared to be made of granite in a similar color.

"Do you want a glass of red?" he asked.

Hollis weighed the amount of time she planned to spend there against the full glass of wine. "I'll take a glass."

The dinner was almost fully prepared when she arrived, so it was finished in moments. Quillen handed her a plate and led the way into his bedroom. She was relieved to see a table was placed just inside the door.

He seemed to read her mind. "You didn't think I was going to make you eat on my bed, did you?" He pulled out her chair for her, balancing his plate in his other hand. "I wouldn't want to roll around in crumbs."

At first, they ate in silence. Hollis enjoyed the cabbage steak and she told him so.

"Thank you. It's just an old recipe I found online when I looked up what to fix in place of turkey one Thanksgiving."

Hollis winced. "That is a hard holiday for animal lovers."

He took a sip of his wine and cleared his throat. "Yeah. One year, my mom eliminated the butter and milk in her recipes, but she put cheese on almost everything, so Rosie and I snacked on raw veggies there and had frozen pizza at home. My mom meant well, but she was trying too hard after Beth..." He trailed off but picked back up before Hollis felt too awkward. "I promised Rosie we'd do Thanksgiving at home after that."

"Beth?" she asked and regretted it when the little bit of good humor in his features vanished. She had heard Quillen mention his wife's name on their last date, and part of her wanted to know more about her.

"She was my wife," he told her. "We were together almost twenty years before— "

A loud objection rang out. Quillen and Hollis looked at each other and bolted out of their chairs. Hollis followed him through the kitchen and down the hall, almost bumping into him when he rounded into a room.

"Rosie!" he called frantically.

The room was dark, but the moonlight allowed her to see a small form on a bed. Quillen switched on the light and Hollis scanned each corner, looking for an intruder.

Rose sat up and shielded her eyes from the overhead light.

Her room was as simple as the rest of the house, except for the roses and violets in a pattern across her quilt. It was homemade, and it appeared to be old. It put Hollis in mind of hand-sewn baby blankets that had been stitched together. The top half was light-colored and faded, but the bottom half was more vibrant. Matching pictures of Rose faced each other above the bed, but one looked a little off, as if someone else's expressions were pasted on Rose's face.

"Are you okay?" Quillen asked her, a touch of mania in his voice.

"What?" Rose looked from one of them to the other, her face puffy with sleep.

"We heard you cry out," Hollis clarified. She stayed in the doorway, unwilling to cross the threshold into the teenager's sanctuary.

"Are you sure you're okay?" he pressed.

Rose nodded her head and winced when the remnants of her migraine threatened to flare up again. Quillen hesitantly withdrew from the room and met Hollis in the hall.

Hollis felt a little strange about seeing Rose in her pajamas after only one real date with Quillen. She saw their home as a private place, and she was an invader.

"I think I should go."

Quillen's blue eyes held her. "Please don't. I'm a little overprotective, but we can still have a nice evening." He put his hands on her arms, kneading them in small circles. "We could watch a movie or stream a show?"

His touch tingled like his kiss, but Hollis tried to keep her face neutral. It would be easy to fall for this handsome man who usually said and did all the right things, but she had the feeling that he was still in love with his wife.

He talked her into following him back to his bedroom. Hollis was surprised by the lack of pictures, and she asked him about it. Usually, parents had at least one family picture or an individual school photo on the wall or an end table.

He was leading her, so she couldn't see his face, but his tone was melancholy when he responded. "Pictures remind us of the past when we should be fully in the present."

Quillen's mood changed when he reentered his bedroom. He slipped out of his shoes and hopped onto the bed. He patted the spot beside him.

Hollis was mortified. *How could she sit next to a beautiful man in his bed and think about any television show?*

Quillen intentionally ignored her reaction, as if to ask her about it would make his invitation more awkward. He wanted her to feel at home in his bed, but Hollis was having trouble trying to analyze the possible outcomes of cuddling in Quillen's bed with him. Finally, she silenced the objections in her brain, kicked off her shoes, and climbed onto the bed with him.

She sat down rigidly and rested her back on the hard, wooden headboard. Quillen took one of the pillows from behind his back and placed it behind her. It was still warm from his body heat, and it brought a fresh woodsy smell to mind.

"What kind of shows do you like?"

Hollis grimaced. Should she tell him about her interest in the true crime shows that gave her ideas for how to dispatch and dispose of her victims?

"Why don't you pick tonight?" she said sweetly.

Quillen hesitated, but seeing her smile softened his gentlemanly reflexes, and he hit a button without looking at the screen. Something started to play in the background, but neither of them watched it.

He kissed her before she knew his intentions and their teeth knocked together. They laughed at their juvenile mistake and Quillen spoke to her as he trailed his fingers down the back of her arm.

"It's going to be hard not to fall for you."

Hollis was used to the lines men say when they have a woman in bed with them, but she wasn't used to the open-eyed kisses and gentle caresses that seemed to give weight to his words. She let him pull her as close to him as possible, while laughter echoed from whatever show he'd turned on.

Hollis had wanted to see and feel his strong arms and chest since she glimpsed their form under his shirt, so she flicked her hand a few times until three of the buttons pulled away. She was so swift with her movements that she was certain Quillen had no idea what she'd done. She eased her hand into his shirt and put it firmly on his skin. He jumped at the touch, but then let out a low growl as she unbuttoned the rest of his shirt.

Hollis was completely caught up in Quillen. She returned his heated stare and decided she was ready to throw her reservations to the wind. The only thing that kept her from going any further was that Rose was sleeping at the other end of the house. She wouldn't let Quillen's hands roam too far, and he kept them where she placed them.

Glass broke and Hollis shot out of the bed before she fully registered the sound. Quillen was behind her this time as Hollis ran to Rose's room. When she got there, Rose was wide awake on the edge of her bed. She shook as she stared at her broken window. A dark figure stood in the room, with a knife in hand.

Chapter Twenty

Hollis came to her senses in the back of an ambulance. She sat straight up on a stretcher while a medic asked her questions. She tried to answer the young woman, but she couldn't concentrate hard enough on the words she spoke. Her mind drifted away before she could focus, causing her to ask the medic to repeat herself.

"Any luck?" called a voice from the back of the ambulance.

The woman yelled back. "I think she's coming around."

He tapped the door to the ambulance twice. "Let me know when she's lucid, okay?"

The tap had startled Hollis and she became a little more aware of her surroundings. She could hear the heat rush through the vents, but it did little to combat the air invading the ambulance through the open door. The woman in front of her didn't give off a smell, and it seemed like she had absorbed the scent of her environment.

The woman stared at her, but it didn't make Hollis feel awkward. She tried to focus on the freckles that danced across the bridge of the woman's nose and the soft rise of her lip that made it seem to pucker, even though the woman wasn't smiling.

"There you are," she said to Hollis. "Can you tell me your name?"

Hollis fought hard to remember which name she should give the woman. She decided on her birth name.

"Good," the woman told her. "Are you in any pain?"

Hollis ran a mental check of her body. She didn't seem to be feeling any pain.

The woman didn't move her eyes from Hollis's. She asked her a few more questions about her physical state and then she took a deep breath. Hollis wondered why the woman seemed to be so concerned about whatever she was going to say.

"Do you remember what happened?"

Hollis's silence answered the question.

"Can you tell me the last thing you do remember?"

Hollis thought back. She had trouble placing memories, so she chronologically went through her day in her mind. She had ridden with Josie to school, she had to endure an hour of Zach popping his gum in class because she didn't want to write another detention for him, and she'd gone to the bank.

Once an image of Quillen came to mind, everything came back to her. The medic must have seen the light dawn behind her eyes because she patted the side of her arm.

Another knock on the ambulance door startled both women. Hollis stared down at her hands and wasn't surprised that they were covered in blood.

"Is she ready to talk?" the man asked.

The medic must have given some sort of silent response because the floor creaked when the man stepped inside. He sat down on the other end of the stretcher.

"Hello, Hollis. It's been a long time."

Hollis had known his voice as soon as he'd spoken, but she had willed herself not to react. She looked up into the face of a man who knew one of her best-kept secrets. He had been studying the blood on her hands, and she imagined that he had finally caught her in the act.

"Hello, Detective Saldana."

Chapter Twenty-One

Asher, Part Three

Hollis watched his brown eyes close. She thought they'd stay open, like the other ones from the past, but his eyes seemed to shut as the last breath left his body.

"I loved you!" she yelled at him, and realizing she still did, let out a primal scream.

She let go of the gun, and it slipped to the floor. She thought about the message that had driven her to kill her lover.

Hollis hadn't known what to do when she had seen Martina's message. She had begged Asher to meet her, promising to stay at the bottom of their long driveway until he could sneak away from Hollis. He had responded with excitement and had messaged her back that he would see her soon.

The number wasn't labeled, but Martina was the only other woman Asher had ever loved. She scrolled up to see previous messages, but Asher had erased anything prior to that day's communication.

Once she saw his deception, Hollis couldn't catch her breath. A heavy weight pressed on her chest and the room spun. She heard

Asher turn off the shower and yell her name, but she didn't know how long it took him to find her.

He dropped onto the floor, with only his towel around his waist, and gathered her in his arms. She was small against his stout frame but sharing the chores around the cabin had made her stronger. She tried to push him away, but she was still finding it hard to breathe.

"It's okay, baby. I've got you," he said as he rocked her.

Asher was no stranger to Hollis's panic attacks. Certain smells and raised voices triggered them, and they had both worked hard to reduce the number she experienced. She hadn't had one in three months, but she was convinced she was having the worst one since she had known him.

Usually, Asher could talk her down in twenty minutes, even though she still felt physical aches from her body's rigidness during the attacks. But now, his presence only intensified her distress.

"I love you, baby," he said to her, talking like he was speaking to a small child. "You're my whole world."

Something in Hollis's mind popped and her attack ceased immediately. The weight rescinded and her breath returned. She had closed her eyes as she fought for control, but when she opened them, everything seemed to be hyper-focused. She allowed Asher to rock her until he noticed the change, and he smiled at her improvement.

"That was a bad one," he remarked.

At first, Hollis thought if she looked at him, then it would give her away. She stared at her shirt where a bright blot of crimson had stained the edge of her sleeve.

She looked up at Asher. His eyes, which had once reminded her of comforting pools of milk chocolate, looked down at her.

"Are you going to be okay?" he asked.

Even though he was happily cheating on her, Hollis was drawn to him. He had been safe. He had been her first love.

Before she thought about what she was doing, she kissed him. It was a deeply passionate kiss that tingled from her lips to her toes. She breathed in his fresh scent, like pine needles in the coldest part of winter.

A thought pressed against her mind that he had been showering to meet Martina, and he would brush her kiss out of his mouth before meeting her at the end of their driveway. *Would he kiss her before he rinsed Martina away? Would she know her if she tasted the difference on his tongue?*

"I think you're right about the storm," he said. "I need to check our traps before the snow gets here."

It was the perfect excuse. Before she had read the message, she would have gone along with whatever he said, staying home and waiting for his return.

"Do you want me to go, too?" she asked as he lifted off the floor.

He stopped, considering her words, or looking for an alternative. "No. I'll go. You stay home and take a shower. Maybe I'll join you when I get back." He turned around and winked at her, but it fell just short of believable. For the first time, Hollis realized that her boyfriend wasn't a good liar. She had merely been too trusting and easy to deceive.

"Okay. Do you want to eat before you go?"

"No," he called back, already going down the short hallway to their bedroom. "I'll eat when I get back."

Hollis turned over the betrayal in her mind, curious about how long it had been going on. She thought about the trips into town for supplies which had gotten more numerous over the past couple of months. He'd returned with some necessities, but not nearly as many as she had expected for his lengthy trips.

She felt the weight threaten to return to her shoulders, and she rushed outside. The cold air was bracing, and her surreal focus returned. An unusually long icicle reflected the light from the kitchen.

Her mind went to the gun just inside the door. Asher had told her it had been his grandfather's gun, during a time when the man had been making white liquor. Hollis had been around guns since she was small, and she wasn't intimidated by it.

"Hollis," he shouted from the bedroom. His tone was merely inquisitive; he didn't know where she'd gone.

She stepped back inside, sweetly returning to her lover's call.

He was in their small bedroom, looking through his flannel shirts. He glanced up when he saw her, a look of concern on his face.

"What's wrong, baby?"

"Martina."

He seemed genuinely confused, or was he a better liar than she'd thought? She advanced two steps and brought the gun up, firing it at his naked chest.

He stumbled backwards, staring at her in surprise.

"I found your messages!" Hollis yelled at him.

Asher busied himself with trying to pull the bullet from his chest, but his attempts stopped almost as quickly as they started. He could no longer hear her, but Hollis continued to talk to him.

"What made you think it'd be a good idea to cheat on me after what I told you I'd done?" she yelled at Asher's body.

Tears started to run down her face, but she swiped them away. There was still more work to be done.

• • • • ●• ● • • •

The truck idled at the end of the driveway. Hollis moved just out of view, unable to see the dark figure inside the cab.

She had messaged Martina and told her that she'd be there in fifteen minutes. She had thrown on her coveralls and grabbed the pistol.

She almost ran down the driveway until it became too steep for her to do more than shuffle her boots along the gravel. Once the truck came into view, she inched closer to the tree line, knowing that it would keep her hidden.

Her heart broke into painful shards when she saw the fire engine red truck against newly fallen snow. Her boyfriend's mistress was inside.

Hollis carried the pistol and all her pain with her until she was at the back of the truck bed. She decided she wanted Martina to see her before she died. She should know that Hollis had been the one to end her life.

She held the pistol at her side and tapped the window. The figure inside seemed to startle before the window slowly receded.

Hollis had never met Martina, and she'd neglected to ask for a description of her boyfriend's first love, but the person inside the truck was clearly not Martina. He was a middle-aged man with cool, blue eyes and a smooth complexion. And he was holding a gun.

Chapter Twenty-Two

Gus

He looked down at the gun in his hands and put it on top of his console. "I'm sorry, ma'am. You can't be too careful when you're out in the country this far."

Hollis was glad he had put the gun away quickly. Her astonishment had been so great that she was too shocked to hold up her pistol.

"You must be Hollis," he said. He smiled, but it wasn't warm. "I'm Gus."

"It's nice to meet you, Gus," Hollis spoke automatically.

"I'm glad to hear you say that," he said through a breathy chuckle. "I can only guess Asher's told you about us since he sent you to meet me."

In an instant, a plan formed in her mind. For months, these men had been playing on her trust and innocence, and she wasn't going to let them get away with it.

• • • • ● • ● • ● • ● •

"Thank you for the beer," he said, angling the cup at her. He took a sip and tried to hide his reaction to the bitterness as he surveyed the bottle. "Moon Walker is an old label. I could never figure out why Asher liked it so much."

It's a beer for liars, Hollis thought.

"You're welcome," she said sweetly. "It's the least I can do after you trudged up that long driveway with me."

Gus had left his truck at the end of their steep driveway. Without four-wheel-drive he worried he might get stuck, and since he wouldn't mind getting stuck with Asher, but was unwilling to be stuck with Asher *and* Hollis, he decided to leave it.

"When do you think Asher'll be back," he asked.

Hollis took in his long appendages and the tufts of hair peeking out of his shirt and sleeves and wondered how she had been replaced by him. *Was this man a better listener than her? Was he everything Asher had envisioned in a lover?*

"He should only be about ten more minutes," Hollis told him.

She sat down in front of him, a mug of tea in her hand. "While we wait on him, tell me how the two of you met."

He looked down at his tea to avoid her gaze, sharp patches of color appearing on his cheeks. "I should probably leave that to Asher, if it's all the same to you, ma'am."

Hollis leaned back in the chair as if she were unaffected, when in reality, she wanted to pull an icicle off the porch awning and jam it through his eye.

"I just thought we could have some polite conversation while we waited," she said. "I'm not your enemy, you know."

His shoulder's slumped. "You're right. Not many people would be kind to me after what Asher and I've been doing."

She smiled at him, thinking of Asher's arms around him after he'd told Hollis that she was his whole world. She fought the urge to beat the man in front of her until he felt the pain she was feeling.

"We were getting a haircut," he began, still not looking at her. "There was a long wait, but we spent almost an hour talking and laughing."

Asher only cut his hair through the summer months, preferring to keep it longer during the cooler months as an added protection. The affair had lasted longer than she'd previously thought.

Gus's mouth stretched into a silent yawn. She dared him to look at her, but he only stared at the floor or his tea. *Coward.*

She got up and paced the length of the kitchen. It was a short walk, as the room was only nine feet by nine feet.

"How did he tell you?" Gus asked her, glancing up from his cup, but not meeting her eyes.

"I saw your message today," Hollis answered honestly.

He closed his eyes and sighed, his posture deflating. "That's my fault. I wasn't supposed to message him today, but I needed him. My mother passed on today."

"I'm sorry," Hollis replied reflexively.

"Thanks. She was the last of my family." He shrugged. "Well, the last one to acknowledge me after..."

He trailed off, but Hollis could guess his meaning. She'd had some friends in high school whose families excommunicated them after they had revealed their lifestyle choices. Hollis supported them, and she would have liked Gus, if he hadn't been sneaking around with her boyfriend.

Gus's left leg jiggled under the table, rattling the keys in his pock-et. "When did you say Asher'd be back," he asked again.

"It should be any time now," she told him, and after she noticed his eyes beginning to droop, she added, "There's something else I'd like to ask you."

Gus finally met her eyes, his mouth drooping open. "I don't feel so good."

"You're dehydrated," Hollis told him. "It happens a lot during the winter months." She nodded to his tea. "You should drink more."

Gus looked down at the mug in front of him, and Hollis thought he was going to take another drink, but he had just enough presence of mind to push it away. He glared at her.

"What'd you put in my tea?"

"Belladonna," Hollis answered honestly.

Gus couldn't stand, and he fell out of the chair when he tried. Hollis easily dodged his attempts to attack her. Finally, he sat slumped against the cabinet doors in almost the same place Asher had held Hollis only a short time ago.

"Why?" His eyes pleaded with her.

Hollis paced as she talked. "You may have known about me, but I didn't know about you. Asher made me believe I was the only girl for him, but then I found you waiting for my boyfriend."

Gus tried to laugh, but only a dry cackle came out. "You never would have been the only one for him."

"Shut up!" Hollis yelled at him.

Gus's lips tugged up in the corners. "Asher was like me. We loved a lot of people." He knew he had nothing to lose, and he was taunting her.

Hollis lifted her head up. "He was happy with *me*."

Gus had closed his eyes, but he said, "And he got what he needed from *us*."

Hollis crossed the distance between them and slapped him. She kept hitting him until she realized he wouldn't be talking to her anymore.

Hollis went outside and put on Asher's coveralls, tucking her hair under a toboggan. She put on a pair of plastic gloves and fished the truck keys out of Gus's pocket. She drove his truck up her driveway and loaded his body and a shovel onto a black trash bag she spread across the truck bed.

It was snowing, but it wasn't sticking to the road, so she drove several miles before she pulled the truck off the road and into the trees. The police would eventually find the truck, but it would look like he had veered off the road accidentally.

Hollis thought about propping him up in the driver's seat, and leaving him, but she had left some pretty severe marks across his face. There was the issue of the Belladonna in his system, too. She decided to go through with her original plan to bury his body.

She dragged Gus, the black bag, and the shovel for what felt like forever before she found a place with softer earth. Her arms were so tired she wondered if she would be able to dig a shovelful, but when she thought about getting caught, adrenaline spiked through her body.

The cold earth was unwilling to come up, so it took her hours to dig a hole suitable enough for him. Even then, she knew it wasn't deep enough. She tossed Gus's corpse and the black bag into the shallow grave, and she fell over several times as she filled it.

When she was finished, she picked up her shovel and cleaned off the dirt with some leaves. She had a compass, and she took off in the direction of the house she shared with Asher. She walked about a mile before the sky lightened, and she saw a tree with a hole in its trunk like a gapping mouth. Her outdoor gloves had survived the experience, but she didn't know if there was DNA evidence on them, so she stuffed them deep into the hole in the tree, covering them with several layers of leaves and topping the leaves with a dead squirrel that she'd found inside the tree.

"Goodbye, Gus," she said, whistling a tune as she made her way back home to her dead lover.

Chapter Twenty-Three

Asher, Part Four

Hollis watched the chest that should have been moving. By now, he would have made an excuse to his lover, or lovers, and he would be back in her arms.

Hollis's mind whirled around the information she'd learned. She went between feeling hurt to emotions of intense grief and remorse for what she'd done. Asher had never physically hurt her. He had only lied to her and broken her heart. She was not a judge, but she had executed his punishment with ease. *What did that say about her? Was she truly irredeemable?*

Yes. The answer was yes. Asher shouldn't have cheated on her, but she didn't even give him a chance to defend himself before she had ended his life. There would be no chance of finding out the whole story. They couldn't have a fight and work it out or peaceably go their separate ways. Hollis had eliminated that possibility. *And why?*

She had an idea about how to answer that question, but she couldn't think about it. She had buried her reasons in a dark place, and she needed to keep them there.

When she got back from dumping Gus's body, Hollis had used Asher's phone to dial the police, but the call wouldn't connect. Asher had used a small radio for emergencies, and she was able to reach someone on an open frequency. The lady asked her a lot of questions, but when Hollis realized it was more for her personal interest than to relate to the police, Hollis told the woman she was feeling faint and had to lie down.

The snow was accumulating quickly, and Hollis wondered if the police would reach their house before it was too dangerous to drive. It had already been hours si

nce she'd shot her boyfriend, and from her perch in the cabin's bay window, Hollis could tell the town was receiving more snow than usual. *Would they leave her with a dead body?*

She had relayed a story she had devised while she was walking back through the woods. It was critical for her to be dressed in the same fashion if the authorities arrived in the early morning hours, but as time ticked away, Hollis became convinced that she wouldn't see them.

She visited Asher's body periodically, and she wondered about spirits and if there was any truth behind them. She spoke aloud to Asher, focusing her words into the air around her, but still glancing at his body from time to time.

She reminded him about her past and asked him why he had fallen into the pattern of so many other men. She had believed he was perfect, and in truth, he was very nearly so, but that made his betrayal even worse. She could believe other men were depraved, but if Asher was kind and good to her, yet he was morally corrupt, then who could she trust?

Asher made no answer. His eyes stared at the ceiling, and he refused to be upset with her. Even in death he was a passivist, for if he was a spirit, nothing flew at her head or knocked over to let her know his feelings about her questions.

When sky cleared, and the sun pushed its way through the window shades, Hollis decided it was okay to take a shower. She scrubbed herself with bleach, having watched a show about gunpowder residue, and lathered Asher's honey-scented soaps afterward. She emerged with a clean scent, so the smell of blood and human remains assaulted her nose when she walked back into the bedroom. She didn't look at her boyfriend's corpse, but she addressed him.

"You were alive at this time yesterday," she spoke conversationally. "You told me you wanted to store more food for the winter while we ate oatmeal with cinnamon." A period of time passed before she spoke again. "How long did you plan to string me along?"

She almost expected him to answer; she could hear his voice so clearly in her mind. *I'm sorry, baby, but I meant it when I said you were my whole world.*

Tears threatened to spill over, but she held them back. Asher had loved her. She had felt it acutely, and she didn't doubt it.

Suddenly, Hollis needed to see more about the secret life her boyfriend had lived. She wanted to discover how far he had traveled into the lifestyle to which Gus had eluded and when he'd planned to leave her.

Apparently, the people he knew didn't just have sex. Gus had said they loved each other. After all, Gus had sought out Asher after his mother had died. Admittedly, Asher was full of love, and he had treated everyone with kindness, but he had led her to believe that she was the only recipient of his affection.

Stricken by her urge to uncover all the lies Asher had told her, she started going through everything. She had assumed there were no secrets between them, so she hadn't bothered going through his side of the bedside table or the drawer where he stuffed bills and collectable correspondence. She tore through the house in minutes, but she found nothing. She was headed outside when she was struck by a thought. She wondered back into the bedroom, and her stomach rolled from the smell. Moments before, it hadn't been so strong, but when she had reentered the room, it hit her full force.

She didn't try to pick apart the scents that were mingling in the air. She tried not to distinguish whether the smell of blood, human excrement, or decay was more powerful.

She stepped over one of Asher's legs and stood in front of the closet. The smell was strongest there and she had to put her shirt under her nose to keep from passing out.

Asher's clothes were on the left and her clothes were on the right of the closet. She only had a couple of coats and two or three jackets, so most of the items dangling from the hangers belonged to her deceased boyfriend. She went through his clothes, checking every front and side pocket. She found a receipt for a hardware store, but it didn't surprise her. Something always need to be repaired.

Asher's tan suede jacket was next to the last piece of clothing on the hangers. Hollis plunged her hand into the pockets, and she was surprised when she found something. Hesitantly removing her hand, she surveyed the box in her hand and her heart dropped.

She knew it was an engagement ring, but she opened it to prove her theory. A small, half-carat diamond blinked back at her in the early morning light. Shaped like a teardrop with a golden band, it was everything Hollis had told him she wanted. But that had been months ago. *How long had he held onto the ring?*

Her mind shot to the cruise they had planned to take during the first week of the new year. *Had he planned to ask her to marry him then?* She'd never know.

Hollis stayed with Asher's body and had little concept of the passage of time. Whether it was from the smell or feelings of remorse, she couldn't eat. She could sleep, though, and she laid her head on Asher, feeling his cold skin on hers. She imagined she was in a grave with him, serving penance for her crime of passion.

Sometime in the night, she thought she heard Asher whisper to her. *You're my whole world, baby. Will you marry me?*

Hollis grabbed his frigid, lifeless hand. "Yes."

"I'm sorry I have to ask you these questions," the detective said.

Detective Saldana was a kind man with coal black hair and a bushy mustache. He was short and thin, with a good demeanor and deep brown eyes. He had taken her under his personal care from the moment she let his coworkers and him into the cabin.

Some of the policemen barked questions at her, but he shouted back at them. They finally left her alone and let him question her.

A notification illuminated his phone and a picture of a girl in a blue prom dress flashed onto the screen. She had the same dark hair and eyes as Detective Saldana, but her smile was lighter, and she seemed freer. Hollis didn't recognize the girl, but she appeared to be her age.

"It's okay," she told him. "I've had some time since I—" She couldn't finish her sentence and the detective patted her hand.

"It's okay. We like to have a fresh statement, but you don't have to talk about anything you're not ready to."

The other police officers were in the bedroom collecting evidence, and one of them passed as Detective Saldana spoke. He gave him a hard stare and Detective Saldana glared back at him.

His expression was kinder when he addressed Hollis. "How about you tell me everything you can from the moment you came into the house?" He put a thin, black device between them. "I'm going to record our conversation, okay?"

Hollis nodded. She waited to start talking until he pushed the tiny button on the side of the recorder, and even though she sped through some of her retelling, she didn't stop speaking until she was finished.

"We had just shot a deer and dragged it back to the house. It was Asher's turn to take a shower first, so I checked on the soup beans and started a pan of cornbread." Asher usually let Hollis take a shower first, but Hollis didn't want to tell the detective why her boyfriend had deviated from his usual behavior.

"It was starting to snow outside, and Asher had told me that it seemed like it was going to be a bad one, so I decided to see if we'd caught anything in the traps we put out." She started to explain their traps and where they were located, but Detective Saldana held up his hand. He had grown up in the country and knew what she meant.

"I came up the porch steps, but nothing really struck me as strange until I opened the door," she falsely recounted. "When I left, Asher was singing in the shower, but when I got back, the door wasn't all the way shut and it was really quiet."

She drummed up a rattled breath and continued. "I yelled for Asher, and when he didn't answer, I went to the bedroom." She looked away and blinked her eyes several times. "He was on the floor with so much blood." She looked back at Detective Saldana. "I tried to pull out the bullet. I really did."

Hollis put her hand in the pocket of her coat and held on to the black box. The tears came easily when she imagined the perfect deck side proposal during the cruise they'd never take together.

She recovered quickly and told him about the rest of her story in one breath. She even relayed that she'd slept while holding on to Asher's corpse.

He waited thirty seconds after she stopped talking and leaned over the recorder. "The preceding was an account of the events that transpired on November twenty-first. The speaker will now verify her name." He motioned to Hollis to speak into the device.

She leaned forward slightly and spoke her name. She confirmed that the events she described were true to the best of her knowledge after she was prompted by Detective Saldana.

Hollis settled back in the kitchen chair and seemed to watch minutes, hours, and days unfold as if they were on a time loop relaying before her eyes. She moved from the chair, but it was only to go to the bathroom. She slumped into the chair, using her arm as a pillow against the wooden table.

She had a vague memory of consenting to something. Moments later a blueish light passed over her body and several adhesive strips were applied to her skin and clothes. The police bagged the samples, but one of them stopped before she made it out the door. "Were you wearing those clothes when you found your boyfriend?"

Hollis had used her time wisely, and she'd had plenty of it to wash her clothes and stuff them under a stack of wood next to the tree line. She jerked her thumb toward their tiny washroom. "They're in there," she said about the clothes.

The lady nodded once and collected the entire basket of clothes. Hollis almost lunged at her as she passed with it, but she wouldn't have been able to explain her need to grab one of Asher's shirts so she could smell it.

Hollis told another officer about Asher's guns, and they took all of them, even the pistol she'd used to kill him. An officer leaned over the detective and whispered to him.

"Have you touched the pistol?" Detective Saldana asked.

Hollis nodded, distracted by her own thoughts.

"When did you last handle it?" he pressed.

"When I found it in the hallway," she stated, looking up at the men.

Her response created some commotion, and she had to point out exactly where she'd supposedly located it. They weren't surprised when she couldn't tell them the angle or temperature of the gun when she'd picked it up, but the officers were more forceful when they questioned her about people who might have wanted to hurt Asher or her.

Finally, their machine-gun questions died down, and Hollis settled back into the kitchen chair. She wanted to protest when Asher was carried out on a gurney, but she could only watch the form under the sheet as it was wheeled solemnly to the coroner's van.

At some point, the police left, but Detective Saldana checked on her every day, just before dark. He tried to persuade her to eat and shower, and he even brought her bags of food. She'd nibble it while he was there, and he'd return the next day, throw away the remaining food, and replace it with a fresh bag from a different restaurant. He'd joke that his daughter liked whatever food was in the bag and laugh dryly when she didn't eat much of it, saying, "I should've known a home-grown country girl wouldn't like this stuff."

Hollis liked everything he brought her, but she could hardly eat. Her guilt weighed on her heavily, causing her stomach to twist in knots.

Asher's parents came, and his father demanded that she leave. His mother spoke to him, and they agreed to let Hollis stay in the cabin until the spring. It was a few weeks before Hollis learned that

Asher had left the cabin and the surrounding property to her, so his parents' demands were meaningless.

Hollis tried to block out the wails that Asher's mother let out when she saw the place where her son had died. Hollis cried, thinking about the grieving parents who could have been her own by the following year.

They comforted her, even though they should be condemning her. She saw the same compassion and acceptance in them that she saw in Asher, and it broke her heart.

Hollis had killed Asher, the only person who could have really loved her. In doing so, she'd darkened her soul and sentenced herself to a life of grief and regret.

Chapter Twenty-Four

Detective Saldana was clearly past the age of retirement, but here he sat, reminding Hollis of her past mistakes. He had the same mustache and thick hair, but both were streaked with silver. Years of eating on the run had softened his once-thin frame, and the lines around his mouth sagged from decades of expressions.

"How have you been?" he asked.

Hollis glanced at her hands, saw the dried blood, and looked back at him. "I've been okay. How's Vanessa?"

"He brightened momentarily as he listed his daughter's accomplishments. "She's doing well. She's a pharmacist, married, and has two kids."

Hollis thought back guiltily on the way she'd dismissed him after he'd cared for her. They hadn't officially parted, and she felt like part of him had been hurt when she'd neglected to stay in touch.

"How long have you been back?" he asked.

The truth was, other than the first time she stayed with Josie and her last mission, Hollis had visited her hometown frequently, pausing in her missions to spend a couple of days in the beauty of the Appalachian Mountains, but she decided to tell him how long she had stayed with Josie.

"I've been here about four months."

The frown lines around his mouth deepened, and he looked at the pad in front of him. "This is a strange situation," he commented.

Hollis fought off the urge to say, *We've got to stop meeting this way.*

"Can you take me through the events of the night?"

Hollis was familiar with the procedure, so she glanced over the parts about her date with Quillen. She may have overexplained their presence in the bedroom, seeking to justify the reason she'd been on the other side of the house with Quillen while at the same time underplay their activities.

"The daughter, Rose, said she had to call for her father a couple of times," he mentioned.

Hollis colored. "We ran to her room the first time we heard her."

"Did the father check her room the first time she had cried out?"

"Yes. We both checked the room. We didn't find anything."

"So you staying over" —he motioned in the direction of the house — "is a regular occurrence?" he asked, eyeing her.

Hollis held his gaze. "No. I wasn't going to stay overnight."

He nodded as if he had a good picture of her relationship with Quillen. Hollis wanted to yell at him that nothing had happened, but she couldn't find the strength.

"Can you continue from the part when you noticed the window was broken?"

Hollis took in an uneasy breath. "I saw the outline of the gun before Quillen turned on the light. I didn't know who it was or why they were there, but I saw a weapon and reacted to it."

"You spent some time in the Navy, right? Do you think your reaction was guided by your experience in the military?"

Hollis nodded, surprised that he'd kept up with her. "Probably."

He was jotting down notes on a white pad of paper as she talked. Without looking up, he motioned for her to continue.

"I ran at the woman and knocked her down. I think something cut me." She looked at her arm and a bandage confirmed her suspicion. As if it only needed her acknowledgement to hurt, the pain awakened and sizzled up her arm. "She was yelling the whole time about revenge and hate, but I was just trying to keep her from shoting me."

He stared at the notepad, the skin on and around his face fell forward and made him look fuller and a little sullen. "What were the reactions of Mr. Banes and his daughter?"

She was shocked by the question. "They were terrified. Rose kept screaming, and I think Quillen tried to grab the gun once."

His head bobbed again. "Can you describe the woman?"

Hollis tried to pull every shred of memory from her mind. "At first, all I could see was the gun in her hand."

"But you knew she was a woman," he interrupted.

Hollis waved her hand dismissively. "Yes. I registered a medium build and feminine features."

"What's feminine about a person in the dark?"

Hollis concentrated on her answer. "The curve of her body." She outlined her meaning with her hands, cupping the air around the placement of breasts and hips.

Detective Saldana seemed satisfied with her answer. He waited for her to go on.

"The woman was stronger than I'd expected." She had heard madness could make a person more powerful, as if their state of mind sent their muscles an unlimited supply of strength. "She wrestled me to the ground and held the gun to my temple." She looked at her hands which she wished hadn't started twitching as she recalled the memory and willed them to stop moving. It took some effort, but in a couple of heartbeats they were still. "She would have killed me if she hadn't spoken."

She didn't wait for Detective Saldana to ask for her words. "She called me some names and told me I had destroyed her life."

Hollis hurried and finished her story. "Then Quillen pulled her off me, I grabbed the gun, and I shot her in the chest."

Detective Saldana's eyebrows went up when she spoke so casually about the murder she had committed. "You know, there are some parallels—"

"I know what you're getting at," she practically spat before she checked her tone. "It was self-defense."

He took a breath and stretched his legs. Even though they had only spoken for a short time, a lot of information had passed between them.

"It certainly looks like self-defense." He gestured to the house, the corner of which she could hardly make out in the revolving red lights on the ambulance. "Their statements match your story." He stared at her for almost a full minute before he added, "Even though it's downright weird."

She didn't need Detective Saldana to tell her how outlandish it seemed. She waited for his pronouncement.

"It seems like a clear case of self-defense," he said. "Your injuries and statement match the description of the events given by the two other occupants in the house, so I have no reason to believe otherwise.

"Did you know the woman?"

"No," Hollis lied.

He nodded his head as if he'd expected her answer. "Wait here while I release you for further medical attention." He climbed out of the ambulance with an effort, wobbling dangerously as his first foot planted on the asphalt. He stood with his back to her. "I hope everything works out for you."

Hollis watched him walk away. Arguably, he had been a father figure to her during the time before her missions started, but now he could hardly look at her without— what was it— contempt?

She thought about her statement and the lie she'd told Detective Saldana. If he looked back— and he probably would— there was an old court case that had involved a restraining order. She'd have to get her story straight before he tried to blindside her when he found out the truth.

She had known the woman who had attacked her, but she hadn't known her for long after they'd met years ago. Nor had she given her much thought over the past eight and a half years.

Hollis had a long line of victims, all male and between the ages of twenty-two and fifty-five. She had never murdered a woman until she shot the bullet into her attacker's chest. It had mostly been in self-defense, but Detective Saldana had been right. Hollis could have incapacitated her without killing her. She could have shown restraint, but after the words she screamed at her when Quillen pulled her off Hollis, she couldn't let her live.

The woman had screamed, "I know you killed Asher and Gus!"

Hollis had several beats to pull her thoughts together, but while her blood pumped wildly, her mind thought viciously. She couldn't let those old wounds be reopened, especially in a town that clung to secrets and scandals like the laundry on their outdoor lines. She recalled the scene in order to continue misleading Detective Saldana when he followed up with her.

She had shot the woman in her chest. The woman had stared at her, reminding her nothing of the beauty she had first encountered years ago. Broken blood vessels stretched across a pale complexion and her eyes dimmed as they lost their purpose. The woman had gasped and shifted from side to side, as Quillen continued to hold her in place. Hollis had jumped up and ran out the door before the woman's body fell to the floor.

It hadn't been right. She usually planned her murders, even if they happened within minutes of her formulating a scheme. This had been different. It had felt wrong, and she could take no satisfaction from its success. The police would be called, and she would be investigated. Her mind had swirled and threatened to go dark as she breathed rapidly. She had fallen in Quillen's hallway, a lump of jittery nerves, with saucer-like eyes and trembling limbs.

"She's dead," Quillen had said from somewhere near her. He may have touched her, but she hadn't felt it.

And so, Sarah Johnson laid in a pool of her own blood. One of Hollis's biggest secrets was safe. For now.

Chapter Twenty-Five

Sarah, Part One

Hollis waited until the woman went on her lunch break, parking in an empty lot across the street. Vehicles passed, but no one glanced in her direction. The townspeople were used to cars pulling over there.

She'd been there most of the day, and early that morning she'd walked inside the bank. It was busy, and only two tellers were serving customers while a third handled drive-through transactions.

The building had high ceilings and a model train ran on a track along the wall, reminding the customers that the area had been a booming railroad town less than a hundred years ago. A little boy pointed to the train and the overhead lights danced in his eyes. His overwhelmed mother let him stop for a moment and watch it, more for a moment of peace than for his amusement. Hollis watched the toy train make several loops around the spacious room before someone addressed her.

"Can I help you?"

Hollis had chosen her line for a reason, but now that she looked at her, really looked at her, she wanted to turn and run away. She couldn't help but stare.

The woman's brass name plate displayed her name, Sarah Johnson, and she was the opposite of Hollis. Short, perfectly styled blonde hair fell around a round face and green eyes. Voluptuous curves were clearly defined in her royal blue dress, offsetting her cream-colored skin. Everything about Sarah was full, from her rounded hips to her large breasts and puckered lips. Hollis was completely captivated by her.

"Can I help you?" Sarah repeated, a little less sure of the customer in front of her.

Sure, you can help me, Hollis thought. *Why don't you tell me why you were sleeping with my boyfriend?*

"I need change for a twenty." She lifted a crumpled bill.

Sarah smiled, placating her. "Do you have an account?"

Hollis was thrown off. She was a few months shy of eighteen, and she assumed that banks would exchange cash for cash. Asher had opened an account with the bank, but if she used his name, then it would tip Sarah off about her identity. Although, with the condescending look she was giving her, Hollis thought she might already know her.

Had Asher told everyone he was in a relationship with her, and they still didn't care to sleep with him? Did everyone know how foolish she was?

"No," Hollis answered. "I just needed change for the laundry mat."

It was a reasonable excuse. The laundry mat was within walking distance of the bank.

Sarah's smile stayed plastered to her face, but Hollis could tell it took her considerable effort. "I can't cash your twenty unless you have an account here. Sorry."

Sarah didn't look apologetic, but Hollis managed to find her own ersatz smile. "That's okay. I'll see if Gus can make change at the hardware store."

That shocked her. The smile ran off her face like the chalk colors on a sidewalk during a hard rain.

Hollis turned on her heel and walked out, knowing she had given herself away, but feeling satisfied by the change in Sarah's expression. She pushed open the double-doors with ease and walked back to her car.

She waited for bank security to step out and look for her, but the only people who came out were the patrons who had successfully completed their business. Then she expected the police to pull into the parking lot and spot her sitting across the street, but the only cruiser she saw passed without glancing in her direction.

Sarah had clearly recognized her, and Hollis had mentioned Gus, who did, in fact, work at the hardware store, but who now had been missing for over a week, so why hadn't Sarah told the bank's security team? The details of Asher's death had been on the news, and even though she had been cleared as a suspect, a lot of people still thought she had killed him. Hollis could see it when they looked at her, whispering behind cupped hands at the funeral and graveside service.

Asher's sister had been nice to her, but when Hollis bent down to talk to Asher's niece, her mother had picked her up quickly and made an excuse that she was needed elsewhere. Asher's parents had spoken to her with cold civility, and no other friend or relative approached her.

She found Sarah's name in the guest book the funeral director had handed to her at the end of the service. Feeling its rightful place was with his family, Hollis had given it to Asher's mother at the interment, but not before she had looked through it and copied some names down.

Sarah had been first on her list, and she was the only woman who wasn't part of Asher's family or one of his known friends. She had looked her up on social media and had found her standing next to Gus at the ribbon-cutting ceremony for the new hardware store. The store had belonged to someone else, but Gus had worked there. Hollis could only assume they hadn't filed a missing person's report because they thought he was on bereavement leave.

Sarah walked out of the building at eleven-thirty, carrying a stylish green lunch bag with her. Hollis wondered why she'd need to leave if her lunch was in the bag. *Couldn't she have eaten it in the break room?*

Sarah got into her car and pulled out. Hollis's car was mostly concealed by another building, so Sarah wouldn't have seen her in the driver's seat.

It was easy to follow Sarah's mid-sized luxury vehicle to the ranch-styled brick home just off Main Street. An alley that ran between the backyards of the houses on the block made it easy to find the house and park where Sarah wouldn't see her.

Hollis walked through the yard and noticed the decorated stepping-stones. Several handprints commemorated the year the stones were placed.

She opened the polished wooden door and stepped inside. The smell of baked goods met her nose, and she noticed a candle on a warmer by the door.

Hollis wasn't worried about making her presence known, but when she found Sarah, the bathroom door was in her way. She could either bust it down or wait for Sarah to finish her business. She leaned against the wall and crossed her arms.

A lot of sniffing echoed from the room, and Hollis wondered if Sarah was sick or crying. The situation was a little clearer to her when Sarah opened the door, and her eyes were glassy. Hollis had seen that look before, and she realized why Sarah hadn't eaten her lunch at work.

When Sarah saw Hollis, she was slow to react. It was all the time Hollis needed to put the rag over her mouth. The chloroform's effect was almost instantaneous, and Hollis let Sarah's body fall to the ground.

Chapter Twenty-Six

Sarah, Part Two

"Please don't do this," Sarah begged.

She'd promised not to scream, nodding her agreement when Hollis asked her, so Hollis had taken out the gag. Sarah had coughed, but Hollis had refused to give her water.

"What're you on?" Hollis asked.

At first, Sarah tried to deny her drug addiction, but after Hollis reinserted her gag and pulled off one of her fingernails, Sarah was more forthcoming about her decent into drugs. Hollis listened half-heartedly. She didn't need to hear about Sarah's hard job and depression.

She interrupted her. "See a therapist," Hollis said simply. "You don't have to use drugs. It's a choice, not some part of a blame-game inevitability."

Sarah closed her mouth with an audible pop. "You sound a lot like him, you know."

Hollis didn't ask for clarification. She knew who she meant.

"*Well, he was my boyfriend.*" She focused all her feelings into every word.

Sarah was humble enough to hang her head. "I know. I'm sorry."

Hollis jumped up, waving the tweezers she found in the bathroom around as she spoke. "What are you sorry for, Sarah?" She must look crazed, she hoped she looked positively mad. "Are you sorry you slept with my boyfriend, or are you sorry you stole any shred of a possibility for happiness away from me?"

Sarah wore a strange expression as she processed her words, and Hollis was hit with the sudden realization that Sarah was one of the few people in town who didn't believe she had murdered Asher. Sarah didn't respond until Hollis clicked the tweezers together, indicating her thoughts on pulling out another one of Sarah's fingernails.

"I'm sorry I slept with Asher. Are you happy now?"

Hollis was a little happier. She had one of her dead boyfriend's sexual partners sweating in a chair and at her mercy.

Suddenly, Hollis was overcome with emotion. It was one thing to know it happened, but it was quite another thing to hear it confirmed. "Why did you sleep with him?"

Sarah looked at the tweezers in Hollis's hand and took a deep breath. "You didn't really know Asher sexually, did you?"

Hollis jumped up. She forced the gag into Sarah's mouth as she shook her head in resistance. Resisting the urge to stab her in the eye with the tweezers, she took off three more of Sarah's fingernails with them before she stopped herself.

The shell-pink skin stood out and bubbles of blood appeared. She'd have a lot to clean up if she wasn't careful.

Sarah cried and thrashed her body from side to side, but the rope Hollis had picked up from the hardware store held her in place. Finally, she calmed down enough for Hollis to take out the gag again.

Sarah gave Hollis a look of pure hatred, but she spoke to her with respect. "All I wanted you to do was think about Asher and what he may have asked you for."

"He didn't ask if he could cheat on me." She spit in Sarah's face, and the woman lowered her eyes as the saliva made a trail down her cheek.

"He was pansexual." The words were almost a whisper.

"What?" Hollis cried. "What does that even mean?"

Sarah gave her an exacerbated look. "He said you were sweet and innocent, but I had no idea you weren't able to talk to him about who he was."

Hollis advanced on her, and Sarah winced. "I'm not sweet and innocent," she asserted, waving the tweezers. "How about you start to make some sense, or I'll poke these in your eye."

"Okay, okay," Sarah said. "What do you want to know?"

Hollis backed off, wishing she could run a hand through her hair, but she had put it up in a bun. She didn't want the police to find one of her loose hairs on Sarah's body.

She sat down in her chair. "Why do you say he was pansexual?"

"Asher loved you," she started. Hollis glared at her, but she let her continue. "He told all of us about you. We never saw pictures of you, but he said you were the most beautiful girl in the world."

Hollis snorted. "I wasn't beautiful enough for him to be faithful to me." She picked one of her nails with the tweezers and smiled when she realized that Sarah saw it as a threatening gesture. "Who is 'we'?"

Sarah looked at the bloody beds where her fingernails had been. "I'm part of a group that met on an app. It was developed for people who enjoy more than monogamy."

"What does that have to do with Asher?"

Sarah looked at her like she was daft. "Asher was on it. He was part of the group before I joined."

Hollis's heart dropped and settled somewhere around the bottom of her stomach. *Had he been part of the group before he'd met her, and if he was, did it make it her business?* Hollis decided it did. She thought they had been in a sexually exclusive relationship, but he had been with other people without telling her. Hollis should have known so she could have decided if she wanted to expose herself to the potential of diseases. Asher's sexual desires weren't the issue; it was the lies he told to Hollis to fulfill them. She spoke her feelings aloud and Sarah nodded.

"You're way too wise for your age," she said, even though she looked only a few years older than Hollis. "I won't guess what made you grow up so fast, but I can tell you that you're right. He told us all about you, but we weren't allowed to meet you."

Hollis felt her anger boiling again. "What was your group? One big orgy?"

Sarah laughed dryly. "No. We all slept together but not at the same time." A tear fell from her eye. "We all loved Asher, and he loved us."

Hollis's rage spilled over and before she knew it, she had her hands around Sarah's throat. She shook her until Sarah's eye's bulged and little capillaries showed on her face.

When Sarah's breathing stopped, Hollis assumed that was the end of their conversation. There were purple bruises forming around her neck, and Hollis was worried about sneaking a body to her car in the middle of the day.

A minute or so later, while Hollis was deciding what to do with her corpse, Sarah gasped for breath. It was both a relief and a disappointment to Hollis, who stuffed a dishtowel in her captive's mouth.

Hollis went over a new plan in her mind before she spoke it to Sarah, who was still breathing rapidly through her nose and trying to cough around the rag. She attempted to shush her, but Sarah wouldn't stop until Hollis put out her hands and approached her, meaning to choke her again. Sarah settled into soft sobs, but she listened to Hollis.

"I'm going to untie you and we're going to walk to my car. You're going to take me to all the people who slept with my boyfriend while I thought he was in town getting supplies."

Sarah nodded when she asked if she could stay quiet. Hollis pulled the dishtowel out of her mouth.

"I have a family," she cried, tears coursing down her cheeks.

Hollis needed her to willingly go with her to her car, so she told her, "I'm not going to hurt you anymore. I just want to meet the other people in your group."

It was a necessary lie to try to calm Sarah. Sarah wasn't buying it, though. She knew she wasn't going to return if she left with Hollis.

"Please. I have a seven-year-old daughter." She nodded behind Hollis and Hollis looked at a staged family photo. A man hung half his body out of a food truck and offered a hot dog to his daughter as Sarah lifted her a little to receive it. The girl had Sarah's blonde hair, but her eyes matched her father's. Even though the members were posed, their smiles seemed genuine.

Hollis looked back at Sarah. "I can't let you live," she said plainly.

For one terrifying second after she had revealed her intentions to Sarah, she thought she was going to scream for help, but she only opened her mouth and shut it again. Hollis waited for her to speak. The words came, but they were forced. She hadn't noticed before, because Sarah had been sobbing, but she was already experiencing pain and soreness in her throat as a result of Hollis's throttling.

"Her name is Alissa." She tried to hold Hollis's eyes, but Hollis was determined to stay indifferent. "She goes to preschool just down the road from here. Her favorite doll is on the table behind you and her favorite—"

"Enough!" Hollis barked at her. "I'm not going to feel sorry for you because you have a kid." But truthfully, she did. She didn't want to take a parent away from a child. "You'll have me arrested for this."

Sarah shook her head vigorously, tears spilling from the sides of her eyes. "No, I won't. I'll tell everyone I'm sick until I can talk better, and I'll cover my neck with a scarf. No one will know."

"Your husband and daughter will see the marks."

"I'll keep the scarf on at home and tell them it's to keep me warm from my sickness. I'll stay in the guest room until I feel better."

Hollis was still skeptical. "How do I know you won't tell on me?"

"Because if I tell on you, then you can reveal the group. My husband will leave me, and he'll take our daughter. I don't want that."

Hollis looked down at her face and thought about the moments when she'd thought she'd killed Sarah. Her death hadn't made her happy. She also considered the child. *How could she kill Sarah while she thought about her daughter coloring a picture for her mother or playing happily at school?*

"I'll need something else for insurance." She reached down and picked up the doll Sarah said had been Alissa's favorite. It was made of cloth with yellow yarn hair and blue button eyes. There were no pupils or irises in the eyes, and they made her uncomfortable. "I'm taking this doll, but I'll take something closer to you if you betray me. I may have to serve a few years in prison for what I did to you today, but I can promise there will be a moment in her life when Alissa's guard is down, and then I'll take her from you."

Hollis wiped everything down with bleach before she left. She took the rope that had bound Sarah's hands and Sarah grabbed her wrists, rubbing them until the circulation returned. Hollis leaned over and stared at her, almost touching her nose, watching her fearful eyes dart from left to right.

"I'm serious. If you say anything about me, you will never see your daughter again."

Chapter Twenty-Seven

"What happened?"

Josie ran down the steps as Hollis came through the door. Her short pink bathrobe was pulled tightly around her, and her hair was pulled up in a messy bun.

"I thought you'd be in bed by now," Hollis said. The outside and hallway lights were on, but Hollis had assumed Josie had left them on in case Hollis came home.

"I was reading," Josie replied, but her bloodshot eyes and puffy face indicated she'd been going through old pictures of Cotton again.

Hollis hadn't gone back into Quillen's house after she had refused further medical treatment, so her hands were still bloody. She'd used some hand sanitizer in her car, but with nothing on which to wipe it, she only rubbed the blood into her hands like some sort of sanguine lotion. She wondered why the medic hadn't cleaned her hands, and she decided it was either because she was afraid the police would need to take samples of the blood or because she wanted Hollis to be reminded that she literally and metaphorically had "blood on her hands." Since the latter was less likely, she assumed it was due to possible police evidence.

She went straight into the kitchen and grabbed the disinfectant wipes Josie kept next to the sink. Every teacher in the school had disinfectant wipes in their classrooms, even Hollis, who had been gifted several containers of them when Josie visited her classroom.

She ran out to her car and wiped it down, and cleaned the doorknob, her keys, and her phone. After she had cleaned her car, Josie had followed her until it was clear Hollis didn't intend to divulge the night's happenings to her.

She put her hand on her arm. "What happened Hollis?"

"I need a shower," she told her friend.

Josie let go of her arm, but Hollis could feel her eyes on her as she climbed the steps. She knew it was hard for Josie to let her go, but Hollis lacked the mental and physical energy it would take to give her friend the type of retelling she'd require. It was better left until the morning.

Hollis showered quickly, already familiar with all the tricks to get blood out of her fingernails. She didn't look at herself in the mirror as she ran a brush through her hair and jabbed a toothbrush back and forth in her mouth. After the taste of wine and Quillen was gone, she climbed into her bed and pulled the quilt up to her shoulders.

Usually, death didn't affect her. She could plan it out like a journey on a map. Once her destination was reached, it was no more than a moment before she was planning her next trip.

But Sarah's death had been different. It gnawed at her in a way it shouldn't. She had punished Sarah, so her debt to Hollis had been paid. Unfortunately, Sarah hadn't liked her punishment and she'd gone after Hollis for revenge.

Chapter Twenty-Eight

Sarah, Part Three

Sarah didn't keep her promise.

Gus was reported missing two weeks after his death, and they found the truck easily. Gus was a known hiker, so the authorities didn't seem surprised that his truck was found in the woods. They were even less surprised when the K9 unit found his body. Amazingly, though, they theorized that he had picked up a hitchhiker and that person had killed him. There had been some reports of a murdering hitchhiker in a neighboring state, so it wasn't a shock to anyone.

Two weeks after they found Gus's body, the police brought a warrant for Hollis's arrest. Despite her attempts to plead that she didn't know Sarah, a bank camera showed their exchange. It had been harmless, but the green bruises on Sarah's neck and the video, coupled with the word of a respected member of the community had given them enough evidence to arrest her.

Hollis tried to remain strong. She merely gave the detectives wide-eyed denial whenever they asked her about the incident and the threat she made against Alissa. She told them she had only had one conversation with Sarah at the bank and had gone on her way. She claimed that she didn't know why Sarah would make up a lie.

The police turned her house upside down looking for Alissa's doll, but they never found it. Without proof, it looked like there wasn't much of a case.

Sarah had called her bluff. Hollis had no intention of uncovering her sex club because it could reveal she had a motive for attacking Sarah and killing both Asher and Gus. It had taken Sarah a little while to get to that conclusion.

Hollis was technically a minor, so she was sent to a holding area for juvenile offenders until her hearing. Sarah sat behind the prosecution and delivered a moving recount of her terror during Hollis's attack. Hollis appeared sympathetic and confused during the retelling, as if she were sorry for Sarah but upset that she was blaming her experience on her.

Hollis purposely misremembered some of the things the detectives had told her during the questioning. Sarah had told the bank employees that she'd been sick, so Hollis said she believed Sarah was having a fever dream about her, and she had misplaced "Lisa's" toy. When she was asked how the marks got around her neck, Hollis offered to have her fingers examined, but the bruises had faded too much to provide a positive match. In the end, there wasn't enough evidence to convict Hollis, so she returned home within the month.

At first, Sarah kept a good eye on Alissa, staying with her as soon as she got off work until she went to bed. Soon, she became complacent, as it seemed Hollis wasn't going to retaliate. In truth, Hollis had gone away during that time, so she wasn't in town hounding Sarah's steps.

Hollis had pulled Alissa's doll from the hole in the tree where she'd placed her gloves, and she took it around her house with her as she performed household chores. It smelled like the dead squirrel she had placed it beside, so she tumbled it through the washer and dryer.

Hollis watched Alissa from her car when she played outside. Sarah was less than guarded, paying more attention to her phone than to her daughter. She talked to everyone within range, but she shooed Alissa away when she approached her with a flower. She went inside often, leaving Alissa outside alone, but there were always neighbors within sight, tending in their gardens or playing with their own children.

Within moments of Sarah's disappearance, a notification would usually ding on Asher's phone. There were several times Hollis wondered how Sarah had gotten undressed and taken a picture so quickly. All the men and women on the app seemed to like it immediately, and Hollis had to admit, Sarah was a beautiful girl.

Hollis had learned many of the ins and outs of social media, and even though Sarah hadn't been forthcoming with more than two names to add to her list, Hollis knew there were others on the funeral guest list that matched the people who belonged to the app on Asher's phone. She focused on two men that she thought Sarah might really like.

At first, she couldn't distinguish patterns in any of their behaviors. They seemed to go to work and do work-related activities, but two weeks after Hollis was released from the juvenile detention center, an opportunity presented itself.

Hollis had been following one of the men from the funeral list, Steven Lingerfelt. On weekdays, she took long walks behind him as he passed people on the sidewalk and talked to them on his way to lunch. One day Steven didn't walk to lunch at his usual cafe. He pushed open the double doors of the agency where he worked and crossed the parking lot to his car. Hollis was in her car, waiting to follow him at a safe distance, so she was ready when his black SUV pulled out onto Main Street.

He turned down a familiar alley, and she drove around the block, entering the alley and parking behind his SUV and another car. A plan formed in her mind, and she never questioned it.

Hollis watched Alissa and her father as he pushed her on the swing set. `The girl swung her legs out and arched them back, ready for another soft push from her trusted parent.

Hollis had followed the rumors about his divorce. Somehow, Sarah's husband had been given enough evidence to support a claim of infidelity and, due to the circumstances, a temporary custody order for Alissa. Sarah's husband seemed vindictive, and after he learned about her affairs with multiple men while Alissa was home, he was able to get the judge to grant him temporary custody on an emergency basis. Sarah was expected to leave her home and it seemed it would be awarded to her husband in the divorce.

Contrary to the pleas she made to Hollis, Sarah had not fought for her daughter. She had moved in with another man, other than the ones with which she was photographed. To Hollis's knowledge, she wasn't contesting the divorce or the custody arrangement.

Alissa jumped off the swing and her father scolded her. He had been frightened when she'd jumped, but he hugged her tightly to him when she started to cry. Soon, they were wearing matching smiles as they walked to the parking lot.

On the way, Alissa spotted an ice cream kiosk and begged her father for one. At first, he resisted her, but then he gave in, either because he had made her cry or because he was a push over. He turned around to speak their orders to the attendant, and Alissa was left to play behind him.

This was the chance Hollis had been waiting on for a month. She opened her car door and lifted herself out. She walked casually across the bridge to where Alissa sat playing.

The girl was full of bouncing blonde curls and happiness. The seat of her plaid shorts was covered in dirt, and her vintage ugly doll shirt betrayed her obsession with baby dolls. She piled rocks on top of one another as she gave them the voices of a family.

Hollis couldn't believe how scared she felt. She had committed murder, so it should be easy.

Hollis pulled the doll out of the pocket of her jumper. Without uttering a sound, she motioned Alissa over. When Alissa saw her treasured doll, her face lit up. A smile climbed all the way from her mouth to her light blue eyes, and she clasped her hands to her chest.

Hollis held the doll out to her, making sure she was within running distance to the car. Alissa's father was deep in conversation with the attendant, asking about the ingredients in his daughter's frozen treat. He didn't know his daughter had moved beyond his sight.

Hollis shook the doll in her hand as if she were playing with it, offering the girl a wide, friendly smile. Alissa reached out for her toy.

• • • • ● • ● • • •

Tom frantically looked around for his daughter, but she wasn't behind him. He slung their ice cream cups onto the counter.

"Did you see where my daughter went?" he asked the attendant.

"No," the attendant replied. "I was talking to you."

He could feel the panic rise in his chest as he spun in circles, looking for a flash of Alissa's blonde hair or green shirt. He yelled her name until it became a chant.

Sarah had warned him that the woman who had strangled her had threatened to kill Alissa if she went to the police. *Had she made good on her promise?*

"Daddy."

It was the only voice that could calm his racing heart and settle his nerves. He turned and grabbed her under the arms, lifting his daughter up to him so he could smell the outside air in her hair.

Once he had spent a few moments in grateful prayers, he put Alissa on her feet. "Where were you?" he said, and remembering her tears at the swings, he added, "I was so scared when I didn't see you behind me. Can you tell me what happened?"

By way of an answer, Alissa held up her doll. Kelly had been her favorite toy until it had gone missing. It was another thing Sarah had blamed on the woman she'd said had assaulted her.

"Where did you find it?" he asked her.

"Kelly was hiding," Alissa told him. "I found her."

Alissa seemed happy to have her favorite toy back, but she kept looking at the parking lot as if someone was watching her. She wouldn't say anything more when her father pressed her about it.

He didn't find out the truth until years later, and even though he'd gotten over his feelings for Sarah, it made him wonder if she'd been telling the truth about her attack. One day, he mentioned the doll to Alissa, and she told him she had been afraid to tell him at the time, but a woman had given the doll back to her. When he asked her to describe the woman, Alissa said, "She was a red-headed lady who looked like she was almost ready to have a baby."

Chapter Twenty-Nine

"I don't need a break," he said.

Hollis smiled despite herself, pacing as she held the phone to her ear. "I killed a woman in your house. I think that requires a little processing, especially for Rose."

Quillen didn't budge. "I have a therapy session lined up for Rose on Monday, but her therapist spoke to her earlier, and she seems fine. She said Rosie was glad you were there to defend us." He chuckled, despite the gravity of the conversation. "Too bad I didn't save the day. It may be the beginnings of some hero worship."

Hollis was a little distracted by his treatment of the murder that happened in his home. A woman was dead. He acted like it was a street fight or an uncomplicated mugging and Hollis had overcome the odds.

"I'm no hero," she spoke firmly.

"You're right." His tone finally had the reverence it needed. "I'm sorry. I've just recently learned my defense mechanism is avoidance, and how better to avoid a situation than to make light of it and act like it never happened."

Hollis understood his explanation. Her mother was similar in nature.

"Are you sure Rose is okay?"

There was a snap in the line like he had opened a door and stepped outside. His whisper confirmed her suspicion that he had moved out of the house to speak to her privately.

"Rosie was pretty shaken up when it happened, but she's dealing with it well." She heard a car pass and rev its motor. "She asked about you."

"Me?" Hollis couldn't hide her surprise.

"Yeah. She really believes she'd be dead if it wasn't for you."

The incident wouldn't have happened if Hollis hadn't been there, but she didn't want to get into that with Quillen over the phone.

"When can I see you again?"

She was shocked by his insistence and fumbled for an answer. She needed to give them some space, but she wanted to talk to him face-to-face before Detective Saldana revealed her connection to Sarah.

"There's a holiday fair at Pale Woods Academy this Friday," she suggested.

She had been dreading attending the activities. She was scheduled to chaperone the event, even though caregivers were supposed to be responsible for their charges, some misbehavior was expected. She assumed her military background had made her a prime candidate for the low-level security Mrs. Bailey had suggested.

"It sounds like fun," Quillen said. "But it'll be a working date, so it doesn't really count."

She rolled her eyes. "It counts."

They finished making plans and she ended the call. Quillen wouldn't hang up first, and Hollis was too practical to draw out their goodbye.

She could hear Josie rustling around in the kitchen. Her friend was loudly moving pans and dishes. Hollis guessed it was an unnecessary act, considering Josie was probably only eating a granola bar with her coffee.

She went over her story in her mind one more time and took a deep breath. It wasn't the first time she'd told her friend the truth laced with lies, and she guessed it wouldn't be the last.

"That's crazy," Josie said, her eyes not leaving Hollis while she finished her coffee.

"I know," Hollis agreed, unsure if she should say more.

"And you knew her?"

"Yeah," Hollis answered and held up her hand, "But no one needs to know it but us."

Josie mimicked locking her mouth and throwing away the key. "But it's weird that she hated you all these years and just now tried to kill you."

Hollis shrugged, lifting her juice glass, but pausing before it reached her lips. "Not really. She may not have seen me the last time I was here."

Josie tilted her head back and forth, weighing Hollis's words. "I guess that's possible. But why would she have seen you now?"

Hollis thought she knew the answer, but she deflected Josie's mind away from it. "It's a small town. It was bound to happen eventually."

Hollis knew how Sarah had found out about her reappearance in town, though, and it had nothing to do with chance.

Chapter Thirty

"Alissa Johnson," Hollis called out without looking up. She had to get through her ruse before Rose walked into class.

"She's not here," Katey said. "I think she'll be out for a while. Her mom's dead."

One of the boys mocked falling with his hand on his chest. Hollis opened her mouth to say something against his behavior, but Zach beat her to it.

"Have some respect," he barked at the boy. "How would you feel if someone killed your mom?"

Hollis was reminded that there was some speculation behind Zach's mother's death, and it seemed the rest of the class thought about it, too. The boy lifted himself off the ground and said, "I'm sorry, man. I was being stupid."

Zach turned away from the boy, but his reproach had stung. The boy was humbled, and he kept his head down for the rest of class. Hollis told the kids to warm up by jogging laps around the court.

Amazingly, Detective Saldana had managed to keep her name out of the press reports by mentioning that a minor was involved. His wife was an editor with a local newspaper, so she could have aided him, too. The reason he wanted to cover for her, baffled Hollis, but after all their years without communication, she was thankful for his kindnesses.

Hollis had looked into Sarah's life since Hollis last saw her, and Alissa hadn't been close with her mother. The death still stung, though, and it may have been worse due to her mother's inattention over the years. The chasm created by an absent parent is so immense that their death can push their child over the edge into the abyss.

Hollis could tell something was wrong when Rose came into the gym. She hovered around Lisa and Katey, but she made no move to join in their conversation.

The bell signaling the start of class hadn't rung yet, so Hollis stared at Rose until she caught her eye. She motioned the girl over with a wave of her arm. Zach was the only other student who looked up, but he quickly returned to jogging at the lead of the line.

Hollis studied Rose. Her pupils were marginally dilated, and her bottom lip was trembling, even though she pressed it against the top one frequently.

"What's wrong?"

At first, Rose dismissed her interest, but when Hollis pointed out her shaking hands and the way she shot looks at the entrance every time there was movement, Rose relented. She crossed her arms over her midsection and moved beside Hollis so they could speak and watch the opening to the gym at the same time.

"I think someone's watching me."

Hollis scanned the room instinctively, but she saw no one there but the kids in the class. She glanced at the bleachers that lined three sides of the court. Someone could be behind them, but it would provide them little opportunity to escape unnoticed if they were located.

Hollis put her hands on her hips. "Who do you think it is?"

"I don't know," Rose said too quickly.

Hollis raised an eyebrow in her direction, but Rose pretended not to notice. Her face was dewy with perspiration.

Hollis tried another approach. "Why do you think they're watching you?"

A tear slid from the eye closest to Hollis, but Rose wiped it away quickly. "Because they're sick."

"Do you know the person?"

Rose glared at Hollis. "What does it matter?" She had raised her voice and a couple of kids looked over at them. She continued at a much lower volume. "Every time this happens, we have to move again."

Hollis bought up a long sigh from her chest. "I'll take care of it," she promised. "As long as you're at school, no one will hurt you." She nodded at Rose's hand where she clutched her phone. "Put my number into your phone contacts." Rose dutifully entered the digits. "Call or text me if you feel danger."

The bell rang, and Rose jogged to her assigned spot. Hollis called the students back to their assigned places, and when her eyes met Zach's, she thought she saw something there.

It looked a lot like respect.

Chapter Thirty-One

Greg

"You lost it?" he yelled. "I can't believe you lost it!" The man tore through the rolling luggage and looked up at his wife. "You had one job." He held his index finger in front of her.

The woman pulled her hands away from her face. "I'm sorry, Greg. I was trying to get the kids ready to stay at your mother's, and the repairman showed up late to fix the dishwasher, and— "

Greg, a plain-looking man with a shaved head and ciga-rette-stained teeth, held up his hand. "It sounds like you're making excuses, but you know who to blame."

She hung her head and nodded.

Greg zipped up the luggage and pushed the smaller one to his wife. "I have a conference here in eight days, so I have to stay. You, however, lost your ticket, so you'll need to go back."

The woman glanced up, horrified. "You mean you plan to go on our anniversary cruise without me?"

"You lost your ticket," he repeated.

The woman let out a sob and bolted for the bathroom. The man watched her go, and when the door clanged shut, he pulled out his phone and dialed a number.

"Hey, baby," he spoke to the person who answered.

Hollis had been watching the exchange between Greg and his wife from two seats away. They hadn't noticed her glances, and she pretended to play a game on her phone to draw attention away from how intently she listened to them.

"It worked," he said. "Jennifer thinks she lost the ticket, but I have it in my back pocket."

Hollis thought she could hear a squeal of excitement on the other end of the line, but she couldn't be certain. The port was a mix of unfamiliar sounds, so it had thrown her perception off.

She thought about what she would have done if Asher had been with her and had witnessed the same spectacle. She would have talked him into distracting Greg while she pulled the ticket out of his back pocket. Then Asher could have pretended to find it on the ground and given it to Jennifer when she returned.

Hollis stared down at the scuffed tile. Asher wasn't here, though.

"Go ahead and drive the rest of the way out," he said into his phone.

Hollis tuned out the rest of their conversation. Emboldened by a new resolve, she picked up her suitcase and made her way to the bathroom, gently knocking into Greg as she went by him.

The man's face was almost as pale as the puffy, white clouds behind him. "What?"

The woman's smile only stretched wider. "This woman" — she motioned to Hollis— "found my ticket."

Hollis stood beside Greg's wife, who had told her to call her "Jenny" after she had given her the ticket. Jenny was a kind woman with small, round eyes and an angular face. Hollis guessed she was at least a decade younger than her husband, somewhere in her late thirties, but that was only because she seemed more mature than the people Hollis knew who were in their twenties.

Hollis had found Jenny washing her face at the sink, and she smiled sadly at Hollis when she approached her. Hollis had admitted to hearing their conversation and produced the ticket. Jenny blinked several times as if she thought the ticket would dematerialize in her hand.

Greg's dark eyes widened, and he looked just beyond his wife and Hollis. "That's not your ticket."

Jenny cocked her head and followed Greg's eyes. Whatever, or whoever, he was looking at had blended into the crowd.

His hand went to his back pocket, and the action wasn't lost on Jenny. She didn't voice her suspicion aloud, though, choosing instead to live under the guise of a mutually loving marriage.

Greg scrubbed his face and glanced behind them again. Hollis moved to the left and noticed a blonde woman with a white sunhat and long, tan limbs. She locked eyes with Greg momentarily, before her smile fell and she seemed less sure of herself.

"You lost your ticket," came his final feeble argument.

Jenny looked at the dock, shifting her weight from one foot to another. Her husband's excuses colored her face, and she tried to reason with Greg by showing him the ticket was marked with their cabin number.

Hollis narrowed her eyes. "I saw how upset you were when your wife ran to the bathroom."

Her words had the desired effect, and Jenny lifted her head and watched her husband's reaction. Greg looked from Hollis to his wife, aware that Hollis knew his secret and had prevented his ruse from affecting his wife's trip.

"I'm thrilled, honey," he said to his wife, flashing her a smile. "I was just a little thrown off. Most people aren't that helpful anymore."

Jenny practically jumped into his arms. "I know!" She beamed at Hollis. "You really saved the day, Holli!"

Hollis almost corrected her, but she stopped herself. She didn't know why, but "Holli" seemed like a good name.

Hollis had decided to visit the people she thought had slept with her boyfriend after she got back from the cruise. She planned to visit a bank teller and a realtor who were on a strange app on Asher's phone. She tried not to think about that side of Asher, opting instead to have an experience as close to the one she would have had with him if he had been there. Unfortunately, Hollis had the worse bought of sea sickness of any passenger. The ship may have practically glided across the ocean, but she could pick up on every rock and jolt of the waves.

The nurse gave Hollis a medicine to calm her stomach, but two days into the cruise, Hollis was still moaning and retching in her cabin. She had hardly come out for meals, even though there were buffets of every culinary delight imaginable, after she'd noticed her table was next to the seafood. Her sickness had made her hyper-sensitive to the smell.

On the third morning, she trudged to the nurse and asked for another dose of anti-nausea medicine. As the nurse fulfilled her request, Hollis told her about her symptoms of haziness and her aversion to fish.

"Could you be pregnant?" the nurse asked.

Hollis's knee jerk response was, "No," but she stared pensively at the floor. *When was her last period?*

"You don't look so sure," the nurse said, and when Hollis didn't comment, she brought a pregnancy test out of her purse. The package had been opened, but it had contained two tests, and the other test was sealed in white plastic.

The nurse explained that she had bought the test for her sister. Her sister had received a positive result, and she was so sure about it, that she didn't need the second test.

Hollis tried to return the nurse's smile, but she couldn't make her face work. She wrapped her hand around the wrapped test and followed the nurse to the bathroom.

The nurse handed her the box and Hollis read the directions. She looked up at the nurse in shock.

"It's going to be okay," the nurse assured her.

No one knew any part of her story besides Jenny, whom she'd confided in about Asher's death, and she had seen very little of her. The nurse didn't know that a positive test would alter Hollis's life in a way that was slightly different than most women.

She peeled the wrapping open and laid the test, collection cup, and dropper in her hand. The test was a slender piece of plastic with a shiny white strip contained inside. There were two windows that allowed Hollis to see the interior strip. One was the test window, and a dark red line would appear if the test wasn't faulty. The second window revealed the results: one line, not pregnant; two lines, pregnant.

Hollis followed the directions on how to "catch" her urine, and before she knew it, she was holding the dropper above the test. She pushed out two drops of her urine and watched as it traveled the length of the strip.

A straight red line appeared first, indicating the test was reliable. Hollis waited in agony for the urine to coat the next window. When it did, Hollis stared at it for so long that the nurse knocked on the door to ask if she was okay.

Hollis emerged, with distant eyes and a face completely drained of color. She held up the test where the positive result was clearly visible, and then everything went dark.

The nurse's name was Joy. Hollis learned it after she had revived her and wheeled her to her cabin. She checked on her every day, sharing stories about her own pregnancy and her experience during the short time she was a pediatric nurse.

Hollis looked forward to her visits. Joy brought her some sort of shake that didn't make her sick and her conversation was a welcome break from the loneliness.

During the next two days, Hollis took walks around the ship's deck and visited the attractions. She laid on a lounge chair and closed her eyes, listening to the sounds of children splashing in the ship's pool.

She noticed Jenny and Greg as she settled into her periods of people-watching. Jenny was always crying, or very near it, when Hollis spotted them. Greg was usually yelling or throwing things around like a toddler.

On the fourth day of the cruise, Hollis was enjoying a ginger ale by the pool, when she heard Greg yell, "I told you to put it in the bag!"

Jenny offered apologies, but he kept heckling her until she ran away. She covered her face to keep the other passengers from seeing her tears.

As soon as she was gone, a self-satisfied smile stretched across Greg's face. He pulled his phone out of his pocket and dialed a number.

One of the passengers made a comment to him that he wouldn't get service that far out. Greg assured him that his phone was linked to a satellite.

Sure enough, someone responded to his call, and he spoke to the other person on the line with a voice dripping in sweetness. A sweetness that should have been reserved for his wife.

Hollis only heard one thing, but it was enough to upset her.

"Yeah, baby," he said loudly enough for the other passengers to hear him. It was almost as if he was daring one of them to tell his wife. "She's always around, unless she's off crying in the cabin. We'll have a much better trip when we go on *our* cruise next month."

Hollis jumped off the lounge chair and almost ran to her cabin. A sharp pain near her right hip caused her to slow her steps.

She had to think of the new life growing inside of her, but she boiled with rage every time she saw the way Greg treated Jenny. It wasn't her business, yet she couldn't stop thinking about it.

· · · ● ● · ● ● ● · ·

Hollis had taken the trip so she could feel closer to Asher. Sure, she was living where they had shared many good times together, but he had planned the trip with her, and it would have been a shame not to go.

She had decided to use the time as a period of reflection. Hollis had murdered her boyfriend and one of his lovers. *Could she ever move past it, or would the murders haunt her the rest of her life?* Hollis had just turned eighteen, but she was certain that her nightmares would always star Asher, with his cold, dead eyes. The dreams hadn't started yet, but her guilt and grief were so strong that she expected nightmares about her deceased boyfriend to begin any time.

Hollis had walked to the edge of the lower deck and peered off the side of the ship. The base of the ship cut through the water, chopping it to either side. She entertained the idea of jumping into the sea and allowing herself to be sucked under the ship. Maybe she could jump from a point high enough so the impact against the water would kill her, or perhaps she'd hit her head on the ship's metal husk, causing her to slip out of the world without experiencing the feeling of drowning.

Then she thought about the baby, and she regretted her dark fantasies. Death would have to wait.

She tried not to think too much about the reason she had killed Asher. Instead, she tried to imagine what it would have been like to have shared the cruise with him. They could have laughed over the tiny octopi staring at them from the seafood bar while they ate and taken walks along the deck at sunrise and sunset.

The ship docked on a beautiful island filled with lovely sights and friendly locals. After Hollis had her hair braided and declined the offers of a multitude of drugs, she wondered back to the ship early.

Most everyone was on the island, and the ship was quiet, other than the staff who were preparing for the big variety show.

Hollis was so preoccupied with pretending to be with Asher that she almost didn't notice Greg at the end of the deck. He hung his arms over the railing, holding a phone in one hand and a Moon Walker beer in the other.

"Hey, Holli," he said to her, clearly drunk and struggling to stand. He put his arm around her, and Hollis was slammed by smells of hops and man-sweat from her past.

"Jenny's on the island," he slurred, cupping the hand that dangled above her chest over her breast. "Do you want to hang out in my cabin?"

Suddenly, it was very clear to Hollis what she and "Holli" needed to do.

Hollis found Joy and sat down beside her. The variety show had just started, and a magician was on the stage, wiggling his nose at a rabbit that had popped out of his hat.

"It's cruel to make animals perform," Hollis commented, surprising herself. She'd never known she felt that way until she had spoken.

"You may have an aversion to meat because you're pregnant," whispered Joy, "but you sound like someone who really loves animals."

Hollis rolled her comment around in her mind. She had never been allowed to have a pet, and Asher had been grieving over the loss of a dog he'd had since he was a young boy, so Hollis hadn't had the opportunity to bond with an animal. She liked them, though, and she hoped to have one at some point. Maybe she could adopt a dog or a cat when the baby was old enough to pet them and not hurt them.

Hollis sat through the rest of the program, and two significant pains stabbed her lower belly. One of the pains was so strong it blurred her vision.

She saw Jenny five rows in front of her. The variety show was amusing, but it didn't seem to hold Jenny's attention, as she kept checking behind her. Presumably, she was waiting on Greg, but he never showed up.

The next day, everyone prepared to disembark. The ship was buzzing with activity, and at breakfast, Hollis was able to catch snatches of news. One of the tables nearest to her briefly discussed a missing passenger.

When she got off the boat, Hollis passed several uniformed officers. They didn't look like what her mother called "street cops," but they had badges on their shirts that signified their occupation. They looked at her, but they didn't stop her. One of the men even smiled a little, like it wouldn't be hard for her to talk him into meeting her for a drink. Hollis noted the gold band on his left hand and anger threatened to overtake her. She needed to get out of there with as little attention as possible, so she calmed herself, smiled back, and left the ship behind her.

Goodbye, Greg.

Chapter Thirty-Two

"I'm tired of moving," Rose argued, but her voice had less bite to it.

"I know," Quillen returned with a patience and gentleness he only found for her. "To be honest, I'm just as tired, but we can't allow that sick piece of—"

"Dad," Rose interrupted. "We've already allowed it. We let the messages control our lives, but now I'm ready to stand up and fight."

"Rosie," he cooed, embracing her. She melted into him, just like the first time he'd held her and her sister after they were born, and he'd thought their breath was the sweetest scent in the world. "You can't fight a depraved person."

She broke from him, crossing her arms. "I took karate when I was eight and you got me those self-defense classes."

He tried not to laugh in her face, but he couldn't help smiling, and she narrowed her eyes. He told her softly, but he doubted she'd understand. She had taken a month-long course in taekwondo when a studio offered it to her second grade class, and she'd hardly moved up a level.

"You only took martial arts for a short time, and the self-defense lessons are only something for you to fall back on if..." he trailed off.

They both knew what he meant, but Rose's posture crumpled. She grabbed her pillow and pulled it to her stomach.

"I froze the other night, didn't I?"

She wasn't crying yet, but he sensed it was about to happen. He put his arm around her, wishing he could make her life better, and hating himself for his parental failures.

"You weren't feeling well," he said. "And you were asleep."

"That's no excuse," she shot back. "Attacks can happen at any time. That's what you and Dr. Fields say."

It was true. He had echoed the words of her therapist many times.

"But you'll be more prepared—"

She shot up off her pillow. "I don't want to be prepared! I want to live like a normal teenager with boy problems and too much social pressure. I don't want to think about the man that took my family away and wonder if he's going to come back and finish the job!"

Quillen wanted to say that he was part of her family, and he was still there, but that wasn't the point, and they both knew it. He wrapped his arms back around her, and even though she fought against him at first, she settled her head on his chest while the tears of anger and frustration spilled over.

Chapter Thirty-Three

Hollis could hear the music blaring before she stepped inside. The windows were closed against the chilly December day, but Josie's choice of monster ballads pounded against the frames. Madonna, The Tubes, and Warrant were among her favorites, leftover from a compact disk collection her mother had passed on to her when she'd died.

Hollis winced when she opened the door. The lyrics to a Poison song reminded her of a video she wanted to forget. She found the speaker in the living room, and pushed the volume button a couple of times, but it was only one of the four speakers in the house. Still, it gave her ears a break.

Several things prompted loud music in the house. There were times when Josie would celebrate her victories, like when she was granted tenure at Pale Woods Academy or when her class received high scores on college entrance exams, and she would throw on a Tiffany or Madonna song and dance around the house. There were lovely gestures when she'd turn on Michael Jackson or Culture Club and try to persuade Hollis into a better mood. Her efforts worked like a charm, even if Hollis didn't recognize most of the lyrics her friend belted out as if she'd written them herself. But there were darker times, like today, when the music was as foreboding as the burning smell in the kitchen.

Hollis remembered the days Josie and Cotton would fight. Well, Cotton would yell and scream, and Josie would go along with whatever he said, sacrificing pieces of her dignity. The time after he left was the worst. She had played the first song they'd danced to at their wedding from the time she'd woken up until she laid her head down. She'd refused to eat and couldn't remember if she'd fed the animals or collected the eggs. Hollis had taken over the farm work for her, even though she wasn't one hundred percent certain that she was caring for the animals properly. Luckily, Josie snapped out of her depression after a week, and the farm was as functional and healthy as it had been before Cotton left.

Hollis looked around for the source of Josie's apparent mood. It didn't take her long to find it. Sitting on the end table between the chairs Cotton and Josie used to share was a stapled group of papers. Hollis imagined the pain her friend must have felt when she opened the envelope with the neatly typed address in the left-hand corner. Josie's eyes must have widened at the "Marital Disillusion" on the front page, falling into her chair as her hopes for her husband's return were obliviated.

Hollis returned the papers to the end table and stepped gingerly down the hall. The blaring beats of Cinderella covered her footfalls, but she didn't want to startle her friend.

Josie was in the kichen with metal muffin pans, bowls, flour, and butter on the counter. She balanced a milk jug over a measuring cup, eyeing it closely. A burnt smell rushed up to meet Hollis and she guessed that whatever was already in the oven was inedible.

Hollis turned down the music. She made sure it was loud, but lowered enough to say something, if needed. She was glad she could read lips, because her eardrums were already ringing.

A large bottle of whisky sat on the kitchen table. It had been Cotton's favorite, and along with his usual beer, he had enjoyed it almost every evening Hollis had stayed with them. Two shot glasses were stationed at its sides, but they had been abandoned for the juice glass Josie poured down her throat as Hollis watched.

She was unsure about the best way to approach her friend. On one hand, Josie enjoyed physical touch, so she might like a hug, but Hollis shied away from contact, so the effort might feel forced. On the other hand, Josie needed someone, even if it was her emotionally stunted best friend, so Hollis threw aside her reservations and put her arms around Josie's waist.

Her friend didn't even jump. It was as if she had known Hollis was there, or maybe her reaction time was reduced to a snail's pace due to the half a bottle of liquor she'd downed. Josie patted her hands and turned around to face her.

"I guess you saw it," she slurred at Hollis.

Hollis nodded. She didn't know the best way to proceed.

"I knew he was cruel, but I never expected this!" She waved a wooden spoon in the air and batter dripped onto the toaster and coffee pot.

She turned back to her futile project. Josie could cook almost anything on the stovetop, but she couldn't bake. Maybe it was because her oven was on the highest setting, or maybe it was self-sabotaged because her mother was such a fantastic baker who won prizes for her blueberry and strawberry muffins.

"I mean, he always told me he'd take the house if I ever left him," she went on, stirring the mixture to quickly.

Hollis inched over to the stove and clicked the off button on the oven's screen. The food inside still burned, but no other baked goods would accompany it.

Josie's head snapped in her direction, and Hollis thought she'd been caught, but her friend didn't look at her hands. She pointed her stirring spoon at her, and a glob of the blueberry mixture dripped onto the tile.

"You know, he stayed gone so long, doing who knows what, but I always thought he'd come back to me when he was done."

Hollis was glad to see her friend's anger, but she knew it was empowered by alcohol, and it would soon be followed by tears. She didn't have long to wait.

"Why couldn't he tell me to my face?" she said, her voice rising to a manic level. "Why get a divorce now? Did he find someone else?"

After her last question, she looked away, staring at the spoon in her hand until another drip of batter dropped at her feet. She stared back at Hollis, a world of hurt in her eyes. "Why am I not good enough?"

"Oh, honey," Hollis consoled, bringing her friend into her arms. "You are more than enough."

She didn't say anything against Cotton, even though it was obvious that he wouldn't be back. She had learned a long time ago to never speak ill about another woman's husband, no matter how mean he had been to her.

Sobs rattled Josie's body, and she and Hollis sank to the floor. At some point, Josie's spoon hit the tile, and Hollis carried her friend to her bed. It was difficult getting her up the stairs, but Hollis pushed herself to make sure Josie was placed comfortably under her covers.

She took the empty juice glass out of her friend's hand and cut the sound on the speakers. She wasn't sure when her ears stopped ringing, as she heard the residual guitar riffs the entire time she cleaned the kitchen. She baked the muffins Josie had placed in the pan and dumped the rest of the batter down the sink. It was hardly six o'clock when she finished, and she checked on Josie before she made herself an individual macaroni and cheese bowl.

Josie slept peacefully propped on her left side when Hollis slipped back into her room. The blankets and pillows she'd pushed behind her kept her friend from rolling onto her back. Hollis was certain she had drunk enough alcohol to vomit at some point, and she didn't want Josie to asphyxiate.

Hollis grabbed one of the pillows off her bed and laid down on the carpet. During the night, she shivered, and she regretted not getting a blanket until Mage curled up beside her. His body heat kept her warm.

All of this upset was because of a man who had hardly cared about the life he'd lived with a caring wife he'd taken for granted. There wasn't one redeemable quality about Cotton. She put her arm around Mage and firmly believed he was the best replacement for Josie's husband.

Chapter Thirty-Four

Cotton, Part Two

"When are you gonna cook dinner?" he yelled from his recliner.

Hollis looked at Josie, who was trying to grade a stack of essays. "Can we order out tonight?" she asked her husband.

"I'll pay for it," Hollis volunteered.

Cotton sucked in a string of snot from his nose and seemed to twirl it around his tongue before he swallowed it. "And I suppose I'm the one who'll have to pick it up?" He stared from Hollis to Josie. "I want a home-cooked dinner."

Hollis was good at reading the emotional temperature in a room, and she could sense his hostility. Many times, she had held her tongue when men had barked commands, but she had always made them pay for it in the end. She hated to watch her friend suffer from her husband's verbal abuse, but she could do nothing. Josie made her own choices, and Hollis couldn't interfere with them. To do so would cause a rip in the fabric of their friendship.

"I'll make some tacos," Josie said.

Cotton's fingers tightened on his armrests as he stiffened in his chair. "What? That's hardly a home-cooked meal! I want pork chops, mashed potatoes, and green beans. You can throw some biscuits in, too."

Josie sighed and moved to get out of her chair, but Hollis jumped off the couch. "Can I do it?" she volunteered. "I have a new marinade I'd like to try with the pork chops."

Cotton's round brown eyes studied her. His favorite meals featured pork, and he didn't want his food compromised. "Just don't mess it up."

Josie glanced at Hollis as she walked out of the living room, mouthing "Thank you."

In the kitchen, Hollis threw together a quick marinade, and peeled and cut potatoes. In cooking, timing was everything, so she gauged the progress of the meat and potatoes as she kneaded the biscuit dough, lamenting that the biscuits would be ready several minutes after the other foods. When she served the meal, she purposely forgot the biscuits, so they would be fresh and warm when Cotton requested them. Thankfully, he didn't yell at her for her forgetfulness.

Hollis doubted he tasted the flavor of his food as he sucked it into his maw and swirled whisky around with it. She found herself hoping that he'd choke on his meal and hated herself for wishing harm on her friend's husband.

"You might be useful for something," Cotton said, picking his teeth with his pocketknife. "Josie can't make a decent biscuit to save her life."

"That's not fair, Cotton," Josie said. "Hollis pays a third of the bills and groceries."

He put a finger in his nose, looked at it, and wiped it on a linen napkin. Hollis closed her eyes, willing her food to stay down.

"Maybe she could teach you a few things while she's here," he said. Josie lowered her head.

He laughed. "Maybe she could help you out in the bedroom, too. After last night's miserable performance, you could use a little—"

"Enough!" Hollis said.

He lunged across the table, knocking over his open liquor bottle and the jelly jar and dragging his plate along with him. He grabbed her shirt and brought her to meet his brown eyes.

"There's only one good use for women like you," he seethed, drops of spittle flying into her face as he spoke. His head tilted, studying her nonreaction. "Oh, you're scared of me."

He flung her against her chair and Hollis struggled to stay upright. Josie remained in her seat with both hands planted on the table. Her soda had spilled, and it ran off the table and onto her legs.

Cotton had slithered back to his side of the table, and he was surveying the damage to his liquor bottle. He drained the last of it, but it only amounted to about three-fourths of a shot.

"You spilled my liquor," he commented, not looking at either woman. "Get me a beer."

Josie blinked, but her reaction wasn't fast enough. He stood up and pushed her out of her chair, knocking her into the wall. Her head cracked against the frame.

Hollis was up just as fast, but she had enough sense to check her hands before she used them against Cotton. If she started, she wouldn't stop, and Josie would never forgive her.

Josie was too scared and shocked to cry. She could only stare blankly at her husband and wait for his next move.

"I'll get it," Hollis said, marching past the horrific scene.

She grabbed a bottle and stared at it. She could solve all Josie's problems with one quick substitution. The Moon Walker beer bottle taunted her, reminding her of past beatings and crimes that had only passed her lips once when she had described them to Asher. *Wasn't Cotton just as bad if not worse?*

She made her decision quickly, and she regretted nothing.

Chapter Thirty-Five

Quillen caught them kissing in the boy's car as he sat idling in front of the house. They were so wrapped up in each other that they didn't notice him pull beside the car and get out. Maybe he should have walked inside the house and waited on her to notice his car, but he couldn't stop himself. He tapped on the window and they both jumped. The boy pulled his hand from inside her shirt, and she rushed to close her blouse.

To his credit, the boy didn't leave Rosie to clean up the mess. He climbed out of the car and extended his hand. "Hello, sir," he said shakily. "I'm Zach."

Quillen shook his hand, but he narrowed his eyes. The boy was attractive, with dark hair that fell carelessly in his green eyes but didn't seem to block his vision. He was lanky, but there was some musculature around his chest and arms that could easily be developed if he ate more. His lack of nutrition was clear in the lack of shine in his hair and the purple, half-moons under his eyes.

Instantly, Quillen understood his daughter's attraction to the boy. Rosie loved underdogs, and Zach came from a hard life. There was something more to him, though, a deeper tone or a maturity in his eyes. Quillen hoped it was due to his upbringing.

"How old are you, Zach?"

The boy looked at Rosie and her eyes widened. She gave a small shake of her head.

Quillen spoke gruffly. "Don't look at her. You know how old you are."

When he faced him again, Zach stood to his full height. "I'm seventeen, sir."

Quillen relaxed a little. "See, that wasn't so hard." He thought better of his easy acceptance. "When will you be eighteen?"

Zach answered quickly and proudly. "In a month and a half."

"I see," Quillen said. "Zach, I think it's time for you to leave." He looked at his daughter. "Rose, you need to go inside."

Quillen watched Zach back out of the driveway before he joined his daughter inside. She admonished him with lips puffy from kissing.

"What were you doing?" Rose yelled at him. She stood with her hand on her hip. Her brown silk blouse was wrinkled down the sides and at her waist. She had left it untucked, and Quillen was reminded of how familiar she seemed to be with Zach.

"How long have you known that boy?" he countered.

Rose registered her lack of moral high ground and glanced away. "Since school started."

"Are you going out with him?" Quillen asked carefully.

He and Beth had dated, but it didn't consist of many dates. When their parents had asked if they were "going steady," they had laughed. Quillen couldn't help feeling just as out-of-touch as he watched the look that crossed Rose's face.

"We've been hanging out a lot."

Quillen had been sitting on the couch, but he jumped up. "You mean to tell me you let that boy put his hands all over you and the two of you are only 'hanging out?'"

The color deepened on Rose's cheeks. "Well, how can you expect me to have a boyfriend when you keep moving us around?"

She had him there. They had moved around so much that it had made long-term attachments impossible, and even though Rose was a beautiful girl, there were very few teenage boys who wanted to have a long-distance relationship.

He threw his hands up. "Why do you need to have a boyfriend anyway? Concentrate on your schoolwork and worry about boys later when they're men and they're ready for a commitment."

"You and Mom didn't," she shot back. "You used to tell everyone that you were high school sweethearts."

She'd made another good point, but he wasn't going to let her win. "Your mom and I weren't like our friends. We were committed to each other, and it was mutual. That boy" —he pointed toward the driveway where he'd met Zach— "moves too fast."

Rose rolled her eyes and crossed her thin arms. "Spoken like a true grandpa."

"Maybe," he conceded, "but I wasn't trying to put my hands down your mother's shirt before I'd taken her on a proper date."

"I wanted him to," Rose insisted. "I want to be like everyone else!" She uncrossed her arms, dropping her hands and her posture. "Did you know that was my first kiss?"

He wasn't at all shocked by her words, even though he knew it was a lie. Rose had never brought a boy around before he met Zach, but there was more experience in their entanglement than he wanted to admit.

"And a kiss would have been fine," he said, pacing, "but you don't need him to paw all over you. I was a boy once, and I remember what they think."

"You're no different," she shouted. "If I would've stayed with Katey Friday night then you would've hit it and quit it with Mrs. Bradshaw."

He was always a little surprised by youthful slang. The words seemed to have an angsty edge.

"I think you mean that I would have slept with Hollis if you hadn't been here," he said.

Rose made a gagging gesture with her finger.

"First of all, it's none of your business, but since you brought it up, I am over the age of eighteen and I'm not romantically linked to anyone else, so that's my decision to make."

Rose shook her head. "Gross. That's just gross."

"Maybe you could talk to Hollis about Zach," he suggested.

"No, Dad. That's not something I want to discuss with my teacher." She hung her head, and her next words were barely above a whisper. "I want to talk to Mom or Violet."

He tried to embrace her, but she waved him off without lifting her head. At first, he'd thought she was acting melodramatic to keep from getting in more trouble over Zach, but after she'd sulked her way into her room, he heard the song she always put on repeat when she was thinking of her stolen family.

The notes drifted to him and assailed his mind, threatening to send him into madness. *Why did she want to play that song?* There were so many songs they had liked individually or shared as a family as they danced in the kitchen or built a project in the backyard. *Why did she have to play the song that had played on the day they lost Beth and Violet?*

Chapter Thirty-Six

Warrant blasted through the speakers when Hollis stepped out of the shower. She wondered down the hall and into Josie's bathroom. Her friend was lining her eyes with coal-black liner and teal eyeshadow. On anyone else, to her, the effect would have been a little trashy, but it was pretty on Josie.

Josie was singing along, and she had a great voice. She stopped and smiled at Hollis, but she didn't say anything. The music was too loud.

Hollis grabbed some of Josie's eyeliner and found some white eyeshadow. Josie had told her the white eyeshadow was meant to detail the lid at the crease, but she applied the powder to her lower lids lightly. The effect of the color and the liner added more appeal to her green eyes and oddly thick lashes.

She hardly ever put on makeup, and she never used concealer, but she was satisfied with the way it brought out her features. Her face was a little thin from too many salads on busy nights, but her jawline was determined, and her eyes lacked the circles Josie had to cover on her own eyes after Cotton's divorce papers had arrived.

Mage wondered into the room with his mouth open. He wagged his tail and closed his eyes when Josie scratched him behind his ears.

Josie ended the rash of eighties music she had played while getting ready to go to the festival. Hollis's ears rang, as she walked down the steps and it was a bad combination with her low heels, knocking her equilibrium off.

They took Josie's car. It was a much more reliable vehicle and it had heated seats. The temperature had dipped into the twenties, and their coats only did so much to cover them when their legs were bare, but Josie had insisted that they wear spring green dresses. She believed they were the perfect color for the holiday season, but Hollis thought she and her friend looked like they were dressing for warmer temperatures.

Quillen was waiting for her at the door. He was handsome in his usual creme button up and black pants. His hair was pulled into a ponytail, and it reflected the light, like he had added a little hair gel to the finished product. He offered an arm to each lady before they entered the academy.

"Thank you, kind sir," Josie said, winking at Hollis.

Hollis was glad her friend approved of the man she was dating. Josie had wanted her to get along with Cotton, but the only person who could truly stand that man was himself.

Every time she remembered him it made her skin crawl to think that her beautiful, kind friend had laid down with that monster every night.

After many years, she thought she understood Josie's draw to Cotton. After her parents had died, he had swooped in and provided her with the protection she thought she was missing. Without her parents there to vet her choice, Josie was left to rely on her own eighteen-year-old feelings, and she was married in less than a year.

"Where's Rose?" Hollis asked Quillen.

Quillen's face screwed into an expression with which she wasn't quite familiar. "She went inside with a boy."

"That's sweet," Josie said. "Who is she dating?"

He scoffed. "She's walking around with a boy called Zach." He almost spit out the name.

"I like Zach," Hollis volunteered. "He's a good kid."

"If you like nose rings and tattoos," Quillen responded.

Josie looked at him until she got his attention. She casually tapped the side of her nose where a small diamond stud shined. The day after Cotton left, Hollis and Josie had driven into town and gone to the first tattoo parlor they saw.

"I have a tattoo on my shoulder, too," Josie revealed.

All his teeth spread into a wide grin. "And I'll bet it's a cute little fairy." He looked at Josie and batted his eyes.

She swatted his arm playfully. "It is not." Her nose rose a little higher. "But just for that, I'm not gonna tell you what it is."

He let go of their arms to open the door to the gym. Hollis had taught her classes in an auxiliary room that day so that the parent volunteers could set up tables for the activities, food, and vendors.

Hollis spotted Rose and Zach at the skeet table. Zach had just won a stuffed duck for Rose, and she threw her head back and laughed when he presented it to her.

"Hey," Hollis said to Quillen when she noticed him watching them. "Will you walk around with me?"

She and Josie signed it to work their mandatory hour and it passed quickly. Principal Bailey acknowledged her and stared at Quillen as he walked around beside her.

When it was time for Hollis to sample the wares of the festival, she practically ran to the funnel cakes. Quillen laughed at her eagerness and told her that the funnel cakes were really called "elephant ears."

"I thought you came from Kentucky," she said to him. "We southern folk call them by their proper name."

He reached over and ruffled her hair. He did it in good humor, but she wasn't happy about the gesture. She liked him, but she didn't want anyone to touch her head when there had been too many times she'd been smacked or punched in it.

Josie threw a five dollar bill into the DJ's tip jar to play an eighties song, but she rolled her eyes when the first beats of "Sugar Me" played. She motioned to the guy, with a buzzed haircut and cowboy boots.

"He doesn't know good music."

"Maybe you should've been more specific," Quillen said. He threw another five into the tip jar, but the kid shook his head when Quillen asked about several other well-known songs from the decade.

He walked back over to them, shrugging his shoulders. "I guess you were right, Josie. The kid didn't know what I was talking about."

"What did you ask for?" Josie asked.

Quillen named off a few chart-topping eighties songs. He counted off a few on his fingers that Hollis knew, even before she had a best friend obsessed with slap bracelets and leg warmers.

Josie cringed. "He didn't know any Journey songs? 'Only the Young' is perfect for the high school group!"

Hollis could think of a few better-known Journey songs, but looking around, she had to agree with her friend. Most of the students who were left were fourteen or older. The other children had been pulled away by their parents to settle into a nighttime routine at home or had been paired off with a friend's parent for a sleepover.

Quillen led Hollis over to a table with various pies on display. "Pick your poison," he told her.

In her mind, Hollis sometimes laughed at small ironies. The invitation to choose a piece of pie was certainly something that brought a smile to her lips. It would be so easy to talk Quillen into buying a pie and taking it home where she could entertain him until morning and feed him bites of the pastry until he drifted off from whatever poison she chose for him. But he didn't know about her hobby. Even though she was on a break, and she was trying not to think about the ease with which she could snatch life from unsuspecting people, he had no idea he was dealing with a monster.

• • • ● ●• ● ● • • •

The festival ended at nine o'clock, and Hollis was glad that she and Josie weren't part of the clean-up crew. They signed out as the last students filed out of the gym.

Quillen stood against the wall, listening to his daughter as she pulled on Katey's arm. Hollis sidled up to them.

"Please let me stay, Dad," Rose begged.

"You didn't seem to want to hang out with Katey tonight," Quillen said. "You hung out with Zach."

Rose sighed. "Yeah. And Katey hung out with Jeremy. Now, we want to spend the night together." She put her hands together and brought them in front of her face. "Please, Dad. We didn't get to spend the night together last week."

Katey smiled and glanced over her shoulder. Hollis was familiar with the ruse. Jeremy and Zach stood at the door, pretending they were talking, but Hollis knew they didn't run in the same circles. Josie had joined them, picking up on the same vibe, but not giving anything away.

"Okay," he said. "You can stay with Katey tonight, but I'm picking you up early tomorrow morning. You have an appointment."

He didn't elaborate in front of Katey and Josie, but he had shared his daughter's mental health visits with Hollis, and she had congratulated them both on seeking professional guidance. There was a stigma about it in the area, but Hollis encouraged their visits. Maybe she would have turned out differently if she had spoken to someone when she was Rose's age. Maybe not.

Rose squealed with delight, but Josie caught her attention before she made her way out the door. She took her out of range of Quillen, and when Hollis saw Rose's face pale, she distracted Quillen. She lidded her eyes and ran a hand down his cheek. Fine stubble should have prickled her fingers, but his jawline was as smooth as the back of her hand, indicating he had shaved before the festival.

He slid his hand up her arm and put his fingers through hers. "Stay with me tonight."

Hollis thought about the way her mind had wondered to the poisoning the pie when he had asked her about it. *Was she ready for a relationship, or had she slowly killed the part of her that could receive love as she had murdered the men who had tried to love her?*

When she saw Josie stuff something into Rose's hand, she inched herself closer to the exit. The shiny happiness that had been on Rose's face was replaced by a faraway look when she rejoined Katey.

Hollis took one look at her friend and realized that her night wasn't over. Either Josie would go home without Hollis and drink herself into oblivion or she would go home with her and continue helping her friend cope with the divorce.

She flashed a pointed look from Josie back to Quillen which she hoped he understood. "I need to go home tonight. We started health class today, and I have some papers—"

"He can come to the house and hang out with us," Josie suggested. "That is, if he doesn't mind gin and good music."

Hollis was surprised by the agreeable look on Quillen's face. "You can pick the music, but gin? I'll have to pick up something a little more refined."

"Suit yourself," Josie said, smiling.

Hollis and Josie made it back to the farmhouse first. Josie had given Quillen her address and directions to it, in case his GPS didn't recognize her rural home.

In the car, Hollis had asked Josie about her conversation with Rose. She had admitted that Rose had been reluctant to tell her about her true plans, but she finally opened up when Josie had quickly shared her own experience.

Rose and Katey planned to meet Zach and Jeremy at Jeremy's mother's house. His parents were divorced, and his mother was away for the weekend. Rose hadn't elaborated on what she thought would happen, but Josie had given her a condom and tried to counsel her on the value of safe sex.

They continued the conversation as they waited for Quillen.

"Do you think she'll have sex with him?"

Josie shrugged. "She's sixteen, and there's a piece of her heart missing since..." Her mouth made a thin line. She didn't need to say more.

"I didn't know you were carrying condoms," Hollis commented casually.

A slight smile crept up Josie's profile. "I bought them today."

Hollis's eyebrows drew together. "You thought you'd meet someone at the festival."

Josie laughed, a full, throaty laugh. "No. Well, maybe." She threw her hands up. "I just wanted to be prepared, okay?"

"It sounds good to me," Hollis said, and then she added, "I'm glad. I hope you find the perfect person for you."

Josie looked at her thankfully. She couldn't tell if it was because she was pleased with her reaction, or if she was happy to end the conversation. Josie had only had two boyfriends, and despite her interest in Hollis's and everyone else's love lives, Josie was unwilling to talk about her own sexual feelings and needs. Unfortunately, Cotton may have quelled her desire to talk about her own sexual wishes, but it was a blessing that he hadn't turned her against finding another partner.

Quillen's SUV crunched the gravel beside the house. His car door slammed, and Mage ran past them, growling and pawing at the edge of the closed door like he wanted to simultaneously attack and bounce on the person on the other side.

Josie calmed Mage, and Hollis opened the door just enough for Quillen to squeeze inside. He slipped into the foyer, and Josie tried to pull Mage upstairs.

"Wait," Quillen said.

He put his hand out in front of the dog. Mage snapped at it and licked it. Hollis had never seen an animal so conflicted about a person.

Quillen continued to hold out his hand, the picture of patience, as Mage went through a rainbow of emotions. Quillen held his eyes on the dog and Mage snapped again.

Josie pulled on his collar. "Okay. I'm taking him upstairs."

"Please wait," Quillen insisted, talking from the corner of his mouth.

Another uncomfortable moment passed with Nina and her red balloons playing in the background. Finally, as the last notes of the song played, Mage tilted his head. He didn't just lick his hand, he almost devoured Quillen's fingers with his tongue.

Hollis was glad when Josie let him go and Mage almost jumped into Quillen's arms. Mage stood on his back legs and Quillen held him, stroking his head.

"What happened?" Josie asked. "I thought he was going to eat you, but now he wants to be your best friend."

Quillen laughed. "I didn't know you had a dog, or I would have told you." He placed Mage gently on his front legs and Mage wandered away, tail wagging. "Animals are uncomfortable around me. It's always been that way."

Red warning sirens blared in her mind as Hollis thought back to the way animals had received her. As her number of victims mounted, most of them didn't like her, and she had to try for weeks before she had won Mage's affection.

Quillen pulled a bottle in a brown paper bag out of his pocket. "My mom wasn't good with animals, but my father seemed to draw them. My mom's allergies kept us from having pets, but when I went on errands with my father, all the feral cats would run alongside his feet." Hollis didn't know what look he saw on her face, but Josie seemed skeptical, and he chuckled nervously.

"I learned a way to relax animals from my father," he went on. "My father told me to calm my soul. He said that animals can sense our emotions, but if you're tranquil, they respond to it in a similar manner."

"So, you just cleared your mind," Hollis said, disbelief etched in her voice.

"Yes," Quillen replied. "I was thinking about Rosie and that boy she was with tonight, but when I approached your dog" —he looked at Josie for his name, and she provided it—"Mage, I threw away the worries and rested my heartrate."

Hollis wasn't completely sold on it, but Josie seemed interested in his technique. They spoke for a few minutes about whether Quillen's methods could be used on pigs and horses, and she was thrilled when he'd told her he used it to break horses.

"But why don't they like you to begin with?" Hollis broke in.

Quillen looked a little sad. "My mother was a little volatile, and I guess I carry some of her spirit in me," he said miserably. "At least, that's what my dad used to say."

"Did she hurt animals?" Hollis asked.

"Hollis!" Josie shouted.

Quillen held up a hand, but he looked stricken. "No. She was bipolar."

Embarrassment flooded over Hollis, consuming her in a fiery wave. She couldn't believe she had been so rude to him, making him reveal something about his family that he would not have mentioned.

"I'm sorry," she said. "That wasn't any of my business."

He looked at her, extending a warm smile, uninhibited by alcohol or deception. "That's okay. You didn't know." He gestured to the direction in which Mage had gone. "And that was a dualistic reaction."

Quillen's good humor returned quickly, but Hollis sat on the couch, almost sulking. He helped Josie pick out a song and he pulled Hollis to her feet to dance while Josie made some cookies.

"I like the song, but I never understood the cows in the video." He laughed, but Hollis didn't join him. "Hey, what's wrong?"

It took some prodding, but Hollis finally told him the reason for her sulkiness. "I feel badly for asking you about your mother. I don't like those kinds of questions, and I shouldn't have made you feel like you had to answer mine."

He smiled indulgently, pulling her a little closer around the waist, her dress coming up a little on her thighs. "I'm not worried about it, but we can talk about it if you want."

His face showed the same signs of avoidance as her, from his uneasy smile to the tension in his jaw. Hollis declined, satisfied with his answer and the similar feelings they seemed to share on the subject.

Josie rounded the corner with a plate of fresh-baked cookies and a deck of cards. She spotted their closeness and tried to back away, but Hollis caught her and yelled over the music for her to join them. They decided to play cards at the table as they could spread out their snacks and drinks while Josie beat them at gin rummy.

Hollis was letting her friend win, but she didn't realize Quillen was throwing his part of the game until she saw him looking over at Josie's cards. As the alcohol made its way through her body, Josie held her fan of cards further away, even dipping them down when she drew a card.

Quillen winked when he saw that she knew.

After three games, Josie looked between them and pretended to yawn. Her attempt was disastrous, throwing her off-balance, and she fell out of her chair, proving that she needed to go to bed for another reason.

Quillen helped her friend up the stairs to her room, and Hollis wasn't worried. It was a strange feeling she hadn't felt since she'd been with Asher. Somehow, she knew Quillen wouldn't hurt Josie.

When he returned, he reported that he'd left her on the bed with the covers pulled up to her chin. Mage was guarding her for the night.

"Is she on her side, in case she gets—"

He put both his hands up. "She's okay," he reassured her. "For someone who doesn't have children, you really are a mama bear."

His words stung, but she turned away before he noticed it. "I just care deeply about the people I love."

Quillen walked up behind her, putting his arms around her. "I hope I can be one of those people one day."

A blush traveled up her cheeks and burned brighter than normal due to her indulgence in the gin. She hoped her color would fade before Quillen saw it.

She patted the hands clasped around her waist and tried to think of words that would express a similar sentiment without giving away too much. She came up blank, so she settled for action.

Quillen didn't have time to study her before her lips were on his. Their tongues slammed together, and she tasted the bitterness in the whisky he'd drunk, as she searched his mouth.

They didn't say anything else until morning, and by then, Hollis was hopelessly falling in love with the man with ice-blue eyes and a warm heart.

Chapter Thirty-Seven

It felt strange the first time she woke up in bed with someone new. Whether she was at their house, or she opened her eyes in her own bed, there was an uncertainty that loomed until she knew the other person's intentions.

Hollis had experienced one-night stands that didn't stay the night, and she'd walked the path of shame to her own place, but she'd not had a relationship—except for the missions she'd completed—since Asher. Part of her wondered if, despite his pretty words before bed, Quillen would get up, silently dress, kiss her head, and leave without a promise to call. She found herself hoping it wouldn't happen.

She laid awake, the anxiety building inside her as she counted the seconds between his rhythmic breathing. Sometimes he'd snore, throwing off her count.

Finally, his body moved against her. She pulled away a little and his grip loosened, momentarily unsure.

Hollis couldn't see his face, and she closed her eyes quickly as he lifted his head. "Is everything okay?"

She was happy he didn't try to shift the focus completely on her by asking if *she* was okay. She didn't like it when men made it seem like there was a problem with her if she didn't do exactly as they expected.

In answer, she pulled his hand against her skin. He kneaded it, tickling her.

"I smell coffee," he announced, pulling her tightly against him once but releasing her quickly.

Hollis liked the decision he was giving her. She could remain in bed with him or join Josie for coffee downstairs.

"I'll pass on the coffee, but I'm going to need some water," she said, lifting out of bed. "I drank a little too much last night."

Quillen propped himself up on an elbow. "Should we have waited? I didn't know you had had too much to drink."

He seemed unsure of himself. Hollis recognized his worry and addressed it.

"No. I knew what I was doing, but I feel a little dizzy this morning." She rubbed her hand down his stubbly cheek.

He kissed her fingers before he got up and dressed. His suit was crumpled, but he looked handsome in a disheveled way, with sleepy eyes and bedraggled hair. She loaned him her hairbrush, and he smoothed his hair back into his usual bun.

Josie tried not to jump out of her skin with excitement when she saw the two of them in the kitchen. She handed Quillen a cup of steamy coffee and Hollis a glass of cold orange juice. They all sat down together at the table, but awkward silence won out around the table where much conversation had been shared the previous night.

Quillen looked outside at the animals. "I didn't know this was a functional farm. I didn't hear the animals last night."

Josie smiled over her cup of coffee before she took a sip. "You may have been occupied." Hollis cleared her throat, and Josie dropped her knowing grin. "Most of the animals are old. I'm just caring for them because they were babies when mom and pop died."

"I'm sorry," he said, real sentiment lining his words. "That must have been hard."

Josie sighed, looking at the mug of coffee like it could funnel her some support. "It was, at first, but then I married Cotton, and he was able to help me with a lot of it. He even won us some prize money from entering the pigs in competitions."

Quillen had the good sense to realize that Cotton wasn't around anymore, so he tried to steer the conversation to another subject. Josie engaged in their dialog, but she wasn't the same. Her eyes often drifted to the sunlight hazily slanting through the window or to the floor.

Quillen left to pick up Rose from Katey's house, where Hollis was convinced the girl hadn't stayed. She waved at him from the door with one arm wrapped around her middle. Part of her wished he'd stay and follow her back to her bedroom, but the other part felt relieved to see him drive away. She was free to be herself without worrying if a stray comment might upset him. Quillen had never treated her differently for expressing herself, but she felt guarded around everyone except Josie. She supposed she'd have to work on that if she expected to have a good relationship with Quillen.

She still felt like she had so much to learn about him. He had been open with her, but Hollis had neglected to ask some very important questions, like *Was he still in love with his wife?* She also strayed away from telling him about Sarah. She'd cross that bridge when she came to it.

Josie hardly spoke to her the rest of the day and retired early with a tumbler full of gin and cranberry juice. Its pale pink color suggested there was more gin than juice in the cup.

Hollis had hoped the appearance of the divorce papers would allow her friend to move on with her life, but the papers seemed to have set her back. Hollis supposed Josie was mourning a relationship she had created in her mind, or perhaps her lost time, so she indulged her friend's misery by turning a blind eye to her overindulgence in liquor and a deaf ear to the woeful melodies blasting out of the speakers in her room.

Mage had been lying on the kitchen tile, and his head darted up, ears perked, searching the area. He barked once, and Hollis wondered if an intruder or an unfamiliar animal might be lurking around the house. Her opinion changed when he leapt onto his legs and bolted up the stairs. Hollis followed him, more out of curiosity than concern, until she saw him pawing at Josie's door.

The notes of the first song Josie had danced to with Cotton rang into the hallway, echoing off the walls. Hollis knocked, and yelled Josie's name, but her friend either didn't answer or it was impossible to hear her over the music.

Hollis tried to turn the knob, but the door wouldn't open. That's when Hollis started to panic. Josie never locked her bedroom door in case Hollis wanted to talk.

Hollis pushed against the sturdy wooden door, and after a few more attempts to call her friend's name, she decided to break it down. Mage stood obediently to the side while Hollis shoved all her weight repeatedly against the door. Luckily, it was an interior door, so its design was less thick than the front door. It gave way after several tries, and Hollis had to cover her ears.

Mage ran into the room, barking wildly and growling once. When he found Josie, he sat at her feet.

Hollis hurried around the bed and found her friend sprawled on the floor. A bottle of pills had been placed on the nightstand and the tumbler of gin had been spilled, drops of it were on Josie's forehead and had soaked into her hair. The pinkish liquid had spread over her off-white rug, staining it a light blood color.

Hollis shook her friend and Josie groaned. Relief rushed over Hollis, but it was short-lived when she couldn't get her friend to stay awake.

"What did you take?" she screamed over the music. Josie's phone was on the nightstand, and the app to control the speaker was open. Hollis turned off the music and the silence rang.

"Josie!" She shook her friend again. "What did you take?"

"Why wasn't I good enough?" Josie slurred before her face slackened.

Hollis grabbed the bottle of pills and read the label. They had been a bottle of Cotton's pain medicine and they were years out of date.

Hollis used Josie's phone to call for an ambulance as she shook her friend. She tried everything she could to rouse her, but Josie wouldn't wake up.

Chapter Thirty-Eight

Cotton, Part Three

Hollis gave Cotton enough Belladonna to knock him out for the night, but she didn't dare do more. He may have been a horrible person, but she had to respect Josie's decision to attach herself to him.

Bruises crept up from Josie's collar and peaked out from her sleeves, and Hollis tried to talk to her about her options. Josie was unmovable. She loved Cotton, and she claimed he was only going through a rough time.

Hollis wanted to shake her, but Josie wouldn't speak against her husband. Her parents had shared a supportive marriage, and Josie had witnessed some rocky patches, so she was convinced she would have the same relationship with Cotton, once he was better.

Cotton had been involved in a work-related injury at a machine shop and he hadn't worked since the judge awarded him a nominal settlement. He ran through it quickly and took odd jobs to afford alcohol and pay the most necessary bills. He had some experience with animals, having grown up on a farm, and he was overjoyed to help Josie with her farm when she advertised for a handy man.

Sensing her need for structure and direction, he took an upper hand, and Josie followed him around the farm, soaking in his words. Cotton saw her naivety and beauty and took advantage of both. He wasted no time locking in his newfound fortune and proposed to her only days after sleeping with her.

Thinking his gesture was a chivalrous display, Josie accepted, and they were married the following month. She never said, but Hollis assumed the abuse started soon after the wedding, because Josie was a shell of her former self when Hollis spoke to her from the ship during a deployment.

Josie had always wanted to be a teacher, so she took classes and had her certificate before Hollis left the military. Cotton didn't want Josie to work until her inheritance money was depleted and he realized that either he'd have to get a job, or his wife would have to work.

Josie started a fulfilling career and came home to repeated outbursts when dinner wasn't on the table at five o'clock. She found ways to hide her unhappy marriage from her coworkers, but Hollis noticed the shift in her eyes before she spoke, and her tightened posture when Cotton was around, as if she was expecting a blow at any time.

Hollis tried to help Josie without condoning the situation, but she felt like her aid was only facilitating her friend's abusive marriage. She wanted to end the tirades and unfair treatment, but she was stymied when Josie announced her pregnancy.

Her friend was elated, bouncing on clouds over Cotton's corrosive comments and staying away from him to keep herself safe. His hands still found her though, and marks appeared on her face, as she protected her stomach during his attacks.

Hollis was conflicted as she watched her friend's hopes and belly grow. She took on Cotton's roll many times, helping Josie paint a neutral color in a spare bedroom and going to doctor's appointments with her friend.

Josie rejoiced over her weight gain, and every stretch mark she claimed as a badge of honor. Her only disappointment was when she learned she wasn't having twins.

"I wish there had been more than one," she confided to Hollis. "I always wanted two children, but this one wasn't planned, and I doubt Cotton will let me have another one."

Cotton was upset about Josie's pregnancy. He complained that her belly got in the way of certain activities, and she was always too tired to cook a decent meal.

Hollis picked up many of Josie's responsibilities, as in her exhaustion Josie forgot to do many of her routine chores. She also tried to prepare as many meals as possible, to keep her friend off her swollen feet.

One night, Hollis was aroused by wailing. She ran out of her room and down the steps, gasping in horror at the scene before her.

Josie lay on the landing holding her belly, a large pool of blood flowering out from her pale pink nightgown. She was terrified, her blue eyes locking on Hollis, begging her to help.

"What did you do?" Hollis yelled at Cotton.

He stood two steps up from his bleeding wife with a smug look on his face. "She fell." He offered nothing else by way of an explanation, but a smile tugged up the corners of his mouth.

Hollis knew she should attend to her friend first, but years of frustration had bubbled over, and she struck Cotton. He had been holding a glass of whisky, and it shattered on the floor. She held his face on the shards of glass as she pummeled him. Finally, her friend's weak voice called out for her to stop, and she listened.

Josie held her phone. It had been in the pocket of her nightgown when she had fallen, and she had used it to dial emergency services.

The ambulance pulled up several minutes later. The timing surprised everyone, as the farmhouse was well away from town.

Cotton presented himself to the medics, but they went around him and assessed Josie's injuries. Hollis held her friend's hand in the ambulance as they rode to the hospital.

Cotton wasn't there when Josie was informed about her placental abruption. He didn't pace in the waiting room during her emergency caesarian section, and he was absent from the room when Josie was told that her baby girl had died moments after she was placed in an incubator.

Hollis held her friend as she broke down, ripping out her IV and screaming in anguish. She stayed with her for two days before Josie asked her to go home.

"You need a shower," she told her plainly. "I'll get to go home day after tomorrow, but you can't stay here the whole time. You have to take care of yourself, too."

Hollis had felt helpless when Josie had needed her the most. After everything she had been through, Hollis wondered if anything she did for her would ever be enough. She slept in the chair beside her, denying the comfort of the pull-out sleeper. She wanted to be on hand in case Josie needed anything.

After Hollis raised her objections, and Josie shot them all down, Hollis left the hospital. Cotton, who had successfully avoided visiting his wife during her hospital stay, picked her up.

"Aren't you going to visit your wife in the hospital?" Hollis spat at him.

He made a grunt that Hollis interpreted to mean that he had no intention of supporting his wife. They drove down the road, and she couldn't take it any longer.

"Did you push her?" she yelled.

He turned on her so fast that everything became a blur. The back of his hand connected with her face, and tears stung her eyes. After a couple of blows, she tasted her own blood, and its metallic scent was the only thing she could sense through her swollen nose.

Hollis was strong, but she was no match for the trained muscles of a farm worker. He stopped her defensive punches effortlessly and took advantage of her surprise by hitting her frequently. She could hardly catch her breath.

He held her down with her face in his lap until they reached the farmhouse. The noises from the chickens and pigs were amplified, even though her ears were swollen.

"The problem with women like you is that you've never been broken," he said as he dragged her out of the truck. She slid along the ground as he dragged her by her hair. "Women are like horses. You need to break them, and then they're docile." He lifted her head and she saw his eyes. They looked almost coal black.

Hollis never talked about what Cotton did to break her, but after he was finished, she didn't come out of her room for days.

Cotton grudgingly picked up Josie, acting enough like a dedicated husband to get her out of the hospital. When they returned, he yelled loudly down the hall.

"For all her talk, where was she the last two days?"

Josie made no reply, but Hollis worried about what her friend thought. *How could she face her, though, after what Cotton had done to her?*

Deep in the night, when the house was still, Hollis's door creaked open. She closed her eyes in fear that it might be Cotton, ready to take even more of her dignity away, but a soft bounce on the bed indicated that her friend had sat on the end of it.

"What has he done to you?" Josie asked.

Hollis didn't answer. *Maybe Josie would think she was asleep, and she'd leave.*

Josie tugged on her blankets, and any hope of Hollis keeping her secret vanished when Josie gasped. "Hollis, we have to get you to the hospital!"

Josie touched a tender spot on her head, still caked with blood, and matted to her head. More injuries were revealed as the blanket slid down her body. Each mark brought a fresh sob from her friend.

"I never thought he would do this to you," she whispered to Hollis.

The blanket slipped just beyond her hips. The black bruises were still in the shape of his fingers.

Josie stood up quickly. "You'll have to give me a couple of weeks." Her words were almost inaudible. "I'm going to get us out of here."

That night, Josie didn't return to her husband's bed.

Hollis waited until the next day to peel herself off the bed. She cried out as the warm water hit her broken flesh, but no one was there to hear her.

Josie had asked Cotton to take her somewhere, and it must have been somewhere he wanted to go, or he wouldn't have left. They were gone for an hour before Hollis found the will to move herself.

She hadn't eaten in days, so a heavy weight pressed against her as her blood sugar crashed. She finished cleaning herself on the floor of the shower, watching the flecks of blood run down the drain.

She washed it all away, and when she emerged from the bathroom, she was determined that no one would know what had happened to her.

When Josie came home, she approached Hollis secretly, but Hollis stared stiffly forward, dismissing her friend's concerns. When Josie touched her face, Hollis flinched, showing more emotion than she had since Josie had been home from the hospital.

"I'm working on getting us out of here, and he won't be able to follow us."

Something inside Hollis, pride or something like it, caused her to let out a forced laugh. "I've been telling you to leave that man," she told her friend. "But you don't need to do it on my account." She lifted her arm. "These bruises are from riding Blaze out into the woods. Something spooked him, and he tossed me down an embankment."

Josie's expression changed from concern to surprise. She turned around, pointed at Hollis, and brought her finger back to her lips. "You're lying to me."

It was the first time she'd called Hollis out on a lie.

Hollis worked hard to pull her best acting face up from the depths of her mind. She plastered on a wide smile and explained her lie again in more detail.

Tears formed in Josie's eyes. "But there were finger marks on your hips!" she whisper-shouted. "I've had the same—" She stopped herself, backing away.

"There are lots of hard little roots when you roll down an embankment," Hollis explained.

Looking back, Hollis realized that she had hurt Josie's chance to leave Cotton. Seeing Hollis hurt had empowered Josie in a way her own bruises and tears had not. When Josie looked at herself in the mirror, with bruises from black to yellow dotting her flesh, on some level, she saw a woman who deserved the abuse. Uncovering the same abuse on Hollis had jerked her out of the lies Cotton constantly fed her and emboldened her to make a change. With her dismissals and lies, though, Hollis had caused Josie to question her perception. In hindsight, Hollis understood she had treated her friend in a similar way to Cotton, making her question what she had seen, even though it was true.

It didn't really matter, though. He was gone before the end of the month.

• • • ● ●•● ● • •

Hollis begged her. "Please go to your Aunt, Jos. She needs you."

Josie paused with her overnight bag in her hand, barely holding it in her fingers. If she let it drop, she'd stay, and Hollis would feel responsible for preventing her final reunion with the aunt who had helped Josie so much after her parents' death.

Hollis had tried to leave twice. She was paying rent on a house near the beach, an investment she'd made the morning after she'd lied to Josie about the source of her bruises. She'd wanted a quiet place to reassess her feelings and determine whether she should begin her missions again. Cotton's attack had been meant to break her, but it had only encouraged her to continue her work. There were a lot of men like Cotton in the world, and she needed to remove them before they could traumatize young and trusting women.

Her mother had been a lot like Josie. She had tried to fix men who didn't think they needed the repairs.

Josie had begged Hollis to stay. Finally believing Hollis's lie, Josie pleaded with her friend to stay a few more months while she healed from the fall and emergency caesarian section. Hollis had reluctantly agreed to face her attacker's snide looks in the mornings and drunken tirades at night.

Josie squeezed her keys, moving them toward and away from the key ring. Hollis watched her back and forth motion, aware that one word from her could change her friend's plans.

"Are you sure you'll be okay?" Josie asked, flicking her eyes to the living room where the monster slept in front of a roaring car race.

Hollis was certain that she would be anything but fine. In fact, she planned to gather her things and leave as soon as Josie's car disappeared in the distance. She could call her and meet her in public places, but Hollis would never subject herself to another moment around Josie's narcissistic husband again.

She pulled up everything she had learned about eye movement, body language, and facial expressions, and she used it to push her friend to the door. She didn't know Josie's aunt, or she would have gone with her, but she told Josie she needed to hold her dying aunt's hand or she'd regret not saying goodbye.

She hugged Josie a little too long at the door, knowing that she wouldn't see her for a long time, if ever. Once her car was out of sight, Hollis crept into the living room. The monster, as she'd started calling him in her head, was snoring in his chair with his mouth open.

How Hollis longed to take the couch pillow Josie's mother had sown and stick it over his mouth until he breathed no more. She'd never met her, but she doubted Josie's mom would be opposed to her using it that way.

But what if he overpowered her again? After her bruises had faded to a light yellow and green, Hollis had doubled her workouts, training her muscles to appear larger and her strength to improve. She had no idea if her strength matched the monster's, and she was unwilling to find out.

She almost ran up the stairs on her toes, so she wouldn't make a sound. The cars still rushed across the pavement as she slung clothes out of the drawers and into her suitcases. There would be nothing of hers left in the house when she traveled down the driveway, and if she missed anything, Josie could mail it to her at the post office box she kept in another state.

She was in such a flurry to throw items into her suitcases, cursing herself for becoming so comfortable in one place, that she didn't hear the stairs creak. The races zoomed on, and they blocked out the quiet footsteps that padded down the hall.

Her back was turned when he spoke, and she closed her eyes at the sound of his voice. She'd been caught trying to leave, and he had told her what he'd do to her and to Josie if she tried to go.

"Now, where do you think you're goin'?"

Chapter Thirty-Nine

Hollis paced the hall of the hospital, wondering when she'd hear news about her friend. Josie was admitted to the hospital hours ago, and the nurse had promised Hollis that she'd update her, as Josie had no other surviving family members. Thankfully, Josie had kept her last name when she'd married Cotton, a topic he hadn't argued since it was discussed before their union, and his name had been removed from her emergency contact form.

She debated calling Quillen and decided against it. *What could he do to help?* He could only comfort Hollis, which she needed desperately, but at what cost? *How would he feel when he learned that his words, or what they did the previous night, could have started Josie to spiral into suicide?*

Hollis had visited the chapel, but she left before the chaplain spoke to her. He had been comforting a young girl, but he had looked up at her and smiled as if to say, "I'll be with you in a minute." Hollis couldn't imagine speaking to him about her concerns, and she felt so wrong in the chapel. She stole the lives of God's children when he wanted her to love and forgive them. She remembered enough from her Sunday school classes to feel uncomfortable about her presence in a Christian sanctuary. *Would God strike her down for what she'd done?* She'd thought He'd be especially angry about Asher.

She left the chapel and blazed into the cafeteria, sitting down at the first empty table. She wasn't hungry, and if she would have been, the smells of various cooked meats would have destroyed her appetite. She just needed to be close to other people, and their chatter and laughter helped keep her tears from spilling over.

How could she have missed the warning signs? Josie had been declining since the divorce papers had arrived. They should have made her feel better, but they'd made her doubt her own worth.

Hollis regretted her lies. She wished she'd have let Josie execute a plan that would have catapulted Cotton out of their lives. Maybe then, Josie would have felt like it was her decision, and she would have held firm to it because of what happened to Hollis.

She started to worry that she'd been absent too long from the waiting room and hurried back. She asked several people if her name had been called, and they all shook their heads with limp mouths and solemn eyes.

She poured herself a cup of coffee. She didn't drink it, but the warm, heavy weight of it in her hands helped her feel grounded.

The clock moved, and Hollis's anxiety grew. There were so many things that could happen to a person who had tried to commit suicide. Josie could be brain dead, or she could have upset her digestion tract so much that she needed surgery.

A nurse called her name, and Hollis walked numbly over to her. When she motioned her into the hall, Hollis's hopes fell, and she braced herself for the worst news of her life.

Chapter Forty

Cotton, Part Four

Hollis was there, but she allowed her mind to travel to other places. She was good at imagining her happy place, an area of fields and flowers, with laughter and golden sun. She imagined its rays on her instead of the slaps across her back as Cotton sought to break her spirit.

He grabbed her chin, and she could smell the minty tobacco on his breath. "I told you to make my dinner." The belt smacked across her hips where fresh bruises had flowered during the night. "I want pork chops and mashed potatoes!"

His rising voice put more fear into Hollis than being caught for the murders she'd committed. *How was he so much stronger than her?* He didn't work out. He only drank liquor and worked a little on the farm. It was hard work, but she had trained specifically to defend herself against him and she'd failed.

The monster had taken the keys to her car. He had only allowed her far enough to feed the pigs and collect the eggs, and he was afraid that she'd ride one of the horses, so he'd opted to care for them, whereas it had been her job to do so when Josie was around.

He sang the first line to an Outfield song. Josie wasn't on a vacation, but it didn't matter. She was far away, and she couldn't help Hollis. She had decided that she would ride it out until Josie returned, but every night Josie called, she reported her aunt was still hanging on.

Cotton allowed Hollis to talk to Josie when she called. She'd had to lie and say that her phone was broken, when in truth, it was in Cotton's back pocket. He'd press a knife against her neck when she spoke, so she wouldn't reveal anything to Josie about the games he was playing in her absence. Hollis wasn't scared for her life, but Cotton told her about the cruel list of atrocities he had planned for Josie if Hollis hinted that things were different at home than Josie imagined them.

Hollis played her part well, and she was usually rewarded with a smack to her head after the call had ended. Then she'd have to serve him beer and liquor as he watched shows about western heroes and rogue gunmen.

Hollis fought against him, but it was like her strength left her and gave him power. He'd go from a methodical beating on her back and legs to pummeling her chest. She'd lose her breath and fight for air as he smiled above her.

Hollis had decided no end was in sight. Cotton had talked about adding Hollis to the household routine when Josie got back. At first, Hollis didn't know what it meant, and then she started to realize that he never planned to let her go.

One day, after a week of torture, Cotton asked Hollis to get the mail. She'd looked at the fields and mountains stretching out before her and decided to take her chances in them. Maybe she could find a phone and reach Josie before she came home. As if he had read her mind, Cotton appeared, and he snatched the mail out of her hand. He dragged her back to the house by her arm.

He laughed as he held one of the envelopes. "This is our ticket outta this dump!" he declared, slapping it in Hollis's face. He opened it and read it, letting out a big whoop.

"Bring me a beer!" he commanded. "It's time to celebrate!"

Hollis looked down at the paper. It was an active life insurance policy with her friend's name in dark letters at the top and Cotton as the beneficiary.

When Josie pulled up, Hollis was standing at the pig's pen. Bacon snorted as Hollis scratched her head.

"You made a friend," Josie commented, after she rolled down her window. Her genuine smile was like an elixir to Hollis's tarnished soul.

Hollis stared down at the animal, thankful she couldn't talk.

From her vantage point, Josie couldn't see the other side of Hollis's face, which showed some signs of Cotton's handiwork. When Josie had texted her about her impending arrival, Hollis had thrown on a pair of jeans and a long-sleeved shirt, applying makeup over the noticeable bruises.

Hollis hopped into the passenger seat, and Josie drove them to the house. Josie's hand paused on the door handle.

"How were things while I was gone?"

"I'm not going to lie to you," she said. "It was hard."

"Did Cotton hurt you?"

Hollis turned so Josie could see the marks on her face. They showed in patches, a purple mark falling down from her eye where it had once been black and green. Purple marks dotted the side of her mouth.

Josie's face morphed into something like pure terror. She was mortified by the evidence of her friend's abuse.

"You lied to me," she said softly. "The blood in your hair..."

Josie started to cry. Whatever she was feeling went to the deepest part of her heart. Hollis felt like her friend had absorbed her pain and was feeling the most innocent part of it.

"I'm leaving him," Josie declared, and started the car. "We can send for our stuff later, but we're getting as far away from this place as possible."

"You don't have to leave," Hollis told her.

The car had already started to move. "Yes, Hollis. I should have done it years ago, but I'm not strong like you."

"Me?" Hollis said, truly surprised. "I stayed around and took it. I couldn't fight him. He held me down and—"

"I'm so sorry," Josie cried as sobs racked her body so hard that she had to pull over. They were within view of the house, and Josie kept looking back at it as if Cotton would charge through the front door at any moment.

"He's not there," Hollis consoled her.

"Where is he?" Josie asked, possibly thinking that her husband was out getting feed for the animals or at the barber in town.

"He's gone." Josie stared at her for a long moment before Hollis added, "There's a note."

Josie drove them to the house and glanced at the empty spot where Cotton usually kept his truck. She ran inside, yelling the name of the man who had abused them both.

Hollis got out of the car and walked into the house. She had some chili in the electronic pot, and she stirred it. She made a pot of tea and put a glass on the table for Josie.

Josie moved almost blindly to the table, but the note was nowhere to be seen. She sat, stunned, through most of the afternoon.

When she was sure it had cooled, Hollis encouraged her friend to drink her tea. Josie took one sip, obeying Hollis's instructions automatically.

"He left me," she said.

Hollis was a little confused by her friend's reaction. She had been ready to leave Cotton moments before she learned he was already gone.

In the days that followed, Josie kept watching for Cotton's truck, especially in the evening. She was convinced he'd return to her and created stories about what he was doing and what they would do when he returned. In his absence, she'd created a vision of her husband that hadn't existed, but it helped her deal better with his absence.

Hollis tended to Cotton's chores, spending extra time with the animals. She especially enjoyed the pigs, and they had grown to love her.

She waited several months before she moved into her beach house. Josie thought she was signing up for another tour of duty, and Hollis left her to her assumptions.

Hollis's beach house was the perfect place for her to find some solace. She lived there quietly in a quaint two-bedroom cottage by the sea, listening to the ocean at night. The waves drowned out the screams in her mind, and she imagined her late-night swims washed away the blood on her hands.

Finally, she could stay there no longer. There were too many men out there like Cotton, and she was ready to get back to work.

Chapter Forty-One

"Hey there," Hollis said.

Josie's eyes fluttered open. She stared forward for a moment, without speaking, until it registered that she was still alive.

She sat up a little, and Hollis noticed deep frown lines around her friend's usually happy face. *Had they formed during the years she'd spent with Cotton?*

Hollis offered Josie a cup of water, and Josie drank from the straw, sipping and then gulping as her thirst awakened. The refreshment seemed to loosen her tongue, and the friends talked about what led Josie to such a desperate act.

"I'm unhappy," Josie said.

Hollis had known that for some time, but she had chosen to ignore it. She related her feelings of selfishness to her friend, but Josie waved them away.

"We're friends, and you were expecting me to come to you with my feelings." She held Hollis's hand but looked away. "I didn't want to bother you with my problems."

Hollis searched for her eyes, but Josie was unwilling to look at her. "I want to help you. You can always tell me anything."

Josie's mouth tugged into a sad smile. "It's always the same, Hols. I'm always going to miss him." Tears cascaded down her cheeks. "Yesterday would have been Rio's birthday." Hollis held her friend's hand as she cried over her lost child.

Josie looked down at the IV snaking into a vein in her hand. "It's not fair to you or my baby." She looked up and met Hollis's eyes. "Cotton hurt you both, and in a lot of ways, he hurt you worse than he hurt me." The tears spilled over again, even though Josie was battling them. "I'm a horrible mother and friend, because I still love him."

Hollis stood up and leaned over the bed, pulling her friend into a hug. Josie gave in to her emotions, so Hollis soothed her, speaking reassuring words into her hair.

"You're a great friend," she said, and determined to show Josie the truth of the statement, she continued. "You met me at my lowest point, and you took me in. You let me stay with you when I needed a break from this crazy world, and you were willing to leave your husband when you thought he was hurting me."

"But he *was* hurting you!" Josie cried, pulling away. "I should have left him the moment I found you beaten and bloody in your bed."

Hollis cringed at the memory but recovered herself. "Neither one of us was in a condition to move that night." She looked away and narrowed her eyes. "And you know he wouldn't have let us leave without a fight."

Josie nodded. "I know, but I should have fought for you."

Hollis thought back on all the lies she'd told her friend and stayed as close to the truth as she could manage. "You know I lied to you about what that monster did to me the first time."

Josie nodded, even though it wasn't a question, and wiped her face with the back of the hand that didn't have an IV attached to it. There were some unspoken understandings between the two women, but Hollis wondered if she needed to give them a voice.

"I fought back every time, but—"

Josie gasped. "Every time? How many times did he hurt you?"

Hollis steeled her nerves and prepared to reveal everything to her friend. Maybe if she knew how broken she was, then Josie could feel more confident about her inaction when she'd found Hollis bruised and bloodied.

"I've been attacked many times," she said. "When I was young, I couldn't do anything about it, but then something happened that kind of"—she turned one hand over the other in the air— "turned the tables. I decided I wasn't going to let anyone hurt me again, and anyone who did, has paid for it."

Josie touched her arm, and Hollis turned to meet her eyes. She saw love and acceptance in them. Their blue was more brilliant in the morning sun, and her tears had left a brightness that reflected Hollis's image. Hollis saw herself through her friend's eyes. Her posture was slumped, and her face was slack; her soul was laid bare.

"I hope you made him as bloody and bruised as he made you," Josie whispered.

There was a venom behind her words, and a sureness in her speech that made Hollis wonder if her friend knew more about what she had done to Cotton, and about her, than she had previously thought.

Chapter Forty-Two

Bob, Part One

"Hand me that skillet," her mother said.

Hollis picked up the cast iron skillet and it bobbed before her mother's hands swooped in to help catch it. They steadied it together and brought it to rest on the counter.

"I swear, girl," her mother said. "You need to do some push-ups or somethin'. You couldn't lift a feather."

Hollis smiled at her mother's joke. She had always been weak, but Penny had been the strong one, taking up for her until a car crash had claimed her life.

Liz Bradshaw was a firm parent, but after her eldest daughter's death, she placed stricter rules on Hollis. She had been fifteen for over half a year, but her mother hadn't taken her to get her driver's permit. Her friends were driving with their parents, but she was stuck watching the world pass by from the back seat.

Her mother took out the rest of the cornbread and stuck it in a plastic bag. "You remember," she told Hollis, "you gotta put applesauce in the batter to make it moist and give it a little sweetness."

She was always giving Hollis little tidbits of knowledge, and Hollis stored them away. One day, she hoped to pass them on to her own children.

Her mother flipped her honey-gold hair over her skinny shoulder. The red roots were showing, so she'd dye it soon. Her mother's curly red locks were lovely in the pictures from her early teens, but she refused to deviate from the same bottle-blonde color she'd worn since Hollis had been young. She was thin, but her muscles were well-developed from carrying bundles of garments at the factory where she worked. Her hands and face showed more years than she carried, but smoking, drinking, and working since she was fourteen had put a lot of wear on her body.

"Where are *you* goin'?" Bob said, shuffling into the room.

He was hung over, as usual, and he'd slept all day, preventing him from searching for a job. He shook a cigarette out of the pack and lit it, inhaling deeply. He scrubbed the hand not holding the cigarette over his round face, and fixed his beady, brown eyes on her mother.

"I got a game tonight," he said.

Her mother whirled around and put a hand on her hip. "*Another* game?"

"Yeah." His movements slowed, and he sat still, staring at her mother as if they were facing off in a western dual. He moved his stubbly chin forward and raised his eyebrows, challenging her.

Her mother turned around and finished closing the bags that held the cornbread. "I just don't see why you can't find a job, but you can play cards all night."

He slammed his fist on the table, causing Hollis and her mother to jump. "It's poker, Liz!" he yelled. "You act like I'm playin' bridge with a group of old ladies!"

Her mother turned back around and stared him down. Hollis wondered why her mother didn't leave him.

After two separate men abandoned her after they impregnated her, Liz Bradshaw swore off relationships. She brought men home, but none of them were there in the morning when Penny and Hollis woke up.

After Penny died, though, her mother had a big, gaping hole in her heart, and even though Hollis was going through the same thing, her mother refused to share her grief. Bob was the first person she slept with after Penny died, and Hollis was shocked to find him there the next morning, eating their cereal and putting his dingy socks on the table.

Hollis often wondered if Penny had somehow kept the men away. She had been old enough to remember Hollis's father, even though he was gone before Hollis was born. Penny had told her he was nice until their mother got pregnant, and then he had beaten her frequently.

"If daddies are like that," she had told Hollis, "then we don't need them."

Penny and Hollis had run into the woods and played whenever they could sneak away from their yard. Pale Woods Forest was dark and cold, even in the summer, but it didn't keep Hollis and Penny from imagining princesses and golden carriages in the spaces between the trees.

They played everywhere, from the streams that ran through the area next to their house to the fort where they watched two little boys battle with foam swords and soft bullets.

There was one place she would never go, though, and it was inside the cave near their house. Hollis could see it from her bedroom window, its mouth yawning wide like it was ready to swallow her up. One time, when it was raining, Penny had tried to pull her inside the cave so they could be out of the weather. Instead, Hollis had run all the way home and cried in the shower.

Most of the time, Hollis liked playing in the woods with her sister. There was a peacefulness that seemed to caress her face when she and her sister spun each other around happily.

"I'll be Princess Audrey and you'll be Princess Hollis," Penny had told her.

"But I want to have a made-up name like you," Hollis had argued.

Penny's bright blonde hair fell around her face as she bounced, her baby blue eyes never losing their light. "You already have a good name," she said, matter-of-factly. "I should know. I gave it to you."

It was true. Hollis's mother had asked Penny to help her name the baby. Maybe their mother wanted to help her feel closer to her new sister, or it could have been because Penny was the only other family Hollis had.

Penny scrunched up her nose. "Mom gave me my awful name." She pretended to gag herself. "And it's not even a nickname for a prettier name, like Penelope." She turned around in a circle with her eyes closed.

Penny would never have let Bob stay, but she was the one who always spoke out. She had been with their mother for four years before Hollis was born, and she'd been allowed to have a fiery spirit, while Hollis's flame was extinguished with discipline.

Finally, her mother dropped her eyes. "Who're ya playin'?"

Bob smiled, showing all four of his oddly angled teeth. "It's just Freddy and Marshal." He took a puff of his cigarette and squashed it into the gold ashtray. "But we need food."

"I made soup beans and corn bread."

Bob scoffed at Liz's offer. "That's not poker food. Don't you have anything better?"

Her mother strode over to her pocketbook. Once red, it barely held on to a dusty maroon. She fished out a twenty.

"You can order pizza," she told him. She pointed at Hollis. "Make sure she gets some this time, though. She's gettin' too little."

Bob sneered at Hollis. "It's not my fault that she missed the boat last time. We ate all the pizza before she came in here." He chuckled. "She doesn't seem to like us. She thinks she's too high and mighty for the likes of us."

Hollis took a step backward, pressing into the corner next to the stove. Her mind registered the cast iron skillet that always sat on it when it wasn't in use.

Her mother had turned back to preparing her lunch pail and was unfazed. "Let her pick her slices when it gets here. Ladies should eat first anyway."

"Is that so?" he challenged, taking a sip of the coffee her mother had kept on the burner for him all day. "A lady should eat before a hard-workin' man?"

"I'd be willin' to argue the point with a hard-workin man," her mother quipped, giving him a pointed look.

Bob grumbled something unintelligible.

Freddy and Marshal whipped in the back door as her mother was leaving. Marshal whipped his hand behind her, like he was either smacking her firm bottom or pushing her out of her own house.

Freddy was tall and lanky, with dirt-brown hair that hung in strings over his acne-scarred face. Marshal had probably been a nice-looking man at one time, but years of drinking had busted blood vessels in his face and a beer belly erupted over his waist line.

Hollis avoided both of them. She ran to her room, pulling her hoodie over her head and hugging herself.

It was mid-July, so she should have been in a pair of shorts and a tank top, but she hadn't dressed that way since the first comment Bob made about the way her butt formed a perfect heart in her shorts. Her mother wondered about her changed appearance, so she wore clothes that covered her body at all times.

She hadn't liked Bob when she met him, but the events of the past month had caused her to hate him. He mostly ignored her when her mother was around, but when she left for work, Bob would drag her to the woods and into the cave she'd feared when she was young.

There was a knock at the door, and a couple minutes later, Bob called her name. She went into the kitchen reluctantly.

"I don't want any," she said to him when he held out the box.

He shook his head and his jowls quaked. "No, missy. You're gonna eat this pizza or I'm gonna stuff it down your tiny throat."

Marshal and Freddy sniggered and whispered. She didn't dare look at them and give power to their words.

She took two slices of pizza and headed back to her room.

"Eat it in here," Bob commanded. He motioned to his friends. "You always hide when Freddy and Marshal are here." He poked his lip out in a mock pout. "It hurts their feelings."

The men sat around the old cherry wood table that her mother, Penny, and her had shared, and they put their aluminum beer cans on its polished surface. They chewed, drank, and played poker, telling raunchy stories that made her want to spit up her pizza.

She'd heard somewhere that aluminum was linked to Alzheimer's Disease, and she secretly wished the men at the table would be suddenly struck with it, forgetting the filthy things they had stored away to share during their card games.

Marshal always dealt the cards. Hollis assumed it was so he could blame the hand he received on someone besides himself. She understood the reason Freddy wasn't allowed to touch anyone's cards besides his own. He cheated. Bob and Marshal caught him a couple of times, but Hollis saw him slip an extra card twice while they were distracted.

Freddy knew she'd seen his deception and winked at her. She fought to keep her food down.

"What's that boy of yours doin' now?" Bob asked Marshal. "Is he still married to that swimsuit model?"

The men all grinned at the idea of sharing a bed with a beautiful woman. It made her sick to see them lick their lips and nudge each other as if it were a possibility.

Marshal scrunched up his nose. "She's pregnant again. Another girl."

"That puts an end to all the fun," Freddy said, almost snorting with laughter. "You gotta put 'em out to pasture when they get so big." He held his hand out from his stomach as if envisioning how far a pregnancy would stretch his belly.

Bob appeared thoughtful. "Naw. You can still have a little fun. You just gotta be creative." He moved his eyebrows up and down.

Hollis was reminded that Bob had a daughter. She didn't have anything to do with him, refusing his gifts and phone calls.

Hollis edged her way around Bob and stood with her back to the stove, and she stuffed the last bite of pizza into her mouth. The men were in the middle of a hand, Freddy smiling at his cards while Bob and Marshal groaned over the cards they were dealt, and spit tobacco into empty beer cans. She eased around them, moving slowly in hopes that she didn't catch their eyes. If she could turn the corner, she could lock herself in her room until her mom got home from work. She thought she had almost escaped without incident until Bob clucked his tongue.

"That's no way to treat our guests," he said. "You're makin' 'em feel unwelcome." Chair legs scraped against the linoleum.

Hollis stood still and closed her eyes. She felt Bob's breath on her neck, putrid with rotting teeth and stale tobacco. "Now what can we do to make them feel more comfortable?"

Bob stroked her hair, and she hated him. She wished she could light her nerves on fire, and he would burn up when he touched her. She wished she could make him feel scared and in fear of his life. She wished she could make him do her bidding by threating to smother his mother in her sleep.

"I can think of a few ways I'd feel more comfortable," Freddy piped up.

"There's a cave not far from here," he told them. "I take her there when I want to let off a little steam." He paused before he said the last three words with emphasis.

"Does she go spelunking?" Marshal laughed. It was his way of making a joke about the crime they planned to commit.

Bob's voice was cold and commanding, devoid of any of the forced humor he used with his friends. "I don't mind sharing, boys, but if I do, my gaming debt is wiped clean, and you guys owe me a carton of smokes."

It didn't take them long to agree, and Hollis was dragged to the cave to satisfy the dark fantasies of monsters, nicotine cravings, and fifty dollars gambling debt.

Chapter Forty-Three

Josie took six weeks off work. Thankfully, Principal Bailey had known Josie's parents, and she appreciated Josie's work ethic, so she covered her absence by telling the other administrators and staff that Josie had fallen and broken her foot. It wouldn't have worked in a public school, but at Pale Woods Academy, Principal Georgia Bailey called the shots.

Josie started seeing a therapist, Margie Bronson, who insisted she was simply called "Margie" by all her patients. At Josie's request, Hollis was called into one of their sessions, and she liked the easy-going, free-spirited woman in a three-piece suit and purple, plastic glasses.

Margie asked them about their schedules and routines, and they responded with chronological accounts of their days. Margie listened along agreeably, but she was looking for a deeper account of their friendship patterns.

"Do you eat dinner together?"

Hollis and Josie looked at each other to see which one would answer. After a silent exchange, Josie answered. "Yes."

"Do you still have nights where the two of you go out?"

Hollis jumped on the question. "No, we don't, and that's my fault. I've been dating a man, and when I go out, I go out with him."

"In her defense, she's offered to take me along," Josie amended.

Margie smiled sadly. "No one wants to be the fifth wheel."

Josie and Hollis looked at the ground. Hollis promised she would make more time for Josie.

"That's not really fair to her," Josie said. Her eyebrows pulled together, and her fists clenched. "She's not dating me or part of my family, so why does she have to pick up where Cotton left off?"

Margie folded her hands, still keeping her face as calm as a lake in the morning sun. "Hollis is interested in your mental health, and as a member of your household, she has a direct connection to it." She turned to Josie, her voice soft and light, causing Josie to release her hands into a more relaxed position. "Josie, would you have tried to kill yourself if you had felt more connected to Hollis?"

Josie's face colored. "It's not Hollis's fault. I tried to kill myself over my stupid husband."

Margie wasn't shaken by Josie's reaction. "I'm not blaming Hollis; I'm blaming you."

It was almost like someone flipped a switch. Josie went from defensive to reflective. Margie gave her a minute to settle into her feelings but prompted her to give them a voice.

"I should have told Hollis about my feelings," Josie said, staring hard at the wooden coffee table in front of her. Smiling women with seemingly carefree lives rode bicycles and planted flowers on the magazine covers.

"Can I say something?" Hollis asked.

Margie spread her hands in a welcoming gesture and Josie looked up at her expectantly. Hollis grabbed her hands and squeezed her fingers together.

"I know it's not my responsibility to make sure that everything goes well for Josie, but I'm her friend, and I want to help her when she needs it."

Margie opened her mouth to say something, but Josie interrupted her. "But you just started a relationship with Quillen, and—"

"Quillen will never be more important than you," Hollis promised.

Margie jumped in. "Do you think it's wise to put a low value on your relationship with Quillen so soon?"

Hollis knew the angle the therapist was pursuing. "I'm not capable of having a healthy romantic relationship."

"I hope you've explored that in your own therapy sessions," Margie said gravely, and she turned the rest of the session directly on Josie.

Hollis didn't speak until Margie thanked them for sharing their thoughts and feelings with her. Even then, Hollis only issued a vague acknowledgement.

Hollis spread a thick layer of peanut butter over her toast. She took it to the table where Josie was enjoying a robust salad.

Josie scrunched her nose. "How can you eat that? I'd choke when I tried to swallow it."

Hollis laughed, taking an extra-large bite. When she was finished chewing, she said, "I've always eaten them this way."

Josie was still appalled by the thickness of her peanut butter spread. "At least drink some milk. I don't want to perform the Heimlich Maneuver on you."

The doorbell rang, and the women looked at each other. Neither one of them was expecting anyone. Hollis saw a momentary flash of hope in Josie's eyes. Even though the divorce papers had been signed, she still wanted Cotton to appear at her door.

Mage bounded down the hall, growling and wagging his tail. Hollis jumped up and answered the bell.

Quillen stood on the porch with two vases of flowers in his hands. After he calmed Mage, he came into the house.

"Where can I put these?" he asked Hollis.

Hollis led him into the kitchen, and Josie stood up when she saw Quillen was carrying flowers. "Those are beautiful!"

"I heard there were two beautiful women living here, and I couldn't resist treating them to flowers and a movie." He winked at Hollis, who smiled at his cleverness.

"I love the flowers," Josie said. "But shouldn't the two of you go on a date by yourselves. It's easier to get to know each other without someone else tagging along."

Hollis had an answer prepared, but Quillen held out his hand to Josie. "I was shocked when Hollis told me you were in the hospital." He shrugged apologetically. "This is a small town, and news travels fast. I hope you're not going to do anything like that again."

Josie shook her head. "No, I don't plan on it." Color was creeping up her neckline, and it seemed she wanted to find an excuse to hide her embarrassment, but Quillen held her eyes and her hand gently.

"I hope you consider me a friend," he told her. His eyes flicked to Hollis, and she nodded her encouragement. "I hoped we could all go out as friends tonight."

"But you and Hollis are—"

Perhaps her friend was going to say "dating" or "more," but Hollis cut her off before she had the chance. "Quillen and I haven't talked about a relationship yet." Her voice was a little harsher than she intended, and Quillen's smile faltered.

Josie had turned away from Quillen who was still holding her hand. "Okay. Let me change, and I'll be ready to go."

When Josie was upstairs and out of earshot, Hollis said, "Thank you. She really needs this."

Quillen motioned up the stairs. "Josie's a great person, but I did this for you."

She smiled at him and took her plate to the sink. She felt his arms wrap around her, but she rounded on him before she realized it was him.

He jumped back with his hands up and a wounded expression. "I'm sorry." He lowered his hands. "Is there something I'm missing, Hollis?" He took a tentative step toward her, but he didn't offer to touch her. "I thought we were together. I mean, after the other night—"

Hollis looked away. "I like you, Quillen, but—"

Quillen stopped her by kissing her. At first, he kept his body separate from the action, but when Hollis kissed him back, he pressed himself to her hungrily. When he pulled away, Hollis could hardly catch her breath. Josie had come downstairs during their kiss, but she had stayed in the living room to give Quillen and Hollis some privacy.

"You were saying?" He said, letting her head fall back on his hand and trailing kisses down her neck.

"About what?" she asked, distracted by his slow-moving lips on her skin.

"Exactly," he responded, believing he had made his point.

Hollis didn't want to feel claimed, and it brought her out of the moment. She was ready to open up a dialog about it when a huge crash sounded from the front of the house.

When they explored the source of the disruption, they found Josie in the living room with a pile of books at her feet. "I'm so sorry guys," she said. "I was trying to move these research books to the bookcase in the dining room, and I guess I wasn't strong enough to lift them."

Hollis looked at the tomes. It would have been an impressive feat if her friend had been able to lug them to the dining room.

Quillen picked up three books at a time and hauled them into the dining room, placing them on the polished table. Josie looked at her with concern, and Hollis realized her friend had purposely dropped the stack.

During one of his trips into the other room, her suspicions were confirmed when Josie whispered, "Just try. Let him like you and lavish attention on you. What can it hurt?"

Hollis shook her head at her friend's elaborate ruse. She had a point, though. Hollis was taking a break, and if she was going to give it her all, then she should accept Quillen's kindnesses and romantic gestures.

They let Josie pick the movie, and she chose a psychological thriller about a stalker. Hollis pegged the killer before the middle of the movie, and she thought of five different ways the movie could have been more intriguing or the killer could have been more creative. Josie and Quillen seemed to be held in the suspense, and they were surprised when the murderer was revealed.

Josie spied the ice cream parlor next to the movie theater, and she dragged them inside. Hollis appreciated the owner's initiative for placing the establishment just outside the movie theater's exit. It seemed strategic, as families and weekend dads and their children filled the tables.

Hollis was the first to pay, and since she already knew Josie's order, she paid for both of them. They had a game of rushing to see who could pay the bill first when they went out.

Josie put her hand on her hip. "I should have known," she said when the clerk waved away her card and pointed to Hollis.

"I should have gone first," Quillen commented. "I would have gladly paid for your ice creams."

They rolled their eyes at his outdated chivalry, but they didn't do it where he could see it. They were used to paying their own way.

"When do you plan to go back to work?" Quillen asked Josie when they sat down at one of the round metal tables. It had been recently vacated and someone had left behind a napkin with the evidence of their strawberry selection on it.

"I'll go back next Monday," Josie replied. "I can't wait to start teaching William Faulkner and Flannery O'Connor to my students!"

"I'm sure Rosie will love it," he said sarcastically.

Josie gave him a strange look. "Rose isn't in my class."

Quillen may have thought her recent episode had damaged her memory, because he carefully said, "Yes she is. That's the reason Mrs. Bailey assigned you to give us the tour of the school."

Josie tilted her head, and her lips formed a thin line. "Rose spent the first couple of days in my room, and then she transferred to Mrs. Bartman's class."

Hollis thought back to her sudden appearance in another one of her classes. "I had some students switch around, too."

She hoped it would help the situation, but it only seemed to make it worse. The heat she felt off Quillen seemed to double in intensity. "Is Zach in Mrs. Bartman's class?"

Josie looked at Hollis. They were both uncomfortable, but Hollis took her cue from Josie, and she kept her friend from further awkwardness. "Yes."

Quillen got up quickly and shoved his ice cream into the garbage. When he returned to the table, he was barely holding onto his composure, but he spoke to them evenly. "I'm sorry, ladies. I think I need to go home."

They had taken separate cars, so Hollis and Josie weren't worried about finding a ride home, but it was a harsh way to end their nice evening. Their ice cream dripped down their hands and dropped onto the table as they watched him swing open the glass door and step out into the frigid December air.

Chapter Forty-Four

"I asked you a question," Quillen spat at his daughter. "Did you change classes for *him*?" He couldn't even say Zach's name.

Rose washed the last dish and placed it in the drainer. She looked around for a towel next to the sink, and finding none, she flicked the water off her hands into the sink.

"You're being weird, Dad. People switch classes all the time."

He couldn't believe how calm she sounded. "You were in an accelerated English class, and now you're—"

"—in a class that's just as good," Rose finished for him. She pressed her back to the counter and put one hand on either side of her as if she were debating lifting herself onto it. "Look, all the classes are good. I'm going to an academy."

"No," Quillen argued. "They have dumb, rich kids who they put in certain lower-level classes, and you're in one of them."

"Why do you say that?" Rose pushed herself up onto the counter, and her posture sagged. "I'm learning exactly the same thing as any other kid in my grade."

Quillen ran a hand across his eyes, pushing on his lids with his thumb and forefinger. "No, you're not, Rosie. You're in the dumb kids' class."

She thought about his words and said, "It's not nice to call people 'dumb,' Dad. I don't like it."

Quillen stared at her, trying to remember when she had changed from the little girl he had pushed on the swings at the playground to a young lady with her own views and opinions. She had transformed without a clear sign. Or maybe he hadn't been paying enough attention.

"Did you change classes for *him*?" he asked again, keeping his anger at a slow boil.

She shrugged her shoulders. "Maybe. What does it matter?"

It took every ounce of his restraint to remain in place. "After what happened to your sister? You're going to risk your life—"

"It was one boy!" she yelled at him. "How was anyone supposed to know about what his father was?"

"There are ways to tell," Quillen said, pacing the room.

"What? Should I hire a private investigator to research both sides of his family?"

Quillen nodded, even though Rose was being sarcastic. "Yes. It's called vetting, and it's perfectly legal. The senior members of the bank do it when they hire—"

Rose closed her eyes and waved her hand. When she opened them, one eyebrow dipped lower than the other. "Zach's not interviewing for a job. He's just my boyfriend."

Rose realized what she'd said when Quillen's eyes widened. It was too late to take back the words.

"He's your *boyfriend*," he said, nodding along like there was rhythm in his statement. "I knew it."

"It's no big deal," Rose said. "We only hang out and—"

"And he puts his hand down your shirt," Quillen said.

The two of them stared each other down. Rose finally broke the silence.

"People my age are doing a lot worse."

Quillen clapped his hands. "Way to go, Rosie. You're ahead of the game in teenage pregnancy." He stopped clapping and narrowed his eyes. "But how long will that last with a boy like that?"

Rose jumped off the counter. "I thought you were worried about his family, but now you think I'm going to get pregnant!" She put her hands on her hips. "Which one is it?"

"Both!" Quillen barked.

"Well, I'm not pregnant, and I don't plan to be."

He thought she was done, but she continued when he opened his mouth to speak.

"And good luck on finding information about his parents. His mom's dead, and his father ran off."

Quillen recognized her attraction to the boy. Aside from his aloofness, Zach had lost his mother, and Rose could identify with that part of him. Quillen flipped his phone out of his pocket.

Rose approached him, suddenly concerned. "What are you doing?"

He opened the browser on his screen, searching for a number. "You just told me his father left him. I have to report it to child services."

Rose grabbed the phone out of his hands and took two steps away. Quillen reached for his phone, but she moved back even more.

"You can't call them," she begged.

Quillen shook his head. It was more emotion than he had seen from her during their entire conversation. "Why? Do you think they'll take Loverboy out of the academy and put him in a foster home?"

She nodded vigorously. "Graduating from Pale Woods is his only chance to make something of himself."

He held out his hand for his phone. "I can't let him raise himself."

Rose looked down at the floor and hugged herself. "You don't have to," she said. "He turns eighteen in a couple of weeks."

Quillen hadn't realized Zach was so close to adulthood. He couldn't remember most of what he said, and he had no idea how Rose calmed him down enough to accept her terms. In the end, he had agreed not to call child services, so that Zach could fend for himself until his eighteenth birthday. In exchange Rose had promised to break up with him.

Quillen tried to sleep, but he kept waking up at the slightest sound. Someone had tried to break into the house, but she was dead. Unfortunately, Detective Saldana wasn't forthcoming with the reason for the dead woman's animosity, so he roamed the house, and checked on Rose frequently.

When he eased open her door, Rose was sleeping on her back with her mouth open. He gently guided her onto her side. Beth had always been worried that the girls would asphyxiate in their sleep, and Quillen found himself catering to his wife's anxieties in her absence. He didn't want to lose Rose, too.

He laid down in his bed and willed himself to go to sleep. He needed to rest, or he wouldn't be at his best as an employee or a parent.

His mind drifted to Zach and his wayward father. He'd seen the man at a bar one night, hanging all over the bar flies and stumbling drunk. He could tell from his stained A shirt and dropped face that he wasn't someone he wanted to know. He had searched him out when he'd found Rose in his son's car. It wasn't hard to locate a man called "Saint" in a small town.

Saint had been in a biker club, and he carried the nickname from the years when he was considered their Sargent at Arms. He'd come a long way away from his youth, and any muscle he had carried had withered away. But the women in the bar seemed to be drawn to his big brown eyes or his largely embellished history in the motorcycle club.

Quillen was a little surprised that Saint had left Zach. He wasn't much of a father, but he had appeared stationary. With a little more research, Quillen learned that their trailer and the land it sat on were paid off, so Saint always had a place to go.

Maybe he ran off with a woman. Zach was almost an adult, and he could certainly fend for himself.

The situation was strange to him. He couldn't imagine leaving Rose. Even when she was an adult, he imagined having Sunday dinners together.

He turned on his side and tried to push the thoughts out of his mind. At least Rose would break up with Zach, and that was enough for him.

Chapter Forty-Five

Hollis left for Christmas, and when she returned, she found Josie in a reasonably good mood. In her friend's absence, Josie had taken down Cotton's pictures and given all his clothes to a charitable organization.

She sipped wine and offered Hollis a glass. Hollis accepted it and hugged her friend with one arm.

"You left pretty quickly," Josie said. "Did you get in touch with Quillen yet?"

Hollis shook her head as she dragged her suitcase behind her and sat it upright in the hallway. "I'll call him later."

"You don't want to face the music, do ya?"

Hollis raised an eyebrow. "I'm not dating the man, so I don't know why he kept calling me."

"Well, when he couldn't reach you, he called me," Josie said, falling back into her chair. "Thanks for that."

Hollis rolled her eyes. "Why are some people so clingy?"

"I don't think he's overly-attached, but he probably thought you liked him well enough to tell him you were skipping town over the holidays."

Hollis took a sip of her wine and made a face.

Josie acknowledged her grimace. "Yeah. It's a dry one."

"I didn't have work obligations, so I went away for a few days," she defended.

Josie raised her glass in a mock salute. "And I'm so glad you can do that. Just don't leave your love-struck boyfriend without a clue about when you'll be back."

Hollis sat down next to her friend, slumping in the chair. "How many times did he call?"

Josie replied swiftly. "At least ten times."

Hollis put her hand on her friend's arm. "I'm sorry, Jos. The next time I leave, I'll tell him I'm going somewhere."

Josie readjusted her position to meet Hollis's eyes. "Do you plan on doing that a lot?"

Hollis smiled at her friend's concern. "No." She reflected on her friend's words. "Do you really think he likes me that much?"

Josie's eyebrows drew together. "He is pretty nearly in love with you." She shook her head. "You two are so different, but there's something about the way he looks at you."

Hollis stared at her friend and wished she could find her a man who would pine over her. Josie was beautiful, strong-willed, and hard-working. The only reason people weren't banging down her door for a date was because she still wore a silver wedding band on her left finger. As she thought about it, Hollis's eyes traveled to her friend's hands, but the ring wasn't there.

Hollis jumped out of her chair, startling Josie and causing her to spill a little wine on her black dress pants. "You're not wearing your ring!"

Josie stared at her for a moment before she looked down at her finger. She held her hand out in front of her and examined the white flesh around her finger where her wedding band had rested for over a decade.

"It was time."

The resignation in her tone kept Hollis from asking anything more, but she found herself staring at her friend's hand as they talked.

"Now, what are you going to do about Quillen?" Josie asked, clearly eager to change the subject.

Hollis shrugged her shoulders. "I can call him."

Josie winced. "Or you could invite him over."

Hollis put a finger on her chin thoughtfully. "He may be too mad to —"

Josie interrupted her with a laugh. "Believe me, he won't be too mad to jump in your bed."

Hollis smacked her friend playfully on her leg. "Josie!"

Josie took a sip of wine and raised her eyebrows over the rim of her glass.

Josie wasn't wrong.

Quillen was sulky when he spoke to her over the phone, but after she led him to her bedroom, he opened up about his damaged feelings and Hollis did her best to repair them. They laid in her bed, and she promised to be more open with him about her plans.

"Where did you go?" he asked, trailing his finger down her thigh.

Hollis wanted to tell him it was none of his business, but Josie had told her that she needed to try to have a relationship with him. Quillen was a likeable man, and Hollis decided to open up to him a little more.

"I had to get away for a few days. Sometimes I need a break."

He raised up on his elbow and stared at her in the dark. His eyes were cast in shadow, and he looked more like a soulless shadow than her lover. "I thought *this* was your break."

"It is," Hollis said carefully. "But I needed some time to get away and reassess what I want."

He caressed her face from her jaw to her chin. "Is it because you want to make your life here more permanent?"

In truth, Hollis hadn't given any thought to staying after the school year was over. She wondered if giving Quillen the idea that a future with her was a possibility was a bad idea. She liked him, but she could never share her darker side with him. He would never hear her true confessions. He would never be Asher.

"Hold on a minute," Quillen said, getting out of the bed.

Hollis watched him sprint in the moonlight to the pile of his clothes on the floor. He dug through his pants until he found what he wanted and returned to the bed.

"I got you a gift for Christmas," he told her, placing a gray case in her hand.

It was square, and too large to be a ring case. Hollis let out a sigh of relief.

Quillen flipped on the lamp by her bed, and they both squinted as their eyes adjusted to the light. Hollis ran a finger under each eye to try to wipe away any smeared mascara.

She opened the box and smiled at Quillen. "It's beautiful."

Quillen had selected a heart pendant on a golden chain. Three hearts adorned the bottom of the heart, leading to the point at the bottom.

"Can I put it on you?" he asked.

Hollis was sweaty and her hair was unkempt, but she held her hair up as he fastened it behind her neck. She studied herself in the mirror on the dresser. Naked and bejeweled, she felt worshipped by her lover, and she gave him a slow kiss of appreciation.

"Let me love you," Quillen spoke as they laid together with their hearts beating rapidly in their chests. And even though she nodded and allowed his touch, part of her was screaming that he wasn't the right man for her.

She thought about her reluctance for a moment. *Was she backing away from commitment because she never let go to Asher, or was she stepping back because she knew she was tied to a different future of brokenness and despair?*

When Quillen's breaths sounded steady against the quiet of the room, she couldn't help feeling trapped. *Was this how people ended up in relationships? Did one person choose another person and they fell together, planning their lives as society beamed and dictated the rules of their engagement?*

Hollis found herself plotting ways out of the commitment. She couldn't just tell Quillen that she was unwilling to move at his speed. She couldn't let him leave tomorrow morning and never call. He'd only harass Josie until Hollis decided to speak to him.

Hollis imagined his bank getting robbed, and the gunman killing him, relieving her of the obligation to be with him. Then her mind rolled to the next morning, where a small push down the steps could break his neck.

Her freedom would be Rose's misfortune, though, and she quickly dismissed the ideas. She drifted slowly to sleep, wondering if she was really cut out for the life she'd created or if she had spent so long disguising herself as a wolf in sheep's clothing that now all that was left was an animal.

Chapter Forty-Six

Bob, Part Two

Hollis stared at the patterns on the ceiling. She imagined the popcorn dots were stars, making tiny, spackled constellations.

A knock sounded at her door, and her mother staggered inside. She swayed as she shut the door, and she stumbled over Hollis's backpack. She plopped down on the bed and placed a shaky hand on Hollis's leg.

Hollis could feel the physical heat from her mother's touch, but she was detached from the sentiment. She'd made herself numb to all of it. Nothing made her happy or feel safe, but she could keep herself from being scared and hurt, too.

A rat skittered across the floor, running over her mother's foot in its haste to get away. Her mother cried out, but she stayed in place, making sure the pest was truly gone.

"Those darn things," she said breathlessly. "I have to put more poison out." She looked at Hollis. "You put some in here, right?"

"Yeah," Hollis lied. There was no way she was going to kill another living being, even if it was considered a disease-carrying nuisance.

Her mother surveyed her emaciated form. "You need to eat somethin'," her mother said. "The doctor said he'll have to admit you to the hospital if you don't."

Hollis actually liked the idea of going to the hospital and receiving forced nutrition through a vein in her arm. At least she wouldn't have to stay at her house and get dragged into a cave almost every night or watch her mother sink further into alcoholism.

Her mother had never fallen victim to drug abuse, and she had only drunk socially, but Bob had put a beer or liquor bottle in her hand every day since they'd been together, and a habit had finally formed. Hollis rarely saw her mother without bleary eyes and a red, shiny face.

Hollis stared back at the woman she loved and wanted to respect. "I'll eat if you make him leave."

"Who? Bob?" Her mother was truly bewildered. "He talks trash, but he's a stand-up guy."

Hollis rolled her eyes. Her mother was simply repeating the same words Bob spoke about himself.

Her mother's hand squeezed her leg just below the knee. "Is he mean to you?"

Hollis stared hard at the imagined stars on her ceiling, wishing she could fly into them. There was no air in space, but at least she'd be far away from Bob when she died. She could turn and watch the world spin, while happy families had taco nights and camped in four-man tents.

"No." She forced the word out. It made a hollow sound that matched the way she felt.

"Will you eat then?"

Hollis nodded her head. She was unwilling to make a verbal commitment when she had no intention of eating.

Her mother brought her toast, butter, and juice. She sipped the juice, and her mother gave her a thumb's up. Hollis flashed her a plastic smile, and her mother closed the door.

Hollis got up, and crossed the room, opening the window to spill out the food her mother had given her. It joined countless other meals that her mother and Bob would have seen if they had walked behind the house. It was winter, though, so the grass didn't need to be mowed, and Bob always came for Hollis in the dead of night, so he couldn't see the mound of food under her window. It probably didn't help their rat infestation, but Hollis didn't care.

She sat her plate down at the foot of the bed and focused on the star pattern. She couldn't control a lot, but she could control what she put into her body. Once, Bob had made the comment that he liked women with a little meat on their bones. Hollis rejoiced every morning when she slid her fingers along her protruding ribcage, happy for their rigid swells as she traveled along her midsection.

She opened her backpack and finished her science assignment. She had started biology after the holiday break, and she thought she may have found her life-long passion. She enjoyed the classroom discussions about all living things, and her notebook was divided and color-coded with plant facts.

She loved learning about weird vegetables, like fiddleheads, and the Castor plant, which was revered as the deadliest plant in the world. She preferred Belladonna, though, and she had collected some of the berries as she'd walked through Pale Woods in September. She thought about swallowing the "Deadly Nightshade" and ending the tormented cycle of her days. She wasn't ready to leave her mom, and she was almost certain her death would send her mother over the edge. She'd kept the berries, and even though they were shriveled, they'd probably kill her if she ate all forty of them.

With a sigh, Hollis exchanged her science notebook for her math worksheet. She didn't like going to school, but she did well in all her classes. She rarely had to study, and she was good at creating mnemonic devices to make good grades on her tests.

Her school counselor had told her that she could graduate early if she completed all her course credits. Hollis poured herself into her studies, hopeful that she could obtain a scholarship and graduate just after her next birthday. She could start college at sixteen and try to get as far away from her mother's house as possible.

The sound of raised voices calmed nerves she didn't know were on edge. When it was quiet, Hollis feared sudden outbursts, but when her mother and Bob were fighting, she knew what to expect, and she wasn't blindsided by a sudden cry or screaming.

She listened to their conversation, and fear swallowed her when she realized she was the reason for their fight. Her mother was talking to Bob about Hollis's refusal to eat.

"Why did she say she'd eat if you'd leave then?" she yelled at him.

"Because she's crazy, just like her mother!" he yelled back. "I'm not stoppin' her from eatin'!"

"Have you been mean to my baby?" her mother said with quiet venom.

"I got news for you, Liz, your *baby* is grown, and you need to quit hoverin' over her like a mother bear." He paused, and Hollis heard ice rattling in a glass cup, indicating that he'd finished his juice glass of liquor. "She's probably just pinin' over some jock that broke her heart."

Hollis laughed to herself. She'd not even looked at the boys in her school. She couldn't imagine letting one of them touch her the way Bob did.

Her mother said something she couldn't hear, and a slap sounded off the walls as the furniture scraped across the floor. Hollis closed her eyes and covered her ears, but she could feel the vibrations of wood hitting the wall behind her.

The movement stopped, and she lowered her hands just in time to hear her mom squeak out the word, "Please."

Hollis rushed out of her room and saw her mom on the floor, clawing at Bob's chest and arms. Bob held her down with one hand around her neck. Hollis jumped onto his back and tried to pull him away, but Bob shook her off effortlessly, and she fell onto the wooden coffee table. Her weight didn't upset the balance of the piece, so she quickly got to her feet and tried to get Bob away from her mother again, earning her the same reward.

Her mother's face was crimson, and her jaw worked up and down. She stared at him with protruding eyes.

Bob released her seconds before she lost consciousness. He simply walked into the kitchen, picked up a fallen chair, and sat in it, turning his back on the scene he'd created.

Hollis helped her mother into a sitting position. Her mother coughed and gagged, finally releasing bile, meat, and potatoes onto the floor.

"Clean that up and go to work," Bob commanded from the chair. He lit a cigarette and slumped over onto the table.

Her mother tried to speak several times before she could communicate that she couldn't go to work. The effort made her cough more.

Hollis retrieved a bottle of water for her mother, but she waved it away and asked for a beer. Now that her mother and Bob were both full-blown alcoholics, cases of Moon Walker beer were always in their refrigerator.

"You'll get fired if they smell the beer on your breath," Bob cautioned. "Drink the vodka."

He turned around in his chair to look at her and Liz glared at him. She still couldn't speak, and purple bruises dotted her neck.

Bob let out a slow puff of smoke. "And don't even think about tellin' anyone where you got those marks, or I'll give your daughter some to match."

Chapter Forty-Seven

Quillen stared at the beautiful woman in front of him. She was breathtaking, with her long limbs exposed after she slipped them through the straps of her black dress, and her hair falling as it framed her face. Her features were symmetrical, but there was something in her expressions that seemed to hide a secret, guarding it with every fiber of her being.

That was fine with him. She could have her secrets, because he had his own, but he found himself wanting to reveal parts of them to her. She had a calming effect on him. Most other women wanted to talk about themselves or make future plans, but Hollis was only concerned about the present, and she let him lead the conversation. They'd spent many evenings in comfortable silence, while he breathed in her jasmine scent, and she was left to her thoughts.

He asked her what she thought about, but she only gave him lies. He knew she was more concerned about whatever plagued her than she was about the sale at a local grocery store or the vet's visit to see one of their sick pigs.

Quillen wanted Hollis to be happy, so he tried to get closer to her in every way. For a time, it seemed like he was smothering her, so he didn't message her for a couple of days, and he was happy when she called him.

Christmas had been hard for Quillen. Since he had lost part of his family, the holidays had been tough, but he shared a quiet day with Rose, and drank enough liquor to put him to sleep.

He had called Hollis, but she had been too busy with her vacation to return his calls. *Where had she gone? Why didn't she invite him to go or tell her best friend where she was going?*

Josie had been great, telling him that it was something Hollis did all the time, but her words did little to relieve his stress. He didn't want to have feelings for a woman that could pick up and leave at any time, but he was already falling hard for her. Again, he stopped trying to get in touch with her for a couple of days, and Hollis called him.

She'd promised that he was her only lover, and she'd been wearing the necklace he had given her every time he'd seen her. It seemed like she cared for him, but something was holding her back.

He wondered if she suffered from PTSD, and he supposed it was to be expected. Josie had hinted about the missions she had gone on, and even though Quillen knew very little about the military, he thought it might be tough.

As they laid on their pillows, he tried to get her to talk about her past. She wasn't forthcoming, often changing the subject to focus on him. She was especially volatile when he asked about her lovers. She looked at him with such venom that he glanced away and let the subject drop.

Quillen was disappointed that he couldn't get his girlfriend to open up about her past. In fact, he didn't even know if she considered herself his girlfriend. They went out in public and slept together sometimes, but she pulled away when he held her to him, and she'd only hold his hand for a few minutes until she flicked it off like she was shaking water from her hand.

Quillen wanted to get close to her, but he was unable to break through her guard. He asked Josie about it, but she was very little help. She claimed that, even though they were close, there was a lot about Hollis she didn't know.

There were times he wanted to give up, but he was determined to win Hollis's trust. Lately, she had been pulling further and further away from him, though, and he hoped she wasn't getting ready to run again.

Chapter Forty-Eight

Hollis pulled into the gas station and got the bags out of her trunk. She avoided the stares of the men at the pumps as she walked under the unforgiving lights over the gas pumps. She carried the bags across the street, stopping on the center line when a car rounded the corner a little too quickly.

She spotted the trailer and looked around for curious neighbors. They all seemed to be asleep, or otherwise engaged, so the cover of night and their indifference kept her mission a secret.

The plastic bags rustled as she placed them against the door. Nothing needed to be refrigerated, so it could stay out all night, but she hoped the supplies would be found soon after she made a hasty getaway. She ran to the road and walked casually to her car.

She'd had another successful drop off, and she sighed in relief when she was finally behind the wheel of her car with the doors locked. She had honored her commitment, and she planned to do way more than she'd promised.

· · · · ● · ● · ● · · ·

Talk of spring break buzzed through the school. Many of the students had plans, as their families were wealthier than those of the students in public school, and the two-week break provided a true vacation from scholastic endeavors before the teachers prepared them for tests that would satisfy state requirements and place them in the proper classes the following year.

Due to her dual responsibilities to teach physical education and health awareness to her students, Hollis taught the same students the entire school year. She had to prepare almost seventy students for their end-of-term tests, but the other teachers sometimes had almost two hundred children to review, and in some cases, reteach.

Hollis wasn't looking forward to the break, but she could see the excitement in the way the students smiled more often and were more alert in her classes. The gymnasium didn't have windows, but she imagined they would have spent most of the week before classes paused staring out of them if it did.

Quillen had asked her to go with him to a Floridian beach, and Hollis was supposed to give him an answer soon. Even though he said he'd pay for separate rooms, Hollis didn't feel comfortable going on a trip with Quillen and his daughter. Maybe she would feel differently if she were as committed as him, but she couldn't bring herself to lower the wall that would allow him into her world.

She and Josie enjoyed a beautiful friendship, but they had grown closer over a decade, and they had met during a difficult time for both of them. Maybe she wasn't meant to have more than a good friendship. She had murdered many men who had given her their hearts. Perhaps that was the reason she didn't feel comfortable when Quillen spoke about long-range plans with her.

Quillen was a handsome man who treated her well, so she should be jumping at any chance to get closer to him, but the closer he tried to get to her, the more she wanted to run away. *Could a person* make *themselves fall in love with another person?* She certainly hoped it was possible. Maybe she could have a good life with Quillen and help him finish raising Rose. From what she'd heard, he could definitely use the help.

Zach walked Rose up to her friends and she kissed his cheek before he took his assigned spot on the gym floor. Hollis was supposed to write them a detention for the romantic contact, but she couldn't do it. Quillen had ranted about his daughter's boyfriend since he found out about them. He had quietened his concerns over the last few weeks because he believed Rose had broken off her relationship with Zach. In truth, it had made them a stronger couple, and when she had given her sexual education class with the girls, she had given Rose two bags of contraceptives.

Zach's appearance and demeanor had changed since Christmas. He walked straighter, and his clothes were fresh, instead of rumpled and stained. The circles under his eyes had faded, indicating better sleep, better nutrition, or both. He contributed more to class discussions, actually speaking up about potential damage to the xiphoid process when they discussed the Heimlich Maneuver. But most of all, he didn't have new bruises and burn marks on his body when his shirt sleeves or pants legs moved up accidentally.

Hollis had heard that Zach had gotten a job stocking shelves at a local discount store. It provided an income for him, while not interfering too much with his studies, which if the other teachers were to be believed, had improved significantly. It had an effect on his social life, too, as he had less time to devote to Rose, but he seemed to make up for it in other ways by giving her extra attention at school and sneaking her into his trailer when she was supposed to be spending the night with Katey.

Hollis was quiet about their secret rendezvous, even though she wondered how Quillen was blind to them. He must have had more trust in Rose than she'd realized, and it would be shattered if he ever found out the truth. Hollis was certain Zach and Rose had established a sexual relationship, and there was no way her father was going to rip Rose away from him.

Just before the bell rang, Andy strode across the floor. His face was crimson, and it stood out against his bright blond hair. He carried a piece of paper in his fist, and he waved it at Zach.

"Stay away from Julie!" he shouted, and his words echoed off the concrete walls and empty spaces in the gym.

The paper seemed to be a note with large, blue ink letters on it, but Hollis couldn't make them out. Andy shook it in Zach's face.

Zach looked completely bewildered, staring at the paper Andy held inches away from his nose. He held his position, neither giving away his fear nor readying himself for a fight.

"Look, bro. I think you've got the wrong—"

"Is your name Zach?" Andy yelled. He pushed the paper just under Zach's nose. "It's signed with your name."

Rose had been watching the scene with obvious concern for her boyfriend, but after Andy said Zach's name was on it, she stared at the floor. Her thumbnail went to her mouth, a habit Hollis hadn't seen since her first day of class.

It crossed Hollis's mind that she needed to decelerate the situation, but her feet were planted to the floor, watching the incident unfold with the other students. Her paralysis broke when Andy grabbed Zach's shirt, bunching the collar in his fist. The note fell to the floor, and one of Rose's friends shuffled into the danger zone to retrieve it. She handed it over, and Rose took it automatically, not looking at it right away.

"That's enough!" Hollis shouted, surprised by the authority in her volce. She strode over to Andy and Zach, forgetting her educator training momentarily as she detached Andy's hand from Zach's shirt.

Andy looked at her in surprise. "You're taking up for him!"

If there were sides to be taken, Hollis would have been on Zach's, but she had to play her role as a responsible teacher. "It's time for both of you to go to the office."

Rose was reading the note when Hollis snatched it out of her hand. She marched both boys to the office and left her class in an unmanaged chorus of chatter.

"He put it in her locker at work!" Andy yelled.

Principal Baily was unmoved by the scandal in his tone. "You need to lower your voice."

Andy realized he was dealing with an adult who had an immense amount of say over his time at school and whether he'd be able to finish the basketball season. He spoke at a volume slightly higher than his regular speaking voice. "Zach works with Julie, and he put that"— he pointed at the note in Hollis's hand— "in her locker. She found it when she clocked out last night."

Hollis handed the note to Principal Bailey, and she put on the dated reading glasses that hung from a loose silver chain around her neck. She looked over it, her face void of emotion.

Hollis had only glanced over the note, but she was certain Zach hadn't written it. She excused herself, grabbed a teacher's aide, and directed him into the gym. The noise of the gossiping teens had reached a dull roar, but the teacher's aide quietened them with a clap of his hands. Before she returned to Principal Bailey's office,

Hollis visited her filing cabinet, pulling a slip of paper from one of the manilla files.

She pulled open Principal Bailey's door and handed her the paper. Principal Bailey's eyes found Hollis, and something passed between them.

She put both sheets of paper in front of Andy. He had taken the seat to the left of where Hollis stood, and Zach had fallen into the seat on the right, massaging his temples.

"As you can see," Principal Bailey began, "this is the note"— she pointed to the crumpled paper on her desk and then to the paper Hollis had retrieved— "and this is a paper Zach wrote in health class." She waited for Andy to understand, but he remained silent. "The handwriting doesn't match."

"He could have disguised it," Andy said simply.

"That would defeat the purpose of signing his name to the note," Hollis pointed out.

Andy glared at her. "Why are you still here? Everyone knows Zach's your little class pet."

Zach huffed. "Hardly. Did you see the grade she gave me?"

A big red "C" headed the paper. It wasn't a terrible grade, but it was a little low for the subject matter. She kicked herself for not pulling out a more recent assignment.

Andy sneered at Zach. "They may not be doing anything about this, but I'll be watching you, and if you go near Julie— "

"I won't sit here and listen to you threaten another student," Principal Bailey told Andy. She leaned forward in her seat, her eyes boring into both boys. "And I don't need to remind you, Zach, that you're eighteen, so you can be arrested and taken to jail if you fight a minor."

Hollis wanted to slap the smug look off Andy's face. She reminded herself that he was a good kid, but he had misdirected emotions over the note Julie had found in her locker at work.

Both boys were dismissed separately to go back to class, but Hollis lingered a little longer in Principal Bailey's office. She took the note, full of vulgar language, and put it in a folder in her desk.

"Who do you think wrote the note?" she asked Hollis.

"I don't know," Hollis replied. "But whoever it was, doesn't like Zach."

"Do you think it was his father?"

Hollis's eyes widened. "No," she answered quickly, earning her a strange look from Principal Bailey. "I mean, I don't think he cared enough to do something like this."

"Cared?" Principal Bailey's eyebrows drew together. "Has something happened to him?"

Hollis kept her gaze steady. "I heard he ran off."

Principal Bailey shook her head. "That leaves Zach without a parent. I was there when they buried his mother. Half the town showed up to support Zach. We all knew his father had— " She stopped speaking and held her hand up, shaking her head. "I'm talking too much."

"Say no more," Hollis said. "I'll pretend I didn't hear anything."

Hollis found Zach in the hall, as if he had been waiting for her.

"Do you really believe me?" he asked.

Hollis watched his unsure posture and tried to reassure him. "I wouldn't have gone to the trouble to bring your test to compare the handwriting if I thought you were guilty."

It seemed to relax him, and they walked back to class with matching strides. Before they entered the atrium that led to gym, Hollis chanced a question about Zach's home life. "Has your father been back yet?" She called him a "father" deliberately, as a dad wouldn't have abused his child.

Zach shrugged. "He's not been to the house yet, but he keeps sending someone to drop off groceries. I thought it'd stop when I turned eighteen, but whoever it is brings stuff to the house once a week."

"I'm glad you have something to help supplement household expenses," Hollis said.

"I wish I knew who it was," Zach returned. "I'd find a way to pay them back."

"Oh, I'd say they don't want to be reimbursed."

Zach looked over at her, sighing deeply. "I wonder if they know where my father is."

"Do you miss him?" Hollis asked, and she was surprised to find that she was anxious to hear his answer.

"It's not that," Zach said, lowering his voice just above a whisper. "I think whoever is bringing the groceries knows where he is, and I'm glad they're keeping him away."

Chapter Forty-Nine

Quillen had expected her answer all evening, and now that they were lying in her bed, he believed it was time for her to give it. Hollis could tell he anticipated a conversation, as he was sliding his hand up and down her bare back, instead of drifting off to sleep.

"I want to talk to you," he spoke into the quiet night.

Hollis rolled over and gave him her full attention. She was prepared to hear a number of reasons, detailing his desire for her presence on his vacation, but his next words shocked her.

"I'm falling in love with you."

Hollis's room was dark, but the shadows she could see in the moonlight tilted as she lost her breath. She tried to steady her breathing and come up with a response befitting his proclamation.

"I— "

Quillen held his finger up to her lips, stopping words that weren't forthcoming. "Please let me get through this. I've tried to tell you so many times."

Hollis pressed her lips together and waited. In the range of moonlit hues, Quillen's eyes looked liquid black. He spoke steadily, and when he was finished, he turned their darkness on her.

"Two years ago today, I had an adoring wife and twin daughters," he began. "I ended the day without Violet and Beth."

Hollis had known Rose had been a twin. Other than her matching flower name, there was still evidence of it all over her room, from the roses and violets on the bedspread, to the matching sets of pictures on the wall.

"Josie told you about it, didn't she?"

Hollis nodded in the night, and his eyes had adjusted to the dark, so he saw the movement. He took in a breath and let it out slowly, blowing warm air from his nose onto Hollis's bare arms.

"I told Principal Bailey everything the reporters plastered on the news about it, but I didn't tell her about walking in and finding them."

His voice broke, and Hollis took it as a cue to put her hand over his arm. He recovered quickly and continued.

"I knew something was wrong when I came home. Usually, our dog, Peppa, would come running to greet me, but she was gone. Beth had taken her to the vet that day, and I wondered if they'd kept her there for some reason.

"I walked down the hall to the kitchen and poured some juice. That's when I noticed the back door was open. A set of boots had made muddy footprints in the kitchen leading to the sink. I traced them to the yard."

Quillen took another minute to recover. When he spoke again, his voice picked up speed in his attempt to purge the events quickly before he lost his resolve.

"The news covered the stab wounds and their botched backyard burial, but the reporters didn't mention that Beth was holding Violet in that pitiful attempt of a grave in our own backyard, or the way I beat the killer before I realized he'd shot himself. They didn't discuss the dirt and clay I dug off their bodies with my bare hands before I saw Violet's dark hair and recognized the moon on the friendship bracelet Rose had given her.

"The whole time I kept thinking he had killed all of them. I thought after I'd pulled Beth, Violet, and Peppa out of the hole that Rose would somehow appear in the same hole."

He was crying, and Hollis did her best to console him, kissing his temple and wrapping her arms around him. She held him as he told her about his grief and the funeral, but she waited for the reason behind the murders, and he finally spoke about it.

"I don't know who called the authorities that day, but they showed up at my house. Thankfully, they kept the reporters at the front of the house and smuggled in Rose through the garage when they picked her up from basketball practice. They left it to me to tell her about what had happened, and part of me hated them for it. I remember looking into her confused eyes and wondering about the link they say twins share. I learned later that she'd had pain in her stomach at the same place where Vi had been stabbed, but she hadn't 'felt' her die."

He lifted out of Hollis's embrace and sat up, scrubbing his face with his hands. From that angle, his words echoed off the walls.

"The police use a killer's full name when they arrest him. John Paul Barton was dead when I found him in my back yard, and the reporters used his full name when they described what he did to my family." He spoke with conviction. "They put his name out there, like they wanted people to remember *him*, while Vi and Beth were mostly called 'the victims'."

Hollis put her hand on his back. Quillen faced away from her, not acknowledging her or her touch. The part of him that had been in the room with her was now back in the past, and she wondered if a piece of him was buried in that hole where he had found his wife and daughter.

"Vi had dated Teddy, her murderer's son," Quillen went on. "Of course, she didn't know her boyfriend's father was a murderer. That all came out eventually, but no one understood why he had targeted her until Rosie found Vi's diary."

Quillen had stumbled into a part of the story where Hollis could ask questions. "The killer didn't usually target women, did he?"

Quillen's voice was cold when he answered. "No. That animal targeted businessmen who cheated on their wives."

She regretted asking the question, but she wasn't as angry about the killer's usual modus operandi as Quillen. After his curt answer, his tone resumed the same sadly reflective tone he had maintained through his story.

"Rosie had been going through some of Vi's things and she brought me her diary. She told me that she'd made a promise not to read it, and she was going to honor it.

"I thumbed through the pages. I was really hungry for anything that reminded me of my wife and daughter, so I took my time. I skipped over the parts that talked about Teddy and her feelings for him, but I found a scribbled page almost at the end of her entries that caught my attention.

"Vi had gone out on a date with Teddy, and his father had volunteered to drive them to the mall. On the way, he said he'd forgotten his cell phone, and he had stopped at his house to get it.

The kids noticed the basement lights turn on, and Vi asked Teddy why his dad was looking for his cell phone in the basement. Teddy told her that his dad spent a lot of time down there, and they didn't think much more about it, until his cell phone buzzed.

Thinking they had solved the mystery of the missing cell phone, the kids went inside and knocked on the basement door. Vi wrote that she heard a man screaming until it became muffled, and Teddy's father appeared at the door. He barely looked at his phone and yelled at the children to get back into the car.

"When he rejoined them, Vi wrote that Teddy's father kept looking at her in the rearview mirror, like he was scrutinizing her. When he dropped her off at home, he told her to 'be careful out there,' and Vi thought it sounded ominous.

"I gave the diary to the police, and they obtained a search warrant. They combed the house, and they found a dead man in the basement with his heart removed. They never found his heart." Quillen paused for a moment before he added. "Or mine."

Hollis understood the metaphor and chose to remain quiet. She thought Quillen was finished until he turned around and took her in his arms. "You were the one who found my heart, Hollis."

He kissed her gently across her mouth and she pursed her lips to receive his affection. She had never been with a man who had such a tortured soul, and she wondered for a moment if fate had thrown them together, laughing in her mind at the irony.

In this moment with Quillen, she wanted to be a better person. She didn't want to be the killer whose full name appeared on the news, no matter how valiant her efforts were to rid the world of scum. She wanted to be the supportive partner who helped heal her lover's damaged heart.

She gently pushed him back, just enough to see the flecks of blue in his moonlit eyes. "I'll go on vacation with you." She swallowed hard. "I'm falling for you, too."

Chapter Fifty

The clock in her office ticked, reminding her that time was running out before she was supposed to travel five hours to a beach named after a tree with her boyfriend and his daughter. She didn't realize she had been clicking the top of her pen vigorously until Josie called her name.

"Huh?"

Josie smiled at her knowingly. She stood in the doorway of Hollis's office holding a flowy pink dress with white flowers. "I thought you could borrow something for your trip to the beach."

Hollis looked down at her white tee shirt and navy blue cotton shorts. "What's wrong with what I have on?"

Josie rolled her eyes. "You're going on a trip with your *boyfriend.*"

She placed extra emphasis on the word, and Hollis wondered the reason for Josie's sudden interest in her attire.

"What's going on, Jos?"

Josie's eyes went wide. "Nothing." She walked over and placed the dress over Hollis's lap. "I just thought you could look nice today."

"For a road trip?" Holis asked skeptically.

"You never know if you might stop somewhere, and..." she trailed off.

Hollis felt like cold water had been splashed on her. "He's not going to propose, right?"

Josie couldn't contain herself any longer. "Yes!" she shouted, as if Quillen had asked *her* to marry him.

Hollis's lunch rolled in her stomach. "What am I going to do?"

"What do you mean?" Josie asked. "I thought you really cared about him."

Hollis couldn't answer her friend. Her mind was racing. *It was so fast! Why did he want to propose so quickly?*

Without her knowledge, Hollis had spoken her last thought, and she wasn't aware of it until Josie answered. "Men like Quillen are romantic, and when they know they're in love, they rush at it full force."

That explained why Hollis felt like the wind had been knocked out of her. She doubled over holding her stomach.

Somehow Josie was able to coax her out of her position in her chair and lead her to a bathroom for female teachers. She helped her change, with Hollis throwing the dress over her head automatically. Once she was back in her office, she felt a little better.

"I don't have to say 'yes'," she told Josie.

Josie's eyebrows shot up. "Sure. But what kind of relationship will you have when you refuse a man's proposal."

Hollis hadn't reached that far in her thinking. She supposed she'd have to break up with him.

"Please don't throw it away," Josie begged. "I want us to live in the same town, be pregnant at the same time, and have our babies grow up and get married."

Hollis almost vomited. She was frightened enough about marriage but having children with Quillen scared her to death.

The bell rang, and Josie whispered some encouragement as she slipped out the door. Hollis lifted out of her chair, feeling like her body was floating. Rose was already at her place on the gym floor, and Zach was at her side. *Could she be the girl's step-mother? Would she be able to soften Quillen's heart when it came to Rose's relationship with Zach?*

Hollis rubbed her eyes without caring about the black mascara smearing across her face. *Could she marry a man she hadn't known for a full year?* She supposed they could have a long engagement, but she doubted Quillen would agree to it after his hasty proposal.

Then her mind landed in a spot that was always just below her surface thoughts. *Did she deserve happiness after all she'd done?*

She had killed the only man she had ever loved, and fully realized her role as a predator of wicked men. She couldn't live in the same house with people who had suffered from the effects of similar crimes. She was just as much of a serial killer as the man who had murdered Beth and Violet.

She grabbed the keys to her car and walked out, making a decision that would affect the rest of her life. When she started her car and drove away, she knew exactly where she was going, even though she drove around for hours before she climbed the familiar gravel drive.

That night, she used the key under the pot that held marigolds in the summer and crept inside the quiet house. She slid onto the couch without a sound and closed her eyes, listening to the sounds of peaceful breathing that echoed down the hall.

Even though she was in a place where her heart desired to go the most, the dreams still came. And with her nightmares, came the truth of the events that shaped her into a monster.

Chapter Fifty-One

Bob, Part Three

Hollis and her mother cleaned up the vomit, and Hollis offered her one of her scarves. She shook her head, opting instead for a red turtleneck shirt.

Her mother left, pointing to the microwave. Hollis saw the outline of a plate stacked with food and understood that her mother had made it for her. They hugged, and her mother stumbled out the door just as her coworker's old Datsun pulled up to their house and blew the horn.

Her mother had been gone for less than five minutes before Hollis was dragged to the cave, this time by her arm and hair. She imagined the star pattern on the ceiling in her room and flew away in her mind to a distant constellation until it was over.

She limped back home beside her abuser. He seemed to walk straighter with a smug smile on his oily face.

"You thought you could get rid of me, didn't you?" he said. When she didn't answer, he grabbed a fistful of her hair and pulled down hard. Hollis cried out.

He hadn't really wanted an answer, so he continued without one. "You thought you could tell your mommy that you'd eat if she'd get rid of mean ol' Bob." He let go of her, pushing her to the ground. "I told you I'd kill her if you said anything about us."

There is no us, she thought. She hated the way he made it seem like she was voluntarily with him.

"What the—" He squinted at the house.

Hollis was numb to external threats. She hoped the house was covered with robbers, kidnappers, or anyone else who would take her away. When she looked up, though, her blood ran cold. Bob had found her pile of food.

He examined the mound beneath her window, toeing it with his boot. "Is this where you've been putting your food?"

Hollis stared at him, admitting nothing.

He picked through the food, shouting obscenities, and yelling about his disgust. Hollis stayed where Bob had thrown her. She could feel the moisture from the dirt soaking into the knees of her sweatpants.

He picked up a handful of the food and threw it at her. Bits of toast and spaghetti landed on her, sticking to her hair and face.

When she was unmoved, Bob stalked over to her and picked her up by the nape of her neck, guiding her to the pile.

"Eat it!" he commanded.

She struggled against him, but he was too strong, and before she knew it, her face was buried in week-old mashed potatoes and macaroni and cheese. She could smell the stale decay, but she couldn't move her head away. Her stomach rolled.

Bob grabbed her chin and held her nose closed. She held her breath as long as she could before she gasped for air.

Bob forced her to eat the food like a dog. She vomited it back up, adding bile to the mix.

Finally, Bob was tired of his sick game. "Clean this up," he demanded. "It's no wonder we have a rat problem."

You're the only rat around here, she thought.

Hollis washed her hands at the sink while Bob smoked a cigarette at the table. She hated his eyes on her, and she imagined pressing them in with her thumbs until he couldn't see her anymore. Then she'd never have to look at his smirks whenever he saw her fail, or he'd caused her pain. In her mind, if he couldn't see her, then he couldn't judge her, but she knew it wasn't true. He would hear about her mistakes, and then the same smug smile would cross his lips, so she'd have to rip those off, too.

As she ran down the list of Bob's body parts that she'd destroy, he moved his chair back and walked over to her. He touched a strand of her hair. His assaults always began that way, and her body tensed without realizing it.

He rubbed the strand between his coarse fingers. "You know, men like blonde women better."

It was an odd thing to say to her. Her mother dyed her hair bright blonde, and it felt crispy when it pressed against Hollis's cheek.

"Red reminds men of fire, and they don't want to get burned," he went on.

Hollis imagined her hair was the flower of flame, engulfing Bob in a fate he couldn't escape. She wished it so hard that blood marched through her ears at the effort she threw into it.

"We'll work on dying it tomorrow."

"I don't want to change my hair," she said before she realized she'd spoken.

Usually, she made herself as insignificant as possible around Bob, but there was still spirit left inside of her, and it couldn't be extinguished. She meant her words, but she wished she hadn't spoken them.

Bob grabbed a fistful of her hair and led her to the living room. "You'll do whatever I tell you to do."

He pushed her onto the carpet, and Hollis hid her face against the mangy brown fabric. His fists dove into her back and legs, adding to the purple and green bruises that already covered the parts of her body no one else saw. When he was finished, he stood up and pulled his belt from his jeans.

Hollis was used to the belt. Even though she was sixteen, he had insisted on disciplining her with it. But he didn't use it. He just stood over her slapping it against his hand.

She pretended to quake with fear. The more afraid she seemed, the less he punished her.

"Now, I think we know who the boss is here," he said, smacking the belt against the coffee table. "Get up."

Hollis stood up on shaky legs.

Bob motioned to the spilled furniture around them. "Clean up this mess," he ordered, pushing her.

Hollis landed on the coffee table.

She spent the next hour cleaning up the house. Her stomach growled audibly for the food in the microwave, but her mouth was still slick with the bile and rotten meals she'd thrown up. She'd clean a room, thinking about warming up the food after she finished, but by the time she got to the next room, she'd feel a wave of sickness and decide that she'd just take a shower and go to bed.

Bob sat at the table the entire time she cleaned, drinking beer and smoking one cigarette after another. Hollis vowed she'd never smoke. The stale smell covered her hair and clothes, and it made her mother cough every time she woke up.

"You're disgusting," he said from his chair. "Take a shower, and I'll be in there in a minute."

Hollis closed her eyes with her back turned. Tears stung, but she blinked them away. He had never attacked her in the house. If he thought he could get away with it then they'd be moving to a new level of abuse.

Hollis gathered her clothes to take with her to the bathroom. Before she closed the door, wishing she could lock it, he called to her.

She approached him cautiously with her head bowed. He saw it as a sign of respect, but Hollis didn't want to stare into the cold, dark eyes of her tormentor.

"Get me a beer," he said and motioned to the microwave. "And heat up that food for me."

Hollis could feel anger boiling beneath her skin. Bob hurt her in almost every way imaginable, and now he was taking the food her mother had left for her. Her fists clenched when she thought of her mother coming home from work and seeing the empty plate. She'd think her daughter had eaten the food, not the loathsome creature at the kitchen table.

The microwave hummed and the food popped as it warmed, causing a mouse to run out from behind the appliance. Hollis jumped back, and Bob tried to beat the rodent with his belt, missing every time it slapped a surface.

"Get the poison," he yelled at Hollis. He cursed the mouse and shoved the table, causing it to almost spill over. "Now!"

Hollis scurried out the door and ran into the outside building. The night was cold, but she barely felt the temperature on her skin.

The container of strychnine sat on the shelf next to the paint her mother had purchased to use on the living room. She grabbed the poison and ran back into the house.

The heat felt good on her face, and she looked forward to her shower, until she remembered Bob wanted to join her.

"Put it everywhere!" he shouted from his chair. "I want every one of them dead!"

Hollis stood there, conflicted about putting out a poison that would kill the pests in her home. On one hand, she didn't want to kill anything. On the other hand, Bob would beat her within an inch of her life if she defied his wishes.

She opened the container and took out a spoon, dipping it into the white powder and pretending to sprinkle it behind the microwave. Bob slammed down his beer bottle, causing her to jump, and a small amount of the powder fell onto the counter.

"Why are you using a spoon?" he yelled at her. "Use the plastic scoop!" He picked up the container and started spilling the powder over the counters.

"Get me a beer and get ready for our shower," he shouted. "I'll take care of this."

He mumbled about rats and doing things himself if he wanted them done right, but Hollis didn't mind his ramblings too much until he brought up the subject of their shower again. She hadn't felt safe since Bob had started living with them, but he hadn't violated her in the house, preferring to take her into the cave where no one could hear her cries.

He reminded Hollis about his beer again, and she pulled one out of the refrigerator. The orange label had been damaged, and the silhouette of the werewolf on the front had been scuffed around the neck.

Hollis used the edge of the counter to pop the cap and she watched as the gas rose. Her eyes fell on the strychnine she had dropped when Bob had yelled.

She wanted to hand him his beer and run out the door, but her limbs wouldn't move. All she could manage to do was stare at the white powder she had spilled and wonder if there was a way to get rid of *all* the rats in the house.

• • • ● ● • ● ● ● • •

Hollis dragged Bob until he was against the cave wall. She left his phone and wallet with him, hoping when he was found, that the police would think he'd wondered off while he was drunk.

She put a bottle of Moon Walker beer in his hand. She'd poured out its contents in the woods as she'd dragged him along. A couple of times she'd almost passed out, but the food she'd eaten before she'd left the house and her adrenaline had lifted her blood sugar enough to help her complete her mission.

Hollis ran back to the house, her footfalls echoing against the hard ground. She didn't meet another animal in the cave or hear the wind through the trees. It was like the forest had stopped time for her, absorbing the soul she had brought to the cave like a sacrifice. She'd heard stories about the woods, but she'd never believed them until that night. Many people talked about the terrible things that walked through the trees, but they had never shown their hideous faces when Bob had assaulted her, and they didn't pop out to frighten her that night. It was almost as if she were one of them, a sinister being behind the guise of a teenage child.

She had committed a murder. She hadn't hurt him in all the ways she'd imagined, but she'd put an end to his demands and snide smiles.

She burst through the door and busied herself with cleaning up the mess. The vomit was the hardest part. She used a washcloth to soak it up and rinse it down the sink. Afterward, she popped it into the washer by itself. She righted the furniture Bob had turned over before his muscles became rigid, and she washed out the bottle that had effectively hidden the taste of the poison, wrapping it in a plastic bag and throwing it in the garbage can outside.

Hollis expected the enormity of what she'd done to hit her in the shower, but all she could feel was relief. She wanted to shame herself for Bob's murder and go to the police, but as the water rushed over her bruises, she found she lacked remorse for her actions.

Bob was gone!

She wanted to shout it from the rooftop and write it in the sky. She and her mother were safe now. They could live their lives without beatings and rapes. It was all over.

But it wasn't over.

Hollis waited for the police to pull into the driveway with their sirens blaring and lights flashing. Her thoughts often drifted to the final clicking of the handcuffs over her wrists and the cold dank cell that awaited her.

Her mother had asked her about Bob as she stood in amazement over the empty drawers that had once been Bob's. Before her mother had arrived home from her shift, Hollis had stuffed their contents into a large plastic bag and carried them into the forest. She had dumped his clothes into an old tree truck that looked like a fallen soldier in the formation of branches around it.

"I just don't get it," she said, swaying to the tune of the liquor she'd drunk. "I didn't think the fight was that bad."

"He said he was done," Hollis said, shrugging her shoulders. "I wouldn't worry about it, Mom. He was a piece of garbage anyway."

Her mother took a deep breath and put her hands on her hips. Her voice was gravelly, but she had mostly recovered from the effect of Bob's hands on her windpipe. "I guess you're right. It's been a long time comin'."

Hollis got ready for school, putting on a navy blue boat neck and jeans that were only a little loose on her. She applied some of her soft tan lip gloss and white eyeshadow, dressing her lashes with a coat of mascara.

Her mother startled when she sat down to breakfast, but she didn't comment on Hollis's changed appearance. She puffed her cigarette and sipped her beer.

"I want you to quit drinking, Mom," Hollis said, and she was shocked by her brazenness.

"I worked last night," she defended. "You wouldn't deny a hard-working woman her beer, would ya?"

"You didn't need it before you met"—she didn't want to say his name, so she searched for another way to describe him— "that man, so why do you need it now?"

Her mother tipped the bottle away from her as if she were reading the label. "It probably wouldn't hurt to go to one of those meetings in town."

Hollis put the rest of her concerns out of her mind and focused on the present. She was going to help her mom achieve sobriety, and then the police could come and cart her away. Until then, she was going to be a good student and an even better daughter.

Her mother stood at the stove, flipping pancakes with one hand and flicking the ashes off the cigarette with the other. She laid a stack of buttery pancakes in front of Hollis, and Hollis surprised her by eating every one of them.

Chapter Fifty-Two

Audrey

"Mommy?"

Hollis's eyes popped open, and a smile illuminated her face. "Hey, sugar bear."

She had perfected her own style, from her rainbow reflective shoes to her side ponytail. She looked similar to other eight-year-olds, but she had a flair of her own.

"Audrey?" a voice called down the hall. "Who're you talkin' to, child?"

"Mommy's here!" the child said excitedly.

Bedclothes ruffled as they were flung aside, and footsteps pounded down the hall. Hollis closed her eyes and waited for them to pounce on her. Four arms encircled her, and squeals of delight pierced her ears. "You're home," they said, even though she'd only visited the tiny two-bedroom house.

Nestled into the side of a mountain, the house had been built around a cabin. The wooden walls were insulated, and Hollis had paid for new, creme siding and stainless-steel appliances before her mother moved in. Little of the original structure remained, but

Hollis could sometimes catch a whiff of pine needles, as if Asher had just drifted through the room on his way outside. The floors were refinished, and an electrician and plumber had been called to make any needed updates before her mother had been presented with the key.

A faux letter from a made-up sweepstakes had arrived in Liz's mailbox and informed her that she had won the house. She had just completed a rehab program and returned to the house she had shared with Bob. Liz was thrilled to relocate, especially since one of the steps involved in her program was to get away from old acquaintances. She didn't question the source of the letter, accepting her prize immediately.

Hollis had paid a man from an acting workshop to answer her call on a burner phone and present her with the house. Thinking he was being paid for his part in a practical joke, he agreed, and he played his part well. He learned enough about the house to answer Liz's questions, and he accepted her appreciation on behalf of the company for which Liz thought he worked.

Hollis had been glad to sneak into the house the night before, but she was happier to have her mother and daughter wake up and find her. Keeping them there, away from the evil men of the world, was her guilty pleasure. She wouldn't rest until all the bad men within a hundred-mile radius of her family were dead, and in eight years, she'd managed to destroy any trace of many of them.

"How long can you stay this time?" Audrey asked. "I want you to meet my friend, Elizabeth. She has the same name as Mom-mom, but she doesn't like nicknames."

She stared at Hollis with big brown eyes that reminded her so much of Asher that a pain stabbed her heart. She tucked a rogue piece of her auburn hair behind her ear, and Audrey shook her head to move it into a freer position.

"I want to take you to Sally's Stables for a picnic and walk down to that river—" She turned to her Mom-mom. "What's the name of it?"

"Nolichucky," Hollis's mother said. She threw Hollis a smile and shook her head at Audrey's exuberance.

"Yes! I want to go to the *Nolichuncky* River," she said, cutely mispronouncing the name. "We could go kayaking, and—"

"Okay, Aud," Hollis's mother interrupted, patting her shoulder. "I think we get the idea."

Hollis had been nodding along, eager to do anything and everything her daughter suggested. "It's okay, Mom. Maybe Audrey and I can do one thing each day I'm here."

"And how long will that be?" her mother asked, her eyebrows rising.

Hollis forced a wider smile in front of Audrey. "I don't know. But maybe I can stay for a little over a week."

Audrey jumped up and down, holding Hollis's hand. "A whole week?" She fell on her knees in front of her grandmother with her hand clasped together. "I'm so glad I'm outta school!"

Hollis's mother was used to Audrey's melodramatic pleas. "You still have your chores, and your helpin' the librarian in town sort books today."

Audrey stood up, flung her head back, and stomped in a circle. "But I don't want to!" she cried. "I want to stay home with my mom."

Hollis's mother looked at her granddaughter sternly. "There's no sense in pitchin' a fit. You know you have to honor your responsibilities."

Soft pink cheeks brushed Hollis's face as Audrey hugged her. "Don't you have any say?" she asked.

Hollis held her daughter at arm's length, locking eyes with her before she spoke. "You know I always defer to your Mom-mom. Whatever she says goes."

Audrey rolled her eyes. "Don't you want to spend time with me?"

Hollis's mother spoke up, her voice booming at first, and then settling into a softer tone. "Now, you know your mom always comes to see you when she has a break from her job. Uncle Sam wants your mom because she's good at her job, and she works to keep us all safe. It's hard on all of us, but we need to enjoy the time we have with her."

Audrey looked at her feet. "I guess you're right. I just miss you." She looked up at Hollis and her voice cracked on the last word.

Hollis pulled her daughter onto her lap. She felt a little guilty about her mother's praise. Sure, she was helping the world by ridding it of bad men, but she wasn't doing it for her country. She was doing it to keep her daughter safe.

Liz's friend, Pauline, beeped her horn when she pulled up to the top of the driveway. Audrey jumped up, casting a look over her shoulder at Hollis before she left. "Do you promise you'll be here when I get home?"

Hollis cringed inwardly. Last time she'd visited, she had left while Audrey was at school.

"Yes, sugar bear. I'll be here."

She smiled and blew her a kiss before Audrey ran out to volunteer with Pauline at the library. Part of Hollis's heart went with her, just like it always did.

Her mother hugged her and turned on the morning news. Hollis did her best to block out the reports, and soon, upbeat morning shows replaced the detailed accounts of horrific casualties of human nature.

Hollis's mother poured her a glass of orange juice and placed a plate of warm waffles in front of her.

"I can go to the table to eat," Hollis offered.

Her mother waved her hand. "I'm sure they don't feed you enough, and they probably make you eat it in the strangest places."

"I eat well," Hollis said.

Her mother shot her a suspicious look that settled on her midsection. "You look beautiful in your dress, but you're barely more than a wisp. You look a lot like I did at your age, with muscles and a trim waist, and I was carrying half my weight around a factory all night."

"Mom, I eat all the time," Hollis responded, and to prove her point, she shoved a large bite of syrupy waffle into her mouth.

"That's a start," her mother said. "I'll make chicken and dumplins tonight." She shook her head, remembering her daughter's lifestyle choice. "Or, I guess, dumplins for you."

Hollis talked to her mother as she went through her morning chores. Despite warnings and finger wagging, Hollis washed the breakfast dishes and made a potato salad for lunch. When they finished lunch, the women sat out on the front porch.

The view stretched out in front of them, almost taking Hollis's breath. A rolling field seemed to drift into rising mountains that were just starting to color from spring's paintbrush. A gentle breeze rolled across them as they talked and laughed.

Hollis's mom looked at her seriously with the same shade of green eyes she had given to her daughters. "When are you coming home, Hollis?"

The question always caught Hollis off guard. "I told you last time that I had signed up for another four years."

Her mother's jaw clenched and unclenched. "You're gonna miss her life, Hollis. You've already been away for almost all of her childhood, and when she reaches her teen years" — she shook her head and let out a slow, deliberate breath— "you might as well forget tryin' to connect with her."

"I wasn't a bad teenager," Hollis defended, in hopes of steering the conversation away from her absence in her daughter's life.

"You had some hard circumstances, though." Her mother reached out and took her hand. "It took me a while, but I finally realized just how hard Bob was on you."

Her mother would never know the extent of Bob's cruelness to her, but Hollis was thankful for the acknowledgement. She squeezed her mother's hand in return, unwilling to talk about an issue that had caused her so much pain.

"You know, they sent me a letter about him," her mother said, easing back in her chair and closing her eyes against the suns rays.

Hollis hardly choked out a response, and her mother opened one of her eyes.

"You look like you've seen a ghost, child. What is it?"

Hollis fumbled for an answer to explain her pale complexion. "I think the potato salad isn't settling well with me." She tried on a small smile. "What were you saying about a letter?"

Her mother sat up and grabbed a case that used to hold her cigarettes. Snapping it open and closed helped quell her desire for nicotine.

"The sheriff sent me a letter and told me they'd found Bob in a cave near the house."

She didn't have to say which house. Hollis knew she meant the house where she'd been raised. The same one that was tarnished with memories of Bob's despicable acts.

Her mother had been talking, and Hollis tuned back into what she was saying. "A hiker found some bones in a cave, and it turns out they were his." She pursed her lips like she was letting smoke from a cigarette flow out of her mouth. "The sheriff said it looked like he'd wondered into the cave and gotten lost. Turns out he didn't leave us after all."

"But what about his clothes and things?" Hollis blurted out. She didn't want her mother to romanticize the memory of the monster who had repeatedly raped her.

"I can't say that the thought didn't cross my mind." Her mouth turned down and Hollis noticed a few new wrinkles on a face she had considered ageless. "I guess I just wanted to think he hadn't left me for a while." Her mouth formed a grim line. "It's hard on a woman when she can't keep a man, especially one like Bob."

Hollis felt rage threaten to spill from her like molten lava. Her mother had grown so much since Bob had been gone. She had shown a lot of personal growth, and Hollis hadn't batted an eyelash when she had left her daughter in her mother's care. It pained her to hear the thinking that had cycled through several generations in her family, and she told her mother how she felt about it.

"You're right," she conceded. "I fall back into that backwards thinkin' sometimes, but deep down, I know he did us a favor when he left."

Hollis put her hand on her mother's arm, and her mother dropped her cigarette case to cover her daughter's hand with her own. Tears glistened in her eyes, and Hollis was glad her mother was touched by the sentimentality instead of the news about her husband's death.

The women spent a moment in silence before her mother startled. "Do you remember that man Bob hung out with?"

"Which one?" Hollis choked out. She tried to keep her voice even and her face expressionless, but it took every ounce of her control just to keep from passing out.

She looked at Hollis. "Are you sure you're okay? Do I need to check the date on that mayonnaise?"

"No," Hollis told her, swallowing back the stomach acid that had been steadily climbing her esophagus since her mother had mentioned Bob. "I'm okay."

"Well, it was the strangest thing," she continued. "The police found another body in the cave. He'd never been reported missing, but they said it looked like there'd been some kind of struggle and Bob had killed him." She stared into the distance. "What *was* that man's name?" she said, tapping her chin.

"Freddy," Hollis answered. "His name was Freddy."

Chapter Fifty-Three

Freddy

She hadn't planned to kill anyone, and she certainly didn't think she'd do it again so soon, but when everything fell into place, Hollis knew it was destiny. It seemed that the universe had seen her struggles and heard her cries, and another wrong had been sent to her to right.

Was she going crazy? It was likely. But in her mind, severe injustices had been done, and no one could stop them but her.

After she put Bob in the cave, she expected things to get better at home. In a lot of ways, they did. She didn't have to walk on eggshells anymore, and she wasn't dragged to a cave to perform unspeakable acts. However, her mother still drank herself to sleep every day after she came home from work and kept a steady buzz through the weekend.

Hollis tried to talk to her about alcoholism, but it earned her contemptuous stares and silence. Finally, Hollis returned the silence and waited for the day her school requirements were fulfilled.

On a sunny winter day, she met a boy who made her feel like she was the only girl in the world when he spoke to her. He was a little older than her, so he was technically a man, but he was close enough to her age to share the same love of music and certain books.

Hollis didn't tell him her age. Thankfully, he didn't ask. She shared that she was graduating from high school soon, but when he asked if she had other plans, Hollis only shrugged. She told him about her interest in plants and animals and his eyes lit up. She wanted to bathe in his milky chocolate orbs, so she continued to talk about the random things she'd learned about plants.

The boy, Asher, told her he attended a college in a nearby city, and he offered to drive her to classes. Hollis applied the same day and asked her school counselor for help filling out the forms for student aid. Her request was approved, but the scholarships and grants wouldn't begin until the fall semester. Hollis didn't want to wait to solidify a daily connection with Asher, so she begged her mother for enough money to attend a class during the spring semester.

Her mother didn't have the money, and Hollis's hopes fell. But one night, as Hollis was washing the last of the dishes, a solution to her problems walked through the back door.

• • • • • • • • • • •

"Where is he?" Freddy asked after he had invited himself in.

"Who?" Hollis asked automatically without turning around. She rubbed the rag around the rim of a cup.

"Bob?" he shot back.

Her mother had been quiet about her husband's leaving, and he'd only had two friends. Marshal had died of a heart attack two days after Hollis had killed Bob, and she took it as another sign that the universe was helping her rid the earth of the people who had violated her. That left Bob with only one friend: Freddy.

"He's not here."

Hollis didn't know why she gave the vague response, but something told her to keep Bob's real and imagined whereabouts to herself. He asked her when he'd get back and she shrugged.

Freddy sat down, tapped his foot against the linoleum, jumped up, looked out the window, and sighed. He was bursting with news of some kind, and he wanted to share it with his friend.

He inched over to Hollis. Hearing him approach, Hollis slid her hand under the soapy water where at least one steak knife was concealed under the bubbles.

"Look at this!" He shoved a piece of receipt paper under her nose. "I won!"

He threw his hand in the air, clutching the paper and danced around the room. Hollis watched with her hands in the soapy water. She moved her hand, but she kept the knife there in case she needed it. Bob had sharpened the knives the week she had killed him, and they were still sharp enough to slice through human skin.

Expending his energy, Freddy's adrenaline wore off, and he fell into a chair. "What do you think your mom will think about it?"

Hollis was thrown off by the sudden mention of her mother.

"Do you think she'd leave Bob for me?"

Hollis felt her blood run cold. Her mother was drinking pretty heavily, and she was hurt over her husband's leaving, so she'd probably fall into the arms of any man willing to give her attention.

Hollis scrubbed the pot she had been working on vigorously, trying to think of a way to keep her mother away from Freddy. It was no use. She was destined to live in a world with depraved men who prayed on women like her mother.

After her mother's shift ended, her weekend would begin, and Hollis was certain she'd wake up to find Freddy in her mother's bed by Sunday. She couldn't let that happen.

Hollis felt more than heard Freddy get up from his chair and stand behind her. "Is your mom as good as you?" he asked.

She could smell his breath. It was the same stale tobacco and rotten teeth smell Bob had always breathed over her before he took what he thought he deserved, but there was a hint of alcohol lingering in the scent, and it gave Hollis an idea.

"Can I get you a beer?" she asked.

Hollis had observed people long enough to understand that they will second-guess themselves if you ask if they want something. Alcoholics may refuse a beer because they don't want to seem like they want it, but if you ask if they will allow you to serve them one, it makes the offer appear more hospitable.

Freddy smacked her bottom. "Yeah. You can get me a beer if you want to."

Hollis walked carefully over to the refrigerator, trying not to seem too eager to fulfill his request. She popped the top on his beer and—checking to make sure he was busy examining his winning lottery ticket—she scraped a little of the strychnine on the counter into his bottle. He looked over at her, and she dropped his cap. To keep his attention diverted from what she was doing, she bent over fully in front of him. Her sweats did little to showcase her form, but it kept Freddy from looking at her fingers slipping the strychnine that had fallen to the floor behind the microwave into his bottle. She gave it a tiny shake before she stood upright.

Freddy licked his lips, and Hollis's dinner rolled threateningly in her stomach. She reminded herself that she needed to win his trust if she was going to pull off her plan.

"Why don't you get one, too," he told her.

"I'm a minor. It's against the law."

He got up from the chair and skipped over to her, picking her up off the floor. "It's a celebration!"

It pained Hollis to join in on his mirth, but she hid her repulsion well until he eased her onto his lap. She used the opportunity to feed him his beer, and he'd drank over half of it before five minutes had passed.

"It tastes funny," he complained. "It's not the same kind Bob always gets."

A quick look at the label would have told him that it was the beer he'd consumed countless times during his card games with Bob and Marshal. The Moon Walker label faced him, but he didn't look at it. He was watching Hollis with greedy eyes.

He put his hand on her leg. "When will your mom be home?"

Hollis shrugged. "That's why Bob takes me to the cave. We never know when she's going to come home early."

She forced herself to say her abuser's name with neutrality. Her suggestion was part of her plan, but she was having trouble getting Freddy to drink the rest of the beer.

He decided he wanted to go to the cave right away, and when she tried to playfully delay him, he grabbed her wrists. "It was your idea," he reminded her. "We can always go to your bedroom."

The thought of sullying the only place that made her feel marginally safe made Hollis's mind race to an alternate plan. She glanced over at the sink, where one pot and a knife still sat under the suds.

"I have to finish the dishes, or I'll get in trouble," she told him. "My mom will get angry and yell at me if she sees I didn't finish them." She looked at her hands and fidgeted like she was a little younger than her age. "Then my mom will be mad, and she may not want to celebrate with you."

Hollis thought she had gone too far. Freddy was silent, and his hand fell from her leg.

"Just hurry up," he growled at her.

Hollis wasted no time. She scrubbed the pot, keeping a close eye on Freddy out of her peripheral vision. When he was staring at the ticket again, she slipped the knife into the pocket of her sweatpants.

Freddy didn't finish his beer before he went to the cave with her. He insisted that she lead him, as it was dark when he was last there, and he was drunk, so he could hardly remember the way.

Hollis was concerned that the strychnine would have no effect on Freddy. *Had its effectiveness expired? Had she not mixed enough in his beer, or did he not drink enough of it?* Whatever the reason, Freddy's steps were sure and straight, and his words were firm, without a hint of a slur.

At the mouth of the cave, he drew her to him, intending to kiss her. She jerked away.

"You had me come up here," he shouted at her. "It better not have been for nothin'."

"Of course not," Hollis said in what she hoped was a sultry voice. "It's just that there's this place further into the cave that's a little more private." Freddy narrowed his eyes, so she added, "We could be as loud as we want."

Freddy pushed up his bottom lip, considering her request. He nodded without a change in his stone-faced expression, and Hollis continued into the cave.

After the first time Bob had raped her in the cave, its darkness and depth no longer bothered Hollis. There was nothing more evil than the heinous act she had experienced, but part of her hoped there was something lurking in the cool shadows. She would embrace it if it would free her from the clutches of men with debauchery on their minds.

Freddy asked her how much longer until they reached the spot, and she knew her time was over. She steeled her nerves, and forced herself to slip into a state of mind where it was okay to kill things that could traumatize you.

"What is that?" she asked him.

Their eyes had adjusted to the dark, but they could see very little in the cave. Freddy brought out his flip phone and used the luminesce of his phone's screen to look in the direction she pointed. Hollis had motioned to a place on the cave floor, and as he bent over to study it, Hollis pulled the knife out of her pocket and cut his neck.

It wasn't as easy as she'd thought. He didn't collapse and bleed out. Instead, it seemed like she'd given him a little better than a flesh wound, so she tried to run the blade across his neck again, but this time instead of slicing skin, the point went into his neck.

She pulled away, bringing the knife with her. This time, Freddy grabbed his neck and fell onto the ground, desperately trying to hold the blood in his body. It shot forth in spurts, and Hollis watched it, until the phone's screen went dark. She remained in the stillness, listening to the sounds of death, and praying that each one would bring him closer to the end. Finally, she heard nothing, but she waited five more minutes before she wiped off the knife and dropped it on the ground. As she backed out of the cave, she bent over and waved her hands over the dirt floor. She hoped she was erasing their footprints, but she didn't know for sure.

Freddy was gone, and she was ready to get out of her house for good.

Hollis was shocked when she saw the lottery ticket on the kitchen floor. It didn't take a lot to convince her mother to take it to the gas station where Freddy had purchased it. It only amounted to five hundred dollars, so Hollis's mother allowed her to take a class at the local college with the money and use the leftover funds to buy the book she needed for it.

Hollis asked Asher about his classes and signed up for the one that interested her the most. Three days a week, Asher drove her and walked with her to biology class. They had a lab immediately after the lecture, and Hollis waited for him while he attended two more classes. It allowed her time to read and finish her homework, and when the weather warmed up, she walked around the campus, taking in the pink blooms on the dogwood trees and the promising warmth on the breeze.

Her mother's drinking worsened, and she was fired. She had worked at the factory for over twenty years, but they insisted that they wouldn't rehire her unless she went through an accredited rehab program.

Hollis was distant and depressed, and Asher caught on to it. He had been showing his feelings for Hollis more, and he told her she was welcome to live with him. Hollis jumped at the chance.

She slept on the couch, even though Asher took her out on special outings she knew were really dates. She wasn't certain why he never pressed her for sex, but she was thankful for his restraint after their heavy make-out sessions.

Hollis kept up with her mother, but it took months before Liz agreed to go to a rehab. Asher insisted on checking her in to the best facility he could find, and Hollis later learned that he had paid for it.

Her mother's condition improved, and after revealing her horrible secret to Asher, Hollis thought she could finally be happy. But a darkness had settled over Hollis, she was just too blinded to recognize it before it grew and swallowed her whole.

Chapter Fifty-Four

Audrey took Hollis to every river and stream she'd ever visited. They explored the depths of Pale Woods, even though it was too cold to roam through the trees for long.

Audrey led her within twenty yards of where she'd buried Gus's body, but his corpse had been discovered and removed long ago. There were other unmarked graves in the woods, though, and Hollis didn't want her daughter to discover them.

Hollis's mother picked up Elizabeth, and Audrey and Elizabeth had a playdate in the front yard. The temperature was seasonable for Northeastern Tennessee, and the girls' noses looked slightly pink after an hour, so Hollis applied some sunscreen to their exposed skin.

Elizabeth was a pleasant child, and Hollis understood why she and Audrey were friends. They made chains out of dandelions and their stems, and they included Hollis in a game of tag, crying out with glee when Hollis intentionally missed touching their shoulders by inches.

Elizabeth ate dinner with them, and Hollis marveled at the kindness Audrey showed to her, allowing her friend to take the first spoonful from every bowl before her. They almost looked like twins with round faces, brown eyes, and hair pulled into matching mid-ponytails.

Hollis spent the next two weeks with Audrey and her mother. The days spun by quickly, with countless activities and afternoon outings, and Hollis enjoyed conversations with her mother at night as they sipped sparkling grape juice.

"Are you sure you don't mind this?" her mother asked, during one of their nightly conversations. Even though it wasn't alcoholic, they waited to enjoy the beverage after Audrey was asleep, making it their end-of-day treat.

"Not at all," Hollis replied, holding up her glass in a mock cheer.

"Some people in my group look down on it," she admitted. "They say that I'm tempting myself by going through the motions of drinking wine."

"Are those the people in your phone group?"

Her mother didn't work, and she lived off social security payments. She was a responsible caregiver, and she worried about allowing anyone to watch Audrey while she went to addiction counseling and group therapy, so she had regular appointments with a therapist on her computer, and she participated in group chats on her phone twice a week.

"Yeah," she said to Hollis, shaking her head. "Some of them are real sticklers, and even though I've been clean for eight years, they think I'm going to relapse because the juice in my glass is the same color as wine."

Hollis's eyebrows drew together. "So, if someone's weakness is vodka, then they should give up water because it's clear?"

Her mother nodded. "Under their line of thinkin'."

Hollis rolled her eyes. "Well, I'm proud of you, Mom. You've stayed strong, and I'd know if you had slipped, since I pop in at random times."

"What's with that, by the way?" her mother asked. "Pauline's boy is in the military, and she knows when he's comin' home."

Hollis didn't remember meeting Pauline's son. Her mother thought Hollis knew everyone she had met, as if their brains were socially linked.

Hollis took some time to answer her mother's question, rolling around several possible explanations and selecting the easiest one. "I'm in a special division. *I* don't even know when I'm coming home."

Her mother's face fell. "I haven't asked you before, because I want you to feel like you're always welcome, but I worry about you, Hollis. It's not good on a woman to ramble around so long."

"I'm not sure what that means," Hollis said.

Her mother closed her eyes and rubbed them. "It means that I want you to find someone to love you. Audrey doesn't need a new father, she had a good one who was taken before his time, but she needs her mother."

"And you think I'll plant myself somewhere if I get married?"

"I do," her mother returned. "You need someone to anchor you. Audrey was your anchor for a while, but you lost that connection to her when you enlisted."

Hollis hung her head. She hadn't been more than a room away from Audrey before she signed custody over to her mother. The enlister had explained, as a single parent, Hollis had to sign over her daughter's guardianship to a family member. Hollis understood the need to have proactive arrangements, but the day she appeared with her mother in court to solidify the documents was one of the hardest days of her life.

Coincidentally, the day she gave up parental rights to her child was the same day she met her best friend. Josie had been in court to contest a cousin's claim on her parent's property. Josie had won the case, but several close family members disowned her after the judge's ruling. Hollis and Josie were both grieving their individual losses, and they formed a fast friendship. Hollis wrote letters to Josie while she trained in boot camp and served her first tour of duty and visited Josie's house to decompress before she dropped in on her mother and Audrey.

She could never tell her mother that she wasn't finished making the world safe for Audrey. After living an almost reclusive life, her mother would never understand the cruel acts Hollis had endured or witnessed and the depravity of human nature.

Hollis felt an emotion bubble inside her, and she spoke before she thought about what she was saying. "I'm kind of in a relationship."

Her mother's copper and silver eyebrows pulled together. "*Kind of?*"

Hollis's face fell into her hands before she looked up and met her mother's eyes. "I already know what you're going to say, Mom, but I'm going to tell you about it anyway."

Her mother pursed her lips, expecting to hear a story she wouldn't like. She crossed her arms over her chest and leaned back in her chair.

"I met a man," she started.

Her mother brightened instantly. "Really?" She released a flurry of questions about his looks, position, and background.

Hollis waved her hand to let her mother know she was overwhelming her. She did the best she could to answer her mother's questions without giving away that she had been living several miles away for over six months.

"His name is Quillen. He works in financing, and he's from Kentucky, but he's lived in other places."

Her mother continued to stare at her, waiting for the answer to her first question. Hollis rolled her eyes and relented.

"He has shoulder-length dark hair and blue eyes, so he's really striking."

Her mother let out a whoop but covered her mouth quickly when she remembered the sleeping child in the house. "I knew he was a looker. Is he good in the sack?"

Hollis spit the grape juice she had been drinking onto the table in front of her and wiped it up quickly with the tablecloth her mother handed her. She and her mother were adults, but her mother was still her mother, and Hollis wasn't ready to discuss her sexual exploits with her.

Her mother laughed at her reaction. "I guess so," she said, winking at Hollis when she groaned.

"So, why didn't you bring Quillen with you when you came home?" her mother asked. "It must be serious if you're mentioning him to me. Don't you want him to meet your family?"

Hollis took a long time debating her next words. Her mother picked up on her reluctance.

"He wants more from you than you want to give."

It wasn't a question, but Hollis nodded her head. Her mother's fingers slipped around her hand and squeezed once.

"Don't you think it's time?"

Unexpected tears fell from Hollis's eyes, tracing soft lines down her cheeks before falling into her lap. She wiped them away, angry at her unanticipated emotions.

Her mother changed the subject, but the spirit of their evening had died. Hollis thought about the love she felt for her daughter and her blooming emotions for Quillen. *Over the years, she'd heard people say that love conquered hate, but could love quench her desire to destroy the men who could make her daughter a victim of their schemes?*

From the time Audrey was born, Hollis had known she was her baby's first line of protection. More than a proactive advocate for her daughter's welfare, she scoffed at the letter-writing and protests that hardly shifted the balance. She had to do something. And she had done it for seven years of her daughter's life. *She had methodically, and mercilessly, killed dozens of men, but was her daughter's safety improved by her continued absence?*

Hollis decided to leave it up to fate. She would give Quillen what he had truly been asking her for over the last few months. She would love him, and she would share her horrible secrets with him. If he accepted it, like Asher had, then she would marry him, and bring Audrey to live with them, making frequent visits to her mother's house. If he was horrified and threatened to turn on her, she would kill him. Either way, Hollis was ready.

Chapter Fifty-Five

It was always hard for Hollis to leave. Audrey didn't make it easy for her, squeezing with all her might around Hollis's waist before she bent down to hug her properly.

"I don't want you to go," the child begged, pulling on Hollis's hand. "When you're gone, I see you everywhere, but you're not here."

"Now stop with that nonsense," Hollis's mom cautioned Audrey. "You'll have your mom thinkin' you're crazy."

"But it's true!" Audrey shouted. "I thought I saw her on the running trail, even though her hair was blonde, and I saw her at school going into the high schooler's gym."

Hollis swallowed audibly. *She had no doubt that Audrey had seen her on the trail in town, but Audrey went to public school, didn't she?* It suddenly registered with Hollis that Audrey had been out of school the same number of days as her two-week visit.

"Does Audrey go to Pale Woods Academy now?" she asked her mom.

Her mother nodded her head. "I told you about it in one of the letters we sent to that PO box you gave us. Didn't you get it?"

Hollis felt weak and dizzy. She fell onto the passenger seat of her car.

"Has she been going there all year?"

Audrey was irritated at being left out of the conversation, so she piped up. "I've been there since the beginning of the school year."

"We were worried about the tuition," her mother said, "but this nice man sent us a letter and said that he'd pay for it since Audrey passed all the entrance exams."

"What man?" Hollis asked, always skeptical of anything a man offered.

Her mother shrugged. "The letter was anonymous."

Hollis ran her hands over her cheeks. "Then how do you know it's a man, Mom?"

Her mother bobbed her head lightly. "I could just tell. It was the way the letter was all formal. If a woman had written it, there would have been an exclamation point after "Congratulations," and it might have ended with "Have a nice day," instead of "Best regards.""

Somehow, Hollis regained her composure and managed to say goodbye to her family. As she pulled out of the driveway, she decided she would quit teaching physical education at Pale Woods Academy after the end of the school year.

Josie welcomed her with open arms. If she could have lifted her, Josie would have swung Hollis around in circles on the porch.

"I've missed you!"

Hollis returned the sentiment but waved away Josie's question when she asked where she'd been. The girls chatted through the afternoon, and when Hollis asked about Quillen, Josie's face grew grim.

"You really hurt him when you skipped out again."

Hollis held up her hand. "To be fair, this was the first time I've skipped out on him."

"That's between you two," Josie said. "But I can see the light all around you, so I know where you've been. How is she?"

Josie hardly mentioned Audrey, as she knew her daughter was a taboo subject, but Hollis was so full of life from her visit, that she told her friend about the love and laughter she'd shared with her daughter over the last two weeks.

Josie was overjoyed to hear Hollis's visit had brightened her outlook. "Are you going to tell Quillen about her? Did he see her picture on your desk at school?"

"I'm going to tell Quillen everything," Hollis told her friend. She didn't expect her friend to fully understand the implications of her words. "If he still wants to marry me after he hears it, then I'm going to do what my mom calls 'settling down.'"

Josie almost knocked her over with a hug.

The girls rushed through their afternoon chores, and Hollis stopped at the pigpen, petting Bacon. "I love it here."

Josie carried the feed bag to the back of the truck. "Just move your fiancé and his daughter into my house. I'll be lonely without you."

'He's not my fiancé yet," Hollis countered. "I still have to see if he's my boyfriend."

"Oh, I think you're safe there," Josie said with a confidential wink.

Hollis showered and dressed to go over to Quillen's house, letting Josie pick out her clothes. She didn't call Quillen, deciding to surprise him instead.

Before she left to reveal her secrets to her boyfriend, she grabbed a bottle of "Holli's" sleeping pills and stuffed them into her bag.

Just in case, she said to herself, but her dark side brightened at the thought of using them.

Chapter Fifty-Six

Quillen

Quillen opened the door, but his expression didn't change. Hollis moved past him into the house and a warm sage scent welcomed her.

Rose's eyes widened when Hollis appeared in the living room, and she jumped off the couch quickly. "Hey."

Hollis smiled at her, trying to imagine if Rose would enjoy having a little sister. "Hello, Rose."

Hollis felt-more than heard-Quillen behind her. Rose met his eyes and excused herself, almost jogging to her room.

Hollis turned around, ready to fill Quillen's head with excuses for her unexpected departure, but she stopped when she saw tears rolling down his cheeks. He crossed the distance between them and pulled her close.

Hollis had been prepared for his anger, but she hadn't expected his tears. She wrapped her arms around him, tugging him to the bedroom, the place where she had always made up for her selfishness.

Quillen allowed her to lead him to the bedroom and close the door, but he stopped her hand from tugging at his zipper. Instead, he went around her to sit on the bed, leaving a space beside him for her.

"I'm sorry," Hollis said after she joined him.

They sat in silence for several minutes, and Hollis wondered if she should add something more to her apology. She remembered Quillen's refusal to give her excuses for his actions, and she decided to let her words have more meaning.

In anticipation of their talk, Quillen had silenced his phone and placed it on the nightstand. It buzzed lightly and he looked at it.

"Rose is going over to Katey's house," he announced.

Hollis was unsure of the best way to begin her story, so she started with their most current issue. "I left because Josie hinted that you were going to propose to me." Josie had told her outright, but she didn't want to throw her friend under the bus completely.

Quillen took a deep breath and scratched the nape of his neck. He tugged at the band holding his hair in a bun until his hair spilled out in dark waves.

"I guess I know the answer then."

Hollis reached over, placing the curve of her palm against his cheek. "No, Quillen. I don't think you do."

His eyes studied her, looking for a missed meaning in her words. "So, you want to marry me?"

Hollis nodded, unable to keep a grin from settling onto her lips. He returned her smile as Hollis heard the front door slam. A vehicle rumbled a little too loudly outside, and she guessed that Zach had picked up Rose, and Quillen was too distracted to notice that change in his daughter's plans.

Quillen's mood had changed, and he put a little pressure on her hips, attempting to guide her onto his lap. She stopped him before he crashed his lips onto her mouth.

"I have a condition."

He fell back against the headboard, his eyebrows climbing. "A condition to what?"

"Marrying you," she said.

He sat up a little straighter in the bed. "Rose already knows how I feel about you, if that's what you were going to talk about."

Hollis shook her head. She picked at the fabric on his blue-green comforter, unable to find a pattern in its nonsensical weave.

Quillen lifted her chin, but she couldn't look at him. She heard him ask for her thoughts, but she couldn't respond right away. Finally, Hollis picked a spot on the floor and started her sad story.

She led with her relationship with her sister, and the accident that ended Penny's life, and she worked her way up to Bob, and what he did to her. She wanted to end her story there, as Quillen's arms moved her into an embrace, but she plugged on, telling him about Freddy and Marshal.

She felt heat off him that she thought might be repulsion, but she later saw his fist balled beside her and realized that he was trying to control his anger. Maybe he loved her so much that he couldn't stand hearing all of the horrible things that had been done to her, or maybe he was picturing what he would do to anyone who tried to hurt Rose that way. Maybe both.

She talked about Asher, reliving the compassion he had shown her and rehashing the way she had ended his life. It was the only time she cried during the story, her heart fully realizing her mistake.

Quillen didn't embrace her, but Hollis understood the reason he kept his distance. If someone was telling her that they had killed their loving partner, she wouldn't know if she needed to worry about her own life. Hollis unconsciously squeezed her purse where the sleeping pills rested. She had taken out a few of them and put them in her pocket before she knocked on Quillen's door.

She continued to recount her list of crimes, from the perverted landlord she had killed after he had attacked her with Audrey in her arms, to the last man she had planned to murder, who may or may not be drawing his final breaths in the cabin in which she'd left him on Christmas morning. The landlord had caused her to leave Audrey in her mother's care and join the Navy, for fear that she would be caught, and suspicions would point to her. She wanted Audrey in a safe place in case she was arrested, but the landlord's remains were never found. The man she'd left in the cabin had been a threat to his son's mental, emotional, and physical well-being, and he needed to be eliminated so his son didn't feel as though he should make decisions based on his father's will.

She regretted none of the killings, except for Asher's and maybe Gus's.

Even though she told Quillen about her depraved landlord, Hollis held back telling him about Audrey. Her daughter wasn't part of her cruel judgements, and she had omitted her from the story. She imagined telling him about her after he'd had time to accept her jaded past.

Hollis hadn't looked at Quillen during her confession, feeling his arms around her once, but noticing his retreat when she spoke of her dark crimes. She slowly lifted her head and turned it in his direction, but he was looking away, an odd expression on his face.

"I need a drink," he said. "Do you want one?"

He didn't glance at her for a response, and she didn't give one. When he returned, he held two juice glasses full of an amber liquid. Hollis took hers gladly and downed the contents. Quillen took a sip of his, running it through his mouth and sucking his teeth before he swallowed.

"You killed Asher," he said.

Hollis had expected him to settle on Asher, as Quillen probably put himself in the place of her deceased lover. She squeezed her lips between her front teeth to keep her expression in check.

"Yes," she replied. "I shot him, and he's my only regret."

"But you still did it? You killed him before he had a chance to explain himself?"

"I knew he was cheating on me, and I was right," Hollis weakly defended, hating herself for the excuse as it left her mouth.

"So, people who cheat should die? You took that man to a cabin at Christmas when we were together. You had to do something to entice him to go. Do you deserve to die for it?"

Hollis had watched fear turn to anger, and she was almost certain Quillen was trying to hide that he was freighted of her. Hollis reached out to touch him, but he pulled away.

"I just need a minute," he said when she shot him a wounded look. "This is a lot to process, and it changes everything."

He took a long drink and shook his head. "I think I'm going to need the whole bottle."

He didn't offer to refill her glass before he strode out the door, but she understood the reason when she spotted his drink on the bedside table. Instinctively, her hand went to her pocket and felt the weight of the sleeping pills.

Hollis glanced at the spot in the room where Quillen had set up the table for their third date. She wished she could go back to that time and erase everything she'd said, but the only way she could do that was if she crushed the pills and mixed them into his liquor.

Hollis took the pills out, watching them roll across her palm. She held Quillen's fate in her hand.

Her eyes settled on a picture of Rose. She was a little older than Hollis when Bob had started abusing her. *What would have happened to Hollis if her mother had died?*

If Hollis killed Quillen, Rose would be placed in child services, and the foster system was cruel. *Would she run away and seek shelter with Zach? Would she get pregnant young and ruin both of their futures?*

Hollis couldn't find an outcome that would help Rose. Every other father she had killed, had left his children with his wife or mother. *Could she really derail Rose's life in such a significant way when Hollis had been the one who had decided to reveal her secrets?*

When Quillen came back into the room, Hollis watched him as he poured a great deal of liquor into his cup. She felt drained from the retelling of her murderous past and her reaction to reliving Asher's death. She curled up on Quillen's pillow and closed her eyes, meaning to open them right away.

"I still need to talk to you," Quillen said, jerking her out of a comfortable doze. She hadn't realized how tired her confession had made her, but now that it was over, she felt as light as a feather, perhaps helped along by the liquor she had downed. She tried to remember the last time she'd eaten, and she groaned when she realized it had been at breakfast when Audrey had fixed pancakes for her.

"Can I have some crackers?" she asked Quillen.

"Yeah," he answered. "As soon as you clear up some things for me."

"I'm sorry." She tried to pull up, but her arms were too weak to lift her. "I don't think I can tell you anything until I eat something. I don't feel well."

Quillen hovered over her, and she felt him place a hand on her forehead. "I just want to ask you one thing."

"What?" Hollis mumbled, barely understanding him.

"Did you think you were the only killer in town?"

Chapter Fifty-Seven

She stared at the electric saw, willing it to disappear. She had wanted things to be different, but there was too much blood on her hands.

She had taken a break that had turned into change for the better. She had created a new life without missions or killing. *Shouldn't that count for something?*

But that wasn't entirely true, was it? She had gone through all the motions, and now, most likely, another man was dead because of her. If not, he lay on the brink of death.

Strangely, she didn't regret it. She would do it repeatedly to save people from their forced burdens.

There was no saving grace for the man she had seduced at Christmas. She had debated it for months and waited until the time was right, watching him and hoping for a small kindness in him, a fondness for animals or concealed giving, but he had been hopeless. He had been a scar on the landscape of a caring community that had welcomed and embraced her.

So she had killed him, committing a murder that she had, in so many words, promised never to do again. *Was her soul too dark for redemption? After so many murders, would this be the one from which she'd never come back?*

He stared at her through the slits in his mask. She knew him, even though his face was covered, his ice blue eyes and long limbs gave him away. He didn't take off the mask, but it wasn't in an attempt to conceal himself. They both knew she wouldn't be leaving the cellar.

"I want to be clear: I knew who you were, or rather, *what* you were, the whole time."

Hollis looked away from him and stared at the cold stone ceiling. She didn't respond. There was no need to try to convince him to let her live, since he had tried and sentenced her long ago for her crimes.

"I never doubted that you'd fail in your attempts to change," he went on.

Hollis wondered if she had ever monologed to her victims before she killed them. She couldn't remember a time when she had cared to hear their responses to her feelings. None of it mattered to her. Once she had decided to kill them, she had just done it and gotten rid of them in the most efficient way possible. Sure, she'd had to get close to them to perfect the kill, but she hadn't tried to carry on a dialog immediately before, or during, their murders.

Hollis assessed her surroundings. A considerable amount of time had passed, and it seemed she had been dragged into a closed space, about twelve feet by twelve feet with stone floors and ceilings and cinderblock walls. A set of wooden steps led up to a plywood door. It was bolted, but it would be easy to knock down if she could get out of her bonds. Hollis guessed she was in the cellar in Quillen's back yard. Under the cover of night, it would have been easy for him to carry her to the building and restrain her.

She was strapped to a gurney around her shoulders, hips and knees. The leather straps were so secure that she doubted she could move even if she freed her hands from the ropes around her wrists.

"Right about now you're probably thinking about all the things you should have done," his diatribe continued. "You shouldn't worry about it. If you could have married, had kids, and lived a good life, you would have done it with Asher."

Hollis couldn't help turning at the sound of her lost love's name. It disgusted her that he had spoken about him.

"It was easy enough to find out about him," he said, holding the saw between his knees with both hands. "When Detective Saldana came to me with the reason you killed the woman who broke into in my house, I looked into Asher and his murder."

Detective Saldana had talked to Quillen about the connection between her and Sarah Johnson. *Why had she thought the investigator had neglected to tell Quillen about her past?* It would have gone against his character. Quillen had just hidden the information until he'd held her captive.

He went on. "You circle around your hometown like a vulture preparing for its next meal." Leaning over her, he added, "Why is that?"

She turned her head and looked at a dark place on the wall. She decided it would be her focal point when he started using his saw. There would be no easy way out for her, like she had given most of her victims. She would suffer through every agonizing cut of the saw until he was ready to stop her torture.

"Where's Rose?" she asked, breaking her silence. "Is she back in the house doing her homework while you torture your victims?"

Quillen stood up, looming over her until she was forced to look at him. She held his gaze with the blankest stare she could manage, glad to see his eyes narrowed in hatred.

"Don't talk about her!" he yelled. "Do you know how hard it was for me to send her to school every day when I knew that you were her teacher?"

"It looks like you used her to fulfil your plans," Hollis responded, liking the effect it was having on him. She could either lower his confidence and strengthen her escape attempts or she could anger him to the point that he'd hasten to kill her. Either way, it would decrease the amount of time he tortured her.

"I don't *use* my daughter!" he yelled again, but then a steely look settled over his eyes, and he took off his mask. "And I won't let little boys, like *Zach*, use her either."

Hollis couldn't control her reaction. Quillen smiled.

"You see," he said, pointing at her. "I knew you liked that boy when you didn't tell me he was still seeing my daughter." He chuckled, but it was a mirthless sound. "I thought I might have pushed them together when I told Rose to break up with him, but when she didn't react to that note I put in Julie's locker, and the other messages I sent, I figured you were counseling her to stay with him."

In truth, Hollis hadn't encouraged Rose to stay with Zach. She had only remained silent when she'd seen them together at school.

"Who sent Rose messages before you moved here?" she asked him, veering the subject away from Zach as much as possible.

Quillen gritted his teeth. "Teddy. At first, he accused us of ruining his life." Quillen stood up, throwing his hands in the air. "As if his father wasn't the one who stole everything away from us!" Quillen sat back down, lowering his voice. "I put an end to that murdering monster when I saw him burying my family in the backyard."

Hollis had wondered why a serial killer would dispose of his victims and kill himself, but she had written it off to a botched attempt to cover the evidence.

"Teddy's notes gave me the perfect excuse to move whenever I needed to, so I make sure to plant a few whenever she asks me for something unsafe, like joining the basketball team. Of course, I had to put a note on your desk at school to really sell it, but I think I can get Rosie to move again soon."

"Basketball isn't unsafe," Hollis countered.

"She was at basketball practice when her mother and sister were murdered!

Hollis didn't argue that Rose's absence from home had saved her life. It was too exhausting to keep up with the anxieties of Quillen's traumatized brain.

He stared down at Hollis and squeezed his hands into fists. "I hate people like you," he spoke. "You're all liars, manipulators, and thieves."

Hollis's eyebrows shot up. She had never stolen anything.

As if reading her mind, Quillen said, "Time. You steal time from people when you kill them."

Hollis rolled her eyes. Almost all her victims were deplorable people. Maybe Quillen should have thought beyond Asher's death. She told him as much.

"Do you think I don't know about Vincent and Marshal's namesake?"

Hollis's head snapped up as far as her bonds would allow. "How long have you been following me?"

Quillen's smile spread across his features. "Long enough to know about almost all your victims, like Freddy, Gus, Andy, and *Bob*." He said the last name pointedly.

His words piqued her interest, but they didn't make her blood run cold. During her confession, she hadn't mentioned any names besides Asher's, but it was nothing a little digging couldn't have shown him.

"I'm not your first, am I?" She locked eyes with him, unwilling to show fear.

They both knew what she meant. The answer to the mystery of why Quillen kept moving didn't involve his attempts to run from his grief or from Teddy's threats. Quillen was following serial killers. The truth hit her so hard that she almost passed out again.

"You're the first one to guess it!" He laughed without humor. "All the other ones thought they were special."

He sat down and wheeled his seat close to her, bending forward enough for her to smell garlic on his breath. "You and your friends are so easy to track."

"I don't have friends!" she spat at him. She thought of Josie but held her resolve. He might hurt, or threaten to hurt, her friend if he thought she was special to her.

"Fine, whatever," he said and waved his hand in the air dismissively. "People like you have patterns, and I study numbers and patterns all day."

Hollis waited a heartbeat before she told him. "That makes you a serial killer, too."

The world tilted as the gurney was knocked on its side. Metal rattled, but all Hollis could see were cinderblocks only two inches away from her nose.

He picked up the gurney, righted it, and plowed it into the ground, lifting and slamming it until her brain rattled. His spittle rained on her as his anger bubbled over.

"Don't say that!" he yelled at her.

He slung the gurney down a final time, and it rolled a couple of feet to the wall. He took a couple of shaky breaths before he pulled her back to him.

"Did you love me?" she asked him. "Was any part of it real?"

"No one could love a monster," he sneered. "I got close to you so you'd let your guard down. My original plan was to rent a boat on our vacation and stab you in your black heart before I threw you overboard with one of these cinderblocks tied to your foot." He motioned to a pile of blocks that had been left over from the cellar's construction.

Hollis wasn't surprised by her lack of emotion over his words. It had been a good plan, and she was sorry that she hadn't used it to kill him.

"You would have been so giddy over the wedding proposal that you wouldn't have seen the knife until"—he buzzed his saw for effect—"Well, you get the idea."

When he cut into her arm, Hollis tried not to cry out, but he pressed the saw down harder than she'd expected, and her screams echoed off the walls as the saw touched bone. Metallic scents flooded her nose, hardly separating the smell of the saw from the blood. The pain was unbearable, and she fought to stay awake. Her brain wanted to shut down to help her cope with the suffering, but Hollis knew she'd either die or wake up to more torture if she winked out. Either way, she wanted it to be over.

Her blood coated his white shirt and light denim pants, and she witnessed the expression her lovers must have seen before she killed them. It was the look of blood lust. Quillen lied to Hollis, trying to convince himself that he wasn't a serial killer, but he had developed the same unquenchable desire for death.

He hovered the saw above her stomach, but just as he touched it, whirling through her epidermal layer, the cellar door burst open.

Footsteps pounded down the steps as Quillen stood, holding the saw out as a weapon. Quillen flipped the gurney, and Hollis's head knocked the floor, blurring her vision.

Something was spoken, but it was only a snatch of conversation, and her head hurt too badly to decipher it. Her mind flashed recognition, but she couldn't put a face or name with the voice before her consciousness faded to black.

Chapter Fifty-Eight

Josie had no idea how long she stood with her cup of coffee and stared at the empty room. Well, it wasn't empty. It still had the furniture and adornments that it had held before, but now it was empty of Hollis.

Her black duffle bag and rolling suitcase were absent, when before they had yawned open, spilling clothes onto the floor. Hollis hadn't put her anything she owned in the drawers, so the dark luggage had comforted Josie. Hollis may not have unpacked, but she had been there.

Josie should have expected it. Hollis left abruptly the last time she'd lived with her. She had gotten her through the initial pain she'd felt when Cotton had left her, but she'd cleared out to work on things of her own. Josie had taken care of her puppy, and she'd created a fantasy world where Cotton would be at home any time.

But she knew it wasn't true. She had known he was gone after she read the first letter. It was almost in his handwriting, but something was off. It may have been the slant of the e's or the lower crosses on the t's, but her husband hadn't written them.

At first, Josie thought Hollis was trying to help her, and in the beginning, the letters gave her some solace. But after a while, it was clear that her husband had left with no intention of returning, or he was dead.

The second letter had come from a California city, and as if by fate, Josie heard a news report about the city the following day. A semi-famous singer was missing, and a neighbor had spotted him with a young, blonde woman. Maybe the name of the singer stuck out to her because Hollis had mentioned him to her over the phone one day. She'd asked her about the lyrics of one of his songs, and even though Josie liked the literary stylings of Billy Joel and Sir Elton John, she wasn't good at decoding the intentions of creatives.

Hollis thought she was careful, but her habits were meticulous, and Josie had known who she was for a long time. She had gone so far as to approach her when she was buried deep in her other life. Hollis made the mistake of returning to their hometown, and when a beautiful young woman named "Holli" started running down the trail that stretched the length of the town, it had not escaped local gossip.

Josie had waited for her friend at a fast-food restaurant situated along the trail. She parked her car at the right angle in the parking lot, and when the blonde girl from the town's whispers appeared, Josie was ready.

When Hollis had seen her, she'd yelled her name, and Hollis had unwillingly approached her. Hollis spoke to her hurriedly and promised to meet her somewhere for an outing at a later date. A month later, she'd called her about a trip to a nearby theme park, and soon after, a Josie's first boyfriend, Robbie, had been reported missing.

Josie started digging into her friend's past and found the only man Hollis had ever publicly dated in her own identity. The news reports of his murder weren't shocking, but it amazed her that Hollis had been able to talk her way out of that one, especially when a hiker's body was discovered, and his truck was found several miles away. The authorities hadn't linked the two incidences, but Josie could piece it together.

She was glad Hollis still visited her mother and daughter, but Josie sometimes checked on them when Hollis was absent for long periods. Under Principal Bailey's discretion, she had paid Audrey's tuition, and she planned to do it every year until the girl graduated. She wanted to keep Audrey close, and it made her feel like she was helping Hollis when her friend wouldn't allow it.

Asher's social media had been full of men and women he'd loved, and she didn't understand why another lover would have been a surprise to Hollis. But her friend had been blind when it came to love, and Josie was no different.

Josie was one hundred percent certain that the signature on their divorce papers was not her husband's, but their marriage had been over for a long time ago. She hoped Cotton was happy wherever he was, but whether he had found someone new or he was dead, it was time for Josie to move on.

Movement out the window caught her eye, and she ran down the steps. Setting her coffee mug on the table by the door and grabbing her coat, she burst through the door, pushing one arm through each sleeve as she ran outside.

He reached over the fence and grabbed something off the ground, but when she reached the pigpen, he was standing with his hands dangling loosely over the rails. She recognized him and relaxed.

"I wouldn't get so close," she warned. "They used to be the sweetest hogs, but Bacon's bitten me a couple of times over the past few years."

Quillen smiled, but it didn't reach his eyes. "I don't think she's going to bite me."

Josie was ready to issue another warning, but he stood to his full height, backing away from the fence and rubbing a noticeable bump on his head. He held something loosely in his closed hand.

It was awkward, standing with the man who had tried to change Hollis without knowing her true history. He thought she was running from her past in the military, but Hollis hadn't been in the Navy for the last four years. That was another thing Josie had checked years ago when she had seen the composite sketch of her friend on national news, just days before Hollis turned up on her doorstep.

Neither of them spoke, and Josie was starting to feel uncomfortable. She pulled the sleeves of her coat over her hands.

"She's gone, isn't she?" Josie said. There was something so final about saying it out loud. It felt different than any other time, like she would never see her friend again.

Quillen looked at the sun. Only the bottom of it touched the mountains, but it lifted almost immediately into the sky.

"Yeah. She's gone," he confirmed.

Josie didn't have to ask him how he knew. Without his knowledge, he had flashed the necklace in his hand when he transferred it to his pocket. Throwing the necklace Quillen had given to her to the pigs had been a clear indication that Hollis was finished with her break.

He was sad, but he didn't seem surprised. "I don't think she could ever have made the changes she—"

"I know," Josie interrupted. It felt too much like she was betraying her friend if she let him finish.

A strong smell wafted to her nose, and she remembered he had grabbed the necklace out of the pigpen when she'd approached him.

"Do you want to come inside and wash up?" she asked, motioning to his filthy hand.

He colored but nodded his head. "I'd appreciate that."

After he'd washed his hands and accepted a cup of coffee from her, they sat down and talked through the morning. Quillen and Josie had shared many comfortable conversations while he had dated Hollis, many of them when Hollis had left both of them. They had more in common than they realized, and there was never another awkward silence between them.

Even though they had scars, Josie felt like she and Quillen had healed, so when it was time for him to go, Josie had no problem accepting his dinner invitation. Hollis had left Josie's house, but this time she was gone, so she wouldn't be back to reignite a flame with Quillen. Besides, Josie knew her friend would wish her every happiness.

When Quillen left, Josie noticed two people pass in a silver car that reminded her of Hollis's Volkswagen. She couldn't make out the driver, and the passenger was slumped over. It was uncommon for an unfamiliar car to travel on the road beside her house, but it wasn't notable.

She sighed as the sight of the car brought back memories of her friend. Josie could only hope that wherever Hollis ended up, she was happy. And maybe one day she would give up her terrible hobby.

The End...of this story.

What happened to Hollis? What will Quillen do next? Will
readers see Josie again?
Find out in the second book of the
Killing Quill Series!

Did You Like This Book?

If you enjoyed this story, would you please write a review on Amazon, Goodreads, and/or BookBub? Something as simple as "I liked it!" helps the author so much! Your feedback can make the book more visible to other readers, and it gives the author a reason to dance a jig when she sees your review!

You can sign up for Courtnee's newsletter, and you will receive exclusive bonus content, like cover reveals, sales, and news about upcoming releases.

Thank you for reading Hollis's Hobby!

Hollis's Killer Pork Chop Marinade

Ingredients

- one-third cup of extra virgin olive oil

- Eight tablespoons of soy sauce

- Two tablespoons of Worcestershire Sauce

- one pinch of ground black pepper

- Fresh garlic (minced)

- one pinch of salt

- Bone-in pork chops

- One cup of brown sugar

Procedure

1.

Mix the ingredients (everything except the pork chops) together.

2. Place in a large bowl or bag and add the pork chops.

3. Marinade for at least an hour but try to leave the pork chops in the mixture for twenty-four hours.

4. Most of us are not serial killers, unless you count the unlucky house plants in compost piles, so make sure the internal temperature of your pork chops reaches 145 degrees before you serve them.

5. Allow to cool and enjoy!

Acknowledgements

As always, I want to thank my eldest daughter, Tosha, for her love and continuous support. She created and maintained my website, and she beta reads every book I write. Thank you for everything you do, Tosha! She has overcome her own situations, and it has molded her into a more empowered woman.

Thank you, Legacee, for your input on Hollis's methods and your deadly suggestions. I hope you read this book, but if you don't, I hope you know that I appreciated our conversations about it.

My mama's favorite genres are mysteries, true crime, and thrillers. I was happy to write a book that could completely grab her from the first page.

I appreciate my family so much! My older children encourage me to write, and my younger children accept it as part of me. I'm so lucky to have children who get as excited over positive comments about my work as me!

My Book Bindings readers are phenomenal people. I especially appreciate my conversations with Linda, Lisa, Elaine, Annemarie, Jane, Judy, and Marjorie. Thank you for your insightful reviews!

Stephen King was my first favorite author. Even though I enjoy multiple genres, his written works helped mold me as a reader and a writer. Thank you, Mr. King, for your influence! (I still hate to "kill my darlings" when I edit, though!)

I appreciate the strong people who helped me manage traumatic events. There are many times that one decision could have changed the course of my life, but my strong support group saved me from spiraling into a self-made abyss. You know your names, and I love you for the sacrifices you made for me.

Thank you, readers! My books would remain unpublished without you!

About the Author

Courtnee Turner Hoyle, author of the award-winning My Brother's Keeper, lives in Northeast Tennessee with her children and husband. She graduated with two undergraduate degrees and a Master of Arts in Teaching from East Tennessee State University. In addition to her published novels, Courtnee has written several short stories that have been anthologized. She's also a travel agent for Courtnee's Magical Vacations, and she tries to talk her anxious husband into taking long trips with lots of people around them. Courtnee enjoys reading, writing, and any reasonable music. She spends her days in her house of secrets, avoiding sweet tea, chocolate, and unannounced visitors. Follow her on Instagram @pale_woods_mysteries, @courtnees_magical_vacations, and visit her website: www.courtneeturnerhoyle.com

Also by Courtnee

Rasputin's Dynasty Trilogy

Rasputin's Scorn
Courtnee Turner Hoyle

Thirteen-year-old Razz enjoys the freedom of his single-parent household until his mother becomes ill. Without involved relatives, he worries about what will happen to his sister, Lexi, and him when their mother dies.

Feeling powerless, he seeks out Scorn, a drug that can give the user unlimited strength, but its effects are

short-lived and the consequences of taking it are high. The user may seem unaffected by it for some time, but eventually, almost all those who take the drug become exceedingly aggressive, using their new strength to tear apart people they feel have offended them. The government collects the users who have pushed past the limits of their strength and taken a life or lives, and places them in a facility from where only one person has returned. Will Razz use Scorn to help him cope with his mother's failing health, and keep Lexi and him together after his mother's death? Or is there something more to Scorn, and is his family somehow responsible for it?

Also by Courtnee

PALE WOODS PARANORMAL SUSPENSE SERIES

SOLOMON'S TEARS
Courtnee Turner Hoyle
A #1 Amazon New Release!

Are the ghosts in her house or in her mind?

Ketron Gouge is puzzled when she feels like one of her children is missing. A quick check calms her panicked mind, but the uncomfortable thought continues to concern her.

Ketron and her husband, Marvin, bought a home they hoped would be perfect for their growing family. Soon, however, Marvin develops a drinking problem and Ketron becomes more anxious about the mysterious shadows and disembodied crying in the house. Most of her five children seem to be conscious of the uncanny events, giving credence to Ketron's worries, but her best friend and therapist think it may be a product of her overstressed mind.

Ghosts from her past and memories of her childhood tumble to the surface, reminding her of her mentally unstable mother, and she begins to wonder if there's truth to the nagging idea that someone is missing. And when she begins seeing things in her house, she thinks it may be time to accept an inescapable truth.

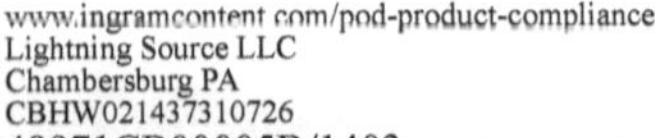